SACROSANCT
& OTHER STORIES

GREAT FICTION FROM THE MORTAL REALMS

D0999259

WARHAMMER
AGE OF SIGMAR

SACROSANCT
& OTHER STORIES

GREAT FICTION FROM THE MORTAL REALMS

C L Werner, Josh Reynolds, Nick Horth, David Annandale,
Guy Haley, David Guymer and Gav Thorpe.

BLACK LIBRARY

A BLACK LIBRARY PUBLICATION

'A Dirge of Dust and Steel' first published in the
Black Library Events Anthology 2017/2018 in 2017.
'The Old Ways' first published digitally in 2017.
'The Dance of the Skulls' first published digitally in 2017.
'Shiprats' first published in the *Black Library Events Anthology*
2017/2018 in 2017.
'Auction of Blood' first published digitally in 2017.
'The Sands of Grief' first published digitally in 2018.
'The Witch Takers' first published digitally in 2017.
The Prisoner of the Black Sun first published as an audio drama in 2015.
Great Red first published as an audio drama in 2016.
'Wrathspring' first published digitally in 2018.
'The Volturung Road' first published digitally in 2017.
This edition published in Great Britain in 2018 by
Black Library,
Games Workshop Ltd.,
Willow Road,
Nottingham,
NG7 2WS, UK.

10 9 8 7 6 5 4 3 2 1

Produced by Games Workshop in Nottingham.
Cover illustration by Lie Setiawan.

Sacrosanct & Other Stories © Copyright Games Workshop Limited
2018. Sacrosanct & Other Stories, GW, Games Workshop, Black
Library, Warhammer, Warhammer Age of Sigmar, Stormcast
Eternals, and all associated logos, illustrations, images, names,
creatures, races, vehicles, locations, weapons, characters, and the
distinctive likenesses thereof, are either ® or TM, and/or © Games
Workshop Limited, variably registered around the world.
All Rights Reserved.

A CIP record for this book is available from the British Library.

ISBN 13: 978 1 78496 792 5

No part of this publication may be reproduced, stored in a retrieval
system, or transmitted in any form or by any means, electronic,
mechanical, photocopying, recording or otherwise, without the
prior permission of the publishers.

This is a work of fiction. All the characters and events portrayed
in this book are fictional, and any resemblance to real people or
incidents is purely coincidental.

See Black Library on the internet at

blacklibrary.com

Find out more about Games Workshop
and the worlds of Warhammer at

games-workshop.com

Printed and bound by CPI Group (UK) Ltd, Croydon, CR0 4YY

Dear Reader,

Thank you for buying this book. You stand on the precipice of a great adventure – welcome to the worlds of Warhammer Age of Sigmar.

Herein you will find a host of great stories that explore the Mortal Realms – a fantastical landscape of mighty heroes, strange beasts, wizards, terrifying monsters, bloodshed and betrayal. Here, rampaging armies clash in brutal conflict, dauntless explorers test their mettle and their swords amongst the cavernous ruins of ancient civilisations, and wild magic causes the dead to rise again.

With this book you will undertake a journey through these realms and meet some of the many characters that inhabit them, pointing the way to even further adventures – recommending your next reads from the extensive and ever-expanding Black Library range.

So strap on your sword or ready your wizard's staff and let us begin. You have but to turn the page...

CONTENTS

SACROSANCT

C L Werner

CHAPTER ONE

Thunder rolled above the vast forest, shaking needles from the ancient pines. Birds took wing, screeching in fright as they rose into the clouds. They wheeled away from the great stream of lightning that crackled through the air. With the storm to spawn it, a bolt struck earthwards and crashed amongst the trees with a deafening roar. A great pillar of smoke and dust was thrown into the sky, rocks and splinters pelting the ground miles from where the lightning struck.

A vast swathe had been gouged from the forest, the ground blackened and the trees knocked flat for a hundred yards in every direction, as though a titan's paw had pressed down upon them. Thick and dark with earth, the pall caused by the impact billowed outwards, throwing a gritty fog across the woods.

Figures moved in that fog, striding from the very midst of the devastation. In such daylight as pierced the smoke, they became more than indistinct shadows. Hulking men clad in armour of gold and blue. Their countenances were hidden behind crested helms with glowering masks. Upon their shields they bore an emblem: a twin-tailed comet, the divine symbol of the God-King, an announcement to all who beheld them that here were Sigmar's mightiest warriors – the Stormcast Eternals.

Reaching to his helm, one of the Stormcasts removed the mask he wore. The countenance locked behind the sigmarite metal was revealed as handsome and cultured. His black beard had a rakish cut and his dark hair was tied back in a plaited braid. There was a severity about the set of his jaw and a troubled cast to his pale grey eyes. With a flourish, the warrior swept his sapphire-hued cloak across his back and knelt upon the ground. His mailed fist reached to the earth, seized a handful of soil and brought it up to his nose. He closed his eyes and took a deep breath.

A tall Stormcast approached the warrior smelling his handful of earth. 'Something is amiss, Knight-Incantor?'

Knight-Incantor Arnhault of the Hammers of Sigmar opened his eyes and stared at his interrogator. 'No, Penthius,' he replied. 'We have indeed descended upon the realm of Ghur. The earth carries the smell of its magic.'

The Sequitor-Prime, Penthius, merely bowed his head. Arnhault was far more versed in the strange laws that governed the storm of magic and its disparate winds. Each of the Mortal Realms was governed by those winds, drawing more heavily from one than all the others combined to define its shape. 'Have you any way of knowing how far we might be from our objective?'

Arnhault let the soil sift through his fingers. There was a faint suggestion of a smile on his face. 'There is a familiar quality to its aura. Something that tells me we are not so very far from where we need to be.'

'Then I shall call your command together,' Penthius said.

'The sooner they are assembled and organised the more–' He cut his words short and stifled a colourful oath. Through the dissipating fog, gold-and-blue-armoured warriors bearing hefty greatbows dispersed between the trees. 'Nerio,' he grumbled. 'Already he breaks with protocol and indulges his whims.'

'The Castigator-Prime would call it instinct,' Arnhault reminded Penthius. 'There is more to strategy than the strictures laid down in tome and treatise. There are times when it is prudent to attend to what one *feels* rather than what one *knows*.'

Penthius shook his head. 'Instinct attends to but one possibility while doctrine seeks a plan flexible enough to confront many possibilities. Nerio's Castigators will be exposed the way he has deployed them. They will not have my Sequitors to guard them. We should adopt a block formation with the–'

Penthius' speech fell into an abrupt silence. Through the forest, a great rumbling could be heard. It took some moments before the noise became distinct enough to be discerned: the cracking of tree trunks and the crash of mighty boles against the earth. There were great pounding impacts as well, as though an avalanche were rolling through the woods.

One of the Castigators, his helm adorned with a great spiked halo, shouted from the periphery of the clearing. 'Knight-Incantor! Something approaches our position!'

'Pull your warriors back, Nerio!' Penthius shouted. 'If there is an enemy come to oppose us, my Sequitors will unleash Sigmar's storm with hammer and shield while your Castigators put a volley into them.'

'Keep your warriors where they are, Nerio,' Arnhault countermanded. 'There is no time to redeploy. We must face the foe from the ground on which we stand.'

The rumbling in the forest was growing louder and seemed to have gathered impetus. The crack and crash of trees was ever more rapid. Now there could be felt tremors that shivered through the ground each time the pounding impacts slammed home. Arnhault knew what it meant, the terrible regularity of those impacts. They were the footfalls of some horrendously immense creature.

'Hammers of Sigmar! Brothers! Whatever comes, it will not stand between us and our duty to the God-King!' Arnhault raised his staff of office, letting its runes catch the fitful light drifting through the fog. At the sight of the Knight-Incantor's staff, a thundering war cry issued forth from the Stormcasts. 'Glory to the Heldenhammer!'

The defiant shouts of the Stormcasts enraged whatever moved through the forest. The violent charge picked up yet more speed. The tremors shaking the ground became a steady shudder. Trees leapt upwards as they were ripped from their roots and thrown into the sky. A heavy, musky stink spilled down into the clearing and caused such small animals as remained in their holes after the stormstrike to flee deeper into the forest.

Trees bordering the clearing were knocked asunder, crashing groundwards and forcing several of the Castigators to scramble from their path. In a spray of splinters and pine needles, a colossal shape emerged from the forest.

Towering over the Stormcasts and even many of the trees, the creature was covered in thick, shaggy black fur that was matted into twisted tangles and clotted with dried gore. Each of its four pillar-like legs was covered in a pebbly crimson skin, and its feet were broad pads with thick, plate-like toes. It had a large hump behind its short, thick neck – a slab of fatty tissue that was almost bald at its very top. The head of the creature was long and broad, with a wide mouth and enormous ebony tusks that curled back upon themselves. Its eyes were small and sharp, clouded with a scarlet sheen of frenzied fury. From the front of its face, a long snake-like trunk sagged and swayed – at least until its beady eyes sighted Knight-Incantor Arnhault. Then the creature reared up on its hind legs and raised its trunk to the sky. A deafening trumpet sounded from the mammoth, and when its tremendous bulk slammed back down onto all four legs, the tremor was such that Arnhault could feel it pulse through his bones.

He could also sense the malign energies that exuded from the creature. It was at once more and less than a mere beast of Ghur. The corrupt touch of Chaos was upon it, twisting it in both body and spirit. Arnhault felt its pain – the mammoth was wracked by the torment of isolation and consumed by a fratricidal madness that had caused it to slaughter its own herd. The bloodlust of Khorne ran through its gigantic frame, manifesting outwardly in spiky knobs of bone that protruded from its shaggy pelt. When the beast trumpeted a second time he detected a belligerence beyond that of a simple animal, rather the fury of a thing lost and damned.

Anger pulsed through Arnhault's veins – not the blind fury of Chaos but the righteous indignation of Sigmar. In his mind's eye he saw an image of what the mammoth should have been, a vision of the magnificent creature before it had been corrupted. Memories flickered before him of great herds of shaggy giants striding across autumnal plains, lending their mighty strength to the last harvest of the inhabitants in return for bushels of fruits and bundles of spring sweet grass. Those mammoths had been wise and gentle, far removed from the crazed beast that now opposed the Stormcasts.

'I will end this torment,' Arnhault vowed, staring into the beast's red eyes. He raised his staff, drawing upon the magic of the storm.

The mammoth bellowed once more and charged towards the Knight-Incantor. The instant it started to move, the Castigators arrayed around it began to shoot. The bulky thunderhead greatbows roared as they loosed a deadly barrage into the immense beast. Mace-like quarrels slammed into the shaggy hide, their crystalline heads exploding in bursts of celestial energy. The condensed breath of Stardrakes was sent crackling across the mammoth's body, searing its fur and scalding its skin. In a heartbeat, the bulky feeder atop each greatbow set another mace into place and the Castigators sent another volley into the raging beast.

A nimbus of light flared from Arnhault's staff as he swept it towards the mammoth. Flung from its head, the light expanded to become a withering wind, hot as the stars and cold as the void. The stellar storm swept across the charging beast, and in that arcane gale its shaggy pelt was peeled back, ripped from its hide in ragged clumps and gory strips. The denuded skin beneath was scarred and wet with blood, pockmarked with the malignant mutations of Chaos. Obscene growths quivered and writhed with loathsome animation as the divine wind ravaged the beast.

The wind Arnhault had drawn down into his staff was enough to bring a gargant to its knees, but the ferocity of the mammoth was such that it thundered onwards, refusing to be bowed despite the magnitude of its injuries. The very gore that bubbled from its wounds gave the beast renewed strength, for the Blood God did not care overmuch from whence the blood flowed.

'Sequitors! Shield and hammer!' Penthius' commanding tone rang out across the clearing. At a run, a dozen warriors stood between the mammoth and Arnhault. Swinging their broad shields before them as the beast pounded forwards, the

Sequitors raised their stormsmite mauls. Blue energy crackled about the head of each weapon, an aura of power drawn from the very essence of Azyr, the God-King's realm. Before the mammoth reached their line, that blue glow was drawn away from the hammers, passing instead into the gilded faces of their soulshields.

When the mammoth struck the line of Sequitors, a titanic shudder swept across the clearing and knocked branches from the outlying trees. Coruscant energies flittered through the air, crackling away in a dazzling display of power. Incredibly, the Sequitors held their ground, their line unbroken. Before them, the giant beast stood swaying from side to side, stunned by the calamitous impact of its charging bulk upon the nigh-impenetrable bulwark of the soulshields.

'Castigators! Loose!' Nerio raised his own greatbow and sent thunderhead maces exploding against the mammoth's flanks. Again the condensed Stardrake's breath was sent searing across the beast's mutated frame.

'Hammer and shield!' Penthius shouted to his own warriors. With the command, the glow left the soulshields and once more infused the heavy mauls the Sequitors bore. As arcane energy crackled about their weapons, the Stormcasts brought them crashing against the mammoth's pillar-like legs and tusked head. Flesh sizzled under their blows. Teeth were shattered in the beast's jaw. Blood turned to steam as it spurted across the glowing hammers.

Yet still the mammoth did not fall. Trumpeting its rage, its trunk coiled around one of the Sequitors. With acute awareness, the beast chose Penthius for its victim, pulling the Sequitor-Prime from the very midst of his Stormcasts. It lifted him into the air, his sigmarite armour creaking as the creature's trunk curled itself into a crushing grip.

Before the mammoth could destroy its captive, a thunderhead mace exploded against its trunk. Nerio, alerted to Penthius' danger, sent the shot slamming into the base of the extremity with unerring accuracy, the missile streaking past the curl of the tusks to detonate against the beast's face. A great mass of flesh and sinew was blasted away by the concentrated Stardrake's breath. All animation fled from the mammoth's trunk as it sagged limply against the ground. Penthius rolled clear of the lifeless coils and brought his maul cracking against one of the tusks. A jagged crack rippled through the ivory, and the mammoth reared back in shock.

'It is time to end your torture,' Arnhault intoned. For all that the mammoth was a crazed and corrupt beast of Chaos, he could not feel anything but regret for the pain his retinue had inflicted upon it. The most merciful thing that could be extended to the beast was the oblivion of a swift death. His voice dipped into a low cadence, invoking the spells of the Sacrosanct Chamber and the lore of High Azyr. A different light gathered about the staff he bore, a pearlescent glow that rippled with celestial power.

'Spirits of storm and sky, let your wrath flow through me.' Arnhault gestured with his staff and the glow leapt from its length, stretching out to become a flash of lightning. The unleashed energy struck against the mammoth's forehead, searing a black hole into its skull. The beast reared up, one foreleg kicking at the air, and then it came crashing down. The impact of its fall sent a shudder through the forest.

Smoke rose from the hole Arnhault's magic had burned into the mammoth's head, yet still the beast clung stubbornly to life. Its eyes retained a berserk fury as they focused upon the Knight-Incantor. Arnhault shook his head. He could not hate this beast any more than he could hate a rabid dog. It was a sick and maddened thing, a creature that had to be destroyed out of necessity. It was pity, not ire, that caused him to turn towards the Sequitors. 'Orthan,' he called out. 'Deliver Sigmar's rest.'

From amidst the ranks of the Sequitors a lone warrior marched forwards. Though armoured in the gold and blue of his brothers, Orthan had forsaken the maul and shield they bore. Instead he carried an immense mace, a weapon with a haft as long as the Stormcast was tall. The head of the weapon was a black bludgeon of enchanted sigmarite through which flickers of divine power flashed. Runes and sigils extolling the might of the God-King were etched across the dark surface and about its neck was a band of purest gold adorned with the emblem of the Hammer, holy Ghal Maraz itself.

Orthan advanced upon the fallen mammoth and halted beside the beast's smouldering head. 'For Sigmar!' the Sequitor howled as he lifted the stormsmite greatmace upwards. The flickers of divine power became a halo of might, suffusing the weapon and the warrior who held it. In a single stroke, Orthan brought the bludgeon crashing downwards. As its smashed into the mammoth's skull, pebbly flesh thick as a man's palm evaporated, inches of skull reduced to crackling cinders. An instant only, and the mammoth's head was reduced to ash. The beast's enormous frame quivered in a final spasm of pain and then was still.

While Orthan visited death upon the mammoth, Arnhault drew a silver vial from a pouch on his belt. An arcane song of eternity whispered across his lips as he held the vessel towards the beast. The instant the creature's life was driven from it, the magic he evoked reached out to the fleeing spirit. He could feel the Chaos contamination drifting apart from the core of the beast's essence, and it was this essence that his spell ensnared. With fingers of aetheric force, Arnhault's magic drew the mammoth's spirit down into the vial, pouring it into the tiny vessel until it was filled with the boiling energies of the vanquished giant. Only when he was certain he had drawn all that remained uncorrupted did Arnhault bring his song to an end. For a moment he could actually see the dark belligerence of Chaos lingering above the mammoth's carcass. Then it began to fade, seeping back into the cursed regions from whence it had come.

Arnhault stared at the vial for a moment and then quickly pressed a sigmarite stopper into the neck of the vessel. A powerful rune fashioned by duardin demi-gods adorned the underside of the stopper, forming a barrier no spirit could penetrate.

Castigator-Prime Nerio approached Arnhault as he returned the vial to the pouch on his belt. 'Forgive my impertinence, Knight-Incantor, but is it wise to try to trap such a spirit?'

Arnhault tapped his fingers against the pouch. 'For all the enormity of its flesh, the beast's spirit is a simple thing. Were it otherwise the taint of Chaos would have befouled it as completely as it defiled its body.' He shook his head. 'No, it is no reckless testing of my arts which you have beheld, merely a practical application of knowledge you too may prove worthy to learn.'

'Nerio would first need to learn how to confine himself to the structure of his lessons.' Penthius walked around the dead bulk of the mammoth to join his brothers. 'I do not think it would be prudent to train an acolyte who insists on learning how to conjure magic before he knows how to safely dispel it.'

The Castigator-Prime rounded on Penthius. 'A versatile mind understands the difference between recklessness and initiative.'

'Yes,' Penthius agreed. 'A versatile mind *does*.'

Nerio patted the thunderhead greatbow slung over his

shoulder. 'If I were not versatile that beast would have twisted your armour into such a state that you would now pass for a marsh crab.'

'If you had kept your archers in formation, we could have settled with the brute before it got to grips with anyone,' Penthius growled back at him. 'It is not for nothing that established procedures are observed. At least by a disciplined warrior.'

Arnhault interjected himself into what he knew would swell into bitter argument if allowed to escalate. Many times he had undertaken missions with Penthius and Nerio in his retinue, but never had he seen them agree upon anything when it came to tactics. Penthius was too hidebound and rigid, doggedly adhering to martial tradition. Nerio, by contrast, was impulsive and headstrong.

'We will save the tactical discussion for a later time,' Arnhault decreed. It was all he needed to say. If there was one thing Penthius and Nerio could agree upon, it was the depth of their loyalty to the Knight-Incantor. When Arnhault gave an order, it was obeyed instantly. The disagreement was forgotten until fresh provocation caused it to return.

Penthius turned towards the Knight-Incantor and bowed his head in deference to Arnhault's rank. 'Your knowledge of Ghur is formidable. Have you any awareness of this place? Do you know how near we may be to where our duty would take us?'

Arnhault's eyes closed as he considered the questions posed to him. 'We stand now in what was once the Wood of Gyr.' He looked to the trees from whence the mammoth had emerged. 'There is a crispness to the air in that direction, a trace of ice on the breeze. If we were to travel that way, we should find Frostmoor and its screaming glaciers. Long ago, it would have been a journey of many days' march.' Arnhault gestured to the pines that dominated the forest around them. 'But I speak of when the Wood of Gyr was home to willow and palm. The land has changed. As the screaming glaciers crawl further from Frostmoor, they drive the beasts and plants of the taiga before them.' He pointed his sigmarite staff at the mammoth's carcass. 'There was a time when these beasts were unknown in Gyr and rare in the Kingdom of Kharza.'

'Kharza is near then?' Nerio asked.

'It is near enough,' Arnhault supplied. 'The royal house of Kharza would ride to the Wood of Gyr to honour the Rites of Taal and hunt the golden boar with jade-tipped spears and sacred leopards trained to hunt no other prey. Their entourages would spend a fortnight travelling to the hunt and back.' He swung around and nodded towards the trees to his right. 'The journey will take us less time,' he stated. 'We are not encumbered by the regalia of royalty and the baggage of the hunt.'

'For all that, we too are hunters,' Nerio said. He reached to the quiver of crystal-headed maces that hung at his side.

'We are not hunters,' Penthius corrected him. 'We are protectors. Our duty is not to simply track some wild brute to its lair. An appeal has been made and that prayer has been heard. We are come to save the faithful of Wyrmditt from the evil that besets them.' He looked back to the mutated mammoth. 'Evil far different to the beasts of Chaos, but no less deadly.'

Nerio shook his head. 'It will not be enough to defend these people. We will have to root out this menace and destroy it utterly if we would bring them a lasting peace. Make no mistake, brother, we are hunters.'

'We are neither protectors nor hunters,' Arnhault said. He donned his helm, locking his face once more behind the stern metal mask. 'We are avengers,' he told his warriors. 'We come not simply to bring relief to the people of Wyrmditt. We will confront the darkness that threatens them and we will make it answer for its manifold outrages.'

Arnhault gestured to his brothers. 'Get our warriors into formation. Nerio, you will abide by whatever deployment Penthius deems advisable. Penthius, you will allow the Castigators flexibility of action should we encounter any unexpected obstacles.' He indicated the mammoth. 'Even before the scourge of Chaos threatened to overwhelm it utterly, Ghur was a place of fearsome beasts. With monsters twisted by the Dark Gods roaming the land, we must be doubly vigilant.

'Wyrmditt lies beyond the Wood of Gyr, across the veldt of the Fangfields and the hill country of Takrahn.' Arnhault nodded to himself as he envisioned the maps he had consulted when this duty had been entrusted to him, matching the place names to his more exacting knowledge. 'The town is deep within one of the border marches of Kharza, at the very edge of the old fiefdoms.'

'That is why the people are imperilled,' Penthius stated. 'They are too near the fallen kingdom. Too close to the shadows of the past.'

Arnhault gave the Sequitor-Prime a reproachful look. 'The shadows of the past hang over us all, brother.' He swept his gaze across the clearing, studying the forest around them. 'Perhaps the past is never a heavier burden than when we do not recognise its weight upon us.'

Mouldering darkness filled the silent hall. The pomp and pageantry of the court was absent now, and in their place there was only an oppressive gloom.

Sabrodt leaned back into the diamond-headed throne. Golden wings cast to echo the leathery pinions of dragons formed a magnificent canopy overhead. The heavy arms of the throne were like scaly coils; the broad feet were clawed talons. If he raised his eyes he could see the fanged visage of the dragon, the huge diamond lodged in its throat. In the right light, an eerie flicker shimmered within the diamond, as though the beast's flame were about to spill forth and immolate those who bowed before the throne.

Since his early childhood, Sabrodt had been enthralled by the Dragonseat. He was captivated by its wondrous beauty, the richness of its settings and the craftsmanship that infused every curve and line, each scale and claw, with masterful artistry. Nowhere, he was convinced, was there anything so grand as this throne. Not in the palaces of the gods themselves could such magnificence possibly be found.

The royal court's splendour was as nothing when compared to the Dragonseat. Artisans from lands beyond a hundred horizons had laboured to create a hall that could complement the throne at its centre. No feat of man or duardin had been equal to the task. Sabrodt had watched them fail, one after another, led away in disgrace to the priest-king's dungeons. As a boy, he had gone down to those benighted vaults to listen to the artists bewailing their fate, begging their guards for even one more glimpse of the masterpiece they had failed to match.

How he had longed to sit upon the Dragonseat and to possess it. Being so near to it year upon year had been a kind of torture to Sabrodt. Always so close, always within reach. Yet he could not dare to reach, for only the priest-king was allowed to touch the throne.

A grisly laugh rose from Sabrodt. Now. Now he *was* priest-king.

His gaze pierced the darkness of the hall, for there was no shadow that could hide its secrets from him any more. He could see the cracked pillars of malachite and obsidian that ringed the chamber, the archways of black marble that stretched between them and helped support the ceiling. Mouldy tatters of tapestry yet clung to the archways, hanging like dusty cobwebs. The lavish rugs that stretched across the floor were faded and frayed, clotted with dirt and grime. The tile frescoes adorning the walls were cracked and crumbling, exposing the grey earth behind them.

The grisly laugh took on a bitter note as Sabrodt stared at the jumbled bones piled about the chamber. It was many years since the court of Kharza had been as he remembered it. The morbid stamp of death was upon it now.

Sabrodt leaned back in the Dragonseat, the throne he had coveted for so very long, and his insubstantial spirit shifted through the ancient chair. He was priest-king, lord of Kharza and the only one with the authority to sit upon the throne, yet it was the one thing he could not do. Only by the greatest exertion of willpower could he impel some semblance of solidity to his being. But to touch the Dragonseat was a thing too keenly desired, too dearly cherished. The moment he tried, his focus would be lost and his phantom hand would pass right through the throne.

A spiteful snarl hissed its way through Sabrodt's fleshless face. He rose from the throne and drew his ragged burial shroud closer around his spectral form. The Dragonseat was a foolishness of his youth, the idle dream of a child. It was not the throne he had coveted. It was the power it represented. The power he now commanded. He, *he* was priest-king!

Ghostly lights blazed within the hollows of the wraith's skull. Kharza belonged to Sabrodt. It was his dominion and would be forever. That was the promise Black Nagash made to him when he had sworn his soul to the Great Necromancer.

That was the curse that would not allow Sabrodt to rest quiet in his grave.

Sabrodt, priest-king of Kharza.

Sabrodt, the Shrouded King.

CHAPTER TWO

The steam of countless geysers billowed up into the morning sky and created a hot rain that pelted the sigmarite mail of the Sacrosanct retinue as they marched across what had once been the frontier of a powerful kingdom. Sometimes the gnarled remains of a watchtower would protrude from the damp earth, its ancient masonry hidden beneath thick growths of crimson moss. The fallen debris of shattered keeps created jagged knolls and stumpy hills on which stubborn thorn bushes sank their roots. Once the empty hulk of an abandoned temple loomed into view, flocks of jackal-bats roosting beneath the empty arches and shattered windows.

'The Kingdom of Kharza must have been rich indeed to lavish such constructions upon its borderlands,' Penthius observed as they moved past the decayed temple.

Arnhault stared at the rubble between the temple's empty walls. 'The margraves drew a generous largesse from their king so that they might better defend his domain from invaders.'

He turned and gazed across the rolling landscape, its vast expanse of sharp-leaved tall-grass broken by clusters of bushes and the occasional stand of trees. 'Many were the grot and orruk hordes that were crushed in the veldt without ever despoiling the heartlands of Kharza. For ten generations, no foreign hand laid siege upon the Koeningshoff or threatened the Dragonseat.'

The Knight-Incantor shook his head. 'But there is no greater enemy of legacy and tradition than Chaos. The legions of the Dark Gods came into Ghur, as they did all the Mortal Realms except sacred Azyr. The chronicles say that the armies of Kharza fought nobly, but against the tide of darkness they could not prevail.'

'Only the might of Sigmar is powerful enough to prevail against Chaos,' Nerio stated and clasped his fingers tight around the holy talisman hanging from his neck.

Arnhault gave Nerio a solemn look. 'Such is true, but the host of Kharza was denied even the choice to perish in battle. Swords raised high. Defiance in their hearts.' His hand closed tighter about the sigmarite staff he carried. 'The chronicles relate that before the battle could be fought, the warriors of Kharza were brought low. Betrayed from within.

'A traitor delivered these lands to the Dark Gods and left them to languish under their vile oppression until Sigmar's might at last forced Chaos into retreat.' Arnhault reached down and knocked over a stone lying atop the loamy earth. An assortment of insects scurried away as he upended their refuge. Deftly he snatched up one of the creatures before it could escape. 'The blight of Chaos lingers on,' he said, holding out to his companions the creature he held. It was a long, worm-like thing with huge mandibles and spiny projections along its sides. Dark burgundy in hue, there were bold white markings across its back, markings that were too vivid and regular to be entirely natural. The white splotches each depicted the skull rune of Khorne.

'Blood-maggot.' Penthius made no effort to disguise his loathing. 'I know this vermin. They feed on the carrion left by Khorne's hordes.'

'How can they exist when the Blood God's murderers have been driven from these lands?' Nerio wondered.

Arnhault dropped the grotesque creature and smashed it with the butt of his staff. 'Like the Blood God, this filth cares not what feeds their malicious hunger. It is enough that their fodder has perished by violence, and in the Realm of Beasts there is a surfeit of violence to sustain them.' He wiped his staff clean on the swaying grass. 'A reminder that even when the hosts of Chaos have been forced into retreat, the corruption they carry with them will remain.'

Arnhault looked back to the desolate temple. 'But it is not Chaos which now seeks to control these lands. A different breed of evil is at work here.' The Knight-Incantor walked towards the crumbling edifice. At his approach, clusters of jackal-bats left their perches and went soaring over the veldt, their eerie laugh-like chirps echoing across the plain.

Penthius called the rest of the Stormcasts to a halt. The armoured warriors broke ranks, using the respite to inspect their weapons. Three of Nerio's Castigators spread out to form a circuit around their brothers, their bulky thunderhead greatbows held at the ready, their eyes roving across the veldt, watching for any threatening sign.

Penthius, however, had his attention fixed in one direction. He watched the old temple and the lone Stormcast who moved steadily towards its crumbling mass.

'A strange humour has come upon Arnhault,' Nerio said, following the direction of Penthius' gaze.

Penthius nodded and watched Arnhault pass through the empty doorway of the temple. 'Maintain command here,' he told Nerio. 'Stay vigilant. I will see if the Knight-Incantor requires help. He is a greater aether-mage than any of us, more attuned to the harmonies of magic. It may be he has sensed something here that none of us can feel.'

'We should make haste to Wyrmditt,' Nerio said, his voice lowered. 'It is there our duty calls us.'

'It is not for us to remind Arnhault of our duty,' Penthius chastised his brother, matching the low tone of Nerio. He did not want the other Stormcasts to overhear the exchange. 'He has served the Sacrosanct Chamber through many reforgings and won for Sigmar many victories. Neither of us are fit to question his decisions.'

'I stand humbled,' Nerio said. 'I can only blame eagerness for putting such thoughts on my tongue. I meant no disrespect to Arnhault.'

'I did not think you did,' Penthius assured him. 'I know your devotion to the Knight-Incantor is as solid as my own.' He clapped his armoured hand against Nerio's pauldron. 'Keep our brothers ready to move on. I will see if I can render Arnhault assistance.'

Penthius moved through the long grass towards the old ruin. Jackal-bats continued to fly up from the temple's darkened interior, their agitated cries sharp in the misty air. The Sequitor-Prime kept a tight grip about the haft of his maul. He was tense with foreboding and uneasy with this departure from the martial strictures of the chamber. He trusted that Arnhault had good reason for this diversion, even if he could not conceive the Knight-Incantor's intention.

The broad archway that stretched above the temple entrance loomed over Penthius as he made his way into the ruin. As soon as his foot crossed the threshold, a feeling of malevolence impressed itself upon him. So strong was the impression that it gave him pause, kept him standing in the shadow of the empty gate. He had imagined the temple had once been devoted to the God-King, or at least Taal or another of the nature divinities honoured by the people of Ghur. Yet there was no hint of holiness about the place, no suggestion of Azyr's light about it. Even if the temple had been destroyed and despoiled by the slaves of Chaos, there should have been some trace of its original sanctification that a Sacrosanct Stormcast could sense.

But there was nothing. Only that nebulous impression of hostility that felt to Penthius like hungry eyes watching him from the dark.

The sound of movement further back in the temple drew Penthius deeper into the ruin. As he moved through the crumbling rubble, around the heaps of debris where the structure's roof had fallen in, the sounds became more distinct. Not simply the flutter of bat-wings or the creep of vermin. There was a stolid regularity about them, a rhythm that might almost have been a low cadence.

Penthius quickened his pace, soulshield held before him and maul at the ready. As he rounded a pile of rubble he came upon a section of the temple where a few remnants of the roof had managed to defy the ravages of time. Beneath it was a patch of ground from which the rubble had been cleared. A simple altar fashioned from a piece of slate stood there, a feeble echo of that which must once have graced such a big sanctuary. He noted with alacrity the morbid offerings resting on the crude table, the fleshless skulls of crows and dogs.

Crouched down beside the altar was a young girl clad in a

deerskin dress and with a serpent-hide belt about her waist. Her ashen blonde hair was tied back in a row of three braids, one hanging across each shoulder while the third dangled down her back. It was from the girl that the sounds Penthius heard came. In her lap rested a small copper drum and she was striking it with a carved leg bone at regular intervals.

'Let her finish the ritual.' Arnhault's voice suddenly broke into Penthius' observations. The Sequitor-Prime spun around, surprised to find the Knight-Incantor standing in the darkness.

'What is all this about?' Penthius asked, slowly lowering his weapon.

There was a sombre quality to Arnhault's words when he answered. 'An old ceremony, something that has been passed down from the days when Kharza was a great kingdom and not merely a wilderness with scattered settlements.' He gestured with his staff at the girl. 'She is rendering prayers to the God of Death, asking that the spirit of her brother be allowed to pass safely into the Underworld.'

'God of Death,' Penthius repeated. He glanced around the crumbling temple. The malevolence he had felt, the lack of even the merest flicker of Azyr's light, was explained. This temple had no part in Azyr. Its energies were those of Shyish and its god was not Sigmar but a far darker entity. 'She prays to Nagash,' he whispered.

'Yes,' Arnhault said. 'Though it was long ago, Nagash was once part of Sigmar's pantheon and permitted dominion over the souls of the dead. It is a dominion he still commands. Only those spirits most precious to the other gods are capable of escaping the Lord of Undeath.'

'We must stop her,' Penthius swore. He started towards the altar, but Arnhault held his staff before him and blocked his path.

'We must wait,' Arnhault said. 'To disrupt the ritual now might prove unwise. It was believed that these prayers would open a channel between the realms. If we interrupt we may cause that channel to remain open and allow the shades of Shyish entry into this world. Moreover, should we silence her prayers we will give warning of our presence here. I would rather know the nature of my enemy before it is aware that I am here to bring its evil to an end.'

Penthius watched the girl as she set the skull of a cat on the altar. With a needle she pricked her finger and drew a single hieroglyph upon the skull in her own blood. He started forwards, instinctively repulsed by the macabre ritual. 'This is indecent,' he growled.

'There are laws to every kind of magic,' Arnhault declared. 'Not all of them are pleasant to behold. The ritual you are watching was old when the Kingdom of Kharza was young, handed down from shaman to mystic and from mystic to priest.' He glanced up at the remaining ceiling, where the faintest remnant of a painted fresco could be found. He drew Penthius' attention to it.

Still vivid upon the fresco was the shining figure of a bearded man in golden armour, a crown of stars upon his head and a mighty warhammer in his hand. Beside him, veiled in darkness, was a shape in black robes and wearing a tall helm that cast the face beneath into shadow. One hand was outstretched, holding in its bony fingers a great book. The other gripped the gnarled haft of a scythe.

'Sigmar and Nagash,' Arnhault named the painted figures. 'There was a time when the Great Necromancer lent his powers to the God-King's design. He was honoured alongside the rest of the pantheon and the people venerated him as the King of the Underworld.'

'That was long ago,' Penthius stated. 'Before the betrayal at the All-Gates, before Nagash raised undead legions across the Mortal Realms to extend his rule beyond the boundaries of Shyish. If ever Nagash's fellowship with the God-King was more than pretence, that time is long past.'

Arnhault nodded. 'These things we know, but they will not help this child. They will not allay her fears for her brother's spirit and the peace it will find beyond the grave.'

The Knight-Incantor's words had a sobering effect upon Penthius. Endowed with the many gifts of the Stormcasts, his body and mind raised beyond the threshold of mortality, it was easy to forget the frailties of mundane humanity. It was a quality that Penthius had always despised when he'd encountered it in other Stormcasts, that self-righteous arrogance and unspoken contempt for common people and their weaknesses. He had always been watchful lest that kind of hubris should find purchase in his own mind. Even then, his vigilance had not been absolute.

'You are correct, of course,' Penthius said. 'Zeal is a poor brother to understanding.'

'Zeal is a powerful tool,' Arnhault told him, 'but you must never allow it to be the only weapon in your arsenal.' A distant look came into his eyes. To Penthius, it seemed Arnhault was no longer even looking at him, or at the temple in which they stood. 'Even so, it is a wise man who knows when to be zealous. Who recognises when the time for compassion and understanding is over and all that is left is the necessity of what must be done.'

'Necessity, brother?' Penthius could not follow the trend of Arnhault's speech.

Arnhault shook his head, the distant look vanishing from his eyes. 'The girl's prayers will be over soon,' he said, ignoring the question Penthius had posed. 'When she is finished, I will speak to her. From her prayers, I have gleaned that she comes from Wyrmditt.'

Penthius looked towards the child with a different appreciation for why Arnhault had taken interest in her. 'She can guide us back to her town,' he said.

'More importantly, she can tell us something of her home,' Arnhault explained. 'She can tell us the nature of this evil that preys on her community. When we know that, we will have a better appreciation for the ordeal ahead of us.' He glanced at Penthius. 'The augurs could divine only so much from the prayers the people of Wyrmditt rendered up to Sigmar. We know only that the evil that hangs over their community is more than the mundane hazard of beast or brigand. The enemy here is such that falls under the auspices of the Sacrosanct Chamber.'

'That could mean the daemons of Chaos,' Penthius nodded to the faded fresco. 'Or it could mean the spectres of Nagash.'

'All the more reason to let her finish her prayers,' Arnhault said, 'and avoid warning those spectres that we are here.' He nodded at the cat skull resting on the altar. Penthius looked at the morbid object with keen interest. Though he'd watched the girl mark the thing with her blood, now there was only the faintest hint of the hieroglyph she had drawn. Before his eyes he watched as even that dim residue began to vanish.

'It will not be long now,' Arnhault assured Penthius.

The two Stormcasts watched while the last traces of blood vanished from the cat skull. The girl bowed her head towards the altar then rose to her feet, her little hands smoothing the folds of her dress. As she turned around, she saw for the first time the armoured giants who had joined her in the ruin. Her eyes wide with amazement, she backed away, almost tripping over the crude altar. Penthius could see the shiver of dread that gripped her as she opened her mouth and tried to scream. All that emerged was a terrified gasp.

Arnhault made a placating gesture with his hands. 'Do not be afraid. We are not here to do you harm.'

The girl kept backing away, her already pale complexion turning still more ashen. She reached to the serpent-hide belt and drew a small knife. In her panic she was oblivious to the absurdity of the action.

'I am Penthius,' the Sequitor-Prime said, tapping his hand against his breastplate. 'This is Knight-Incantor Arnhault.' He paused as he noticed the girl responding to his voice. 'We are on a quest and have come from very far away...'

The girl looked at Arnhault. 'Are you really a knight?' she asked with a quiver in her voice.

'I am,' Arnhault answered. 'I am a knight in the service of the God-King.' He pointed to Penthius. 'We both are. We are sworn to honour Sigmar's justice and protect those who keep the spirit of Sigmar's laws.'

'Tell us, little one, by what name are you called?' Penthius asked.

The question caused colour to rush into the child's cheeks and an embarrassed smile to tug at her mouth. 'My name is Hilda,' she said. 'My grandma used to tell me stories,' she added as she lowered her knife. 'She talked about knights who walked inside the lightning and would sometimes come down to fight monsters.' She pointed at the crow skull lying on the altar. 'Grandma died.'

'And now you have lost your brother,' Penthius said, indicating the cat skull the girl had added to the macabre collection.

'Oh no,' Hilda hurried to correct him. 'He did not get lost. Everybody knows where he is.'

'We mean that he is gone from this realm,' Penthius explained.

'No, they won't let him go anywhere,' Hilda said. 'It isn't allowed. He has to stay where they put him.'

Penthius shook his head. 'Your brother is dead. Of course he must stay where they buried him.'

A puzzled expression fell across the girl's face. She gazed up at the Stormcasts in confusion. 'Berndt isn't dead – he is just where they put him.'

Arnhault stepped forwards and leaned down to look Hilda in the eyes. 'You were sitting here saying prayers for your brother's spirit,' he reminded her. 'Why would you do that if he is not dead?'

Hilda drew away from Arnhault, fear creeping back into her eyes. Penthius walked over to Arnhault and laid his hand on the aether-mage's shoulder. 'Let me talk to her,' he suggested. He reached up and undid the straps holding his helmet. When he removed the sigmarite mask and revealed his own features, Hilda smiled at him and even took a step closer.

'I apologise if we frightened you,' Penthius said, 'but it is important that we know why you were saying prayers if your brother isn't dead.'

'Because Mamma and Pappa said he was going to go away like grandma did. I don't want Berndt to go away, so I came here to ask the god to not take him.' Hilda cast her gaze to the floor, trying to hide from Penthius the tears that now filled her eyes. 'When grandma was sick I came here to ask the god not to take her, but he didn't listen.' She stamped her foot on the floor. 'I did everything just like Pater Mathias does in his chapel, but the god wouldn't listen to me.' She looked up, instinctively turning towards Arnhault when she asked her question. 'Why didn't the god listen? Was it because I was bad?'

Arnhault shook his head. 'There is no easy answer for why.

Sometimes even the kindest gods won't do everything that is asked of them.' He darted a look at Penthius, then returned his gaze to Hilda. 'You say they are keeping Berndt somewhere? Is it somewhere in Wyrmditt?'

Hilda nodded and stifled a sob. 'Yes. We all live in Wyrmditt. They took Berndt and locked him in the chapel.'

'Who did? The other people in the town?' Arnhault waited while the girl slowly nodded. 'Why would they do that?'

Hilda looked at Arnhault, then swung her gaze back to Penthius. 'They have to give him to the king,' she said.

Arnhault rose to his feet. When he spoke, it was in a sombre whisper. 'What king, child?'

'The Shrouded King,' Hilda said. 'The priest-king of Kharza.'

Thick clouds of mist hung above Wyrmditt, pelting the town with warm rain. Brief glimpses of the settlement could be seen from the hills above it, but for the most part it was simply an indistinct mass. Situated on the periphery of the vast geyser fields, Wyrmditt was veiled in the steam exhaled by the boiling pools. The atmosphere was damp and heavy, notably hotter than the veldt and the area around the abandoned Shrine of Nagash.

Arnhault studied the town from atop one of the hills, or at least as much as the heavy mists allowed him to. There were spells he might have evoked that would have dissipated the clouds and afforded him an unobstructed view, but he dismissed the temptation to draw on his magic. From what he had learned from Hilda, he was concerned that the enemy would sense such an aetheric disturbance. If it could be helped, he intended to deny their foe such warning.

'It never fails to be a cause for wonder, the places men will make their own.' Castigator-Prime Nerio touched his fingers to the talisman he wore. He and three of his bowmen had accompanied Arnhault as a bodyguard while the Knight-Incantor scouted Wyrmditt. The armour of all four Castigators was damp with the warm rain, but only Nerio had the habit of cradling his greatbow against his side to protect it from the moisture – a precaution that was unnecessary for the thunderhead greatbow, but perhaps not so eccentric for whatever weapon he'd carried before he was first reforged.

Arnhault rolled that thought over in his mind. A little echo of the past still impressing itself on Nerio. It was one of the terrible riddles of reforging, which parts of the Stormcast remained and which were lost upon the Anvil of the Apotheosis. An old habit devoid of conscious volition endured while the face of a cherished son was obliterated from the mind. There seemed to be no pattern to what was retained and what was lost, yet Arnhault was convinced there had to be some kind of methodology behind it all. Except for the profane magic of Chaos, all enchantments and conjurations obeyed certain laws. Even if an aether-mage didn't know what they were, that didn't mean they were not there.

'Would it be impudent to suggest that these people should move?' Nerio jested. 'Certainly there must be places they could settle where they wouldn't have to drink the air.'

Arnhault pointed to the dirty brown ribbon that snaked its way past the dark mass that was Wyrmditt and its streets. 'That is the Wyrm River, born from the blood of the demi-dragon Zhaan. Men have always plied its waters to trade with their neighbours. In the days of Kharza there were many towns like Wyrmditt on its shores, some even larger. The mist you despise is the price these people pay for their prosperity.' He gestured away from the town and the river to the geyser fields and the plumes of water vapour rising from the boiling pools. 'The geysers throw up more than steam and mist. Rare salts and exotic minerals are cast up as well, dredged from the very roots of the world. In old times there were duardin lords who would pay their weight in gold for the treasures yielded by this land.'

Nerio wiped the condensation from the mask of his helm. 'Greed,' he hissed. 'I could forgive that motivation if it simply asked these people to endure this cloying atmosphere, but this town has sunk far beneath such considerations.' He waved back down the hill to where Penthius and the other Stormcasts waited along with the girl. 'What that child has told us makes me think we should leave this whole place to its fate.'

Arnhault glared at Nerio. 'The mission entrusted to us calls us to this place,' he reminded him. 'Our duty is here. We will defend it.'

'Forgive me, Knight-Incantor,' Nerio said, 'but was it not you who said that we were not hunters or protectors, but avengers? Who is worthy of vengeance if not those who would sacrifice their own people to save themselves?'

'The fiends that have forced them to such an abominable choice,' Arnhault replied. 'The undead creature that has crowned itself king of Kharza.' He cast his gaze out over Wyrmditt, but it was not the town he was looking at. It was the land beyond it, the old kingdom hidden by the low-hanging clouds. 'Do not think this evil will be content with one town. It will seek to expand its dominion, to bring even more of Ghur under the shroud of Nagash.' He turned back to Nerio. 'What we fight here is but a skirmish in a far wider war.

'We will avenge the innocent who have been lost here,' Arnhault vowed. 'But we will visit that vengeance upon those truly deserving of it.' He looked once more upon the sprawl of Wyrmditt. His focus was drawn to one structure that was taller than the others, its slate roof poking through the mist.

'Come,' he said, 'I have seen all I need to see. It is time we returned the child to her home.

'And proclaimed to the people of Wyrmditt that their deliverance is at hand.'

Arnhault led the procession of Stormcasts as they marched into Wyrmditt. The buildings were tall and narrow, their lower walls built from heavy stones while the upper floors were fashioned from wooden beams and panels of lacquered paper. Each structure had an angled roof with slate tiles and leering gargoyles that did their best to spit out the omnipresent rain collecting on them. A few of the buildings sported little workshops that faced the street while others had ornate gateways that led into tiny gardens of rock and sand. Sometimes a larger structure would appear, signs stretching out from their facades to proclaim the trade conducted within. Brewer and cooper, stonesmith and tanner, glass-blower and steelmonger.

The armoured tread of the Stormcasts upon the cobblestones sent a dull roar rolling through the streets ahead of them. There was no question that the inhabitants were aware of their visitors, yet not one could be seen. Arnhault could imagine them hiding inside their homes, peering anxiously through shuttered windows and cracked doors. Perhaps none of them recognised the Stormcast Eternals for what they were, or perhaps they did and hid themselves from a sense of shame over what their fear had driven them to do.

'Do they not know who we are?' Orthan wondered. 'Can they not guess why we have come here?'

Penthius shot the Sequitor a stern look. 'We came here to fulfil our mission and execute our duty, not for accolades and glory, brother.'

From his tone, Arnhault could guess that Penthius shared

some of Orthan's disappointment. It was only natural. They had come to Wyrmditt in part to deliver it from its enemy. Instead they found the inhabitants seeking to placate that enemy and hiding from the warriors who would rescue them from the darkness.

'Honour is a seed which everyone nurtures within their own heart,' Arnhault declared, casting his voice so that each member of his retinue would hear him. 'Only your own deeds will make it grow, not the cheers of the crowd.'

He raised his staff, gesturing to the mist-cloaked street before them. 'We turn at the next corner,' Arnhault commanded. 'From there we will be where we need to be.' He thought of the tall building he had seen poking up through the fog. 'Where we belong.'

The Stormcasts marched onwards, still unchallenged by the townsfolk. Occasionally they would hear a door slam shut somewhere in the distance, but otherwise the only sound was their boots upon the cobbles. Except for a few prowling cats and wandering chickens, nothing moved through the streets.

The change came when Arnhault led them towards the tower-like structure. The Stormcasts bowed their heads in reverence when they saw the carved hammer that stood above the building's entrance and the banners that hung to either side of it, the twin-tailed comet stitched across their blue fields. A temple not to Nagash but to Sigmar. Here, if anywhere in the town, they would be recognised and welcomed.

'It seems deserted,' Penthius said to Arnhault. He indicated the tattered nature of the banners, the faded state of the hammer. Thick clumps of moss clung to the stonework, the wooden supports were splintered and warped, and the paper panels were torn in many spots. Everything about the temple screamed of neglect.

Arnhault kept his gaze fastened upon the building. More attuned to the aetheric harmonies, he could sense the difference between a sanctuary that had been abandoned and one in which a sincerity of faith persisted. 'All is not always as it seems,' he advised Penthius.

A moment after Arnhault spoke, the temple door slid open. An aged man in a ragged robe stumbled forwards. His skin was almost white in its pallor and the few strands of hair that clung to his scalp had a silvery sheen. Around his neck he wore a heavy chain from which a tiny golden hammer hung. When he turned his wizened face towards the Stormcasts, the eyes that regarded them were white with blindness.

Just the same, a look of ecstatic joy seized the old man's features. Clasping the hammer in both hands, he fell to his knees and began to weep. 'Sigmar, mighty God-King, receive my unworthy gratitude! Hear my praise, oh Sigmar, for in your unmatched benevolence you have sent your divine warriors to aid us in our direst need!'

'How can he know who we are?' Nerio asked. 'He cannot see us.'

'He does not need to see us,' Arnhault declared. He stepped forwards and gently lifted the old man onto his feet. The man's thin arms clutched adoringly at his gauntlet.

'I have prayed,' the old man said. 'How I have prayed that this day would come!'

'I am Knight-Incantor Arnhault of the Hammers of Sigmar. How are you named?'

The old man held the hammer icon to his lips before answering. 'I am Friar Mueller, the keeper of Sigmar's faith in Wyrmditt.' Emotion welled up within him, almost choking his words. 'When all others lost faith, I would not lose hope that Sigmar would deliver our town.'

Hilda stepped out from among the Stormcasts and took hold of Mueller's hand. She turned towards the armoured giants. 'Friar Mueller lives here,' she said, 'but nobody else has come here in a long time. Not since the Shrouded King.' She lowered her voice to a conspiratorial whisper. 'He used to see, but everyone was afraid he would make the Shrouded King angry...'

'The scum,' Nerio snarled, his hands tightening around his greatbow. He glared at the buildings around them, as though he wouldn't leave anything for the undead to lay claim to.

'Do not blame them,' Friar Mueller begged the Stormcasts. 'They were afraid and it was naïve of me to think I alone could match the Shrouded King's evil.' A smile pulled at his face as he nodded his bald head. 'But now, now you are here. Now this evil will end!'

Friar Mueller turned and began shouting into the streets. 'Cowards! Wretches! Why do you hide? How can the blind man see and you cannot! Sigmar has heard my prayers! In his divine mercy he has sent his holy warriors to fight for us! Come out! Come out and greet those who will deliver you from the Shrouded King's horrors!'

One by one, across the town, the sound of doors opening could be heard. Gradually figures appeared on the streets, men and women who slowly moved towards the Temple of Sigmar and the armoured warriors arrayed around it. As they came nearer, the suspicion Arnhault saw on their faces changed into wonder. Their pace quickened and soon a large crowd was gathered around the Stormcasts. An excited babble rose from the assembled townsfolk. They gazed in open admiration at the huge warriors and the massive weapons they bore.

Arnhault turned and addressed the crowd. 'We are come in answer to the prayers of your Friar Mueller,' he announced. 'His unwavering faith has brought us down from Azyr to vanquish the darkness that threatens you.' He shook the sigmarite staff at the gathered villagers. 'A darkness that you have too long sought to appease.' The crowd fell silent at the reproach in his voice. 'You did what you did out of fear. The weight of those deeds is a burden each of you must bear alone. But know this – there will be no more appeasement. The Shrouded King will take no more of your people.'

Arnhault pointed to Hilda. 'This child has told me that her brother is being held as an offering to the Shrouded King. He is to be released. At once.'

A man and woman emerged from the crowd and hurried to Hilda. Gathering her in their arms, they bowed at Arnhault's feet and sobbed in gratitude to the Knight-Incantor. Arnhault's attention, however, was fixated upon another pair who had come creeping out from among the townsfolk. One was a fat, elderly man arrayed in a fur-trimmed coat and wearing a jewelled pectoral. The other was a lean slip of a creature, only his thin face poking out from the hooded cloak that enfolded him.

'Burghermeister Vanholf,' Arnhault addressed the man in the coat. 'I have heard much about you.'

The man in the hooded cloak shook his head. 'Surely you will not lend too much credence to a child's stories.'

Arnhault spun around and pointed an accusing finger at the cloaked man. 'I have heard even more about you, Pater Mathias.'

The thin priest threw his head back and tried to assume a haughty posture. 'I did what was needful to save this town. How could we trust that Sigmar would answer our prayers?'

'So you started feeding people to the undead,' Nerio snarled.

'Better that the few die in order that the many should live,' Mathias said, trying to defend himself.

'Spoken like a true acolyte of Nagash,' the Castigator-Prime retorted.

Mathias winced when he noted that Nerio's greatbow was aimed towards him. 'The rituals of the dead must be observed,' he protested. 'If the spirit is not received by Nagash and allowed passage into the Underworlds then it will wander endlessly, without form or purpose.'

Arnhault stepped forwards. Before Mathias could react, his hand had seized the front of the priest's cloak and he lifted the man off the ground. 'It was you who communed with the Shrouded King and made this obscene arrangement.'

The priest's eyes were wide with fright as he saw the disgust in Arnhault's gaze. 'He demanded tribute! Tribute! The Shrouded King claims all the lands of Kharza as his own and will have tribute from all who dwell there.' He cast an appealing look to Vanholf and the other villagers. 'The Shrouded King did not want gold or riches. He demanded lives, vassals to serve in his domain.'

'And you gave them to him,' Arnhault hissed. Contemptuously he flung the priest from him. Mathias crashed down upon the cobbles amid the stunned crowd. 'Leave here, priest! Leave before I think better of my mercy.'

Pater Mathias did not need to be warned twice. Picking himself up from the ground, he shoved his way through the crowd and ran off into the mist.

Arnhault turned back towards Vanholf. The burghermeister's face was beaded with sweat, his eyes bulging in fright. 'You have been led astray, Vanholf. You have attended ill counsel for too long. Now you will listen to me.'

'Of course,' Vanholf gasped. 'Whatever you say, my lord. Whatever you need, Wyrmditt will provide it.'

'Good,' Arnhault told him. 'First we will discuss the layout of your town and what happens when the Shrouded King comes to claim his tribute. Then we will make our plans and decide how Wyrmditt will be redeemed from this evil.'

Within the silent depths of his throne room, the dark essence of Sabrodt stirred. The Shrouded King looked across the mouldering finery of his funereal palace. The splendour he had coveted for so long was hollow to him now, as empty as an open grave. It would take more, much more, to satisfy him.

In a rush of shadow and malice, Sabrodt swept through the desolate corridors of his cairn, past the sepulchres of ancient knights and legendary heroes, past the urns that held the ashes of princes and barons.

Arise, the malignant spectre thought as he passed. Wisps of shadow crawled out from the tombs in his wake. Gradually they took on the merest semblance of shape, the faint echo of form – wraiths called into being by the decree of their sovereign.

When Sabrodt emerged from the hulking barrow mound that held his throne, a seething morass of darkness followed him into the moonlight. Phantasmal skulls leered from the folds of ghostly robes, bony hands grasped spectral blades. Sabrodt turned his crowned head towards the aethereal throng. Among them he could recognise the most powerful warriors of his father's reign and the most renowned heroes of Kharza's long history.

His! All his! Sabrodt whipped around, staring across the barren plain on which his barrow had been raised. It was a place soaked in the blood of battle and the stink of death. How many had died here in that final battle? Thousands? And all of them his to command. Conquered and conqueror alike, all forced to recognise his dominion over them! It needed but a single word, a single command, and they would rise from where they'd fallen, a host of the dead whose only purpose would be to obey!

What other priest-king of Kharza had been so mighty?

Even as Sabrodt exulted in his power, his gaze fastened upon a discongruous patch of green upon the desolate plain. The Shrouded King gnashed his bony jaws in rage as he looked on this defiance of his rule. He knew it would be useless to try to destroy it by force or spell. The grass would always come back, as vibrant and alive as before. More than the sight of this stubborn life in his domain of death, it was what the greenery represented that fed Sabrodt's anger.

Yes, all the souls that had perished in that final battle belonged to Sabrodt, were his to command. All except one – the spirit of the warrior who had fallen where that grass now grew.

Hate welled up inside Sabrodt, a hate that had been with him from the very cradle. A hate, he realised, that had become even stronger than his desire for the Dragonseat.

Somehow, some way, Sabrodt would yet slake his hate.

The Shrouded King turned back towards his shadowy followers. 'It is time to claim my kingly tribute,' he told them. 'It is time to add another vassal to my domain.'

Sabrodt closed one skeletal fist. In response, the earth before him split open and an aethereal steed pawed its way out of the ground. Corroded barding and a tattered caparison covered the phantom stallion, leaving only its fleshless legs and skull exposed. The light that glowed in the recesses of the creature's head echoed the gibbous glow that blazed in Sabrodt's.

With a thought Sabrodt was mounted upon the grisly charger he had conjured from the earth, the Shrouded King's shadowy essence blending with that of his mount. The wraith reached to his side and drew a pitted sword from its rotten sheath. As his bony fingers tightened around it, the corroded blade was transformed, restored into a sharp-edged weapon aglow with a grave-sent power.

Sabrodt held the ghostly sword aloft and called to his spectral warriors. 'To Wyrmditt,' he commanded them. 'To Wyrmditt and the tribute that is my due.'

CHAPTER THREE

The elders of Wyrmditt had a hard time meeting the gaze of Arnhault and his warriors. The burghermeister and his council kept looking around them, frowning in embarrassment as their eyes chanced upon a splintered panel or a faded wall hanging. There was no need for the Stormcasts to accuse them of anything. The cobwebs and dust that lay everywhere already did that far more forcefully than any words could.

The Temple of Sigmar was in a wretched state, maintained for far too long by only its blind priest. Friar Mueller had tried, but the care of the temple was beyond his abilities alone. Decay had set in, as sorely within as without. A few more years and the structure would be a dilapidated ruin.

Arnhault stood with Mueller at his side, beneath the icon of the Hammer behind the altar. He wanted to impress on the elders the depth of their faithlessness and to remind them that it had been the priest's devotions that had brought deliverance to Wyrmditt. Guilt was the quickest way to subdue any opposition that might have presented itself to Arnhault's plans. It was a pragmatic solution to the problem, if not exactly a sympathetic one. The Knight-Incantor was not without an appreciation for the townspeople, but he would not allow such considerations to influence him. To do so would cost Wyrm-ditt the thing it could least afford.

Time.

'The tribute you intended to render this Shrouded King.' Arnhault's solemn tone rolled across the town leaders. 'I understand it was to be claimed in the Shrine of Nagash upon the rising of the new moon.'

The elders looked uneasily amongst themselves, no man wishing to be the one who confirmed the Stormcast's statement. Finally, in a faltering voice, Vanholf addressed Arnhault. 'The Shrouded King has always taken his... tribute... from the Shrine of Nagash. It... he... rides through the middle of town. His very presence causes the flowers to wilt and milk to sour. None sleeps when he makes his midnight ride, and all await the... the scream when he claims his due.'

'There will be no scream tonight,' Nerio stated. His hand patted the quiver of crystal-tipped maces at his side. 'Unless the Shrouded King finds his voice when he does not find his victim.'

Arnhault nodded and pointed his staff at Vanholf and the elders. 'I can see the doubt you feel. I can smell the fear that hammers inside your hearts. You have lived in horror of this monster for too long. You have almost convinced yourselves that he is invincible, that there is nothing which can be done except to appease him.' His voice dropped to a low whisper of wizardry, drawing magic to him. He let the power flow down to the end of the staff. A nimbus of lightning crackled and flashed about the head of the staff in a display of arcane power. The elders backed away, their eyes wide with awe, their tongues muttering in fright.

'This time, the monster will not be appeased,' Arnhault told them. 'This time he will be challenged. This time he will be vanquished.' He laid his huge armoured hand on Mueller's shoulder. 'By the might and glory of Sigmar God-King, this darkness will be banished from Wyrmditt.'

'But… but the Shrouded King is…' Vanholf held up his hands in a hopeless gesture. 'When first he came upon us and made his demands, there… there were men who stood against him. They tried to kill him with swords and with spears and with arrows. Nothing could harm the Shrouded King. He is not a thing of flesh and bone as we are.' The burghermeister closed his fingers into a fist and shook it in despair. 'He is more ghost than anything else, as intangible as the steam from the geysers.'

Mueller smiled at Vanholf. 'Have faith, friends. Great Sigmar knows all and would not send his warriors to us if they could not prevail against our enemy.'

Arnhault held the crackling staff higher. 'There is a dark magic which empowers your tormentor, but we too have magic. We have the magic of Sigmar's storm, the essence of sacred Azyr, to pit against the fell undead.' He let the power gradually ebb from his staff. 'I have fought for Sigmar's justice in more battles than I can remember and against enemies too horrible for you to imagine. Always the power of Sigmar has sustained me and never have I seen daemon or spectre that could deny the God-King's might.' He nodded towards Mueller. 'Be guided by your priest. Have faith. I do not expect any of you to face the enemy. All I ask is for your faith and conviction. Sigmar will deliver Wyrmditt.'

'You will lay a trap for the Shrouded King?' Vanholf asked. 'When he comes to receive his tribute, then you will confront him?'

Penthius stepped forwards, sweeping the elders with a stern look. Of all the Stormcasts, the Sequitor-Prime had the least forgiveness for the obscene bargain they had struck with the Shrouded King. 'The wraith will answer for its evil,' he stated coldly. 'We do not want any of you near when we depose your undead king.' He tapped his golden breastplate. 'We have the armour and weapons to confront this monster. We have the resolve and discipline to defy its evil.' He waved his hand towards the doorway. 'Go and take your people from Wyrmditt. Stay away from your homes this night. When you return in the morning, you will be free.'

Vanholf kept his eyes downcast but shook his head emphatically. 'But the Shrouded King may expect a trap,' he said. 'Always Pater Mathias has acted as... as a mediator between the town and the wraith.' He looked up at Arnhault. 'Pater Mathias is gone! No one can find him. He has left us!'

'In a time of crisis, men display their true quality,' Penthius scowled.

'We will carry out the plan with or without Mathias,' Arnhault declared. 'The wraith may be so certain of its power over you that even without Mathias' welcome, the monster will not be suspicious.'

Vanholf was still uneasy. 'If... if the Shrouded King does suspect...' Suddenly the burghermeister looked up, excitement on his face. 'If we took one of Mathias' cassocks...' The excitement faded as he looked up at the huge warriors. 'No, the Shrouded King would never mistake one of you for Pater Mathias.'

'Then we will need one of your people to play the part,' Penthius stated. Again his uncompromising eyes moved across the elders. 'Who among you will do it? Or are there no heroes left in Wyrmditt?'

A long moment of shameful silence dominated the temple. It was broken at last by a quiet voice from beside Arnhault.

'I will do it,' Mueller declared. 'I feel it is my duty, for I was the one who begged Sigmar to send you to us.'

The Stormcasts looked at the blind priest in astonishment. Even Penthius was impressed by the man's determination.

'Are you not afraid?' Arnhault asked.

'Of course, my lord,' Mueller said. 'But I can control my fear.' He raised his hand to his sightless eyes. 'Now I understand that this affliction is a blessing. Because I cannot see him, my fear will grow no worse when the Shrouded King comes. I can stand outside the shrine and wait for him, just as Pater Mathias did.'

Arnhault was pensive. The risk to the blind priest would be great. Mueller would be standing in the very path of the storm. Yet there was something in what he said about his blindness being an asset now rather than a hindrance. Anything that increased the chance of luring the Shrouded King into their trap had to be considered. Moreover, he thought about the terrible humiliation Mueller would feel if his offer were rejected outright.

'It will be dangerous,' Arnhault advised Mueller. 'Search your heart and if you are certain this is the path Sigmar has called you to follow, then we, the Gilded Sphere of the Sacrosanct Chamber, will accept your help.' He gazed over the elders and saw that, somehow, their dejection was even more pronounced than before. Truly these men had been humbled. Arnhault marvelled at the wisdom of Sigmar.

To be humbled in the presence of the Sacrosanct Stormcasts was something a man could rationalise to himself. To be humbled by the courage of a blind man... That was a lesson none of the elders would ever forget.

The Shrine of Nagash was an imposing pagoda near the centre of Wyrmditt. The morbid tower was not pressed upon too closely by its neighbours. Instead a great expanse of open ground surrounded it, ground that was uncharacteristically barren by the standards of Ghur. A few withered trees and the husks of yellowed bushes were the only evidence life had ever intruded upon this place. The dirt around the dead plants was parched and grey, as though some vampiric scourge had drawn all the vibrancy from it.

The pagoda itself was equally barren, but in a different way to the neglect that afflicted the Temple of Sigmar. Here the walls were in good repair, the wooden beams and doors fastidiously maintained. It was not the rot of abandonment that hung over the Shrine of Nagash, but rather an aura of total decay, a repulsion of life itself. The place made no pretensions about its macabre nature. Every doorway was framed by the fleshless grins of leering skulls. Skeletal gargoyles gripped the edges of the roof, condensation drooling from between their fangs. Around the walls were grim funerary niches where placards bearing prayers to the dead were exhibited for all to see.

Everything about the place was steeped in the darkest of magic, the heavy aether in which the realm of Shyish itself was immersed. Arnhault could feel its essence the moment he approached the pagoda and walked across the desolate earth. It was like a clammy film pressing against his skin.

'Is something wrong, Knight-Incantor?' Orthan asked Arnhault. The very best of Penthius' Sequitors, he had been tasked with being Arnhault's guardian when the trap was sprung. A powerful warrior, he was less attuned to the threads of magic they walked through than the aether-mage.

'This is a vile place,' Arnhault declared. 'It has been abominably used.' He let a ripple of magic course through his staff and back through his body. The aetheric wind dissipated the clammy sensation, but more than that it lent a certain quality to the inimical energy. A quality that was at once unspeakably vile yet strangely familiar to him. 'Long before the first bricks were laid down, this site was blighted.'

'They built the shrine to Nagash here because Pater Mathias said it was sacred to the Lord of Death,' Mueller told Arnhault. The blind priest looked strange in the heavy black robes that now shrouded him. Vanholf and the elders were too afraid of the Shrouded King to fight, but they did lead Nerio's Castigators to the shrine and bring back one of the cassocks to complete Mueller's disguise.

Arnhault gripped the priest's shoulder. 'In that much he told your people the truth. This place is saturated in dark magic.' The Knight-Incantor hesitated, strangely troubled by his own words. He stared at the pagoda, at the town outside the patch of barren earth. In his mind he tried to imagine the place as it might have looked before Wyrmditt had been built.

'Something happened here,' Arnhault continued. 'Something that drew the attention of Nagash to this place.'

Mueller nodded his head. 'Death,' he said. 'Only that would interest Nagash. Many small deaths or one death of greater consequence. Perhaps Pater Mathias knew which, but if he did he never said.'

Arnhault let the spell he'd evoked fade. Gradually the clammy sensation returned and with it came a sense of frustration. He felt he knew the answer to this riddle. Yes, he *felt* it, but he did not *know*.

'A last chance to turn back,' Arnhault reminded Mueller. He stared up at the darkening sky. The day was fast fading. Soon the new moon would rise and with its ascension, the Shrouded King would come to claim his tribute.

'I know,' the priest said. 'It grows cold now, despite the dew from the geysers. That means the sun is gone, or nearly so.'

Mueller shrugged his shoulders. 'I can be of use to you here. Let me stay. Let me show you the measure of my faith in Sigmar.'

Arnhault grabbed the hood of the cassock and drew it over the top of Mueller's head. 'This will lend itself to your disguise. From a distance, even the wraith might mistake you for Mathias. When he draws near... then he will sense the light of your soul and know he has been tricked.' His grip tightened about the haft of his staff. 'Orthan and I will be within the shrine, ready to strike before that can happen. I have three Castigators on the upper floor of the pagoda. Nerio and the rest are in the buildings around the tower along with Penthius' Sequitors.'

'Sigmar willing, the enemy will not escape,' Mueller said.

A grim laugh rose from Arnhault. 'It is the duty of all Stormcast Eternals to be the instruments of Sigmar's will.'

Arnhault peered through the slats to either side of the shrine's doorway. From his vantage point, he could see the disguised Mueller standing out in the middle of the barren ground. His head was bowed as though he were reciting prayers to Nagash as Mathias would have had he been waiting for the Shrouded King.

Past the priest and the blighted expanse, Arnhault watched the streets of Wyrmditt. Though its own light was dim, the new moon appeared magnified by the mist. A silvery glow spilled down onto the land, illuminating the town and the hill above it. The streets were a patchwork of shadows and emptiness. The buildings were dark, brooding bulks, their doors locked and their shutters fastened. From memory Arnhault could have declared which of the structures harboured a hidden Sequitor or Castigator, where Nerio and Penthius stood by, waiting for his signal.

The crucial moment, giving the signal. Arnhault had taken that task onto himself. A flash of arcane lightning from his staff and the Stormcasts would spring into action, closing a circle of righteousness around the infernal Shrouded King. Only when he was certain the fiend was in their trap, that escape was impossible, would he give that signal. Their mission in Ghur depended upon it.

So too did the lives, perhaps the very souls, of everyone in Wyrmditt. If the Shrouded King got away there was no telling the sort of vengeance he might wreak. Even as civilisation began to spread across the war-ravaged Mortal Realms once more, so too did the malefic dominion of Nagash. The ghastly necroquake that sent its shock waves from Shyish had loosed legions of the unquiet dead upon the living. The Shrouded King was part of that terrible scourge and even Arnhault could not say how much of its power might be at the wraith's beck and call. Cheated of its tribute, the spectre might dispense with its pretension of kingly rule and simply annihilate the entire town, each death swelling the numbers of Nagash's slaves.

Such would not be! By Sigmar, Arnhault would not permit it! He had spoken truth to the elders of Wyrmditt. He had fought against the enemies of mankind many times and in all their horrific forms. The Shrouded King was simply the latest of those enemies to cross him, another foe upon which to bring justice and judgement.

Why then, he wondered, did he feel so strange? The longer he spent in Wyrmditt, in the old lands of Kharza, the more Arnhault felt a growing unease. His studies of the chronicles and history of the vanquished kingdom lent themselves to an eerie familiarity, or was it something more? What was this hinterland between *feeling* and *knowing*?

A shadow fell across Arnhault's awareness, drawing his gaze

to the hill above Wyrmditt. There, upon the summit, a lone rider had appeared. Manifested might have been the more fitting word, for the Knight-Incantor swore the horseman had not been there an instant before and there had not been time for his steed to reach the summit unobserved. Illuminated by the lunar glow that suffused the mist, the rider remained a thing of shadows. A dark caparison clothed his mount, rendering it a black smudge upon the hill. The figure astride its back was similarly arrayed, a nebulous blot that exhibited only the vaguest hints of shape within his voluminous robes. Only the head seemed to have substance, a bare skull that rose above the shrouded body.

'The enemy is here,' Orthan stated, peering through the slats and following Arnhault's gaze. 'Look at the crown it wears.'

Arnhault had already seen it. Indeed, his eyes could not leave the sight of that jewelled circlet. An unaccountable fury suddenly welled up within him, an emotion as fierce as it was unexplainable. This wasn't the righteous indignation of Sigmar's warriors towards the infernal foes of mankind. It was something deeper than that. More base and primal. More selfish.

'By my own hands will this atrocity be destroyed,' Arnhault swore.

Orthan gazed at Arnhault, shocked by the passion in the Knight-Incantor's voice. 'Of course,' he said. 'Just as you command. The honour of vanquishing the wraith belongs to you.'

Arnhault stifled a bitter laugh at Orthan's choice of words. Honour? There would be no honour here! There was no honour in crushing vermin under heel. To find honour in battle the enemy had to possess at least some semblance of worthiness. To be more than a thing of contempt.

The Knight-Incantor shook his head, stunned by the emotion that gripped him. It was unseemly, this arrogant loathing for which he could not account. By an effort of will, he fought to suppress the feeling. 'We do not fight for ourselves and our own glory,' Arnhault said. 'We fight to fulfil the duty Sigmar has entrusted to us.' His words were more a chastisement of himself than Orthan, an injunction against the wrath that had so suddenly filled him.

The rider began to descend the hill. The ghostly horse trotted towards Wyrmditt at a confident and unhurried pace. There was a sneering disdain about its progress, bespeaking the mocking contempt with which the Shrouded King regarded the living men he had claimed as his subjects. The display evoked disgust in Arnhault.

Orthan expressed his own revulsion. 'Arrogant villain, isn't he?' the Sequitor remarked.

'His arrogance serves us,' Arnhault said. 'It will lead the wraith into our trap and see him destroyed before he is even aware of his peril.'

Even as he spoke, Arnhault's attention remained riveted upon the crown the creature wore about its fleshless head. He recognised it from his studies as that which had been worn by the priest-kings of Kharza before the hordes of Chaos devastated their land. Together with the Dragonseat throne, it was a part of the regalia that signified their dominion. To see that noble legacy debased by this grave-filth was too much to bear. As Sigmar willed it, Arnhault would end this profanation!

'My lord,' Orthan pointed up at the deserted streets through which the Shrouded King rode. He drew Arnhault's attention away from the wraith's crown and to the lone figure who came creeping out from hiding. It was Pater Mathias, the priest of Nagash.

'I should have seized him as Penthius advised,' Arnhault grumbled as Mathias hurried through the streets. 'I left him free because I thought his capture would upset the people of Wyrmditt and cause them to resent us. I should have anticipated the possibility of this betrayal and taken pains to prevent it regardless of the consequences.'

There could be no question of Mathias' purpose. The black-robed priest was outside the cordon of hidden Stormcasts, beyond their reach unless they stirred from their concealment and exposed their presence. He was set upon a course that would intercept the slow, imperious ride of the Shrouded King.

'What is done is done,' Arnhault hissed. He shook his head. 'Sigmar grant that my mercy has not undone our plans.'

The Shrouded King drew back upon the reins of his phantom steed as Mathias emerged from an alleyway and stood before him in the street. The priest genuflected towards the wraith in an exhibition of obscene deference.

'Sire,' Mathias spoke, his thin voice loud in the brooding silence that hung over Wyrmditt. 'I am your loyal subject, a brother in the service of Nagash.' He stared up at the Shrouded King. 'Attend my words, master, for I am your friend.' He waved his arm towards the pagoda. 'They are waiting for you. Sigmar's knights would deny you your tribute and have laid a trap for you! Like slinking jackals, they wait to pounce on you, sire. But I remain true to you. I bring you warning. Ride from Wyrmditt and escape their trap!'

The Shrouded King looked down upon Mathias, ghostly lights glowing in the pits of his skull. Seconds stretched into an eternity for Arnhault as he watched to see what the wraith would do. Would he believe Mathias or think the warning itself to be a ruse to trap him? The Knight-Incantor prayed it would be the latter.

Arnhault's prayers seemed to be answered. Answered in savage and brutal fashion. A hiss of contempt boiled off the

Shrouded King. The wraith's bony arm lashed out and in its skeletal claw a smouldering sword appeared. Mathias had time to shriek once before the blade swept across him. As the sword passed through his flesh, a weird double-image of the priest became visible. The solid, physical form of Mathias fell to the street whole and unmarked. At the same time, a translucent reflection staggered where he had been standing, a welter of blood spurting from the half-severed neck. The ghostly shade stumbled as it clutched at its gashed throat, then evaporated in a burst of phantasmal sparks.

The Shrouded King urged his aethereal steed onwards, its spectral hooves trampling the physical carcass of the fallen priest. The wraith glared at the pagoda and Arnhault could feel its malignant gaze sweep through him. An electrical shock shivered through his body, a reaction unlike anything he had ever experienced before. With half the town between them, with the walls of the shrine concealing him, Arnhault felt as though the spectre had just reached inside his armour and closed its skeletal fingers around the very core of his soul.

'He knows I am here,' Arnhault told Orthan, and there was a quiver in his voice when he said it. Because there was something more to it than that. Something he could not express to the Sequitor. Something he tried to deny even to himself. *He knows me*, Arnhault's mind raced.

The steed reared back, its hooves pawing the air. From the Shrouded King there issued a ghastly howl. A single word, a word that cracked across Wyrmditt like the snarl of a lash.

'Arise!'

In response to the command, shadows surged up around the Shrouded King. In a matter of heartbeats there was a broiling mass of darkness flowing through the street around the wraith, a black cloud that billowed towards the Shrine of Nagash. As the cloud spilled further and further away from the Shrouded King, it began to break apart. Distinct shapes could be discerned, blobs of shadow that became wispy forms draped in dark robes and tattered shrouds. Fleshless faces grinned from beneath decayed hoods. Bony claws clutched rusty chains and gleaming scythes. Embers of grisly grave-light flickered in the sockets of leering skulls.

A matter of heartbeats, but in that time Arnhault realised that the trap had been turned against the Stormcasts. The Shrouded King had summoned his phantom vassals, conjuring a tide of wraiths to come crashing down upon the foes who dared to defy his dominion.

There was just one chance, a desperate hope that Arnhault seized upon. Just as his own attention had been riveted upon the Shrouded King, if the fiend's own focus was concentrated upon a single point, perhaps the situation could be salvaged. Perhaps he could give Penthius and Nerio a chance to salvage this disaster. He looked at the disguised Mueller standing on the barren earth, shaking from the fury of the wraith's cry but unaware of the infernal host rushing straight towards the pagoda. At the very least, Arnhault would not abandon the brave mortal to the undead legion.

'We will draw them to us,' Arnhault declared. 'If we can keep them fixated on us, then our brothers may yet surprise this fiend.'

Orthan's hands tightened around the haft of his stormsmite greatmace. 'Sigmar smiles upon the bold,' he said. He put action to words, swinging the weapon and obliterating the wooden wall. A hulking figure in golden armour, he pushed through the breached pagoda and strode out onto the open ground. 'Night-haunting wretches!' his bellow rang out. 'Here stands Orthan of the Hammers of Sigmar! Here stands he who will send you back to your empty tombs!'

Arnhault followed Orthan out onto the blighted ground. The undead had displayed no especial attention to the Sequitor's challenge, but the moment the Knight-Incantor appeared in the open, there was a pronounced change. The air itself seemed to crackle with hate. The ghoulish glow in the Shrouded King's skull took on a livid hue. The intensity of the creature's focus felt like a blade piercing Arnhault's breast.

'Volkhard,' the Shrouded King's snarl echoed above the silent tide of wraiths. The name, as it rang out, was filled with venom, spat into the air as though it were poison.

To Arnhault, the effect *was* poisonous. He felt a searing shock burn through his veins. He would have sworn he had never encountered the name 'Volkhard' before, yet when he heard it uttered by the Shrouded King it felt... familiar. More than familiar – at some deep level, some depth of being beyond conscious awareness, he recognised it. Recognised it as belonging to him. As a part of him.

Orthan cried out in alarm when he saw Arnhault stagger. He shifted his hold upon the greatmace and reached out to steady the aether-mage. Even as he did, the enemy came rushing towards them. No longer a silent wave of shadows but a howling gale of undead fury, impelled by the rage that swirled within the spirit of their master.

'Loose!' Nerio shouted down from the roof of the pagoda. The Castigator-Prime and two of his brothers stood up, their greatbows trained upon the wave of wraiths. Crystal-tipped maces shot down into the ghostly throng. Attuned to the necromantic forces that gave the nighthaunts shape, the flasks fitted to the maces exploded as soon as they connected with the ghostly creatures. The draconic breath trapped within burst forth in blazing balls of blinding light. The dark forms of the wraiths were seared by the holy energy, torn into wispy tatters that dissipated in the mist, their tortured souls banished from the realm of Ghur.

A dozen of the wraiths were vanquished by Nerio's volley, yet the destruction of their companions did nothing to slacken the charge of those that remained. The shadowy host spilled across the barren ground, rushing towards Arnhault and Orthan. Castigators in the surrounding buildings now sent their own shots into the undead legion, obliterating dozens more of the spectral creatures. Penthius and his Sequitors emerged from concealment and ambushed the flanks of the spirit army, their mauls shattering the ghosts in brilliant flashes of Azyrian light.

Still the horde continued to pour towards one fixed point, converging upon the pagoda and Arnhault. The Knight-Incantor had prayed he could focus the attention of the nighthaunts, but now that prayer was being answered with a vengeance. Desperately he tried to rouse himself from the shock that had stunned him, but it was like trying to swim against a raging river. His innermost being rebelled against the effort and refused to obey.

Orthan turned and raised his greatmace, ready to defend Arnhault to the last. But there was another who moved to defy the oncoming horde. Blind though he was, Friar Mueller could sense the malign evil of the wraiths. He turned towards Orthan and gestured at Arnhault. 'Take his lordship somewhere safe until his affliction passes! I will delay these fiends for you.'

Before Orthan could react, Mueller was moving towards the undead. As he stepped into their path, a nimbus of divine light surrounded the friar. He raised his arms and cried out. 'Sigmar's will be done!'

The spectral horde faltered for an instant, repelled by the holy aura in its midst. But then an inarticulate shriek of rage rose from the Shrouded King, a command that would brook no denial. The army charged onwards and rolled across the friar in a black wave of death. The priest and the divine light around him were crushed under the phantoms, smothered in the cloying swirl of undead.

The sight of Mueller's self-sacrifice snapped Arnhault from the paralysis that held him. Orthan was already swinging his greatmace to meet the foremost of the shadowy wraiths when Arnhault raised his staff and drew upon the magic of Sigmar's storm.

A gale of aetheric force roared through the undead, crackling with arcane energies. The least of the wraiths were blasted apart by Arnhault's spell; others were hurled back and forced to draw their scattered essence back into a concentrated shape. The cohesion of the horde was shattered. From a single unstoppable tide, the nighthaunts broke into a litter of disparate bands. Into this bedlam of disorder, Penthius and his Sequitors surged forwards. Arnhault could see them, employing their soulshields to further divide the wraiths and push them into pockets where their stormstrike mauls would complete their dissolution.

Orthan's greatmace struck down the leering, chain-wrapped spectres that came shrieking towards Arnhault. With every blow of the huge weapon, a wraith was obliterated, the cohesion of its shadowy form shattered in a spray of spectral ribbons. Continued shots from Nerio and his warriors kept the wraiths from bringing any great numbers to bear upon the Sequitor.

Arnhault employed his staff to aid Orthan in the defence. Crackling with magic, the sigmarite weapon ravaged the undead horrors. A fiend with the fanged skull of a beast, brandishing a glaive, charged at the aether-mage, only to be struck by the electrified staff and boil away in a cloud of smoke. A dark ghost draped in chains was immolated by the arcane force Arnhault sent into it, a brief flash of spirit fire that quickly vanished.

'Volkhard!' The Shrouded King's cry pierced the night, ringing out over the sounds of battle.

Again the name struck Arnhault. His awareness seemed to expand, a cascade of images racing through his brain – confusing flashes of places and things, events he could see but not remember. When he looked at the charging wraiths, faces began to appear, filling out the fleshless skulls. Familiar faces, though distorted by the necrotic powers that had resurrected them as grave-cheating ghosts. He could almost put names to some of those faces. If he concentrated, Arnhault thought he might...

The Knight-Incantor strove to retain his focus. The song of a spell quivered upon his lips and unleashed a bolt of lightning through the oncoming wraiths. Seven of the fiends were banished in an instant while many others were thrown back in tatters, their dark essence only gradually seeping back to reform into grisly apparitions.

If there were names that belonged to the faces Arnhault saw, then they had little connection to the phantoms. These were but the distorted, twisted echoes of the people they had been in life. Whoever they had been, it had no bearing upon what they were now.

This conviction made it easier for Arnhault to vanquish the wraiths that surged around him, but when a gap in their shadowy ranks afforded him a view of the Shrouded King he found cause for doubt. The master of the undead army had kept clear of the battle, marshalling his spectral forces from the streets beyond the Shrine of Nagash. Now when Arnhault looked at the monster, he saw a pale face clothing the leering skull, an almost transparent skein of skin about the bones. As with the others, it was a face that was familiar to him.

Only this face had a name. For the third time, turmoil seared through Arnhault's mind and shock sizzled through his veins. He knew the Shrouded King, or at least the man he had been in life...

'Sabrodt,' Arnhault hissed. Then he added a sobriquet to that name. A title that the villain might not have carried in life but which he had certainly earned in death. 'Sabrodt the Usurper.'

Across the distance, the rider appeared to hear Arnhault. The wraith responded with a bitter peal of laughter, an audible sneer of withering mockery. The Shrouded King fixed his malignant gaze on Arnhault.

'Sabrodt!' Arnhault raged. He could see the nighthaunts surging towards him again, refocused by their master to destroy the aether-mage. Orthan stumbled back as the tide of chainrasps and glaivewraiths threatened to overwhelm him.

A sense of righteous fury blazed through Arnhault's mind. He drew upon that emotion, feeding it into the arcane song that fell from his lips. A tempest of magic swirled through the geyser-born clouds above Wyrmditt. At his direction, that energy came pelting down in a cascade of burning rain. Against the sigmarite armour of the Stormcasts, the searing deluge was harmless. The undead, however, were not invulnerable. Like wax candles melting beneath a flame, the creatures wilted in the rain, clumps of their essence dripping away. Where a seething mass of shadows had filled the cursed ground around the pagoda, soon there was only a stagnant slime of smouldering ectoplasm.

One wraith alone had the force of will to defy the storm Arnhault had summoned. Away in the streets, the Shrouded King glared at the aether-mage. The semblance of a face vanished, leaving the creature's leering skull.

'Sabrodt!' Arnhault cried out again. Before he could muster the energy for another spell, the Shrouded King whipped his steed around and galloped off into the deserted town. 'Sabrodt!' he shouted and started to run towards the streets. As he charged after the retreating rider, Arnhault found he was not alone. First Orthan, then other Stormcasts joined him in pursuing the wraith.

When he reached the spot from where Sabrodt had watched the battle and directed his forces, Arnhault paused. There was a scum of darkness spattered across the cobblestones, residue from the wraith that had melted off in the deluge. A little further on, he could see more drops of ectoplasm.

'We must hasten, my lord,' Nerio advised. The Castigator-Prime gestured with his greatbow towards the hill above the town. Just visible from where they stood was the dark shape of the undead rider. 'He has been hurt by your magic. We can still catch him if we hurry.'

Penthius nodded, taking up his brother's call to action. 'Wyrmditt will not be safe and our mission not fulfilled until we have destroyed the Shrouded King.'

Arnhault gazed up at the fleeing wraith as its aethereal steed carried it over the top of the hill. He looked back at the spatters of ectoplasm. But more than that, he reflected upon the things he had experienced during the battle.

There were questions here. Questions that might prove even more important than pushing back the grasping hand of Nagash and his undead slaves.

'No,' Arnhault commanded. 'Let him go.' He could see the confusion in their eyes. They did not doubt his abilities but that did not mean they understood his intentions.

Arnhault wanted to keep it that way. At least for now. Instead he placated his brothers with a half-truth. 'It is vital we end this scourge not simply for today, but for good. To do so, we need to do more than just destroy the Shrouded King. We must track him back to his lair and purge it of whatever infernal power has concentrated there. We must find the source of this undead plague and ensure it has been disposed of.

'Only then can we say we have honoured our obligations to Sigmar and our Stormhost,' Arnhault told them. 'Only then can we go home,' he added, but there was a strange light in his eyes when he said it. Because somewhere deep inside him, he could not shake the uncanny sensation that he already was home.

CHAPTER FOUR

Cold pain crawled through the spectral essence of Sabrodt as his steed galloped away from Wyrmditt. The searing deluge that had been conjured from the misty sky had inflicted a measure of harm upon the wraith. But it was an injury from which the Shrouded King was already recovered, his black powers drawing from the deathly vibrations left by the necroquake Nagash had unleashed upon the realms to replenish his phantasmal shape.

No, it was the other wound he had taken that wracked Sabrodt's being with a numb, gnawing agony. An old wound, festered and rotten, so long a part of him he had deluded himself that it was gone. Sight of the aether-mage who led the warriors of Sigmar ripped open the scab and let the poison of hate swell through his soul.

He *knew* that one. There was no mistaking the flavour of that spirit, the presence that motivated the reforged body. Through a thousand generations and all the manifold realities of the

Underworlds, Sabrodt would have recognised the being of King Volkhard.

The fires in the pits of the wraith's skull flared into a ghastly crimson incandescence. Sabrodt no longer saw the mist-veiled hills above Wyrmditt or the plumes of steam streaking up from the fields of geysers. It was a different kind of land through which he now rode, a land richer and more vibrant than that he had claimed as part of his domain. He could see great fields of wheat and corn, vast orchards of peach and almond, hills green with grapevines. There were tall manors with ivy-covered walls and roofs tiled in white slate. The villages of tenant farmers with their huts of wattle and daub, each with its little garden and chicken coop.

A bitter hiss rasped across the wraith's teeth. This was the land he'd coveted, the land he'd fought so hard to possess. The memory of it was etched onto his spirit, branded there by the fire of his passion. It was his by right! Kharza and the Dragonseat and all that fell within its dominion.

Even as he stretched forth his fleshless claw, Sabrodt saw the landscape fade and change, shifting back into mist and wilderness. A mirage of the past. All that remained of the kingdom that should have belonged to him.

The Shrouded King looked back over his shoulder, towards Wyrmditt. He would return. He would bring forth all the ghostly legions at his command and he would raze the place. Not one brick would be left standing, no two beams of wood left nailed together. Every soul in the place would be wrested from its mortal flesh and drawn into Sabrodt's undead army. The Stormcasts...

A cruel laugh rose from Sabrodt as he considered the sigmarite-clad knights. He had made a mistake before, allowed his kingly outrage to cloud his judgement. Revenge upon

Volkhard made him oblivious to the might of his foes. The retinue he brought with him from his graveyard court was unequal to the feat of destroying the Stormcasts. More, much more, was needed to overwhelm them. And he knew just where he would bring such a horde to bear upon Sigmar's knights.

Volkhard would not be content to remain in Wyrmditt. Sabrodt had seen him, so too had he seen Sabrodt. Volkhard would pursue the wraith now, hunt for the Shrouded King across the entire realm if need be. Were their positions reversed, had Volkhard done to Sabrodt what Sabrodt had done to him, there would be nowhere the wraith would not follow. The aether-mage would lead the rest of the Stormcasts after the Shrouded King.

Sabrodt raked his talons through his spectral essence, willing his recent wounds to reopen. He watched with abominable satisfaction as splashes of black ectoplasm dribbled onto the ground. A trail for his foes to follow. He would make it easy on Volkhard.

It would be unbrotherly to let him be late for his own funeral.

'There is more of the wraith's ichor up here, my lord!' Nerio called down to Arnhault. The Castigator-Prime gestured with his greatbow at the spectral splotches that marred the ground beside him.

Arnhault felt a sense of relief that Nerio had recovered the trail. Twice since leaving Wyrmditt, the Stormcasts had lost the Shrouded King's track. The spectral steed he rode left only infrequent marks behind – a wilted stem where its flanks had brushed across a bush or a patch of yellowed grass where a hoof had touched the ground. The stains left by the wraith himself were far easier to find, ugly black blemishes that looked like painted shadows and carried with them the rank stench of the grave. Keeping them in sight, the Hammers of Sigmar could be certain of following their quarry back to his lair.

'I do not like this,' Penthius confessed, drawing close to Arnhault so that the other Stormcasts would not hear. They were marching through a system of narrow valleys that wended their way between the hills beyond Wyrmditt. It was terrain to make any soldier uneasy. If an enemy should appear on the hills and spring an ambush, the Hammers of Sigmar would be trapped.

'You have dispatched scouts to warn us of any lurking foe,' Arnhault reminded Penthius. He gestured with his staff at the hills around them. Carefully making their way along each flank were a pair of Castigators with a Sequitor to support them. 'In perfect keeping with the doctrines of Lycaeon. We use the valley to hide our presence, we keep scouts on our flanks to ensure we have remained hidden.'

Penthius shook his head. 'It is not a question of procedure,' he said. He tapped his hand against his chest-plate. 'This feels wrong. I feel it down inside.' He pointed at the black stains left by the Shrouded King. 'This trail strikes me as too deliberate, too easy to follow. I think Nerio would agree with me. Even when he loses it for a moment, it is never too hard for him to find again.'

'The Shrouded King was wounded when I summoned the storm's power,' Arnhault declared. 'Only the most powerful among the undead could recover from that magnitude of divine magic.'

'Then this one should have already faded away,' Penthius said. 'We have followed this trail for several miles now and the wraith still leaves its essence behind like a slug's slime. Surely it has lost enough to lose its ability to manifest and been compelled to fade back into its grave?'

'Perhaps he can draw upon the energies of the necroquake,'

Arnhault suggested. 'I am more attuned to the aetheric vibrations than you, brother, and I can sense the fell energies left by Nagash's ritual. How much more connected to those vibrations would a creature formed from the same energies be? We have already seen that the Shrouded King can call upon the black art of necromancy. Perhaps he can also draw on the necroquake's vibrations to replenish the ectoplasm he is losing.'

'Or perhaps the wraith is baiting us,' Penthius warned, his tone severe.

Arnhault closed his eyes. The Sequitor-Prime had given voice to the worry that nagged at his own mind. Was the Shrouded King leading them all into a trap?

'Some bait is worth taking,' Arnhault told Penthius. 'Employ what precautions you feel are necessary, but we will not abandon this trail. Wherever it leads, the Hammers of Sigmar will follow.'

Arnhault said no more. He did not dare to. It was enough that following the Shrouded King would lead them to the wraith's stronghold and allow the Stormcasts to complete their mission: to liberate Wyrmditt from its undead oppressor and reclaim the region from Nagash's power. This much was the duty that had been entrusted to the Hammers of Sigmar.

There was another reason that drove Arnhault onwards despite the danger. A possibility that was so profound in its potential that he trembled to consider what it might mean.

The process of reforging was flawed. Wresting the spirits of the valiant from the grasp of death at the very moment of their passing gave Sigmar the power to build an army of eternal heroes. But there was a price to such power, a toll that was paid by each Stormcast when their soul was set upon the Anvil of the Apotheosis. An insidious sort of degradation set in, stripping away the memories of what had come before. The

Stormcast who fell in battle was reborn in Sigmaron, but each time he left something of himself behind. There were some who had undergone the process so often that only their sense of duty and their devotion to Sigmar remained. In rare instances even this spiritual anchor was lost and the spirit broke free to become a rampaging lightning-gheist, a near-mindless ghost of awful strength.

Reforging wore down the memories of each Stormcast. *What* they were remained, but *who* they were was increasingly lost. Arnhault himself had no memory of who he had been before his first reforging. The spells, the esoteric lore, even the history he'd drawn from the libraries of his Sacrosanct Chamber, these were all at his immediate recall. The life that had come before then, however, was a blur – mere impressions rather than memories. Seldom had he even given the lost past much thought. It was enough that he had his duty and his devotion to Sigmar.

At least it had been so until now. Arnhault had felt the Shrouded King's recognition like a sword piercing his breast. 'Volkhard', the wraith had named him, and he knew the name was his own. Just as he knew the undead fiend was Sabrodt and that the creature was a usurper with no right to the crown he claimed.

Arnhault did not know how he knew these things; he only felt them to be true, as true as anything he had ever learned – scraps from a forgotten past rising from some buried part of his being. That they could be conjured forth by Sabrodt was a mystery, one that Arnhault was determined to unravel. The Shrouded King had transcended death, just like the Stormcasts, but he had not lost his memories. Further, he had somehow been able to provoke them in Arnhault's psyche, stirring them up from whatever secret place they had been buried during his reforging.

Even more than freeing Wyrmditt and ending the terror of the nighthaunts, Arnhault had to discover how Sabrodt had done this to him. How had the wraith made him remember he had once been named Volkhard? The key to unlock that mystery had implications far beyond simply Arnhault's own lost memories. It could bring about a new age for the Stormhosts and serve to correct the terrible flaw in the reforging process.

If Arnhault could discover Sabrodt's secret, he and all his fellow Stormcasts need never fear losing their humanity when their spirits were set against the Anvil. They would fully become the heroic warriors Sigmar intended them to be.

The spectral trail led across what had been the frontier and deep into the Kingdom of Kharza. Great stands of blackened trees, their branches scratching at the sky like the claws of skeletons, had risen to reclaim the pastures and fields of more civilised centuries. Black buzzards cried out as they flew through the grey sky, their eyes roving the earth below for the merest scrap of carrion. Lean jackals crept through thorny brush, their noses sniffing the air for any hint of rotten meat on the wind. Emaciated hogs, their hides hanging loose over their bones, pawed at the desiccated soil, greedily devouring the few grubs and beetles their efforts exposed.

Through this wild desolation, the golden armour of the Stormcasts made a stark contrast as they marched onwards. Scouts preceded the main column while strings of pickets watched the flanks. In the midst of his retinue, Knight-Incantor Arnhault maintained a stoic silence, marching with the almost mechanistic step that told his companions he had entered a semi-meditative trance. Left to their own company, Penthius and Nerio took position at the head of the column where they could monitor both the main body and the scouts ahead of them.

'Another village,' Penthius pointed out, waving his maul towards a stretch of wilderness where the weeds and brambles exhibited a certain uniformity in the way they had grown. 'The walls are gone, but you can still see how the plants mark where the buildings stood.'

Nerio smiled at the Sequitor-Prime's observation. 'Anything that needs to sink its roots deep can't do it where there's a stone foundation to contend with.' He clapped his brother on the back. 'I explained as much to you three villages ago. You are so vexed by the possibility of ambush that you are becoming forgetful.'

Penthius uttered an annoyed grunt. 'I *still* say we are being led by the nose. The Knight-Incantor suspects as much himself, but he feels it is a risk worth taking.'

'Do you question Arnhault's judgement?' Nerio asked, both surprised and offended by Penthius' words.

'I am not so arrogant that I would be so impertinent,' Penthius replied. 'But it may be that Arnhault is... Well, to me he seems distracted. And I think that has caused him to lose his sense of perspective.'

Nerio gave Penthius a reproving look. 'You *are* questioning the Knight-Incantor's judgement,' he accused. He glanced around, noticing that his raised voice had drawn the attention of the Sequitors and Castigators following them. 'Arnhault has served the Hammers of Sigmar through many reforgings. He is a veteran campaigner who knows his duty.' Nerio's tone became almost derisive. 'What could possibly distract a warrior of his calibre from fulfilling his mission?'

The severity in Penthius' eyes when he looked at Nerio made the Castigator-Prime stop in his tracks. He did not argue when his brother drew him away from the column and towards the ruined village.

'I do not know what it is that has disturbed Arnhault,' Penthius told Nerio, 'but something happened to change him back in Wyrmditt. There is a shadow hanging over his mind. He has not spoken of it, but sometimes, for just a moment, you can see it if you are watching him closely enough.'

Nerio shook his head and pointed back to the column and at Arnhault's trance-like march. 'The Knight-Incantor meditates to bring his powers to their peak. His mind is on the battle ahead of us...'

'That is just the problem,' Penthius interjected. 'Arnhault isn't thinking about the battle. Not the way he normally would.'

'What is wrong, Penthius?' Nerio's tone was curt. 'Is he deviating from protocol too much for your hidebound sensibilities?'

Penthius let the jab go unanswered. Instead, he simply gestured to the ruins around them. 'This is the third village we've seen. The deeper we march into what was Kharza, the more evidence we see of how prosperous this land once was.' He pointed a finger at Nerio's chest. 'Consider how populous this land was before Chaos despoiled it. Now ask yourself how many of those people, how many of their spirits, have been drawn into the Shrouded King's legions?'

Nerio shook his head, rejecting the idea. 'The Shrouded King was not so mighty when we fought him in Wyrmditt.'

'But now we will fight it on ground of its choosing,' Penthius pointed out. He waved his maul at the blackened forests with their skeletal branches. 'Remember when we first descended upon Ghur and how Arnhault showed us the lingering taint of Chaos? Have you seen any sign of that corruption here? Or is it all suffering from a different blight, a blight from Shyish and the black power of Nagash?'

Nerio was silent as he weighed the questions put to him. He had done a fair amount of scouting after they'd left Wyrmditt, rotating the duty between all his Castigators. 'No,' he confessed. 'I have seen no evidence of Chaos, only the decay of death.'

'This is the Shrouded King's domain,' Penthius stated. 'The wraith has led us here on purpose because it is here that it thinks it can destroy us. Among the strictures of combat there is the admonishment to always beware of letting the enemy decide when and where to fight.'

'If all you say is true, then we have no choice but to fight the wraith here,' Nerio said. 'Place our trust in Sigmar that our pursuit of the Shrouded King has been swift enough for us to catch him before he is ready. If we do not vanquish him, then we will fail in our duty here.'

Penthius nodded slowly. 'We will answer the demands of duty and none shall look upon us and say our honour was in question. But when battle is joined, we must be vigilant. This thing that distracts Arnhault...'

'You think the Knight-Incantor would do anything...'

'No,' Penthius interjected. 'Arnhault would do nothing to put the rest of us at deliberate risk. But I would not say he would disdain to take such a risk onto himself. If he thought the gain to be had was worth it, he would not spare himself.' There was a grim look in Penthius' eyes. '*That* is what we must look for. I worry that Arnhault will underestimate this enemy and take chances with himself that he should forego.' He looked back to the column and stared at the Knight-Incantor. 'I think there is some connection between him and this wraith. And I fear that connection may bring Arnhault's doom.'

Into what had been a land of fertility but was now a haunted domain of lingering shadows, Sabrodt's spectral trail led the Hammers of Sigmar. Arnhault could feel the change in the air, could sense the macabre atmosphere into which they marched.

Throughout the long chase, the landscape had grown steadily more decadent, the unburied corpse of Kharza left to rot under a grey sky. Now, however, that sense of things dead and forsaken intensified to such a degree that he could feel it down inside his lungs every time he drew a breath. Nor was he the only one to be afflicted by that uncanny impression. The Sacrosanct Stormcasts were all attuned to the aether to lesser and greater degrees. He could see the most sensitive among the Castigators and Sequitors pause from time to time in their steps, hesitating as they tried to shake the ghoulish influence pressing upon them.

For Arnhault it was something more than just sensitivity to the necrotic aura of the Shrouded King's land. From the corners of his eyes he kept catching fleeting images of the Kharza of old. He saw the peach trees with their furry fruit, watched the wind sigh through a field of golden wheat. A sun-bronzed ploughman working the soil. A big white cow idly chewing her cud. Children playing around the walls of a well, their yellow hair flaring in the breeze. All of these scenes called to him, crying out to some part of his being that was impotent to respond. He felt a sense of regret that he did not recognise these phantasms, for he knew they had once been precious to him. When he turned his head, when he would have focused more directly upon these images, they invariably disappeared, consumed by the grimness of Sabrodt's kingdom.

Sabrodt's kingdom. Merely thinking of it as such made Arnhault's body cold with rage. The wraith had done this. Whatever destruction the hordes of Chaos wrought, it was the blight of necromancy that now assailed these lands. Or perhaps the rot was even older than that. The idea suggested itself to Arnhault and would not go away, nagging at the edges of his anger and trying to fan it into a consuming hate.

Kharza had been remade into the decayed semblance of the Shrouded King. Nowhere was this in greater evidence than when the Stormcasts ascended the narrow pass and stood upon the barren plateau. The morbid influence became stronger still as Arnhault gazed across the plain. Here, he knew, was the very root of the nighthaunts, the font from which the undead scourge drew its hideous strength.

Arnhault knew this because he found that he knew this place. Not with an understanding conjured from books and scrolls, but with the wisdom engendered only by experience. He looked across the plain, at the surrounding heights of jumbled stone, the deathly bulks of barrow mounds and ancient cairns – but he did not see these things.

Instead, he saw a great army assembled. Arnhault could hear the snap of banners flying in the wind, could smell the husky scent of war dogs as they were led from their wheeled kennels. He saw cavalry, a great company of high-born sons astride coal-black destriers, their lamellar armour painted with the glyphs of their household gods. The mounted knights were arrayed on the flanks, screened by a phalanx of common pikemen, freeholders drawn from across the kingdom, each responsible for his own weapons and armour. Beside the pikemen were row upon row of archers, professional soldiers maintained by the nobles and the great temples, each company bearing the colours of their sponsor. At the centre, terrible in their blackened mail, were the royal guards of the priest-king himself, warriors chosen from across the domain and from every caste, selected not for the blood of their breeding but for the blood they were prepared to shed in battle. Among them, fighting afoot as was the royal custom, would be the priest-king himself.

Arnhault shook himself, shuddering as he felt a part of

himself being drawn into the mirage. Quickly he looked around, fighting to orientate himself in the present. The battle-field of yesterday was washed away, receding into the corridors of his memory.

'What is it, my lord?' Penthius asked. There was not only concern in his tone, but also a touch of uneasiness.

'This is the place,' Arnhault declared. 'This is where the necro-quake cast its most malignant energies. The Shrouded King will fly from us no longer. Here is where he will fight.'

'It is a trap,' Penthius said, looking across the ancient graves.

'Yes,' Arnhault agreed. 'Our advantage is that the Shrouded King does not expect us to know it is a trap. Bold is the dragon who enters the snare knowingly and fierce is his wrath when the hunter comes to claim him.'

Penthius smiled as he lifted the sigmarite mask to his helm and fastened it tight. 'What are your orders, my lord?'

Arnhault gazed across his retinue. At Nerio and his Castiga-tors with their thunderhead greatbows, at the Sequitors with their stormstrike mauls and soulshields. He looked again at the echoes of the past, at the army of Kharza arrayed for its final battle. He could see now the priest-king, adorned in the jewelled armour of his estate, the clawed crown of his king-dom circling his helm. He felt those royal eyes upon him and he knew the monarch's name was Volkhard.

'We advance,' Arnhault said. He pointed his staff at a small patch of green amidst the morbid waste. 'That will be our rally-ing point.'

Penthius nodded and motioned Nerio to join them. 'It is too much to think we will get that far without being challenged.' He glanced at the rocky slopes that descended from the sides of the plateau, and to the rocky slopes that bordered its fur-ther edge. 'The nighthaunts are spectres without substance.

Difficult ground will be no impediment to them.' He gave Arnhault a severe look. 'When they come at us, they will come from every side.'

'We march in turtle formation?' Nerio asked. 'My Castigators at the centre with your Sequitors locking shields?'

'No,' Arnhault told them. 'Not a turtle. A dragon.' He pointed to Penthius. 'Divide your warriors into four groups, fore and aft, left and right. At your command, any one section drops down and allows the dragon to expel its flames.' He turned to Nerio. 'Your warriors will provide those flames. Each of your maces can break the arcane cord that maintains the undead. As we advance, the Castigators will maintain a steady barrage. The Sequitors will hold the enemy back with shield and maul – you will finish them with your volleys.'

'As you command,' Nerio replied, excitement in his tone.

'The plan is a sound one,' Penthius said. 'A similar tactic was employed by Lord-Celestant Kadir Lingh at the Battle of the Cursed Fountain and he was able to successfully fend off three thousand beastkin with less than a hundred warriors.' He shook his head. 'Of course, our foes are more formidable than beastkin and–'

'And there is the fact we will be advancing while we are in formation instead of just holding our ground,' Nerio added. He saw the surprise in Penthius' eyes. 'I am familiar with procedure – it is just I seldom find it applicable.'

Arnhault gestured with his staff at the plateau. 'Your Castigators must move and fire,' he told Nerio. 'How quickly they do so will set the pace of our advance.'

Nerio saluted the Knight-Incantor. 'We will not fail you, my lord.'

Arnhault nodded and dismissed his brothers. They had their warriors to make ready and he, he had his mind to prepare.

The battlefield was of Sabrodt's choosing, a place steeped in the blood and death of Kharza's last stand against Chaos. The Shrouded King had chosen this site because it was here that his dominion was strongest.

His eyes drawn again to that small spot of green, Arnhault considered that it was also here that Sabrodt's dominion was not complete.

A chill wind whipped across the plateau as the Stormcasts began their advance. Nerio could feel the clammy clutch of the grave pawing at him, reaching down inside him with cold fingers that scratched across his very soul. He closed his hand tighter about the hammer talisman he bore and whispered prayers until the profaning energies abated. Around him he could hear other Stormcasts following his example; many of his Castigators and even a few of the Sequitors were trying to drive away the defiling emanations.

The Hammers of Sigmar maintained a loose formation. Penthius would give the command to close ranks and become the dragon of Arnhault's plan. The intention was to lull the Shrouded King into complacency, to make the wraith believe that they were haplessly following him into his trap. To alert the their foe early would be to fight for every inch of ground. This way they would be able to gain some distance unchallenged.

Nerio wondered about the point Arnhault had chosen as their objective. He was no aether-mage, but even he could sense the strangeness of the spot. A lone patch of life amidst the Shrouded King's stronghold. Whatever secret was bound into the plot's defiance of the wraith's death magic, it was clear Arnhault thought the Stormcasts could make use of it against the nighthaunts.

'Steady,' Nerio cautioned his Castigators as they moved across the desolate plain. Each step they took brought a magnification of the sense of menace he felt pressing down on him. He could feel a thousand baleful eyes watching him, despising every breath he drew into his body, envious of each pulse that sent blood coursing through his veins. It was something he had felt before when the Hammers of Sigmar were called upon to oppose the undying legions of Nagash. That strange and hideous hate of the dead towards the living, a remorseless need to destroy what they could no longer possess.

Nerio and the Castigators gradually moved further onto the ancient battlefield. All around them, in a loose posture that was deceptively relaxed, Penthius and his Sequitors marched with shields on their backs and mauls at their sides. Arnhault kept pace with the Sequitors, his robes fluttering about him in the clammy breeze.

The change came with such abruptness that Nerio had to blink to be certain that what he saw was not merely a trick of the light. A dark smudge upon the ground, a stain that gradually elongated, slowly expanding before them. From a mere mark on the barren earth, it grew into a wispy shape, definite in form but as intangible as a shadow. What it resembled was a jumble of bones and bits of rusted armour, a decayed sword and a grinning skull. From the skeletal heap, a sense of misery and loss struck Nerio, such that he was forced to stop to shake the impression from his mind.

As he cleared the cobwebs inside his skull, Nerio saw that the phantom remains that had captured his attention were not the only ones upon the plain. Everywhere there were other shadows seeping up from the earth and taking shape. The ground was becoming black with the skeletal images. The carrion of a great battle boiling up from their forgotten graves.

'Sacrosancts!' Penthius called out. 'Close ranks!' At the

Sequitor-Prime's command his warriors pulled the shields from their backs and unlimbered the mauls hanging from their belts. Nerio's Castigators formed a compact square while the Sequitors converged on their position, ringing them with a wall of soulshields. Orthan prowled the inner edges of the square with his greatmace, smashing the phantom corpses before they could get underfoot.

'They will attack soon,' Nerio advised his archers. 'Be ready to loose the instant I give the order.' Around him, the Castigators raised their thunderhead greatbows and fitted the crystal-headed maces into their carriages.

What had been simply jumbles of bone a moment before now began to stir. Like fungi, each shadow rapidly shot upwards, taking on the grisly vestige of a fleshless skeleton wrapped in its own shroud. Great lengths of chain bound some of the apparitions while the bony talons of others clenched phantasmal scythes and mouldy swords. From every eye socket, a green glow shone, a spectral malevolence that glared hungrily at the Stormcasts.

'What are they waiting for?' one of the Castigators cried out as their formation marched past the unmoving masses of nighthaunts.

It was a question for which Nerio had no answer. Each step, each yard, brought more of the spectres boiling up from the ground. Now he could see the malformed muzzles of gors and skaven protruding from some of the shadowy figures. The Shrouded King was calling up not only the vanquished of Kharza but also the restless spirits of the Chaos horde that had conquered their land.

'Sabrodt is here.' Arnhault did not say the words in a loud voice, but they cracked across the tense silence like a peal of thunder just the same. Ahead of Nerio, the Knight-Incantor stared at the great cairn that dominated the macabre site.

There was a patch of darkness between the Stormcasts and the tomb, a darkness that became steadily more substantial until it had assumed the same grisly likeness they had observed in Wyrmditt. A skeletal rider wearing a crown and bearing a sword, his steed draped in black.

The Shrouded King raised his sword overhead. He swung it through the air three times then from his fleshless jaws a single word issued. 'Arise!' And at the wraith's command, the jumbled bones swelled into spectral warriors with even greater rapidity while more dark stains seeped up from the ground. 'Arise!' the monster repeated, and again the ranks of its army grew.

'The judgement of Sigmar be upon you!' Arnhault shouted. He raised his staff aloft, its tip far above the heads of the other Sacrosancts. From above, a crackle of lightning swept down from the sky. The bolt flashed into the aether-mage's staff and then burst forth in a rolling wave of sparks and flashes. The arcane energy flew towards Sabrodt, immolating those spectres caught in its path, reducing them to puffs of ash and cinder. The Shrouded King himself was caught in the blast, the magic crackling through his essence. The wraith sank to the ground as the steed beneath him evaporated.

Protected from Arnhault's spell by his own black magic, Sabrodt pointed his sword at the Knight-Incantor. 'There!' he snarled. 'There stands Volkhard, the faithless king who led you to defeat! There stands Volkhard, the foolish king who thought to defy your conquest!'

At the Shrouded King's shriek, the gathering spectres raised their own howls of rage and despair. A black wave of hate, the nighthaunts came sweeping towards the Stormcasts from every side.

'Stand fast!' Penthius shouted as he locked shields with his troops. The Sequitors' soulshields formed a wall against which the oncoming wraiths crashed. The undead were stunned by the divine energy that emanated from the shields, fed into them by the esoteric discipline of Penthius and his warriors. Scorched and singed, the creatures drew back. As they did, the glow from the shields passed over into the spiked mauls the Stormcasts bore. Before the wraiths could recover, the Sequitors lashed out, striking them with their enchanted weapons. Dozens of the spectres burst apart under the assault, their essence unable to endure the holy aura that infused the mauls.

'Falcon!' Nerio shouted, and at his call the Castigators swung around to the right and raised their greatbows. At the same instant, the Sequitors there dropped to one knee, leaving a gap through which the archers could shoot. Loosing the crystal-headed maces, the Castigators sent an explosive barrage into the horde of wraiths. As each mace struck, whether connecting with the phantasmal essence of a nighthaunt or smacking against the unclean ground, it exploded in a blast of draconic flame. The unleashed breath of Stardrakes consumed the wraiths, extinguishing their deathly energies in an instant, leaving behind only splotches of rancid ectoplasm.

'Eagle!' Nerio cried out, and this time it was the Sequitors at the head of the formation who dropped down and made way for the missiles the Castigators sent into the undead horde. Again the wraiths were consumed by the exploding maces, scores felled in the blink of an eye. Yet still more of them came, surging upwards from the barren earth, determined to claim the lives of the warriors who dared trespass in their domain.

'Our advance is too slow!' Penthius cried out. 'They are too many to keep back!' A second wave of wraiths came sweeping in, crashing against the soulshields. This time, mixed amongst the chainrasps were some of the skaven-skulled apparitions. Baring their chisel-like fangs in grotesque snarls, they brought long glaives to bear, stabbing past the guarding shields to pierce the warriors behind them. Three Sequitors collapsed, spilling into the mass of Castigators behind them. Orthan lunged to plug one of the gaps, his greatmace obliterating the scythe-wielding ghost that came sweeping through the breached shield wall. Arnhault rushed to another gap, his staff crackling with arcane power as he drove it through the ghostly head of another wraith that tried to exploit the lapsed defence.

Nerio ran to plug the final hole. 'Hawk!' he shouted to his men as he hurried to confront the beast-headed phantom that flew into the middle of their formation. While the Castigators turned to loose their maces into the mass of wraiths converging on the left flank, Nerio moved against the glaive-wielding ghost. The thing slashed at him with its weapon, missing him by such slight measure that he could feel the chill of its necrotic blade rush through him. In response he brought his greatbow up and shot a mace through its chest and up into its skull. The bestial ghost disintegrated in a flash of crackling energy and burning shadows.

'Sigmar protect and defend!' Arnhault's voice sang out. 'Sigmar smite and avenge!' The Knight-Incantor's body briefly glowed with aetheric energies as he tapped into the arcane storm and focused his will upon it. An instant later, a tremendous gale descended upon the plateau, lashing across the plain with tempestuous force. Entire clutches of wraiths were buffeted by the punishing winds, shredded by the elemental force unleashed upon them. Phantasmal tatters writhed through the dark sky as the wraiths lost cohesion.

'Quickly!' Arnhault shouted to the Sacrosancts. He gestured with his staff towards the patch of greenery.

'Forwards!' Nerio ordered his troops, urging them to haste. Penthius, too, spurred his Sequitors onwards, seizing the advantage that had been gained.

A momentary advantage. Nerio could see a grey phantom flitting about the plain, a ghoulish lantern clenched in its hands. Wherever its cadaverous light shone, the tattered wraiths began to coalesce while more of their number came bubbling up from the cursed earth. It would not be long before a revivified undead legion came sweeping down upon them once more.

Nerio had served with Arnhault before and knew something of the toll the Knight-Incantor's spells took on him. He would not easily be able to conjure another gale to batter the nighthaunts a second time. Moreover, as he looked ahead, he could see the Shrouded King moving his own forces to intercept them.

The wraith had conjured another steed for himself, this time an assemblage of equine bones that exuded a gibbous glow. Around him, a cadre of spectres wielding long scythes and with blindfolds lashed about their faces came shrieking and howling towards the Stormcasts.

'Eagle!' Nerio shouted, but this time when the Castigators loosed their missiles the wraiths were hardly disturbed by the explosive detonations. Instead an eerie green light enveloped them and absorbed the very worst of the blast. Sabrodt laughed as his undead soldiers came surging onwards.

'Return to the graves which are your rest!' Arnhault shouted. Standing behind the Sequitors, he aimed his staff at the charging mass of nighthaunts. A deafening thunderclap boomed across the plateau, its force hurling the wraiths back with hurricane force. Sabrodt alone defied the power of Arnhault's spell, his steed digging in its hooves and sliding back across the lifeless earth for several feet before the intensity of the storm was expended.

By then it was too late. Only a few yards separated the Hammers of Sigmar from the patch of greenery they had been striving to reach. 'For the Heldenhammer!' Arnhault cried as he dashed through the ranks of the Sequitors and made for the one spot on all the plateau that had resisted the malignity of the necroquake and the spells of Sabrodt.

Nerio was not sure what he had expected to happen when they actually reached that spot. Some infusion of divine energies perhaps, some aura of holy protection that would render them immune to the ravages of the undead.

None of that happened. Instead, Arnhault just stood there for a moment. There was a strange look in his eyes, an expression Nerio had never seen there before. But whatever strange spell held him, it quickly abated. When it was gone, Arnhault did not rejoin the Stormcasts. Instead, he turned towards the Shrouded King.

'I know who you are,' Arnhault hissed, and in his voice there was a measure of hate and rage that chilled even Nerio's heart.

The Shrouded King whipped his steed around and galloped into the huge cairn. Arnhault howled in fury and charged after the wraith, pursuing him towards the tomb.

'Arnhault! My lord! Come back!' Nerio shouted after the Knight-Incantor.

'Castigator-Prime Nerio!' Penthius snapped. He swung around to see the other Stormcast glowering at him. 'The undead are regathering their strength. They will attack soon. I task you with holding them back.'

Nerio shook his head. 'Me? But you are senior in rank! You should be in command.'

Penthius had already broken ranks and was hurrying after Arnhault. 'You are in command,' he called over his shoulder. 'I have to help Arnhault!'

Nerio watched him go, then glanced at the patch of greenery. What was that place? And what had it done to the Knight-Incantor?

He set aside those questions as the spectral horde came sweeping towards them once more. 'Close ranks!' he commanded. 'Sequitors, hold the line! Castigators be ready to loose on my mark!'

CHAPTER FIVE

A fury such as Arnhault had never known roared through his heart. Standing upon the small plot of grassy earth had opened him to something. He could not say if the images that seared through his mind were drawn into him from outside or borne to his awareness by some deep, forgotten fragment of his psyche. Whatever their source the effect was like being struck by a thunderbolt. He no longer merely felt the name Volkhard belonged to him; he knew he *was* Volkhard.

Arnhault could see the barren plain around him as it had been long ago, on that day when he'd led his army at the head of his household guard against the hordes of Chaos. He saw again the horde of marauders and monsters as they came charging up onto the plateau. He braced his forces. It was here and here alone they had any chance of stopping the invaders and protecting the heartland of Kharza. Here the awesome numbers of the Chaos horde could not be brought to bear. Here it would be the quality of the warriors and the righteousness of their cause that would prevail.

So it might have been. But Arnhault knew the strategy was doomed from the first, doomed by treachery. Before battle was joined, a dark shadow appeared atop the stony rise and cast his foul spells upon the field. Magics steeped in the deathly energies of Shyish. A moment of terror and pain, the strangled cries of thousands of warriors… And then nothing. The battle lost, for none were left to fight it.

The dark shadow had a name, one that spurred the fire in Arnhault's soul. Sabrodt the Usurper. The undead filth that dared now proclaim itself the Shrouded King.

Arnhault pursued as Sabrodt retreated into his mouldering tomb. Before it had been duty and necessity that drove him to confront the wraith, his obligations to the people of Wyrmditt and his devotion to Sigmar. Now he pursued Sabrodt for far different reasons. He knew what this creature had done and what his fell deed had cost the people of Kharza. These were crimes that Arnhault would see avenged!

The scythe-wielding spectres came flying towards Arnhault, seeking to intercept him before he could overtake Sabrodt. The Knight-Incantor pointed his staff at the one of the skull-faced haunts, a pulse of lightning snaking away from its glowing head to rip through the shadowy creature and reduce it to a foul-smelling smoke. Another of the fiends rushed for him, slashing its scythe for his helm. Arnhault whispered one of the arcane songs he had been taught and sent a punishing gale of wind tearing across the ghost, scattering its essence across the battlefield.

The Knight-Incantor dealt with the other ghostly reapers in similar fashion, destroying or rebuffing them with his magic. Such was the anger driving him onwards that he gave no thought to conserving his energies, or what the toll taken by so hurried and rapid a string of conjurations might be. Once, he thought he heard Penthius calling after him, warning him against so reckless a course, but Arnhault ignored the cries. None of that mattered now. All that mattered was Sabrodt and meting out upon the wraith the justice he had escaped for so many centuries.

Baleful wards guarded the Shrouded King's tomb. Arnhault could see a red haze flickering before the entrance. He paused for only an instant, then he clenched his staff and pointed it at the virulent light. His head reeled at the terrible strain as he willed his arcane powers to pierce the eldritch barrier. The prudent action would be to slowly unwind the enchantments that shaped the ward, unravelling them gradually until they were harmless. Such caution would mean time, however, and Arnhault would spare none for Sabrodt's reckoning.

The barrow mound was a great heap of jumbled stone, its entrance a gash in its face framed by heavy blocks of marble carved into macabre figures. As Arnhault strove to penetrate the warding haze, he could see the eyes of stone ghouls and gheists smouldering with profane energies. Feeding more power into the wards, the carved guardians began to shiver, trembling as though an earthquake shook the plateau.

Arnhault poured more of his own magic into the effort to break the guarding spell. Liquid dripped down his forehead and only when he tasted it on his lips did he realise it was not mere perspiration but blood sheening his skin, such was the strain. His ears rang with a maddening cadence, his vision became awash with the red haze of the ward so that he was all but blind. A mortal wizard would have been crippled by the stresses Arnhault was allowing his body to endure, much less the fantastic exertion necessary to maintain the ordeal.

Bit by bit, Arnhault pushed through the haze. Each step he felt the hostility of the ward increase. Through the red blur, he could see chips of stone cracking away from the carvings as their quaking became more and more violent.

Finally, he was through. It occurred with such abruptness that Arnhault found himself lunging into the darkness of Sabrodt's barrow. Behind him, the chipped residue of the carvings clattered to the ground, shaken into fragments by their struggle to defy the Knight-Incantor's determination.

'Praise Sigmar,' Arnhault intoned, thanking the God-King for granting him the power to break through the wards. Only for a moment did he pause within the entrance. Then, conjuring a golden glow to surround the head of his sigmarite staff and illuminate his way, Arnhault hastened into the tomb's murky halls.

The inside of Sabrodt's barrow had a musty, decayed stench. The reek of old bones was omnipresent, as was the stink of soil from which all vitality had been drained. Even with Arnhault's spell to light his way, the corridor was cloaked in gloom and shadow. He would almost be upon some niche in the wall before he was able to discern the sarcophagus of an ancient king or valiant knight. There were places where faded murals and tattered tapestries ran along the hallway, their artistry now wasted almost to the point of oblivion.

The hall angled sharply downwards, plunging ever deeper into the cursed earth beneath the mound. The further he penetrated the tomb, the more Arnhault felt a crushing weight pressing upon him. Not the mass of stone above, but rather an emotional pollution that perverted the atmosphere. A miasma of misery and bitterness that dragged at him with almost physical force. The contagion left behind by the Shrouded King's festering thoughts.

Arnhault hesitated when a dust-veiled mural caught his notice. Singing a minor cantrip, he sent a blast of wind across the wall, driving away the dirt and revealing the image hidden beneath the patina. What stood exposed was a scene of the heroine Sofira with her obsidian spear embedded in the primary head of the hydra Rhasst. A shiver coursed through Arnhault, a tremor that magnified the fury he already knew. It was not the memory of the ancient legend that upset him, but rather the memory of where he had seen this mural before. It had adorned the royal palace of Kharza.

The Knight-Incantor quickened his pace, no longer caring that he might trigger some trap left behind by Sabrodt to guard his tomb. Aware now that the Shrouded King had violated the royal palace to decorate his grave, Arnhault began to see other pieces that should have been in the home of the priest-kings. With each discovery, his outrage at the Usurper's effrontery was redoubled.

By the time Arnhault reached the centre of the tomb, to that great hall where Sabrodt had built his morbid imitation of Kharza's throne room, he was ready to tear the barrow mound apart stone by stone. When he saw this ultimate profanation of the royal house he was overwhelmed, sickened by the macabre scene. The Dragonseat, from which the monarchs of Kharza had ruled the land, now dragged down into a cobwebbed crypt deep beneath the earth.

The shadow that reposed on the Dragonseat stirred, turning the smouldering fires in its skull towards Arnhault. There was scorn in that gaze, the smug defiance of a thief confronted with his crime.

Arnhault glared back at Sabrodt.

'You are in my chair.'

Cold malice flowed through the essence of Sabrodt, permeating every corner of his spectral being. The purity that Arnhault exuded, the taint of Azyr that emanated from his golden armour, stung the wraith's senses, an irritation that at once both vexed and provoked.

And the Shrouded King was already provoked. His ire had been roused the moment he had recognised Volkhard in Wyrmditt.

'I looked for you among the dead, Volkhard,' Sabrodt hissed. 'How long and earnestly I probed the Underworlds seeking your spirit.' He raised a fleshless hand and pointed at the Knight-Incantor. 'Now I understand why you were not there. Sigmar stole you from Great Nagash and made you one of his mindless puppets.'

Arnhault raised the sigmarite staff he bore and shook it at the sneering apparition. 'You will not profane the name of the God-King, usurper!' At his gesture, a bolt of lightning flared through the gloomy hall.

Sabrodt did not stir from the throne. There was no need. The lightning fizzled before it could come near to him, shattering into a cascade of flickering sparks. 'How much the God-King has taken from you, wretch!' he snarled, his hands sliding across the arms of the throne. 'This is the Dragonseat, enchanted by the Magi of Yordo to defend the royal blood against all spells that would render him harm. You should know these things, Volkhard. It is useless to turn your magic against the priest-king of Kharza.'

'Then I will pull you down from your stolen throne with my bare hands,' Arnhault growled. He rushed towards the Dragonseat.

A burst of deathly power threw the Stormcast back, repelling him as completely as the arcane lightning he had conjured. Arnhault staggered, his golden armour singed by the repulsing force.

'The Dragonseat protects the king from assassins,' Sabrodt's ghoulish tone descended into a hateful snarl. 'Even those assassins who were once kings.' The last word was poison in Sabrodt's mouth, forcing him to concede that there had been a time when Volkhard ruled Kharza. It was a memory hateful to him, so he decided to evoke one he sensed would be just as unsettling to the Stormcast. He leered at Arnhault, willing his spectral essence to rebuild for a moment the face that had once rested upon his skull.

'Have you forgotten even this?' Sabrodt asked, at once shocked and disgusted by Arnhault's response, his lack of agitation at gazing on the wraith's mortal visage. 'Can so much of who you were have been taken from you?'

Sabrodt could see the Stormcast's confidence falter. He saw the glimmer of confusion in Arnhault's eyes. Just as the name of Volkhard had drawn together the scattered fragments of memory, so now did the Knight-Incantor react to the Dragonseat.

'I was furious when your spirit escaped from me,' Sabrodt said. 'When the power of Nagash raised me from my grave, I sought you, but you were not to be found. Even the spot where you died has defied my influence.' A scornful hiss rattled up from the wraith's essence. 'Now I see there was no reason to be angry. Sigmar has done far worse to you than I should ever have imagined. He has stripped your identity and left you naught but a hollowed shell. A zombie that deludes itself into believing it is still a man.'

Arnhault shook his head, revulsion in his eyes. 'Brother,' was the word that dripped from his tongue.

Sabrodt rose up from the throne. 'Yes. Brothers.' He pointed to his phantasmal face. 'A visage the very mirror of your own. But for the accident of a few heartbeats, I would have been king! But it was you who was drawn from mother's flesh first. I was but a contingency, trained only as successor in case you should perish. Mine was a shadow existence of observing all that could have been mine, yet knowing that it would never be.' He clenched his bony fists, the loathing he felt causing his phantom features to vanish and leave only the fleshless skull. 'So long as you were alive, I was nothing!'

The Stormcast glared at Sabrodt. 'You are still nothing,' he jeered. 'You don't even have a body, a twisted spirit too wretched to rest in its tomb.'

'No!' Sabrodt's roar boomed through the hall. He stretched his arms wide and exerted his hideous will. From the darkness, shadows gathered. 'I rule here now! Kharza is mine! Everything is mine!' He glanced from side to side as the nighthaunts took shape and began to surround the Stormcast.

'I am the Shrouded King! It is you, Volkhard, who are nothing!' Sabrodt gestured to one of the wraiths, a thin apparition draped in black with the crossbeam of a gallows lashed to its back. At his gesture, a billowing mass of darkness spread across the ghost's hands, hardening until it had taken the appearance of a gleaming double-axe. 'You will die, Stormcast. My executioner will cut the gilded head from your shoulders, and this time we will see if Sigmar can cheat Nagash of your soul.'

'By volley! Loose!' Nerio shouted as the black cloud of wraiths came rushing against the Stormcasts once more. The explosive maces detonated only a few feet from the crouching Sequitors, sending crystalline shards clattering against their soulshields. Dozens of the shadowy ghosts were ripped apart in the impact. Those at the centre of the blast were banished entirely, their essence consumed by the Stardrake's breath within. The wraiths on the periphery of the explosions, however, were not completely destroyed.

Scattered by the maces, Nerio did not believe the chain-draped phantoms could have reunited their essence on their own. Certainly not as quickly as they did. It was the ghastly corpse-light held by one of the spectres that was infusing the wraiths with such power. Almost as soon as the sound of the explosions was fading, the disincorporated ghosts were taking shape once more and converging upon the Hammers of Sigmar.

'We could beat them back, brother, if it were not for that accursed lantern!' Orthan snarled to Nerio as he hastened to the latest breach in the shield wall. His greatmace came cracking down upon the phantasmal skull of a scythe-bearing wraith, shattering the creature in a burst of necrotic vapour. The Sequitor the undead had sliced with its ghostly blade struggled for a moment to rise and then collapsed. An instant later he vanished in a bright flash of light, his spirit drawn back into the keeping of Sigmar.

Nerio aimed his thunderhead greatbow and sent an explosive shot crashing through the wraiths that came rushing towards Orthan. The apparitions vanished in a cloud of celestial energy. Before any others could charge the breach, the remaining Sequitors repositioned themselves to repair the shield wall.

Several of the Sacrosanct Stormcasts had been dragged down by the nighthaunts and with each loss, the space within the formation became ever tighter. Orthan was having difficulty manoeuvring and reaching the gaps. Soon there would not be room enough for all of Nerio's Castigators to remain behind the protection of the Sequitors.

'They will wear us down if we continue to fight them this way.' Nerio looked past Orthan to where the pale wraith and its ghoulish lantern continued to draw spirits from the dead earth and reshape the ones the struck down by the Stormcasts. Arnhault had pursued the Shrouded King; perhaps without their undead lord the rest of the nighthaunts would lose their foothold in Ghur and fade back to the Underworlds. But for such an event to help the Hammers of Sigmar, they would have to keep from being overwhelmed.

'By Sigmar, we will hold,' Nerio vowed. He gestured towards the lantern-bearing spectre. 'Either we will be the doom of that fiend or it will be the doom of us!' He looked across the Sequitors and Castigators, proud that these warriors would accept his command even if it was far from anything to be found in the martial strictures Penthius knew by heart. 'It does no good to hold position here. On my mark, we will make a drive for that corpse-calling wretch! I want ten Castigators to alternate with the Sequitors in the vanguard. As you shoot, fall back and allow one of your brothers to take your place. Sequitors will defend you as best they can. It will need speed and boldness to prevail. If the lampbearer flees before us, we must catch it or we gain nothing.'

Holding his thunderhead greatbow high, Nerio shouted to the Stormcasts. 'For Sigmar! For the Heldenhammer! To glory and victory!' On his command the Stormcasts shifted positions. A wave of oncoming wraiths were surprised by the reformation, extinguished by the concentrated volley of crystal-headed maces that shot out at them the instant they came near the shield wall. The first Castigators fell back, letting warriors with loaded greatbows take their place. The redeployment happened even as the armoured warriors marched across the plateau, none of them missing a step.

The nighthaunts came at the Stormcasts from all sides. The Sequitors on the flanks and rear were especially hard-pressed to hold off the undead assault, for this time there was no withering volley from the Castigators to break the attack. There was no alternating glow of maul and shield as the Sequitors made their reprisals upon the nighthaunts. Now the soulshields maintained a steady illumination as the Stormcasts focused their energies entirely upon defence. Trying to present an unbroken front against which the wraiths would crash, they lost the versatility that had served them before. One by one, Sequitors were pulled down, stabbed by glaives and scythes that managed to slip past the warding shields.

Nerio felt the fall of each Stormcast like a knife twisting in his guts. He knew they were being brought down because of his change in tactics, but he also knew that if they didn't change tactics then they would not be victorious. The lampbearer had to be vanquished if they were to prevail.

'Castigator-Prime!' one of the Sequitors in the vanguard cried out. 'The ghostmaster knows our plan! It is sending even more wraiths to intercept us!'

Nerio looked to Orthan. 'I think it will need something even more unexpected and reckless to carry the day,' he said. 'I should appreciate your aid.'

Orthan nodded and hefted the bulk of his greatmace. 'Show me where you want violence.'

Nerio gathered a group of ten Castigators. 'Hold back and do not rotate with the others,' he told them. To the rest of the Stormcasts, he gave different instructions. 'We will rotate archers three more times. On the fourth rotation, the front rank will drop down as they loose. Then the reserves will open up. You are going to cut a tunnel through the wraiths for myself and Orthan to reach the lampbearer.'

Nerio and Orthan kept in the centre of the formation as the Gilded Sphere advanced towards the spectre. The wraiths came rushing the Stormcasts from each direction, attacking with a vengeance. More Sequitors were dragged from the line and even a few of the Castigators in the van were brought down. Then came the moment for the double-volley Nerio had arranged. The front rank dropped to one knee once the fourth rotation was in place. Two lines of Castigators sent a withering hail of thunderhead maces into the tide of undead. Those in the fore were extinguished in flashes of brilliant light. Behind them, scores more were immolated by the draconic energy, the shreds of those blown apart in the first volley evaporated completely by the explosions from the second.

A gap ten paces wide had been opened in the wave of night-haunts. Into this fissure, Nerio and Orthan plunged. The Sequitor led the way, sweeping his greatmace through the few wraiths that moved to block their charge. The apparitions were battered by the heavy weapon, their aethereal substance ripped apart. There was no chance to make certain of their dissolution as the two Stormcasts hastened onwards, leaving their undead foes to reform behind them as the necromantic light summoned them back to battle.

There was no going back for Nerio and Orthan. A spectral mass of ghosts now separated them from their brothers. Only by pressing on could they gain anything at all. Both could see the lampbearer ahead. The spectre appeared to recognise their threat. It raised its skeletal arms and beckoned to a clutch of glaive-armed wraiths. The apparitions came howling towards the two Stormcasts, determined to keep them from reaching the corpse-caller.

'Do not tarry,' Orthan told Nerio. Without explaining himself, he intercepted the stalking wraiths. His greatmace came cracking down on the skull of one, extinguishing it in a blaze of dark vapour and divine light. A second stalker was subdued by Orthan's fury, its essence bludgeoned by the glowing weapon. Such was the havoc unleashed by Orthan that the other stalkers deviated away from Nerio and converged upon the Sequitor. From all sides, the piercing glaives came slashing for him.

As the doomed Orthan had warned, Nerio did not tarry. Accepting the Sequitor's sacrifice, he hurried onwards towards the fleeing lampbearer. At the very limit of effective range, Nerio raised his greatbow and took aim.

The spectre glared back at him with the graveyard glow that shone from the shadows of its hooded face. It raised the grisly lamp higher, beckoning, commanding the restless dead of the plateau to rally to its aid. Nerio felt all the creature's undying hate smash down on him in a surge of wrath.

Then the Castigator-Prime shot the mace from his greatbow. The missile spun across the haunted field, narrowly flying over the cowled heads of the undead as they rose from the earth. The crystal tip of the mace whistled past the heavy lantern, causing its light to flicker. Then it slammed into the shadow-veiled head of the corpse-caller. The unleashed stormbreath billowed out in a nimbus of purifying power. The spectre gave voice to a piercing wail of despair as the celestial energy devoured it, collapsing its tenuous bond with the corporeal world. Like a puff of smoke, the phantom vanished, its extinguished lamp crashing to the earth alongside its empty cloak.

As the lamp's light faded, so too did the ghosts that had been rising from the earth. Like mist before a strong wind, they drifted apart, seeping back down into the cursed soil. Nerio was comforted by the knowledge that there would be no unending tide of reinforcements for the nighthaunts now.

That only left the multitudes of enraged undead already upon the battlefield. Nerio turned from the residue left by the lampbearer to see the rat-skulled stalkers finish Orthan. Pierced by the ghostly glaives many times, the Sequitor lost his hold upon the greatmace. Even as the weapon crashed to the ground, the Stormcast's life ebbed away. In a blinding flare of light, his spirit was drawn back to Azyr.

Their prey gone, the stalking wraiths remembered the other foe they were supposed to destroy. Too late to help the lamp-bearer, they now came rushing to avenge the spectre by dealing with Nerio as they had with Orthan.

Nerio fitted another thunderhead mace to his greatbow. How many of the undead horrors would he vanquish before they could reach him?

Arnhault watched as the spectral headsman emerged from the circle of nighthaunts. The murderous axe glistened in the wraith's grip, its edge alight with fell enchantments. Sabrodt had spoken true; there was death in that blade. Perhaps even death for a Stormcast.

'There was a moment when you, too, knew the menace of this axe,' Arnhault told Sabrodt. A thrust in the dark, an informed guess based upon what he had learned of the spectre. For him, as a Stormcast, the past was only hazy fragments. For the Shrouded King, the past was an obsession, a pattern from which he could not extricate himself.

The thrust struck home. Furious light glowed in the sockets of Sabrodt's skull. The wraith shook a bony talon at Arnhault.

'I spit on your pity,' Sabrodt hissed. 'I rejected it when it was offered! I warned you of what would happen… brother. I warned you that the Dragonseat would be mine!'

Sabrodt's tirade stirred some of the disjointed fragments buried within Arnhault's memory. He saw again the scene as it had unfolded long ago. He recalled the reasons he had spared Sabrodt the first time he had tried to seize the throne. 'It was not for your sake I did not send you to the headsman. Your wife and my nephews pleaded for your life. They begged me to spare you and I was too selfish to risk earning their scorn, to see hate for me in their eyes.'

'You were weak,' Sabrodt scoffed. 'Too weak to rule.'

'You were the weak one,' Arnhault countered. 'Always letting others take the risks. You could not even do your own fighting. You had to let the hordes of Chaos do that for you. A conqueror? A usurper? You are nothing but a scavenger, afraid to fight for what you want.'

Sabrodt's laugh was a steely growl that echoed through the tomb. 'You will not goad me into leaving the Dragonseat, however much you try to shame me. I will sit here and be content to watch you die.'

The ghastly executioner rushed Arnhault. The Stormcast lifted his staff to block the descending axe. In a blur of eerie speed, the ghost's weapon swept past his defence and crashed against his shoulder. There was an icy shock as the spectral blade struck him. His arm dropped, numbed down to his wrist. It was all he could do to retain his grip upon the staff. In another fit of uncanny speed the ghostly headsman pulled away and brought his double-axe up to deliver another blow.

Before the stroke could fall, a golden shape charged out from the darkness. Penthius swept his soulshield between the executioner's descending axe and Arnhault. The weapon cracked against the enchanted barrier, the impact throwing the headsman back. Penthius retaliated with a crushing swing of his maul that disrupted the shadowy essence of the murderous wraith. The undead creature flickered backwards, ectoplasm dripping from its tattered shape.

'Next time I wish you would listen when I call you,' Penthius quipped.

Arnhault slapped his hand against his numbed shoulder, letting arcane heat drive down against the graveyard chill. 'Next time I will,' he promised.

Sabrodt pointed his bony fist at the two Stormcasts. A

blackened blade manifested in his grip, conjured from the cairn where it had physically reposed. 'Destroy them,' he roared at his undead court. 'Your king commands it!'

The wraiths responded to the Shrouded King's decree, flying at the Stormcasts in a ghostly swarm. Penthius brought his maul flashing through the first few creatures, shattering their phantasmal shapes. His conquests were too few to stem the tide. The chain-wrapped nighthaunts forced him to raise his shield and try to hold them back with its magic.

'Sigmar's will,' Arnhault intoned as he drew the vial from his belt and cast it at the undead swarm. As the vial struck the wraiths, it shattered, unleashing the energies of the mammoth's spirit. The crackling power raged through the ghosts, whipping across their aethereal shapes to scatter them about the hall in wispy tatters.

The executioner alone from Sabrodt's court defied the tempest Arnhault unleashed upon them. The creature came charging for the aether-mage, its axe raised to cut him down. This time Penthius was too far away to intercede.

There was no need for the Sequitor-Prime to do so. Arnhault responded to the threat by whipping his staff across the wraith's arm. The glowing head seared through the spectral limb like a flash of lightning. The executioner reared back, the severed arm disintegrating in a flurry of ebon motes. He retained his grip upon the axe, but the weapon had too much solidity to be easily wielded single-handed. Before the wraith could compensate, Arnhault's magic again scorched the cloaked figure. This time the staff raked upwards, flaring through his chest and up through his skull. Bisected from rib to cranium, the executioner struggled for an instant to retain such substance as he possessed, then exploded in a spray of blackened fragments.

Sabrodt shook his sword at the Stormcasts. 'You have won

nothing! I conjured my retainers from their graves once – I will do so again!'

Penthius hefted his maul and would have rushed the throne, but Arnhault warned him back. It would need a different strategy to unseat the Usurper.

Arnhault glowered at the Shrouded King. '*You* have won nothing,' he accused. 'Look at this kingdom you have claimed. A dead place filled with dead things. Echoes and shadows, that is all you hold! Is this the kingdom you coveted, brother? Or is this just a mockery of that dream?'

A howl of anguish wracked the Shrouded King. 'Do not presume to speak to me of dreams, slave of Sigmar! What do you remember of *your* dreams, Volkhard? You mention my wife and sons, but what of your own? Do you remember them?' The skull-face leered at Arnhault. 'Do you even recall their names, or has Sigmar taken even that from you?'

Arnhault felt Sabrodt's words cutting into him, opening all the uncertainties. The haze of his own past refused to be swept away. But when he looked at Sabrodt, he thought he understood why. 'You remember everything, brother. You remember what happened long ago. You remember what you did and what was done to you. You remember what you wanted.'

Sabrodt leaned back upon the Dragonseat. 'And you wish to know the secret of why I remember these things when you do not?'

The wraith's words gave Arnhault pause. Try as he might, he could not recall Volkhard's own family. That memory had been lost, pounded from him upon the Anvil of the Apotheosis. How much had been lost there? And what would he be willing to pay to get it back?

'Yes, monster, I would know that secret,' Arnhault confessed.

The Shrouded King glared down at him. 'Hate, brother. That

is the key! That is the force that is stronger than death and the grave!'

'Hate makes you remember everything,' Arnhault conceded. 'All except one thing – who you were. Where is the man who was Sabrodt? I see only his shadow.' He slapped his hand against his armoured chest. 'I have forgotten much, but I have not forgotten who I am. I remain the defender of the innocent, the champion of the good. I remain true to my purpose. All you do is clutch at a past that is gone and bitterly tell yourself it is enough.'

'It is more than you have, Volkhard. More than you will ever have. You curse my dominion because you are too weak to claim it for yourself.'

Arnhault shook his head. 'Is that what you want, Sabrodt? You want me to be jealous of this charnel house you call a palace and this graveyard you call a kingdom? They are nothing, brother. Empty. A fitting dominion for a weak traitor.

'We were twins,' he reminded Sabrodt. 'It did not matter which of us was born first. We were both taught the same things, instructed in the same ways. We were both watched and judged. Either of us might have become priest-king of Kharza. They chose me not because I was first... but because I was better.'

Sabrodt leapt down from the Dragonseat, his frenzied wail thundering through the crypt. A blur of hate and shadow, the Shrouded King lunged at Arnhault.

The instant Sabrodt was away from the throne, Arnhault raised his staff and sent a crackling spear of lightning stabbing into the wraith. The Shrouded King was transfixed upon the magical beam, but even impalement was not enough to dull his ancient hate. Sabrodt forced himself down the shocking lance, his ectoplasm steaming away as the aetheric power seared his undead essence. His jaws opened in a scream of fury, as he slashed his infernal sword into Arnhault's armoured shoulder.

Against another blow, the sigmarite mail might have lessened the impact, but the blade Sabrodt bore was imbued with a fragment of the merciless ire of Nagash himself. To the spectral weapon's innate power was added the rage of the creature that bore it, the centuries of brooding hate that had given the Shrouded King his kingdom. The blade tore through the armoured pauldron, down into the flesh beneath, through muscle and bone to cut a phantom path through the heart within. Ghostly as a cobweb, the wound did not bleed, flesh did not part, bone did not snap. The only evidence of the cut was the blemished mark on Arnhault's armour and the spectral cold that shivered through his soul.

Sabrodt leaned close to Arnhault, his skull briefly assuming once more the features he had worn in life. 'You were *never* better than me,' he snarled. 'You will *never* be better than me.'

'Sigmar found me worthy,' Arnhault told the fading phantom. 'Nagash simply found you… useful.' He watched as Sabrodt's essence collapsed into a black mist that sank down into the cursed earth of his tomb.

'Penthius!' Arnhault called to the Sequitor-Prime. 'Attend me!' The Knight-Incantor stumbled and fell, the uncanny wound visited on him by Sabrodt rapidly taxing his strength.

'I am here, my lord,' Penthius assured Arnhault. He took hold of the aether-mage's arm and lifted him up from the floor.

Arnhault looked into his brother's eyes. 'Quickly,' he said. 'The wraith's cut is a mortal one. I can feel my life being drained. Only my magic sustains me now.'

'What can I do?' Penthius had a desperate quality to his voice.

'Get me outside,' Arnhault commanded. 'I must die, but I will not die in this place. Not where *he* has fallen. Get me outside, where I can feel the presence of the God-King looking down on me.'

The battle had ended by the time Penthius emerged from the barrow mound helping the stricken Arnhault out from the tomb. The stains of blood and ectoplasm were the only evidence of the conflict. The forms of the fallen had vanished soon after being struck down, drawn back into the cursed earth or else borne aloft to the Celestial Realm. Only the victors remained to meet the two Stormcasts.

Less than forty warriors remained of the Gilded Sphere. The rest of Arnhault's retinue had fallen to the nighthaunts. Castigator-Prime Nerio was not among the vanquished. Penthius felt relieved to see the impulsive warrior come marching towards him. Nerio hesitated when he saw the condition Arnhault was in.

'The Shrouded King,' Penthius explained. 'Arnhault vanquished it, but not before the wraith cut him with its sword.'

Nerio wrapped his arm around the Knight-Incantor's other side and helped Penthius bear him away from the tomb. 'We knew something had happened when the nighthaunts lost interest in the battle. One moment they were all around us, the next they began to sink back into the ground.'

'That must have been when Arnhault defeated their master,' Penthius said. He glanced down at the insensible aether-mage. The Knight-Incantor was scarcely breathing now, his body carrying with it a clammy chill.

'Is there anything we can do?' Nerio asked, taking stock of Arnhault's state. Other Stormcasts joined them now, taking hold of the dying Knight-Incantor and helping carry him.

'Only what he asked of me,' Penthius said. He nodded towards the lonely green plot. 'We will lay him down there, where King Volkhard fell.'

Nerio gave Penthius a questioning look. 'Volkhard? Is he not the one who wrote the history of Kharza that Arnhault was always studying?'

Penthius did not answer. He was not sure what he could answer. From what he had overheard, Volkhard and Arnhault were one and the same, but until Sabrodt had named him such, Arnhault did not remember being the last priest-king of Kharza. Yet for Volkhard to have written the history resting in the Gilded Sphere's archives, he must have known much more when first he was reforged as a Stormcast.

As they laid Arnhault down on the grass, Penthius considered something else the Knight-Incantor had said. Something about remembering *who* he was rather than *what* he was. Perhaps, in some way, Arnhault had allowed those memories to be consumed by his reforging while retaining other ones – memories that would serve his duty to Sigmar, the rites and rituals he had learned as an aether-mage.

Penthius and the other Stormcasts backed away as a brilliant blue light engulfed Arnhault. The light shot upwards, vanishing in the grey sky. It left behind it only an empty patch of grass.

Penthius closed his eyes and thought about what was happening even now in Sigmaron. Arnhault was being reforged, made ready to fight again. What would he remember of this strange homecoming, of this encounter with his treacherous brother? Would the name Volkhard mean anything to him, or would that too be lost?

'Nerio,' Penthius said, turning back towards the barrow mound and pointing his maul at the dark entrance. 'Before we march from this place, I want that tomb sealed. And we will raise a marker here for King Volkhard.

'So that any who chance to pass this way again may remember.'

YOUR NEXT READ

SOUL WARS
by Josh Reynolds

In the shadowy lands of Shyish, Nagash, God of Death, calls forth his soulless legions to reassert his dominion. Will Sigmar's brooding Anvils of the Heldenhammer be enough to stop the onslaught?

For these stories and more go to **blacklibrary.com, games-workshop.com**, Games Workshop and Warhammer stores, all good book stores or visit one of the thousands of independent retailers worldwide, which can be found at **games-workshop.com/storefinder**

A DIRGE OF DUST AND STEEL

Josh Reynolds

Eerie shrieks pierced the gloom.

They reverberated through the broken field of toppled pillars and dust-shrouded statuary, riding the night wind. To Sathphren Swiftblade's ears, there was both damnable pleasure and promise in those cries. The Lord-Aquilor repressed a shudder and bent forwards in his saddle. 'Faster, Gwyllth,' he murmured into his mount's ear. 'We're almost there.'

The long-limbed, avian-headed gryph-charger squalled in reply, and increased her speed, despite the weight of the fully armoured Stormcast Eternal she carried on her broad back. Sathphren glanced back, checking on his warriors. Half a dozen armoured Vanguard-Palladors rode hard to either side of him. Like the Lord-Aquilor, they wore the silver-and-azure war-plate of the Hallowed Knights Stormhost, and rode atop lean, leonine gryph-chargers. The beasts were galloping flat out, the magic that flowed through their muscular frames enabling them to easily outpace their pursuers.

As one, they bounded over the fallen statue of some long-forgotten warden king. The square, bearded face glared sightlessly at the silver-armoured riders and their steeds as they raced on across the broken ground. The duardin had once ruled this unforgiving land. Before the coming of Chaos, the Oasis of Gazul had provided shelter for traders and pilgrims alike. Now, it was a daemon-haunted ruin, shrouded in shadows and dust.

Out of the corner of his eye, Sathphren caught a glimpse of a pack of lithe, inhuman shapes as they raced along parallel to the Hallowed Knights. The creatures, at once serpentine and avian, leapt and scrambled over fallen pillars and broken walls, moving with a speed that defied comprehension. They were urged on by their cackling riders – slim, hideously sensual daemonettes, the Handmaidens of Slaanesh.

The daemonettes resembled women, with thick manes of snaky locks and pitiless, androgynous faces. Chitinous claws snapped wildly at the air, as the creatures gesticulated obscenely. The Hounds of Pleasure were on the hunt, and Sathphren and his warriors were their quarry. 'Looks like they've caught up with us at last, eh, Feysha?' Sathphren called out.

'Took them long enough,' Feysha, his second in command, replied. The Pallador-Prime peered back over her shoulder. 'Though I've not seen such a pack of beasts since the Bitterbark. Every daemon in this desert must be on our tail.'

'Good. The more of them the better.' Sathphren glanced back, following her gaze. Behind them, daemons raced across the dust dunes with quicksilver grace. Brutal beast-kin loped in their wake, braying to the Wraith Moon above. There were mortals among them as well – strange figures those, clad in everything from silks to furs, bearing weapons and musical instruments in their tattooed hands. Some rode atop daemonic steeds, while others capered through the dust. Golden standards, decorated with looted tapestries, mirrors and flayed hides, bobbed above the monstrous cavalcade.

It was not an army. A horde, at best. A moveable feast of frenzied indulgence. A celebration of blood and pain. And at its head, crouched atop a massive chariot made from bone and gold and pulled by a darting, hissing herd of daemon-steeds, was the host – the creature known as Amin'Hrith, the Soulflayer.

The Keeper of Secrets was a monster among monsters. It towered over the tallest of its followers, even squatting as it did on its nightmarish conveyance. Its elongated torso bore a quartet of long, milk-pale arms. One of these ended in a vicious, snapping claw, while the hands of the others rested upon the bejewelled hilts of the various blades sheathed about its person, beneath the cloak of skins it wore. Its head was that of a bull, with great, curving horns capped with gold, and a ring of silver in its wide, flat nose. A mane of thick spines draped across the back of its neck, and its pale form was covered in the marks of ritual scarification, as well as various gemstones clinging to its chest like barnacles.

Sathphren's gaze was drawn to the largest of these – a massive ruby, set between the daemon's uppermost pectorals. Something flashed within the facets of the gem, and he turned away, frowning. 'Into the oasis – go!'

Lone pillars and broken statues gave way to more substantial ruins – stone watercourses and shattered aqueducts cast elongated shadows in the moonlight. And beyond them, the high, narrow summit of Gazul-Baraz. The ruins spread out around the immense tower of limestone, spilling forth from the caverns beneath it, following the ancient watercourses. There were greater ruins by far within those caverns, stretching into the deep darkness. This was but the uppermost level of that vast fiefdom. One the Soulflayer had destroyed, and now claimed as its own.

'Swiftblade – beware!'

Feysha's shout was all the warning he needed. He ducked low, folding himself over Gwyllth's neck. A crustacean-like claw snapped closed where his head had been, as a daemon-steed drove itself into Gwyllth's side. The gryph-charger stumbled and spun, shrieking in rage. Sathphren hauled back on the reins, and snatched his boltstorm pistol from its holster. He levelled the weapon at the daemonette rider and loosed a bolt. The bolt struck it in the eye and sent it tumbling from the saddle. Its serpentine steed staggered, off balance, and Gwyllth smashed it from its feet, tearing open its elongated neck.

More daemons closed in, moving quickly. Sathphren holstered his pistol and unsheathed his starbound blade. The blade gleamed like a distant star as he parried a darting claw, and removed a daemonette's head. It spun away, trailing gory locks.

The rest swirled about him, cackling and shrieking, and he dealt with them swiftly. Even in death, they laughed, as if pain and pleasure were both but a singular sensation. The stink of strange incense rose from their glistening flesh. Black eyes, empty of all save malice, bored into him and their smiles were at once alluring and repulsive. Their claws gouged his silver war-plate, but failed to penetrate. 'Who will ride more swiftly than the storm-winds?' he roared, laying about him.

'Only the faithful,' came the response, as the boltstorm pistols of the others cracked and starstrike javelins hissed, further distracting his pursuers. A moment later, Feysha's lunar blade joined his own, as her gryph-charger bore a squealing daemon-steed to the ground. The surviving daemonettes retreated in disorder, a frustrated tenor to their shrieks. Sathphren hauled Gwyllth around and thumped her ribs. The gryph-charger leapt back into motion, speeding to join the others, followed closely by Feysha. 'Keep moving,' Sathphren bellowed. 'Our allies are waiting.'

They led their pursuers down a slope into a narrow defile, between twinned limestone crags that acted as a gateway into the cavern-city beyond. The crags had felt the touch of hammer and chisel at some point in antiquity, and alcoves had been carved into their inner slopes. Immense statues occupied these alcoves – ancient duardin kings and heroes, Sathphren thought. Their countenances were uniformly, grimly stoic, as if humour were somehow taboo among their folk.

Having met them, Sathphren could well believe it. The Gazul-Zagaz were a sombre folk, as befitted those who worshipped death. Their ancestors had taken the name of their fallen god for their own, in the dim, ancient epoch when Nagash, the Undying King, had warred with the old gods of death and emerged supreme.

Theirs was a society built on a legendary defeat, and the bones of those it had claimed. Where they had once ruled, they now merely persisted, huddled in the ruins of former glory, waiting out the days. Hunted by creatures like those even now pursuing him and his warriors. The servants of the Soulflayer had made these ruins their playground. But not for long. Not if Sathphren's gambit was successful.

It was a simple enough plan. Bait the foe in and chew them apart, piecemeal. With the aid of Sathphren and his warriors, the Gazul-Zagaz might rule the Sea of Dust once more. And in return, they would help the Swiftblades complete their mission. 'So far, so good,' he muttered, as they passed through the shattered gateways and into the cavern-city beyond.

It had been hacked from the stalactites and stalagmites of the vast caverns, built into the very bedrock. Despite the situation, he could not help but marvel at the extent of that ancient undertaking. Crumbled structures and ruptured aqueducts rose over sloped avenues. Moonlight shone through great wells carved in the uppermost reaches of the cavern. The silvery radiance was reflected in the sluggish waters that still slithered through the broken aqueducts, and poured down into the ruins in haphazard waterfalls.

'Look,' Feysha called out. She pointed. Sathphren laughed.

'It appears our newfound allies are as good as their word.'

A line of duardin waited for them, their stocky, armoured forms set in a rough battle-line. They were clad in coats and cowls of burnished gromril. Each wore a steel war-mask wrought in the shape of a stylised skull, and carried a heavy, baroque hand cannon. Dust sifted off the broad forms of the duardin Irondrakes as they raised their weapons. '*Uzkul-ha!*' they roared, as one.

The ancient drakeguns belched fire as the Vanguard-Palladors leapt over their wielders. The volley cut through the front rank of daemons and mortals like a scythe of fire. Mortals fell screaming from their abominable mounts, and daemons were ripped to shimmering rags. In the ensuing confusion, the duardin fell back into the ruins, reloading their weapons with a speed born of precision and experience, clearing the path.

Monstrous chariots rattled on in pursuit, over the broken bodies of the fallen. These were bombarded from on high, by hurled chunks of stone. Many slewed wildly, crashing into one another or flipping and rolling. Daemon-steeds screamed as they were pulled to the ground or crushed beneath the tumbling chariots. Even the Soulflayer's massive carriage was brought to a halt, as a chunk of stone shattered one of its wheels, and killed several of the beasts pulling it. The Keeper of Secrets leapt from the wreck with a bellow of frustration.

'Remind them that we're here, brothers and sisters,' Sath-phren shouted. As one, the Hallowed Knights emptied their boltstorm pistols into the stalled horde. The Lord-Aquilor took aim at the Soulflayer, and sent a shot smashing into its chest. The daemon whipped around, eyes narrowing. Sathphren gave a mocking wave and glanced at Feysha. 'Think that'll do it? I'd hate to think the beast is getting bored of us.'

The daemon flung out a claw and bellowed. Its followers surged past it, clambering over the wreckage in their eager-ness to catch their prey. Feysha jerked on the reins of her gryph-charger and turned the beast about. 'I think so, my lord,' she said. Sathphren laughed and jolted Gwyllth into motion.

Drakeguns spat death from the ruins, as the Irondrakes fired again. Followed by the echoes of that volley, the Vanguard-Palladors split up. Several turned back, arrowing through the ruins. They would harass the flanks, and bleed the enemy, strik-ing and fading as only they could. It was what they had been forged for. The rest continued on, racing down what had once been a grand avenue, pursued by the main body of the enemy.

Sathphren looked ahead. At the end of the avenue, between two crumbled structures, a shield wall of duardin warriors waited. '*Gazul-akit-ha!*' The words echoed through the cavern, accompanied by the crash of weapons against shields. '*Uzkul! Uzkul! Uzkul!*' The wall of duardin shields parted, allowing the Stormcast Eternals to pass through.

Mourning bells, mounted on iron standard poles, tolled grimly as the duardin beat on their shields. Warriors wear-ing white vestments over their armour and golden war-masks lifted stone tablets marked with crudely carved runes. As they paced up and down behind the battle-line, they began to sing an eerie dirge. The sound rolled across the line, and sent a chill down Sathphren's spine.

'That doesn't sound like any duardin battle-song I've ever heard,' Feysha said. The Vanguard-Palladors slewed to a halt behind the shield wall, their gryph-chargers yowling in protest. The beasts hated standing still, almost as much as their riders.

'They're mourning the dead yet to be,' Sathphren said. 'Singing their souls to the caverns of their god.'

'Their god is dead.'

'I don't think they care.' He gestured to the duardin. 'Can you support them until Thalkun gets his Vanguard-Raptors into position?'

Cadres of Stormcast marksmen were even now scaling the broken heights of the oasis-city, seeking the best vantage points to deliver their lethal volleys. They would further bleed the foe, dispersing their strength. The enemy was caught fast in the jaws of the trap now, though they didn't yet realise it.

Feysha nodded. 'Aye, if we must. I still think one of us should go with you, at least.'

'One soul more or less won't make a difference.' He gestured. 'Remember, don't fight too hard. Let the beast through. If we're to win this, it must reach the oasis.' The shield wall was only there to blunt the initial rush of the foe. Once they'd bloodied them, the duardin would retreat, as the Irondrakes had, and regroup in the ruins.

'You can count on us,' Feysha said. 'It's the duardin I'm worried about. They look set on dying here.' The dirge swelled up, rolling through the ruins. The song of a dying folk, as they made what might be their last stand. Sathphren frowned and shook his head.

'They know what's at stake, as well as you.' The Gazul-Zagaz had set the price for their aid, though it meant duardin blood would be shed, as well as that of his warriors. For centuries, they had suffered the depredations of the Soulflayer. Now, at last, they had a chance to free themselves. Whatever the cost.

Feysha met his gaze solemnly. 'Much is demanded...' she said.

'Of those to whom much is given,' he replied, completing the canticle. They clasped forearms. 'Fight well, sister. And don't let them catch you standing still.'

'Never,' Feysha said, cheerfully. 'Hup!' She thumped her steed, and the gryph-charger leapt into motion. Sathphren watched her. She would circle through the ruins in order to flank the horde flooding down the avenue. Several of the remaining Vanguard-Palladors followed her, while the rest readied their javelins and drew their boltstorm pistols.

Sathphren twitched the reins and urged Gwyllth deeper into the ruins, seeking their heart. The beast growled low, unhappy at being denied the chance to savage the enemy. 'Soon enough, old girl,' he said, stroking the bright green plumage on her neck. 'Now let's go bait ourselves a trap, eh?'

Traps within traps. That was how the Swiftblades waged war. Sathphren had learned the art of the oblique approach in those harsh, bloody days before he had been called to Sigmar's side. Those lessons had stayed with him, even as he had been reforged, body and soul, on the Anvil of the Apotheosis.

And if there was one place where such an approach was needed, it was Shyish. The Sea of Dust was a harsh land of broken mountains and dust storms that could strip flesh from bone, as easily as gilt from sigmarite. It had its secret roads and hidden paths, and the Swiftblades had sniffed them out, one by one. This was not merely aimless wandering on their part, but a quest given to them by the God-King himself.

The Swiftblades had been sent to Shyish to find the ruins of Caddow, the City of Crows. And in that broken city was the Corvine Gate – an ancient Realmgate linking Shyish with Azyr. Only a scant few such transdimensional apertures remained, in the wake of the War of Death and Heaven. Sigmar had commanded that it be rediscovered and reopened. Sathphren did not know why they sought it, or what might await them there. Nor, in truth, did he care. That the quarry was named was enough. He would find it, or perish in the attempt, and explain his failure to the God-King in person.

But first, he had a daemon to slay. And a bargain to make good on.

He smiled. It was the Soulflayer he'd set this trap for, and it had proved very obliging, thus far. The creature had been easy to provoke – one whiff of fresh prey, and it had been on their trail. Then, in his experience, daemons were many things, but rarely shrewd. They had provoked and teased it for days, leading it into the ruins. Now, it was time for the trap to snap shut. A thrill of premature satisfaction surged through him. He forced it down. The hunt wasn't done yet.

Gwyllth loped through the ruins, carrying him down long, aqueduct-lined avenues towards the central plaza, where the waters of the oasis still ran fresh and clean within the great temple of Gazul. The remains of that edifice rose up around the softly bubbling spring like a forest of stone. It was a massive rotunda of pillars and glowering statues – as with everywhere in the city, the faces of the dead had been captured forever in stone.

Sathphren could hear the soft susurrus of the water as it swirled about its stony prison, deep within the forest of pillars. It filled the watercourses, which stretched from the base of the temple and connected to the closest aqueducts. He hauled back on the reins, bringing Gwyllth to a stop before the vast, flat steps leading up into the temple. A group of duardin awaited him. They wore soot-blackened robes and armour, and their beards and hair were covered in ashes. Some carried weapons, but most had their hands free. They were rune-singers – the last members of an ancient priesthood. Once, they had guided their kin through life. Now, they warded their souls in death.

One of them stepped forwards. 'You have returned.' The War-Mourner of the Gazul-Zagaz was clad in black, and his armour was bronze. Several heavy tomes were chained to him, the cover of each marked with the Khazalid rune of death. He bore an iron staff, surmounted by a dirge-bell and a heavy hammer. Unlike his companions, he wore no mask, though his face had been painted with ash and soot to resemble a skull.

'As I promised, Elder Judd,' Sathphren said as he slid from Gwyllth's back. Heart pounding, he could hear the whistle-crack echo of the hurricane crossbows wielded by the Vanguard-Raptors. Thalkun and his warriors were unleashing a blistering fusillade against the pleasure-maddened warriors flooding into the ruins. But even that wouldn't hold the Soulflayer back for long. Nor did he wish it to. 'Is our trap ready?'

'It waits, manling.' Judd frowned. 'Are you certain the Soul-flayer will come?'

A roar of frustration echoed across the ruins. Sathphren smiled. 'Fairly certain.' He clapped Gwyllth on the haunch. 'Go. You know what to do.' The gryph-charger screeched and turned, scraping its beak against his war-mask. He caught hold of its feathered skull. 'Go, sister. And wait for my call.'

The great beast squalled and loped swiftly into the forest of pillars, tail lashing. Sathphren drew his starbound blade and laid it across his shoulder. The avenue trembled beneath his feet. He turned, keen gaze sweeping across the ruins. He felt no fear. Only the anticipation of a hunter who closes fast on his moment to make a kill. 'Take your kin, and get out of sight, rune-singer. Best we not distract our prey.'

Judd hesitated. The duardin was old, even by the standards

of his people. So old that he might have witnessed his people's fall in person. His hair and beard were the colour of ash mixed with snow, and his weather-beaten flesh resembled worn leather. But his voice was strong, as were his shoulders. 'Are you certain you wish to do this, manling? It may well mean your death.'

'Then we are in the right realm for it, no?' Sathphren looked down at him. 'I swore an oath. And I will hold to it, with every breath in my body.'

Judd nodded. 'Aye, you did at that. And so did we. If we are victorious, we will guide you to the ruins of the City of Crows. And we will aid you in opening the way for your kin, as best we can.' He patted the hammer that rested in the crook of his arm. 'And if we fail – we will add your name to the Great Dirge.' He smiled mirthlessly. 'It is the least we can do.'

Sathphren laughed. 'Don't start singing yet. There's never been a foe to catch me, if I didn't wish to be caught.' He jerked his head. 'Go. It's close. As soon as I lead it into the temple…'

'We know what to do, manling. And so do they.' Judd glanced meaningfully at the statues that glared down at them. Sathphren grunted, trying to ignore the chill that swept through him. In Shyish, the dead did not rest easy, whatever their race.

'Let us hope so. I have no wish to fight the dead, as well as a daemon.'

Judd gave him a gap-toothed grin. 'Have no fear on that score. They know their enemy.' He turned and barked an order in his own tongue. Swiftly, the rune-singers disappeared into the ruins. The duardin of Gazul-Baraz had learned well the art of vanishing from sight. So skilled were they that even Sathphren's warriors had been impressed.

'We have much to learn from each other,' he murmured. 'Perhaps after this is over.' An old refrain, but a comforting one. It implied an end to strife. Something he had not truly believed possible in his mortal life. But now, he had hope. That, in the end, was perhaps the greatest gift that Sigmar had bestowed upon him.

He sank to one knee and planted his sword point-first into the stones before him. Somewhere in the cavern, he heard the tolling of dirge-bells. He could see the battle-lines breaking in his mind's eye. The duardin would retreat, and the foe would splinter, greedy for victory. Softly, he began to pray. As a mortal, his faith had not extended itself to prayers. Here, now, it was another weapon in his arsenal. Each canticle was a wall, a gate, a tower – defending him from what was to come.

He was still praying when the first of the daemons burst into view. Smoothly, without missing a beat, he rose, starbound blade hissing out. A daemonette fell, its unnatural skull cleft in two. Another leapt on him, claws clacking. He swept it off him, and sent it crashing into a pillar. Before it could rise, he pinned it to the pillar with his blade. He twisted the sword, silencing its shrieks.

Two more came at him and met their end. More of them loped down the avenue – some bore wounds, their limbs stained with black ichor. Over their sibilant cries, he could hear the crash of steel and the shouts of his warriors, echoing through the cavern. They had fallen back, as he ordered, opening the way for his prey. He smiled and lunged to meet the daemonettes.

Before he could reach them, a sudden jangle of bells caused them to stop short. With disconsolate hisses, the creatures retreated. They flowed back up the avenue, around a massive form that strode into view. *'You have teeth, then. Good.'*

The Soulflayer.

The daemon's voice was like syrup over coals. *'It is always better, when the prey has teeth. A bit of fight makes the triumph all the sweeter.'* It flung back the edge of a cloak of mortal flesh and hair, heavy with plundered duardin gold, and clashed its bronze bracers, setting the dozens of bells that hung from them ringing. *'You've led me a pretty chase, little glow-bug. I've followed your scent for days. The stink of your soul teases me in exquisite ways. It is like lightning on the tongue.'*

'You haven't caught me yet,' Sathphren said. His hand dropped to his boltstorm pistol. 'But here I am. Come and get me.' He studied the gems that marked the daemon's flesh. Each one flickered with an inner light, some of them brighter than the rest. Thanks to Elder Judd, he knew that the gemstones held the souls of those slain by the daemon. It was called the Soulflayer for good reason.

The Keeper of Secrets bared lupine teeth in a hideous parody of a smile. *'I will. But in my own time. The hunt is ever more pleasing than the kill.'* It spread its uppermost arms. *'Why else would I leave the stunted inhabitants of this wasteland with their souls intact?'*

'Not all of them,' Sathphren said. The stink of the daemon flooded his nostrils. It was a cloying fug, like perfume over rot. He shook his head to clear it.

The daemon's head twitched, like a bull shaking away flies. *'Ah. Does word of my magnificence reach so far, then?'* A bifurcated tongue slid across the thicket of fangs. *'I am flattered.'* A claw-tip caressed the ruby. In its facets, something that might have been a face, contorted in agony, formed briefly before dissipating. *'Yes. I took their prince. The last prince of Gazul-Baraz. He is precious to me. I keep him with me always and will until the day I grow bored of these arid lands, and the scuttling prey that inhabits it.'*

Sathphren laughed. 'That's not the story I heard.'

'Oh?'

'I heard that you remained here out of fear.' Sathphren forced a laugh. 'Shyish has claimed so many of your kind. They say that Amin'Hrith hides in the wastes, hoping the war will pass him by. That the Soulflayer is nothing more than a scavenger, picking the bones left behind by more faithful celebrants.'

The daemon snarled. It thrust its chitinous claw at Sathphren. *'Choose your words with care, little glow-bug. You are alone.'*

'I'm done with words.' Sathphren snatched his boltstorm pistol free of its holster and loosed a shot. One of the gemstones on the daemon's abdomen burst as the bolt struck home. Amin'Hrith shrilled in rage as a soft will o' the wisp of soul-light fluttered upwards, through the daemon's grasping hands.

'Thief!' The daemon capered, trying to catch the light as it swam upwards and away towards the roof of the cavern above. Sathphren fired again and again, backing away with each shot. Gems burst like blisters, releasing soft puffs of radiance – souls, long denied their rest by the daemon's greed. With every shattered bauble, the daemon grew more enraged. It loped after him.

'I will tear your soul to pieces, to replace that which you have taken,' it screamed. It drew the blades that hung from its war-harness as it ran, and slashed apart a nearby pillar in a fit of petulance. Sathphren raced up the steps and into the temple through the slabbed archway that marked the entrance.

The rotunda was full of pillars, each carved with thousands of runes – names, he knew. Or so the Gazul-Zagaz had claimed. The names of the dead, going back to the founding of the city. At the heart of the rotunda was the vast pool from which all the water in the city flowed. It bubbled and flowed, as fresh as the day the first duardin had discovered it. A colossal statue of Gazul sat atop a dais of dark stone, overlooking the waters. The god's statue was draped in a burial shroud of shadows and dust, his features obscured.

Sathphren lost himself among the pillars, moving as quietly as possible. He could hear the clop of the daemon's hooves on the stone floor. *'I can taste your fear and your desire on the wind,'* it growled. Its voice was thick with silky menace and promise, all in one. It echoed through the pillars. *'I will add your soul to my collection, little glow-bug. You will dangle 'pon my chest, and your screams will soothe me to sleep, 'ere I grow tired of my games.'*

Sathphren didn't answer. He heard a voice chanting – Elder Judd. The rune-singers were gathering outside the temple now. They had waited centuries for this day. The jaws of the trap were clashing shut. He heard the scrape of chitin on stone, and tensed. It was close.

'Why do you not answer me, little glow-bug? I thought your kind liked to talk. So boastful, you storm-riders. You wield declarations like swords.' It chuckled again, and he could almost see the ghastly smile on its twisted features. *'Do you tremble at the thought of my gentle touch, glow-bug? As well you should.'*

A fug of perfumed musk suddenly enveloped Sathphren. He spun. A chitinous claw thrust itself towards him. He leapt aside. The claw gouged a pillar in half, casting rubble across the floor. The Keeper of Secrets lunged into view, hauling itself around another pillar. Its eyes blazed with a monstrous greed. *'Oh, I have such sights to show you,'* it snarled. *'Nightmares and ecstasies beyond any you can conceive. I will flay your soul from the meat. I will make adornments from your bones, and wear your screaming skull into the eternities yet to come.'*

Sathphren lunged, his starbound blade licking out across

the daemon's taunting muzzle. Amin'Hrith jerked back with a shriek of pain. Sathphren twisted aside, narrowly avoiding a wild slash from the daemon's blade. He whistled sharply, and Gwyllth leapt down from the top of the pillars, where she had been waiting. The gryph-charger's weight caught the daemon by surprise, and knocked it stumbling. The great beast clung to the daemon's broad back, tail lashing. Her beak stabbed down into the alabaster flesh, releasing a spurt of sickly-sweet ichor.

Amin'Hrith shrieked, clawing at its attacker. Sathphren ducked beneath a flailing claw and drove his sword into the daemon's elongated torso, twisting it upwards with all his strength. It gave a tooth-rattling shriek and dropped a heavy fist onto him, driving him to one knee. A second blow caught him on the chest, and sent him skidding backwards. The daemon tore the screeching gryph-charger from her perch and hurled her into a pillar. She crumpled to the ground with a muted whine.

Sathphren rolled onto his stomach. Pain beat at his temples, and his chest felt as if it had been caved in. He coughed, and tasted blood. The chanting was louder now, beating at the air like hammer strokes. The air felt heavy with something – anticipation, he thought. He glanced towards the statue of Gazul, and it seemed as if the god's eyes were gleaming.

It was time. The trap snapped shut.

Amin'Hrith touched the ragged wounds opened in its flesh with something akin to wonder. *'How exquisite. It has been centuries since my flesh was ravaged so.'* It fixed Sathphren with its yellow gaze. *'I thank you, glow-bug. Let me show you my gratitude properly.'*

'Let me show you mine, first,' Sathphren wheezed, hauling himself upright. He rose to one knee, spots swimming across his vision. 'For the gift.'

'Gift?' The daemon hesitated, head tilted.

Sathphren held up the ruby. He'd managed to chop it loose, just before the daemon had swatted him aside. It pulsed with an unsettling warmth, as if there were a fire within its crimson facets. Amin'Hrith looked down at its chest, and then back at him. It took a heavy step towards him, claw extended. *'Give it back, glow-bug. Or I will ensure your torments are legendary, even by the heady standards of the Pavilions of Pleasure.'*

'A kind offer, but not one I care to take.' Sathphren slammed the flickering gemstone down on the stone floor, shattering it. Outside the temple, the song of the rune-singers rose to a rolling crescendo, shaking the very stones underfoot. They fell silent as the echoes of the ruby's demise faded.

In the quiet that followed, Amin'Hrith laughed, and Sathphren felt his sense of triumph ebb. *'And what was that supposed to achieve?'* the daemon sneered. *'What did you think would happen, glow-bug? I am no mere courtesan, to be banished at the whim of a mortal. I am Amin'Hrith, the Soulflayer. I have wallowed in the dust of a thousand worlds, and seen reality itself shatter beneath the awful weight of my lord's gentle gaze. I have worn ghosts as baubles and hunted entire peoples to extinction, in the World That Was. And I will do the same here. I–'*

The shards of ruby shone suddenly with a soft light, interrupting the daemon. Blood-red shadows crawled across the pillars and floor. Curls of cerise smoke rose from the fragments, twisting and coalescing with one another, until they became a vaguely duardin-shaped mass. Something that might have been a face turned towards the daemon, and twisted into a wrathful expression. A wordless cry boomed out of the stones and air, and the daemon stepped back. *'What is this? You could not challenge me while you lived, little prince. What makes you think you can do so now?'*

The smoky shape took a step forwards, its hunched form sprouting an amorphous shield and something resembling an axe. The temple seemed to shake with its tread. Sathphren caught sight of ghostly shapes drifting through the pillars – the dead, come to answer their long lost prince's call. 'He isn't alone,' Sathphren said.

While the daemon held the soul of their prince captive, the Gazul-Zagaz had been unable to act against it. Now, with the ruby shattered, and the soul free, the dead of Gazul-Baraz, raised up by the song of the rune-singers, could have their long-delayed vengeance. Sathphren smiled. A good plan. A fitting plan.

A grim dirge rose from the spectres as they gathered, encircling the daemon in a ring of insubstantial bodies. Sathphren could hear the faint crash of steel, and the crack of stone. Motes of pale light floated within ghostly skulls – the eyes of the dead, fixed on the author of their torment. *Uzkul,* they moaned, as one. *Uzkul. Uzkul. Uzkul.*

The Keeper of Secrets turned, trying to keep all of the gathering spirits in sight. *'Begone, shades. There is no joy to be had from your pallid essences.'* It swept out a claw dismissively, trying to disperse the horde. The dead struck, as the claw passed through them. Ghostly axes and hammers caught the limb, and ichor spurted. Amin'Hrith screamed in rage and pain. The daemon jerked its injured limb back. *'No. No, this isn't right.'* It whirled, eyes fixed on Sathphren. *'What have you done?'*

'What I do best,' Sathphren said, as he rose to his feet. Gwyllth was on her feet as well, if somewhat battered. He caught hold of her and hauled himself into the saddle. 'And now, I leave you to it.' He thumped the gryph-charger in the ribs, and she leapt away with a shriek, even as the daemon lunged for them.

Amin'Hrith crashed awkwardly into a pillar as they avoided its grasp, and screamed in fury. It clattered after them, smashing rubble aside in its haste, and the ghosts boiled up around it like storm clouds. A typhoon of spirits – led by the crimson essence of the prince – surrounded the blundering daemon, striking at it from all sides and angles. They blinded it, slowed it. Trapped it.

And there was another presence there as well, something greater than any ghost, and mightier than any daemon. It seemed to gather itself in the limits of the temple, readying itself as Sathphren urged Gwyllth towards the entrance. The shadows thickened and the voices of the dead were echoed by a deep tolling, rising up from somewhere below. Not a bell, this, but a wordless cry, like the crash of stone into the sea.

It roared out as the gryph-charger leapt through the archway and down the steps. Sathphren turned his steed about, sword in hand, to face the archway. The Keeper of Secrets clawed at the entrance, hands gripping either side of the aperture. It strained, as if against unseen bonds. Its mouth was open, but Sathphren could hear nothing save that roaring cry.

A wind rose up from somewhere and caught at the creature, forcing it back. Beneath the roar came a grinding sound, like stone rasping against stone. One by one, the remaining gemstones on the daemon's flesh burst. Ghostly hands clutched at the Soulflayer's limbs and head. The daemon's eyes bulged as it fought against the dead.

'*Uzkul. Uzkul. Uzkul.*'

Sathphren glanced around. Judd and the other rune-singers chanted as they approached, their bells tolling sombrely. With every peal of the bells, the daemon's grip on the aperture seemed to grow weaker, its claws digging deep trenches in the stone. Then, with a final thunderclap, a dark shape, massive and indistinct, caught hold of the Soulflayer and jerked it backwards, into the dark of the temple and out of sight.

It did not even have a chance to scream.

The rune-singers ceased their song. The sound of the bells faded. All was silence, save for the burble of water. Judd thumped the ground with the ferrule of his staff. Slowly, the spirits of the dead emerged from the darkness. Their prince stood among them, his form as indistinct as before, recognisable only by the raw, red radiance.

Judd lifted his staff, and murmured. The spirits of the dead duardin wavered like smoke and dispersed, in shreds and tangles. They drifted upwards, towards the roof of the cavern and the moonlight streaming through. Something like thunder rumbled in the depths, and Sathphren felt its reverberations in his bones. He thought it might be laughter.

Judd smiled sadly. 'Gazul is pleased. Our oath is fulfilled at last.'

Sathphren looked at him. 'They say Nagash devoured the other gods of the dead, and added their might to his own.'

'Yes, that is what they say.' Judd shrugged. 'And yet, what is death to a god?' He scooped up a handful of dust, and let the wind pull it from his hand. 'Dust, and less than dust.' He sighed and looked at Sathphren. 'But that is a matter for another day. For now, we will fulfil our oath to you. We will lead you where you wish to go.'

Sathphren nodded solemnly. 'I expected no less.' He laughed suddenly and turned Gwyllth about, towards the sounds of fighting. 'But first – our task is not yet done. There are still daemons to hunt, and an oasis to free. As I promised.'

HALLOWED KNIGHTS - PLAGUE GARDEN
by Josh Reynolds

During the greatest battles of the War for Life, the Stormcast Eternals
suffered a great tragedy: the Hallowed Knights Lord-Castellant Lorus
Grymn was lost to the Realm of Chaos. Now his fellow Steel Souls venture
into the domain of Nurgle himself in search of their lost comrade…

For these stories and more go to **blacklibrary.com, games-workshop.com**, Games Workshop
and Warhammer stores, all good book stores or visit one of the thousands of independent
retailers worldwide, which can be found at **games-workshop.com/storefinder**

CALLIS & TOLL: THE OLD WAYS

Nick Horth

Armand Callis winced as the marsh strider bucked beneath him. Every time the beast moved, his legs rubbed painfully against the rough hide saddle that was lashed around the creature's segmented body. They had been travelling for hours, and he still hadn't got used to the strider's awkward, rolling gait as it stretched out its six long limbs to balance on the soupy morass beneath them. He sighed as he peered through the gathering fog, hoping to catch sight of their destination looming into view. It was useless. He could barely see more than a few metres ahead.

'How much farther?' he shouted.

'Soon,' grunted their guide, a wizened old fellow with an expression that could turn milk sour.

Callis' marsh strider clicked and hissed, before releasing an arcing jet of fluid from its mandibles. On the whole, Callis decided that he preferred horses.

'Marshpoint is close,' said Hanniver Toll, mounted upon his

own strider to Callis' left. Beneath his signature wide-brimmed hat, the older man's face was chapped pink by the cold and had several days' worth of stubble across his chin. Callis rubbed his own face ruefully. His typically neat and well-groomed moustache was tapering wildly out of control, and a coarse beard itched beneath the scarf wrapped around his mouth.

'Follow my lead once we arrive,' said Toll. 'The feud between the Junicas and the Dezraeds is on the verge of erupting into a full-scale border war.'

'No wonder,' muttered Callis. 'I'd be miserable too, if I lived out here.'

The Brackenmarsh was a featureless expanse of foul-smelling mud and grime that lay to the east of the great city of Excelsis. It was a bubbling pit of slime and weeds that reached to the mouth of the enormous Ulwhyr Forest. They had avoided the winding trade road that led through the marsh to the frontier township, as Toll had wanted to make it to Marshpoint as swiftly as possible. Unfortunately, marsh striders were the only way to cross the fenland – travelling by foot was a sure way of getting yourself drowned or eaten by the primitive beasts that dwelled within its murky depths. Despite their immense size and vicious, barbed forelimbs, the mantis-like beasts were completely docile. Each of their six legs ended in a tangle of thick hairs that spread out across the rippling surface of the water, forming buoyant pads that allowed the striders to skip across the marsh with surprising speed.

'The disappearance of Adrec Junica has turned a tense situation into a volatile one,' said Toll. 'House Junica has long accused the Dezraeds of trying to undermine their trade in silksteel, and now they have an excuse to spill blood.'

'If that happened, the Freeguilds would not receive their shipments of silksteel.'

Silksteel was a substance woven by arachnids found within the Ulwhyr. Thin and light, it possessed a fearsome tensile strength, meaning that it could be woven into light, padded armour that stopped blades and arrows as surely as steel plate. As Excelsis lacked vast natural deposits of metal, silksteel was vital for outfitting the local regiments. Without it, the already undermanned city guard would find itself under-equipped too.

'Indeed,' said Toll, nodding. 'We're here to try and neutralise the fray by uncovering whether Lord Junica's firstborn son was indeed slain by the hands of the Dezraeds, or simply drank too much, stumbled into the marsh and drowned.'

'Hardly seems like vital work for an agent of the Order of Azyr,' said Callis. 'Couldn't they have sent a detachment from the city guard?'

'The city guard is stretched parchment-thin as it is,' said Toll. 'The battle for Excelsis left the city weak and vulnerable. If it comes under siege again, it will fall. Trade has been severely hampered and the people are ready to riot. Callis, this infighting could be the spark that ignites a full-scale uprising.' Toll paused. 'We would have no choice but to set the White Reaper loose. That's not an outcome I would relish.'

Callis fought off a shudder. He had once come face to face with Lord-Veritant Cerrus Sentanus – the White Reaper of Excelsis – and had barely escaped with his life. If Sentanus was loosed upon the inhabitants of the city, the streets would run with blood.

'Here,' growled their guide, pointing one thin finger into the distance. Following his gesture, they could see the lambent glow of torches flickering. Rising up out of the mist like the backbone of some drowned behemoth, a perimeter wall loomed over a short pier of mildewed wood. It was a well-made fortification, as these things went. The wood was smoothed and sanded down to prevent anyone scaling it, and dotted along the line were swivel-mounted arbalests with large, hook-shaped magazines. A great, circular tower loomed above the parapet, and atop the battlements, Callis could see a heavy ballista, aiming out into the gloom.

'The ones who built this place knew their business,' Callis said. 'You'd only require a few men to hold this wall against a horde.'

'You're looking at Junica coin,' said Toll. 'They employed the most skilled duardin siege-smiths when they built this place. You don't survive out here, beyond the city's reach, unless you can defend yourself. Their private armies are larger than many Freeguild regiments. House Dezraed's included.'

Callis' eyebrows quipped. 'I'm surprised that's allowed.'

'Both Dezraed and Junica are old Azyr stock. At one time or another, they've both had figures on the council of Azyrheim. The men we're here to see, though, are minor scions of the great houses. Still, they're powerful figures with a bottomless supply of coin and the ear of the Excelsis council. As long as they pay their tithes and maintain their shipments, the city is content to allow their standing armies.'

As they approached the bank, the marsh striders hauled themselves out of the dank swamp, flicking their long limbs free of foul-smelling weeds.

'Who passes?' came a shout from the palisade gatehouse, where a bucket-helmed face peered down at them, silhouetted against the sickly yellow sky. The figure was leaning against a swivel-gun mounted upon the edge of the wall.

'We are expected,' shouted Toll, dropping nimbly from the saddle, patting the beast's chitinous, armour-plated leg affectionately. The thing gave a shrill chirp and lowered its many-eyed head to the mossy earth, loudly slurping at a clump of moss. 'I am Hanniver Toll, agent of the Order of Azyr. Open the gate.'

Even from a distance away, Callis could see the colour drain from the man's face.

'The witch hunter,' breathed the guard. The figure made a frantic gesture to someone on the other side of the wall, and there was a clanking, grinding sound. Slowly, the great gate began to creak open.

'So this is Marshpoint,' said Callis. 'Hardly a sight to set the blood astir.'

It was far from the worst hovel that Callis had ever laid eyes on – indeed the poor quarters of Excelsis were far more run-down – but a tangible pall of misery hung over the cluttered white stone houses that formed the main street. The construction was simple, functional and rather ugly, with thatched green roofs slanting away into the fog, and uneven masonry.

'Someone threw this town up in a hurry,' said Callis.

'It's more fort than town, truly,' said Toll. 'The only people who live here are soldiers and workers from the silksteel plantations. We're probably the only outsiders these people have seen in months. Few travellers or merchants risk the trade road this far east.'

Shrouded figures hustled across a road of rough-hewn cobbles in the fading light, glancing at the newcomers with nervous eyes. The central plaza, such as it was, featured a statue of an imposing warrior, a Stormcast Eternal with hammer raised to the skies. The grandeur of the craftsmanship was marred by the smear of verdigris and mould, and the hazy green light that filtered through the darkening clouds gave the noble image an unsettling pallid glow. The looming towers and the high wall cast the squat, unremarkable little town in shadow, giving it a claustrophobic feel.

Several shabby-looking guards dressed in leather jerkins stared down at them from a walkway that ran the length of the outer wall. One strode down the steps to meet them, removing a woollen cap as he did so to reveal a boyish, earnest face, dark-skinned and fresh-eyed. He looked barely out of his teens.

'They told us to expect visitors,' he said. 'But we weren't expecting you here for another few days. We thought you'd take the trade road.'

'I would prefer to resolve the situation here as swiftly as possible,' said Toll. As he stepped forward, he removed his wide-brimmed hat and reached into his coat. He withdrew a waxen scroll, marked with the image of a blazing comet.

'Sigmar's teeth,' whispered the guard as he studied the paper. His eyes went wide. 'Sorry, sire. Forgive my blasphemy. I...'

'I have business with Lords Fenrol Dezraed and Kiervaan Junica,' said Toll, ignoring the man's discomfort. 'Send word of my arrival to both.'

'Um... Begging your pardon, sire, but they won't leave their estates,' mumbled the guard. 'Neither of them. We've already seen blood spilled, and with the Junica boy missing, they're readying for war...' He shook his head. 'They've stopped the patrols and blocked the roads. There's only fifty of us defending this entire town. Heavens forbid the orruks come pillaging and burning, or the bog-devils swarm the walls at the White Witch's command.'

'Your name?' said Toll.

'Guardsman Rolkyr, sire,' said the man.

'Send word to both the houses, Guardsman Rolkyr, and return to your post. Your diligence is noted. It would appear that there are some souls yet in Marshpoint who remember their duty.'

Rolkyr seemed surprised. He gave a slight nod and scrambled away up the stairs, shouting orders to his men.

'Son,' shouted Toll. The guard turned. 'Where's the tavern?'

'The Moss Throne,' said Rolkyr, gesturing to a rather shabby two-storey building across the cobbled square. Dim light shone through the lower windows, but other than that it looked more like an abandoned barn than a place to catch a good night's sleep. The sloped roof was thick with ivy, which draped down the mouldy wooden walls like strands of wet hair. The windows were round and the entire structure sat oddly slanted on the street, as if it was about to slide into the bog. Still, it was a tavern, and they'd have ale. Callis had drunk in far worse places.

'Obliged,' said Callis, snapping a friendly salute.

'Tell the Lords Dezraed and Junica that they can grace us with their presence at this fine establishment.'

'Sire,' nodded Rolkyr in agreement. 'Just supposing, but what if they refuse?'

'They will not,' said Toll, 'if they value their continued existence.'

They took a table in the centre of the tavern and ordered food along with a thin, tasteless ale. Gradually the clientele filtered out, eyeing the newcomers uneasily as they left. The common folk were mostly slight, pale figures, lean from hard work but rather sickly looking. No one but the barkeep, a rotund man of middling years with a drooping moustache and sad eyes, spoke to them. Callis, tired though he was, could feel the aura of tension and unease that surrounded them. It wasn't merely their presence that unsettled the locals. The town had the distinct feel of a city facing a siege. A burgeoning sense of dread reminded him of times he had spent awaiting battle, knowing that bloodshed was coming, but unable to do anything other than stand ready until the killing started.

After perhaps an hour, they heard the clatter of hooves outside. Callis moved to the window, while Toll continued to pick at a rather sorry slice of grey meat. Peering out of the misted glass, Callis saw two-score soldiers riding pale mares and carrying long, forked spears emerging out of the haze. They flanked a great carriage of crimson and gold, shining gaudily amidst its unassuming surroundings. These soldiers were a different breed to the ragged fellows manning the palisade. They wore thick cloth tunics with silver pads upon the shoulders and chest, and their armour glittered in the gloomy evening light. The image of an aetherhawk in flight was embossed upon their chest plates and upon the barding of their mounts. Callis recognised the motif – the symbol of House Dezraed. The same image hung from the banners of Excelsis' market square and soared above the Halls of Justice.

He returned to the table and drained the rest of his ale, wincing slightly at the silty, bitter aftertaste.

A few moments later, the door opened, letting in a drizzle of rain and a chill wind. The soldiers entered in perfect parade lockstep, their boots stamping out a staccato rhythm on the wooden floor of the tavern. They spread out in a fan on either side of the door, slamming the hafts of their spears down and raising their heads imperiously. The tavern hound, a morose-looking beast with rheumy eyes and a matted mane of blue-grey fur, got up from its position under Toll and Callis' table, and sauntered across the floor. It paused briefly to idly lap at its hindquarters and gaze at the newcomers.

'My name is Captain Lecian Celtegar,' said the lead soldier in a clipped Azyrite accent. He wore a half-face helm with a bright blue plume, and was the only guard not carrying a long-spear. Instead, he rested his hand on a fine, silver longsword at his belt. He removed his helm, revealing a wave of blond hair and an angular face locked in a permanent half-sneer. Callis disliked the man on sight. 'May I present my Lord Fenrol var

Dezraed, the Eagle of the East, Warden of Marshpoint and the scourge of the forest greenskins.'

Callis glanced at Toll. The witch hunter leaned back in his chair, a long-suffering expression upon his face.

A man entered the tavern. At first, Callis thought it was several men, wrapped up in a single enormous bedsheet. The mighty Lord Dezraed was far from the statuesque patrician his entourage had intimated. He was a huge, wobbling bulge of a human, enormously fat with no suggestion of muscle beneath. A toga of rich crimson silk struggled vainly to lend an air of Azyrite nobility to the wall of flesh, but to no avail. Dezraed's eyes narrowed as he laid eyes on them, two sunken pools of glassy ice within his pink slab of a face. The man's thin blond hair had been separated and slicked back by rain, and he carried a look of utmost irritation.

'So you are the findsman, are you?' he said to Toll, his voice a deep, throaty gurgle. 'You believe it proper to force me out of my home and onto the streets where Junica's assassins lurk? You drag me to this *hovel*, like I am some minor cutpurse to be ordered about at your own will?'

Toll rapped his fingers on the table and stared levelly at Lord Dezraed.

'Take a seat, my lord,' he said, and there was not a hint of irritation or anger in his words. Not for the first time, Callis wondered how the man remained so calm. 'Lord Kiervaan var Junica will be joining us presently, then together we three will unpick this mess.'

Dezraed's eyes widened.

'You invite the very man that seeks my death? Who baselessly blames me for the abduction of his firstborn son, as if I would sully my hands by laying them upon that thin-blooded wretch? I summoned you here to deal with that madman once and for all, not to–'

'You do not summon the Order,' said Toll, and though his voice remained level, there was a sliver of ice in his words. 'You do not make demands of us. Now sit.'

The noble's great lips quivered in astonished rage. He was not a man used to being spoken to so curtly, Callis thought with some satisfaction.

'May I offer you a drink?' said Toll, indicating his cup of ale.

Dezraed snorted, turning his nose up at the humble spread that lay before the witch hunter.

'Wine,' he barked at his retainers, who rushed back outside into the rain. Dezraed snapped his fingers and another two perfumed servants rushed forth carrying an immense curule chair between them. They set it down. The man eased his bulk into it with a groan of protesting timber.

They waited another thirty minutes or so in interminable silence before they heard the clatter of approaching horses. Dezraed's men moved to surround their master, who slurped the last dregs from a horn of pale, sweet-smelling mead. The door swung open and a stocky man in black leather and chain-mail entered. The newcomer took in the scene, fixing on Toll for a moment. The witch hunter met his gaze. Eventually, the man slammed one fist on the door and a group of heavyset men entered, armoured in gold-plated scale armour and long, black hoods. Each carried a black-iron mace fashioned in the shape of a comet. They held their weapons at the ready as they filtered in, glaring daggers at Dezraed and his own gleaming host. Callis let one hand fall to his pistol and readied a foot to overturn the table if things went awry, as they typically did in these situations. If Toll felt the tension, he did not show it.

A thin, aging man dressed in austere black entered, flanked by two more guards. He wore a military-style jacket and breast-plate, polished and buckled with parade-ground precision. His greying hair was shaved close to the scalp, and he wore his moustache thin and curled with wax. This one fancies himself a military man, thought Callis. A strangely common delusion amongst the noble classes, that. Lord Junica took in his modest surroundings with the air of a man examining some unpleasant substance stuck to the sole of his boot. His face was gaunt where Dezraed's was flabby, and his brow was furrowed in a cold glare that only intensified when he caught a glimpse of his rival.

'Lord Junica,' said Toll, tearing a hunk of black bread in half and dabbing it into the thin stew. 'Please, join us. I am Hanniver Toll, of the hallowed Order of Azyr.'

'You ask me to sit beside the man who killed my son?' hissed Kiervaan Junica. 'I should paint the floor with this fat bastard's blood.'

Dezraed spluttered in outrage and his guards stepped forwards, spears lowering threateningly. Junica's men took a pace back, readying their own weapons. There was a muffled yelp as the barkeep dived behind his counter to the sound of smashing glass. Toll took another bite of bread and washed it down with a swig of ale.

'I did not kill your idiotic spawn, but I wish I had,' shouted Dezraed, slamming his meaty fists upon the table. 'The only good Junica is a dead Junica, and if you insult my honour again, I shall seek the satisfaction. I warn you now!'

'Enough,' said Toll, and the two men looked at the witch hunter in surprise. Seemingly oblivious to their disbelief, Toll took up a napkin in one hand and dabbed at his moustache.

'Stand your men down. If there is even a drop of spilled blood at this table, then word will make it back to Excelsis, I assure you. Next time the Order dispatches an agent to your doorstep, they will not send a single man. They will send in the hounds, my lords. Your lands and your profits will be confiscated. Both of you will be dragged before the Halls of Justice to explain why you defied the word of the God-King. Perhaps we shall give you to the White Reaper, so that he may uncover the true extent of your failures.'

Lord Dezraed's red face went suddenly pale, and even Lord Junica looked unnerved at the threat. Callis allowed himself a small grin. There was a distinct pleasure to be found in watching Toll work.

'This is a private matter,' Kiervaan Junica stuttered. 'There is no treason here. I only wish to know the truth behind the disappearance of my son.'

'Disrupting the flow of vital supplies in a time of war is treason,' said Toll. 'If I possessed the same disposition of many of my kin, you both would already be returned to the city dungeons, there to wait for the hangman's rope around your necks. Now sit, my lord.'

Junica eased himself into a chair. His bodyguards stood on either side.

'Pass me the ale,' said Toll, gesturing at Lord Junica.

The noble looked startled at the blunt request, as if Toll had just fired his pistol into the ceiling. His attendants stared at each other in confusion.

'Excuse me?' Junica said.

'The ale,' Toll repeated.

To Callis' surprise, Junica reached out an uncertain hand and passed the jug of sour-smelling liquid to the witch hunter, who took it and poured himself a fresh cup.

'You accuse Lord Dezraed of murder without proof?' said Callis.

Junica glanced at him, surprised, as if he had not noticed him at all before he had spoken.

'Long has the feud between Junica and Dezraed raged,' he said. 'When we forged a path on the frontier with blood and spirit, the Dezraeds followed us like parasites, leeching off our noble work. As they have always done.'

'You dare?' roared Lord Dezraed, spittle flying from his lips. 'House Dezraed desires only to serve the will of Sigmar, as *we* have always done. It is the Junicas who provoke us, stealing away the riches of the land for themselves alone, threatening honest workers and harassing my soldiers at every possible turn. Excelsis is built upon the blood of the Dezraeds. We were here long before the Junicas, and we shall be here long after your ragged house crumbles into dust.'

'My steward, Ghedren, saw your men pursue my son into the forest,' said Junica, indicating the unassuming man in the chainmail hauberk. 'They were drunk, seeking sport. My firstborn son. Aldrec was a strong, brave boy, and your men ran him down like a dog. At your order, no doubt.'

'My soldiers did nothing of the sort. Yet I know that you yourself resort to murder all too quickly, Junica,' snarled Dezraed. 'As did your son. On the very night you claim he was assaulted, it was he who murdered a Dezraed man in cold blood, then fled the scene of the crime rather than face the consequences. Half a dozen more of my men have disappeared also. No doubt their bodies have been dumped in some stinking bog with Junica daggers in their backs.'

'You witnessed this altercation?' Callis asked Ghedren.

'I did,' the man said, nodding. 'It is as the Lord Junica states. Words were exchanged and swords were drawn. I do not know who struck the first blow, but Aldrec was wounded on the arm in the struggle. He fled on horseback. The Dezraeds chased him.' The man spoke with a soft, lilting accent, quite at odds with his coarse and weathered face. Callis guessed that

Ghedren was in his third decade or thereabouts, but he had the rough look of a man who plied his trade in the wilds. Callis noticed the familiar curling lines of blue-ink tattoos emerging from under the man's collar. A fellow Reclaimed. A descendent of the nomadic tribes who had once lived here, before Sigmar's Tempest brought the light of the heavens back into the realms, rather than a great, Azyr-born family like his masters. Perhaps that was why he appeared to possess some humility.

'They went beyond the eastern gate and into the Ulwhyr,' he continued. 'I followed after them, but they were horsed and I was not. I lost them in the darkness, but I heard screams, so returned to seek help.'

'The words of a lowborn mercenary employed by the Junica,' said Captain Celtegar, with a dismissive snort. 'How utterly convincing. I tell you now, upon my honour and that of my men, no such incident took place. This one lies.'

Ghedren simply shrugged. 'It is what I saw.'

'How many days past was this?' asked Toll.

'Five days, sire.'

'And you have returned since to search the area?'

'We have. We found no sign of Master Junica, nor of his pursuers.'

'It is possible, then, that something else could have occurred within the Ulwhyr? Not murder?' Toll continued.

Ghedren shrugged. 'Perhaps, but the Dezraed soldiers were after blood.'

'You will take me and my associate there,' said Toll. 'You will guide us to the spot where you lost track of them. If what you say is true, there will be traces of their passing.'

Ghedren looked at his master for confirmation. Lord Junica nodded slightly.

'Captain Celtegar will accompany you,' said Lord Dezraed.

'Along with two men of his choosing. Just to ensure that this is not some foolish attempt at revenge.'

'I have such a thing as honour, you bloated fiend,' snapped Junica. 'A concept that escapes you entirely.'

Their bickering was about to start over anew, when Toll slammed his fist on the table.

'Silence,' he barked. 'At dawn, we will enter the Ulwhyr and find out the truth of this. My lords, you will remain in Marshpoint until I tell you otherwise. And I warn you both, if blood is shed on these streets, I promise I will ensure that a price is paid. Now leave.'

Callis followed Toll out of the eastern gate of Marshpoint early the next morning, rubbing at his itching eyes. It had not been a relaxing sleep in the cramped guest chambers of the Moss Throne. The room had smelled of mildew and rot, and he had been kept awake by the sounds of buzzing insects and a slow, steady dripping from the roof above his head.

'So, what do you think of our Lords Junica and Dezraed?' Toll asked.

Callis scratched his beard and yawned.

'They would each see the other destroyed if they could,' he said. 'That's clear. But I am not sure about a murder plot. Lord Dezraed hardly seems like a master schemer.'

'Do not underestimate him,' said Toll. 'Marshpoint may not be a glamorous place, but the silksteel plantations are of great value to both houses. They would not send lackwits out here to oversee one of their most valuable trades. Fenrol Dezraed looks like a greedy fool, but clever men often hide behind the mummer's mask.'

'Why the firstborn son?' said Callis. 'Why not the old man himself? If you're going to start a war, why not make that your opening move? If this is a Dezraed scheme, what's the end goal?'

Toll rolled his hat in his hands and nodded thoughtfully.

'Be watchful as we enter the Ulwhyr,' he said, checking the firing pan of his four-barrelled pistol. 'Observe all. Discount nothing.'

'I've patrolled the wilds before,' said Callis. 'I know well what it's like out here.'

'I do not just mean the forest,' Toll replied, but before Callis could ask what he meant, the witch hunter strode over to greet the Junica steward, Ghedren, who was waiting for them on a flooded path that led out towards the distant spectre of the Ulwhyr Forest. The man carried a well-made composite bow and a heavy-bladed knife at his hip. He was wrapped in a large wolf-skin cloak that smelled strongly of wet fur. He dipped his head in greeting as they approached. The vast, ominous expanse of woodland that was the Ulwhyr lurked on the eastern edge of the town, emerging out of the early morning murk. The canopy was an impenetrable carpet of dark green, the trunks of the trees below gnarled and twisted, leading into darkness. A tide of sickly green mist rolled out from the bog, swirling around the mouth of the forest like the breath of a fallen giant.

'So that's where we're headed?' Callis said. 'Seems like an inviting sort of place.'

Ghedren smiled. 'The Ulwhyr is dangerous, yes. But it is also a place of life. For many years, my people walked its secret paths, hidden from those that wished us harm. It protected us, granted us all that we required. One need only show the forest the proper respect and they can walk amongst its shadows unscathed.'

'You almost sound as though it's a sentient thing,' said Callis.

'Perhaps it is. These lands are rife with magic. Within the Ulwhyr dwell things more ancient than a mortal could possibly contemplate,' said Ghedren. 'The forest belongs to them, not us.'

'For now,' interrupted Toll. 'In time, the light of the God-King will reach even the darkest corners of these lands. We will tame this place, and then we will burn away the shadows.'

'Some evils cannot be banished so easily.'

'I did not say that it would be easy,' said Toll, who then went to converse with the gaggle of nervous-looking guards manning the east gate, leaving Ghedren and Callis alone.

'You were raised in the city?' asked the steward.

'I was,' Callis replied. 'Though my family weren't Azyrite. I served in the Freeguild for many years.'

Callis briefly thought to mention his regiment, but decided against it. The Coldguard of Excelsis had been entirely liquidated for their part in the heretical plot to overthrow the city, after all, and he was the sole survivor. That fact tended to set people on edge, for some unfathomable reason.

'I thought as much,' said Ghedren, nodding. 'You have a soldier's bearing. It is surprising to me that a man so young – one of the Reclaimed, no less – is in the employ of the Order. You must be a man of rare talents to be elevated so high.'

'I'm merely a soldier, as you say. Just doing what is asked of me.'

Ghedren gave an awkward, sad smile.

'Aren't we all?' he said. 'Yet it seems that we must work twice as hard for half the praise.'

'Aye,' said Callis. 'I won't disagree with you there.'

'Your master... This witch hunter,' said Ghedren. 'He is Azyr-born, I take it.'

Callis blinked in surprise as he realised he had never thought to ask.

'I confess, I have no idea,' he said.

'He's more alike to them than us, I think,' said Ghedren. 'I worry that he does not understand this place, not truly. He is a creature of the crowded street, the shadowed back-alley...'

They heard boots squelching through the mud, and turned to see Toll leading three soldiers along the muddy path towards them – two Dezraed guards and the captain, Celtegar. All had pistols strapped to their belts and had ditched their spears for more practical longswords.

'Corporals Brujda,' said the captain, indicating the shaven-headed woman, 'and Yol.' The latter was a short, stocky red-headed man with a wispy beard and lazy eyes. The two soldiers gave perfunctory nods, all business. Celtegar cast a withering look at Ghedren.

'Where do you insist that this fiction occurred?'

'They pursued the Junica boy this way, along the path and into the forest,' said Ghedren.

'Lies.'

'He was bleeding from his wounds, and they were striking him with lances.'

'When this farce is over, I'll have your head for this, savage,' snapped Celtegar.

'You'll keep a civil tongue in your head,' snarled Callis, moving to within an inch of Celtegar's face, enjoying the look of surprised fury on the man's angular features. 'The only justice here will be served by the Order of Azyr.'

For a moment, Callis thought Celtegar would swing for him. He tensed his arms, ready to block the man's punch and return it in kind.

'Stand down, Armand,' said Toll. 'This is not the time nor the place.'

Callis stared into the captain's grey eyes a moment longer,

just to let him know the time had long passed where he would suffer the insults and barbs of blue-blooded fools. When he stepped back, Celtegar was all but trembling with rage.

'Lead on, Ghedren,' the witch hunter said. 'I would have us get to the truth of this as soon as possible.'

Callis had never much liked forests. He'd fought in several during his time in the Freeguilds, and these had been amongst his most miserable experiences. The deep woods played tricks on a soldier's mind, made one jump at every sound and every flickering shadow. The Ulwhyr was worse than most. It was a twisted labyrinth of curling boughs, smothered in darkness. Its mist swirled around their legs and up to their knees, making every step a potential hazard. Callis had expected the usual cacophony of sounds, the chattering of insects and the hooting of birds, yet the ominous canopy above them was startlingly silent. He winced at every snapped stick and muttered curse from his companions. If anyone was lurking in wait for them, they would hear the approach from a mile away.

They had been walking for perhaps two hours when Yol stumbled, then let out a curse in shock when he realised what had caught his foot. It was a corpse, face down in the soil. The grey flesh and stiffness of the limbs suggested this was at least a few days old. A man armoured in the silver of House Dezraed.

Callis rolled the body over with his boot. The dead man's eyes were wide, crazed even, like a frightened deer. His mouth was open in a scream, and blood had caked around his eyes and mouth.

'Lartach,' breathed the Dezraed woman, Brujda. 'He went missing a few days back. Around the same time as the Junica boy. He was an idiot and a drunkard, but a decent enough sort otherwise.'

'There are no wounds,' mused Callis. 'Nowhere. How did this man die?'

'The White Witch,' muttered Yol, shaking his head.

'Enough with that nonsense,' snorted Captain Celtegar.

'What's that you say?' asked Callis. 'The guard at the gate mentioned that name.'

'Just a legend,' said Celtegar, waving a dismissive hand. 'A tale concocted by the natives of this region. It's all they ever talk about. The dreaded White Witch of the Ulwhyr, the taker of children. A ghost, whose screams can stop the heart of mortals.'

'Oh, she is real,' said Ghedren softly. 'These are her lands.'

'All you people ever talk about are ghosts, spriggans, tolmickles and bog-devils,' mocked Celtegar. 'Backwards nonsense. This is probably just another fool who got drunk and choked on his own spew.'

Ghedren stood and slowly moved off deeper into the treeline.

'Horse tracks,' he said. 'They lead this way.

'Continue,' said Toll.

Callis squinted. 'I don't know how you can see anything in this fog.'

'My father taught me to hunt in these woods,' said Ghedren. 'He taught me to track, to move unseen, to hide my trail. To understand and respect the dangers of the wild. These men we seek, the Dezraed guards, they may have lived here for many years now, but they have learned no such lessons. Such superstition is beneath them, so they say. They believe only in the power of the God-King, and scorn the wild tales of uncivilised folk.'

'If Celtegar is what counts as civilised, I'll gladly remain a so-called savage,' muttered Callis, and Ghedren chuckled.

They were losing light now, despite the fact that it could not have been more than a few hours since they had set off. The thick canopy overhead cast them into near pitch-black darkness. Every tangled cluster of vine seemed to take the form of a skulking beast of the forest, and every wisping curl of fog seemed almost alive in its movement, drifting towards them out of the murk. Callis shook his head, angry with himself for allowing this miserable place to unsettle him. Eventually, they came to a wide, enclosed clearing, hemmed in on all sides by fat-trunked oaks. A great pool of greenish water spread out before them, dotted by clusters of drooping reeds and sharp rocks. At the far end of the pool, a bank of discoloured leaves rose into a steep mound dominated by a huge, long-dead blackwood tree. In the centre of the marsh was a small island of pale flesh and shining metal.

'Another body,' said Ghedren.

They waded out into the morass to get a closer look. It was a dead horse, half-submerged in the foetid water, pallid and bloated. Something had torn great chunks out of the beast's hide, devoured most of its innards. They shoved against the carcass and found a rider beneath, pinned by the animal's weight. The dead man's face was horribly swollen and his skin a pale green.

'Scavengers,' said Ghedren, noticing Callis' uncomfortable look. 'These are the bites of several creatures. These, however...'

He indicated scores of smaller slices across the flank of the horse and on the body of the dead man. They looked like gouges, ragged and imprecise, rather than the neat cut of a blade. One such tear had ripped open the unfortunate soldier's cheek, and another had torn a bloody line across his throat. It looked as if the horse had been dragged down into the mud, and the rider had become trapped underneath its weight, helpless against his attackers.

'There's something out here,' growled Captain Celtegar. 'Watching us. I can feel it. Whatever did this, it isn't far away.'

Ghedren knelt, placed a hand on the mossy earth and stared off into the blackness of the forest. After a moment, he shook his head.

'I do not sense anything nearby,' he said.

'Who cares a damn what you sense, curseblood?' snapped Celtegar.

Callis had heard that term before. Several of the officers in his regiment had muttered the same insult behind his back, not caring if he heard. It was used to denigrate any who did not hail from blessed Azyr, anyone who was – in their eyes – tainted by native blood.

'Use that word again and I'll break your jaw, you preening shit,' said Callis, slowly and deliberately.

Celtegar's men squared up, their hands on the hilts of their swords. The captain stepped close to Callis, who had to lean his head back to maintain eye contact. He was a big brute, this one, but still, Callis had fought bigger.

'You will withdraw that insult,' said Celtegar.

'You shall first,' said Callis. 'You forget who I represent here, captain. Strike a member of the Order, and see the consequences.'

'Silence,' hissed Toll. The witch hunter's pistol was raised, aimed out into the swirling fog. In a matter of moments, the mist had grown as thick as smoke, and now formed an opaque wall around them. They could barely see more than a dozen feet in any direction. Something stirred with a splash in the water nearby, and they all started, drawing their blades and forming a circle, hostility temporarily forgotten.

'I told you,' said Celtegar, his voice tight with fear. 'Something is coming.'

He had barely finished speaking when something broke the

surface of the bog and closed around his leg. Celtegar shrieked in surprise and toppled backwards, sending up a great wave of water as he splashed onto his rear. An arm, rotted through and draped in weeds, was clamped tightly around his ankle. A head emerged, flaps of decaying skin hanging loosely from a grinning skull. The undead thing began to haul itself along the captain's prone form, reaching for his neck with creaking fingers. Callis put a boot against the undead's chest, kicking it off the screaming Celtegar and into the murky water. He hacked at its neck with his blade. The head came free, sinking into the bog.

Another figure erupted from the water behind Corporal Brujda, wrapping its arms around her neck, teeth tearing at her neck and shattering as they crunched into her plate gorget. She gasped in revulsion and began to awkwardly swipe and slash at its forearms, trying to cut it loose. Yol smashed the pommel of his blade into the undead thing's head, and it fell back into the water, but another was already rising in its place. This corpse looked fresher than the others, and was clad in the same shining metal plate as the Dezraed warriors. Its head lolled at a strange, unnatural angle, but Callis could make out a thin, cruel face with eyes glazed and vacant.

'G-Gaulter?' stammered Yol, lowering his blade just a fraction.

Too much. The risen corpse slashed its own weapon, a rusted sabre, across in a wide arc, and there was a splatter of bright crimson. The Dezraed guard fell, clutching an opened throat, gurgling and choking. He splashed into the water, and his former companion leapt upon him and drove its sword into his chest again and again.

'Move!' shouted Toll, grabbing Captain Celtegar under the arm and hauling the heavyset man to his feet. The water boiled to life as yet more rotting bodies clambered upright. The witch hunter fired and a corpse came apart in an explosion of bone and flesh. The stench of rot and acrid gunpowder choked the air.

'This way!' shouted Ghedren, splashing through the water towards a rising bank of dead leaves.

They staggered after him, weaving their way through the mass of decaying bodies. As they dragged themselves up onto the muddy bank, more dead things erupted from the water, scraping and clawing at their legs. Callis saw a skeleton rise up ahead of him, a curling branch of thorns protruding from its eye sockets. He drew his pistol and fired. The bullet smashed the skull into a thousand shards of wet bone, and the thing slumped back beneath the surface. Then they were out, on their hands and knees, dragging themselves free. Toll grabbed Callis' hand and hauled him up. Callis turned, searching for the Dezraed woman, Brujda. She was wading after them, hacking at the bodies rising around her, eyes terrified.

'Come on,' roared Callis, stretching out his hand, straining to reach her.

She was only an arm's length away when half a dozen dead things surrounded her and bore her down. Her scream cut off abruptly as she went under, and bubbles broke the surface. Callis and Celtegar tried to cut their way down to reach Brujda as she thrashed underwater, but more of the dead were rising with every moment, blocking their path and dragging themselves onto the shore. The foetid surface of the swamp turned a deep crimson.

'She's gone,' said Toll, firing round after round, the grey-black smoke from his pistol churning with the pale, white mist.

An arm wrapped in rusted chainmail reached out of the mist to grasp the witch hunter around the throat. A leering skull appeared over the man's shoulder, its yellowed fangs snapping as it sought to bite down into Toll's exposed neck. Toll drove an elbow into the side of the thing's head and there was a crunch of breaking bone, but its grip did not relent. Callis stepped forward, trying to keep his balance while straining to reach Toll. He lost his footing in the slick mud and fell, slipping and cursing, back towards the marsh water. Somehow he managed to grasp a fistful of gnarled roots to stay his descent. He looked up to see Toll stumbling backwards, the skeleton still tearing at his neck. The witch hunter fell, seemingly in slow motion, swallowed up by the mist.

'Toll!' shouted Callis, crawling forwards on his hands and knees, searching for his companion. There was no reply, and he could see nothing but the ghostly shapes of shambling figures drawing ever closer. He fired and one of the figures dropped to the ground with a rattling groan.

'He is lost, Armand,' shouted Ghedren. He loosed his bow and an arrow sailed past Callis' head to smash a skeleton to the ground. 'We must run! This way! Follow my steps.'

Callis took one last look into the thick fog.

'Hanniver?' he shouted, but heard only the echo of his own words in response.

It was hopeless. To blunder out into the gloom with the dead all around would be to seal his own fate alongside the witch hunter's. He felt numb. It seemed absurd – all that he and Toll had been through, only for the man to fall here. Cursing, he turned and followed Ghedren, who led them higher, along the crest of the mound. It was a strange formation, Callis noticed. There was an almost artificial curve to it, a gently sloping arc through which rose a great, twisted tree of black wood. Ghedren stopped beneath its creaking boughs, watching the others as they approached him. The ground suddenly groaned beneath their weight, the roots splintering. Soil and clusters of leaves tumbled away into a pitch-black hole. Callis tripped and fell, sliding towards the drop, clutching desperately for a handhold on the mud-slick roots. He stared up at Ghedren.

'Help us,' he shouted, but the man did not move a muscle.

'Forgive me.'

Ghedren reached down and tugged hard at a thick cluster of vines, raising his long dagger in one hand. He sliced down, again and again, and with a loud crack the roots came apart. The ground beneath Callis and Celtegar fell away. They toppled end over end as the world spun. Callis tried to grasp a hold, but could find no purchase. Something ripped at his cheek and blood splattered across his face. Dirt blinded him and filled his mouth. Suddenly, he struck something with enough force to blast the air from his lungs. Everything went dark.

Callis was dragged back to consciousness by a stabbing pain in his face. He brushed a hand against his cheek and felt torn flesh. Groaning, he struggled to his feet, spitting foul-tasting soil. He stared up and saw a trickle of light filtering down from above. That snake, Ghedren. He had led them here, like lambs to the slaughter. But where, exactly, were they?

Someone moaned beside him. He saw a gleam of metal in the darkness. It was Celtegar. The Dezraed man stood and teetered, favouring his left leg.

'Are you all right?' asked Callis.

'Just fine,' spat the man. 'I warned you we could not trust that wretch. Now, where are we?'

'Good question,' said Callis. He squinted, waiting impatiently for his eyes to adjust to the gloom. They appeared to be in some kind of tunnel. It looked too smooth to be a natural formation. He ran his hand down the wall to his left and felt something hard and cold. Stone. So this was some kind of ancient structure they had fallen into, built from…

His hand brushed over a stone and he felt a circular indentation. Below that, he ran his fingers over a row of sharp objects, a surface of irregular curves and indentations. A shiver of fear ran down his spine.

'Skulls,' he whispered. 'Skulls in the walls.'

Celtegar bent and picked up his blade. Callis gathered his own and recovered his pistol, his heart thumping. His eyes had adjusted to the light, and he could see that all around them were bones, packed into the earth – row upon row of grinning skulls and the curving beams of ribcages. Fingers and teeth arranged in spiral patterns that turned his stomach. Hundreds upon hundreds of dead things, packed and piled upon each other. Not just human bones, but the fanged skulls of forest beasts and the delicate frames of dead birds. He stepped forward and felt the crunch of more bones underfoot.

'By the God-King,' whispered Celtegar. 'What is this place?'

Ahead, the tunnel curved and descended. Callis moved forwards carefully, the carpet of bone crunching with every footstep. Ahead, the tunnel ended at the mouth of a cave, a pitch-black archway of stone from which hung several objects that clattered and tinkled in the wind. Animal bones, bound together with long ropes of knotted hair, formed into gruesome marionettes. Runes were carved into the black surface, in a language Callis could not read. They were harsh, childlike etchings, and their simplicity somehow made them all the more unsettling. He edged closer and felt the dangling totems clatter against his leather jerkin as he eased past them. Beyond, a low-ceilinged chamber was formed from tangled roots, which curled around each other to create an enormous throne of twisted briar. Upon the throne sat a skeletal figure, head bowed. It was draped in robes of white cloth and a silk gauze covered its face. Around this figure were scores of skeletons, a congregation near one hundred in number, their heads bowed in supplication. Men, women, duardin and aelves. Some were full-sized. Most were small, delicate things. Children, Callis realised with horror. He moved closer. Behind the throne, he noticed another tunnel, thick with vines and thorny brambles. This one appeared to slope up, and he could see the faint shimmer of light.

'This way,' he muttered to Celtegar, who nodded. Together, they began to inch their way through the chamber, between the kneeling dead. They drew closer to the enthroned figure. Its fleshless hands rested upon the knotted armrests of its seat. In its right fist, it clutched a silver dagger.

At the very foot of the throne, kneeling amongst the throng, was a tall, broad-shouldered figure swathed in a black cloak, and a silver aetherhawk embroidered across the back glittered in the dim light. His shoulder-length hair was black, smeared with mud and dead leaves.

'It's the Junica boy,' muttered Celtegar, starting forwards.

The man's head lolled at a strange angle, and his neck was coated in dried blood.

'He's dead,' said Callis. 'We must leave.'

'We need to retrieve the body,' said Celtegar. 'Here is the proof that the Lord Dezraed is innocent of any crime.'

'If we stay here, we'll end up as dead as this one. We have to move.'

The soldier ignored Callis and slowly reached out a hand towards the dead man's head. The wind whistling through the chamber grew louder. Something clattered behind Callis making him spin around, raising his sword. He saw nothing but the sea of smiling skeletons. He turned back, shaking his head.

The figure on the throne snapped its head up to look straight into Callis' eyes.

He cried out and staggered backwards. The figure rose, drifting up from its throne and into the air, throwing its silk-wrapped head backwards to reveal a gaunt and terrible face, a half-necrotised, feminine visage with eyes the colour of deep water. A crown of thorns rested upon the creature's brow.

'*Il thua ca na men,*' it hissed, in a voice like splintering glass. '*Worach mach bar!*'

And then the spirit opened its mouth and screamed.

The sound drove a knife through Callis' heart. He collapsed onto his back, mouth open in horrified agony as his chest tightened and his muscles tensed so hard that he felt the bones of his left hand pop from their sockets. He spat blood, and his vision swam with crimson. That awful sound. It was a keening wail of pure misery and hatred. His heart skipped a beat and he tried to breathe, but found he could not draw in the air. Panic gripped him and he almost blacked out.

Abruptly, the keening stopped. Callis lay there, unable to breathe, unable to move. Slowly, awfully, the spectre drifted above him, staring down at him with malice. The spirit bent down to embrace him, placing its ice-cold fingers upon each side of his head. He gazed into its night-black eyes and saw nothing but a deep and unquenchable hatred. His terror was absolute.

The spirit's mouth yawned open, exposing blackened teeth. It came closer and closer. He tried to scream but could not form the sound.

Suddenly, the wraith's eyes snapped off to the side, widening first in surprise, then in rage. A sword swept through the air. The spectre hissed as the silver metal swept through its incorporeal form. It spiralled away from the strike in a wisp of green-white light. Callis felt a hand grab him by the shirt and lift him upright. It was Toll. The witch hunter raised his pistol, the barrel a mere inch from Callis' temple. As they heard the first awful, discordant notes of the spirit's keening wail, Toll fired. The flash of the muzzle left a scar of light across Callis' vision, and he was thrown backwards.

This close to their ears, in the cramped confines of the low chamber, the effect of the gunshot was akin to a cannon discharging. Callis heard nothing but a painful, piercing ringing. He gasped for breath, blue in the face, and finally sucked in a ragged mouthful of air. He saw Toll, standing before the floating spectre, one hand clasped to the comet symbol around his neck, the other wielding his silver rapier. The spirit rushed forward, its ragged mouth torn open in a silent scream, its dagger seeking the witch hunter's neck. As the ghost swept in, Toll hurled himself to the side, slashing at the insubstantial body of the creature. The banshee screeched, then whirled and came for the witch hunter again. This time, Toll reached to his belt and hurled a handful of white powder. The spirit recoiled, mouth twisted in agony. It slashed its dagger across and Toll fell back, a spurt of blood erupting from his left shoulder. The witch hunter's sword spun away into the field of bones. The banshee swooped towards the prone man, hands reaching for Toll's throat.

Callis scrambled to his feet, almost tripping over the corpse of Captain Celtegar. The man lay staring sightlessly up at the ceiling, blood pouring from his eyes and mouth. Callis dived for Toll's fallen rapier and took it up in two hands. It was light and perfectly balanced – even holding it seemed to still his thudding heart. The banshee wrapped its bony fingers around Toll's throat. The witch hunter kicked, struggling and gasping for breath.

Callis leapt forwards and drove the tip of the rapier into the spirit's side. The banshee arched its back and began to jerk, sickly green light pouring from its mouth as it spasmed. It turned to look at Callis, and the pure, cold hatred on its withered face almost stole the strength from his sword arm. He drove the blade into that awful visage and right down the creature's throat.

The spirit rose into the air and, even through the ringing in his ears, Callis could hear its awful, high-pitched screech, this time a sound of pain. Then, in a blinding flash that hurled him from his feet, the banshee came apart, erupting into a thousand motes of baleful light. Around them, the bones of the kneeling dead crumbled into dust.

Callis collapsed to the ground, panting, exhausted.

It took several minutes for the ringing in their ears to subside. Even then, it did not completely disappear, nor did the pain fade away. They lay there for a long while, neither speaking. Eventually, Toll hauled himself upright and extended a hand to Callis, dragging him to his feet. The ringing in his ears was agonising still, a piercing pain that jolted through his mind like a lance of fire.

'We should return the body,' said Toll at last, his voice muffled as if it were echoing over a great distance. 'That should spell the end of the Junica and Dezraed feud, at least until they find another reason to come after one another.'

'Doesn't feel like much of a victory,' sighed Callis.

'They rarely do,' said Toll. 'Leave the glorious victories to the soldiers, Callis. We deal in solutions.'

They took hold of the body of the lost Junica boy, and began to drag him towards the tunnel at the rear of the grotto. Callis glanced towards the fallen Captain Celtegar as they left.

'We'll send someone to claim his remains and those of his soldiers,' said Toll. 'And a priest to see these folk get a proper burial.'

It was a long, awkward struggle to haul the dead body up the sloping channel, but eventually they clawed their way out of a bank of close-packed soil and back into the gloom of the Ulwhyr. Callis sucked in a mouthful of air and slumped to his knees.

'I never thought I'd be glad to see this place,' he said.

'You slew the White Witch,' came a voice from behind them. They spun to see Ghedren leaning against the thick trunk of an age-old hardwood tree. He had his bow drawn and raised, aimed straight at Callis. Yet there was only defeat in his eyes, and slowly he lowered the weapon. 'You are not the first. Just because she is gone for now, it does not mean she will not return. Nor that our children are safe. Killing you now will change nothing.'

Callis charged at the man, grabbed him by the neck and hurled him to the floor. Ghedren did not struggle, even when he drew his sword and pressed it to the man's neck.

'You led me there to die,' Callis snarled.

It was a familiar sensation to Callis. The bitter sting of betrayal, and the sick surge of shame and rage as he realised how easily he had been manipulated. Was this how it always ended, he wondered? Trusting someone, only for them to drive their rapier into your unguarded spine.

'Do it,' said Ghedren. 'Kill me, if you must. I do not begrudge your fury. I am sorry that it came to this, but I had no choice. She always returns, Armand. She always takes her due. The curse cannot be broken.'

'The children?' said Toll.

Ghedren nodded, a single tear trickling down his face.

'When it began, I do not know,' he said. 'Before my father's time, and before his father's. A tithe borne of her hatred for the living and her sorrow for a life that was taken from her, some say. The firstborn child of the tribal elder must be delivered unto the White Witch, lest her wrath fall upon all others. Every generation, another sacrifice. By giving one life to sate her fury, the people may survive.'

'Lord Junica's son,' said Callis. 'You led him to that beast as well?'

'There are no longer any tribes, but the White Witch still demands her due. The Azyrites rule over us, and so they must pay the blood price. We tried to explain. We tried to tell them what lay within these woods, and the danger they courted by straying into the depths of the Ulwhyr in search of profit. The silksteel plantations, they strayed into her domain. We tried to warn them that her wrath would be terrible unless an offering was made, but they would not listen. They would not believe. And so, for the good of all, I acted.'

'The Dezraed soldiers,' said Toll. 'How did you dispose of them?'

'Their feud with Aldrec Junica was real enough,' said Ghedren. 'It was simple fortune that I was there that night, accompanying my lord's son to the house of his mistress. We passed the Dezraed soldiers on the road. They were drunk and eager for a fight. Aldrec was never one to back down. Insults were exchanged and swords drawn. He slew one of their number and the rest pursued him. I saw a chance and took advantage of it. I led him deep into the Ulwhyr. The Dezraed followed, and one by one they were claimed by the forest.'

Callis slammed the man's head against the ground. 'And what? Murdering us was an attempt to cover up your crimes?'

Ghedren closed his eyes.

'I did not wish to kill you,' he said, his voice soft and sad. 'But I knew you would never understand what is at stake. You would not stop until you found out the truth.'

'The witch is dead,' said Toll. 'If you had trusted us enough to tell us the truth, lives could have been saved. Including, perhaps, your own.'

'You ended nothing,' snapped Ghedren, shaking his head frantically. 'You think brave warriors have not fought the White Witch before? She is tied to this place, to the very spirit of this forest. No blade can lay her low. She has haunted these trails for centuries. Perhaps even longer. She will return, and her vengeance will be more terrible than ever. It is the children that will pay the price for your actions.' He sighed. 'I am ready to face my death. I know, in my heart, I did the only thing that I could have done. Do as you must.'

'My boy,' whispered Lord Junica. There were no tears in the old man's eyes, but his voice broke. Callis looked away. He'd hardly taken to the man, but he knew all too well how it felt to bury a loved one.

Aldrec Junica lay in repose upon the bed of a carriage, his eyes closed and his arms folded across his chest. They had taken him to the local mission – a humble yet sturdy chapel of Sigmar, attended to by an elderly, grey-bearded priest who had performed the rites and consecrated the body with blessed oils. Candles fluttered in the chill breeze. Callis gazed at the benevolent, stained-glass figures that looked down from the chapel's spire. Saints of old. Warriors and heroes, witnesses to this sad little ceremony.

'He was slain by a wraith,' said Toll. 'A banshee of the forest. The Dezraeds played no part in it. In fact, it was one of your own who led your son to his death.'

Two guards dragged Ghedren forward. Lord Junica stared at him, his mouth trembling.

'Ghedren?' he whispered. '*You*?'

The prisoner raised his head and met his master's gaze.

'I am sorry for your loss,' he said. 'But it was the only way. I tried to tell you. The White Witch required your son's life.'

Junica staggered over to the kneeling man and struck him across the face.

'Everything I have done for you,' his voice shook with rage. 'Everything you have been given, and you betray me? You murder my boy? My firstborn son?'

He struck Ghedren over and over, his blows growing weaker every time. Toll caught his arm as it fell again, and ushered the man away.

'Enough,' said the witch hunter. 'Come.'

He led Junica out through the doors of the chapel and into the central plaza of Marshpoint. The guards led the bound Ghedren after them. He met Callis' eyes as they passed, but looked quickly away. There was much that Callis wanted to ask the man, but the time for questions was long gone now. Ranks of Junica soldiers stood in an honour guard outside the Sigmarite chapel, banners fluttering from their raised spears. There were a few-score locals too, crowded around the edge of the square, no doubt wondering what all the fuss was about. Nearby, a small force of Dezraed soldiers mounted on horseback watched the ceremony with bored expressions on their faces.

'Well, a sad business. But over now, at least,' said Lord Dezraed, who sat upon the open step of his carriage, wrapped in thick furs to fend off the blustery wind. 'Only the matter of a formal apology remains.'

'What?' hissed Lord Junica, eyes widening in outrage.

'For your baseless insinuations,' Dezraed said, as if the answer was perfectly reasonable. 'Accusing me of this horrible crime, when it was your own man all along.'

'You'll get no apology from me,' snarled Junica. His hands curled into fists. 'Now leave. I have an execution to prepare.'

He turned to Ghedren.

'You'll suffer for what you've done,' he hissed. 'You'll beg for death, but I will not be so merciful as to grant it. I will break you down, inch by inch, and I will take pleasure in every moment.'

'These natives must be kept in line. I agree we must let them know we will not tolerate such betrayal,' said Dezraed, nodding his great slab of a head.

'I will ensure you live a long time before I am finished with you,' snarled Junica. Ghedren looked up and met his gaze.

'I believe,' Toll began, 'that it is the task of the Order of Azyr to administer justice here.'

He drew his pistol and fired a single shot. There was a burst of pink mist and Ghedren toppled like a sack of grain. He struck the cobbles hard, and a pool of blood flowed out from his broken body.

'No,' screamed Lord Junica. 'He was mine. *Mine!*'

'You will bury your dead son and return to your duties. The plantations shall reopen, and you will restart the patrols. Both of you.'

At this, he turned and jabbed a finger at Dezraed.

'I should have you both dragged back to Excelsis in chains,' spat Toll. 'You have displayed incompetence, foolishness and borderline treason. Your petty feud has not only endangered this town, but it has risked the lives of loyal soldiers by denying them the supplies they require. Now my patience with this farce is at an end. The fighting stops, or I swear I will make you both regret your actions for the rest of your miserable lives. Do you understand?'

'I am a son of a great house,' Lord Junica snarled. 'I have powerful friends in Azyrheim–'

'You are a minor scion of a great house,' said Toll. 'You are here only because the other lords of the Junica House have more pressing matters to attend to. You are replaceable, and you will be replaced if you cannot perform your duties. Do you understand? Both of you?'

There was a long silence.

'Say the words,' said Toll. 'Say that you understand.'

'I… understand,' said Lord Dezraed.

'I understand,' growled Lord Junica through gritted teeth, as if each word was a knife in his gut.

'You have a month to get your affairs in order,' said Toll.

With that, the witch hunter strode off, Callis rushing after him. They made their way to the southern gate, and the guards waved them through. Callis' heart sank a little as he saw the marsh striders looming above the jetty, chewing on clumps of moss. Their wizened guide was back, already stowing their saddlebags upon the beasts' flanks. Another few days of back-aching discomfort awaited. The joy of it.

'I can't deny that was satisfying,' said Callis.

'I'm glad you found it amusing,' said Toll. 'Perhaps we should discuss your own failures.'

Callis blinked. 'What?'

'Why do you think I brought you here?'

'Because it serves you well to have someone who can handle a sword guarding your back?'

'I can throw glimmerings into any tavern in Excelsis to strike someone who knows how to fight. I brought you because you're sharp, and you know when to draw steel and when not to. But that's only part of this trade, Armand. What allows us to survive is the ability to read people, to see beyond the obvious to the deeper truth. I brought you here to see if you were ready to do that. You failed.'

'You knew Ghedren was the traitor?'

'As you would have, had you not been blinded by your dislike of the Dezraed and the Junica. You let your own personal opinions cloud your judgement, and you gave your trust to a man who had not earned it.'

Callis had never truly felt at home in the Freeguilds, but at that moment, he recalled the simple clarity of his former life with a wistful fondness. Recently, it seemed that even when he was sure he was doing the right thing, it turned out otherwise.

Toll hooked one foot into the stirrups on the side of one of the marsh striders, and hauled himself onto its back. He squinted down at Callis, pulling his hat down low to block the hazy light that filtered through the grey clouds.

'This is a lesson, not an admonishment. We all make mistakes, but in this line of work they have a habit of getting you killed. God-King knows I've put my trust in the wrong person before – you know that better than anyone. Learn from this. Next time, I may not be there to haul you out of the flames. Now, come. We must be back in Excelsis within the next two days. We have new business to attend to.'

YOUR NEXT READ

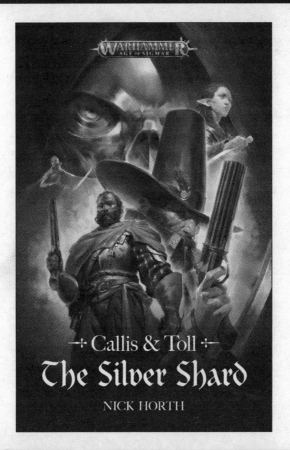

CALLIS & TOLL: THE SILVER SHARD
by Nick Horth

Witch Hunter Hanniver Toll and his companion, former Freeguild
soldier Armand Callis, brave the deadly seas and jungles of the
Taloncoast as they try to prevent their nemesis, Ortam Vermyre, from
seizing an artefact that can reshape reality.

For these stories and more go to **blacklibrary.com**, **games-workshop.com**, Games Workshop
and Warhammer stores, all good book stores or visit one of the thousands of independent
retailers worldwide, which can be found at **games-workshop.com/storefinder**

THE DANCE OF
THE SKULLS

David Annandale

The Mortarch of Blood's party arrived at the royal palace in Mortannis with the coming of full night. Neferata, her handmaidens and her ladies of court swept up the grand staircase leading to the palace doors. On either side, standing to attention, were the elite guards of two cities: Mortannis to the right, Nachtwache to the left. Walking one step behind Neferata, Lady Mereneth said, 'I do not trust the nature of this honour.'

'Nor do they expect us to,' Neferata told her favoured spy. 'This will not be the trap. They know the consequences will be too great. What will come will be more subtle, one our enemies can deny.'

Neferata had come to Mortannis to attend a ball arranged explicitly for her visit. The event was formally presented as an act of fealty and peace. She knew, therefore, exactly what it was. She was entering a battlefield.

She would not have it any other way.

Mortannis lay close enough to Nulahmia for it to be a point

of concern. Queen Ahalaset had never challenged Neferata directly, and the tensions between the two cities had long been unspoken, subterranean. Close to the borders of Mortannis' region of influence lay Nachtwache. It was ruled by Lord Nagen and Neferata had kept a close watch on the relations between Mortannis and Nachtwache. As long as there had been friction between the two, friction that she had encouraged, the two powers had kept each other contained. She had even tolerated temporary alliances in the face of the threat from the legions of Chaos. But the armies sworn to the Everchosen were, for the time being, pushed back from this region of Shyish, and it appeared that the cities' rulers had formed a much more substantial alliance. That would never do.

So she had accepted the joint invitation from Ahalaset and Nagen immediately, after putting on the expected charade of diplomatic negotiations. There was work to be done here, and she knew she was putting her neck into the jaws of a trap. Though she arrived at the palace with only her immediate retinue, she was confident in her assurance to Mereneth. Ahalaset and Nagen would not strike here, with their own guard. Neferata's army waited outside the gates of Mortannis – legions of vampires, skeletons and wraiths cantoned in the lower reaches of the mountains that surrounded the city. Any move by the forces of Mortannis or Nachtwache would see Mortannis burned to the ground.

These were the realities of the game about to be played. They were known by all. The war would take place at another level. There would be no siege, no scaling of the walls. After all, this was a celebration. The war would be invisible, until a point came when the combatants chose to drop the illusion.

Neferata's party passed through the high doors of the palace, down the entrance hall and into the grand ballroom.

Torchlight shone off the gold leaf of marble caryatids that held up the vaulted ceiling of the ballroom. The ceiling mosaic was a wonder of bronze-covered bones. Hundreds of skeleton arms reached from the edges of the vault towards the centre, where a huge skull composed of other skulls opened its jaws in an ecstasy of death.

The honour guard of the two cities was also present in the ballroom, but more discreetly, keeping to positions against the walls. In the fore, lining the path of the procession to the large dais at the back of the ballroom was the gathered nobility of Mortannis and Nachtwache. Vampires and mortals bowed as Neferata passed. She acknowledged their greetings with the faintest of nods. She met the eyes of the nobles, all of them, and watched the spasm of fear and admiration take them.

Queen Ahalaset and Lord Nagen stood together on the dais. Though Ahalaset was host, they were side by side, equals at the event. They bowed too, completing the show of respect that had greeted Neferata.

No one was armoured except the guards, and even their plate was ceremonial, adorned with jewels and golden skulls, more resplendent than practical. Neferata, like her opponents on the dais, had prepared for the kind of war about to be waged. She wore a regal black dress of silk so fine it flowed like water. The train of the dress was much lighter than its length would suggest, and it moved behind her over the marble floor like the touch of night. From her shoulders hung a crimson cape. Its leather, so soft it was a mere breath of wind against the fingers, was made from the tanned flesh of fallen enemies.

'We are honoured, Queen Neferata, that you accepted our invitation,' said Ahalaset as she rose again. Her cheekbones were high, her eyes proud. Her brilliant green robes shimmered with silver thread, which wove the designs of scores of coats of arms, as if meant to remind Neferata that Ahalaset too had long experience on the battlefield.

At the end of his bow, Nagen began to reach out for Neferata's hand to kiss. When she did not extend her arm to him, he turned his gesture into a flourish, though the effort was clumsy enough to be obvious, then straightened. He wore a damask coat and a waistcoat inlaid with diamonds. The buttons of the coat were obsidian and shaped into finger bones. Its delicate fringe was human hair. Nagen's features were narrow and refined, and he consistently let a single fang poke down from beneath his upper lip. 'It is our greatest wish,' Nagen said, 'that you understand our intentions to be peaceful. We want you to know that Nulahmia can trust Mortannis and Nachtwache.'

'Of course you do,' Neferata said, and smiled.

Her hosts hesitated for a moment, uncertain how to take her words. Then they returned her smile and descended from the dais. 'We hope you will enjoy the ball,' said Ahalaset. She and Nagen led Neferata's party to join the other nobles. 'There will be a Dance of the Skulls.'

'Then my pleasure is assured in advance,' Neferata said.

Ahalaset clapped her hands. Musicians emerged from side doors at the rear of the ballroom, carrying instruments and chairs. They mounted the dais. Within moments, the orchestra began playing, and the war began.

'Do they think we do not realise this is a trap?' Mereneth whispered to Neferata as they watched the first of the dances.

'Of course they know that we are not fooled,' said Neferata. 'They believe they can overcome our wariness, and that is what matters. They will act, have no fear. Our journey will not have been in vain.'

A few dances in, Neferata saw, from the corner of her eye, Lord Nagen turn towards her, about to invite her to the floor.

As if she had not noticed, she took a single, graceful step away and began to speak to one of the ladies of Ahalaset's court. Mereneth remained where she was, and Nagen, already committed to the beginnings of a bow, had no choice but to make his invitation to the spy. Mereneth accepted.

Neferata left her conversation as quickly as she had begun it, but though her departure was abrupt, the other vampire was awed, not offended. With a parting glance, Neferata saw the woman shrink before her, overcome with the knowledge that she had not been destroyed.

Neferata walked slowly along the edge of the dance, watching Mereneth and Nagen. Other nobles parted before her, backing away even when they also sought to greet her. She exchanged brief words with the vampires and mortals she passed, but they did not deflect her attention from the ball.

Mereneth was a skilled, graceful dancer. Nagen had difficulty keeping up with her. Her movements were never such that he stumbled, though. She kept him away from the edge of humiliation, and though Neferata could tell that he was a well-practised dancer himself, and prided himself as such, Mereneth's control of their turns made him appear even better than he was. He had to focus on his steps, and he was grateful enough for the guidance of Mereneth's hands that he did not pay attention to what else they might be doing. Neferata kept level with them as they moved up and down the ballroom floor. Twice, at chosen moments, she caught Nagen's eye and gave him the hint of a smile. The first time, he seemed unsure that she had done so. The second time, his face lit up with certainty, and her unspoken, vague promise was enough. He devoted himself with even greater energy to his performance, as if to say, *Look how well we shall dance together.*

Neferata allowed her smile to grow a little broader, though

she hid her amusement. *Are you already forgetting your purpose, Lord Nagen?* she thought. For the moment, it seemed he had.

When the dance ended, he and Mereneth joined her. Nagen rushed to speak before Neferata could escape him again. 'Queen Neferata,' he said, 'will you do me the honour of being my partner for the Dance of the Skulls?'

'It would be my great pleasure,' she said.

Nagen beamed. Neferata held him before her with her smile. He would, when the necessity pushed him hard enough, remember what he was supposed to be doing. He would remember that his purpose this night was not to secure a dance with the Queen of Nulahmia. But he was not remembering now. And while Neferata transfixed him, he was not looking at Mereneth, and he did not see her slip the ring she had stolen into Neferata's hand.

'And now,' Neferata said, releasing Nagen from her gaze, 'I have neglected my other host for too long.' She left Nagen happy and willing to be distracted by Mereneth once again. She doubted he would ever notice the missing ring. The theft was a preliminary step. She had no specific use for the ring as yet. Instead, her possession of it opened up a wider field of action. She would see what possibilities would arise.

Ahalaset was at the feasting table on the other side of the ballroom. She gestured for Neferata to join her. 'You must tell me what you think of this vintage,' she said when Neferata drew near. She filled two crystal goblets from a large decanter.

Neferata accepted hers and brought it to her nose. She sniffed a finely crafted blend of blood. 'Most inviting,' she said, but did not drink.

Ahalaset smiled. 'Please accept it,' she said, and drank first.

Neferata sipped. 'This is extraordinary,' she said, and it was. She tasted the innocence of the newborn, the enthusiasm of youth and the wisdom of age. They existed together on her palate, forming the entire arc of mortal life. She was impressed. 'You have some superb artisans at your disposal,' she said.

Ahalaset raised her goblet in a toast. 'I am pleased you think so,' she said. 'I selected this vintage purposely for your visit.'

'I am honoured.'

Ahalaset lowered her voice. 'I have, if you are interested, Queen Neferata, set aside a gift more potent yet.' Her eyes flickered quickly to the left and right.

Ensuring that I am alone, Neferata thought. She was. She had dispersed her retinue through the crowd, inviting Ahalaset to make her move. 'You interest me,' she said. 'Do go on.'

Ahalaset pointed to a small door in the corner of the ballroom, behind the dais. 'You will find in there my personal choice of slaves,' she said. 'They have been curated for the quality of their blood. They come from the same families whose lives you have just tasted.' She produced a small, golden key. 'Should you wish to savour their delicacies…?'

Neferata accepted the key. 'I should indeed,' she said. *Good*, she thought, *we are done with the prelude. Now we can begin.* With a knowing smile to Ahalaset, she made her way over to the door and let herself in.

She entered a richly appointed chamber. In the centre was a divan draped in crimson cushions and silks. The candles of human tallow on the chandelier were encased in red-tinted glass skulls, suffusing the room with a warm, intimate glow. The light was dim, though, and Neferata noted the many deep shadows in the corners. The shape of the room was an octagon, and chained to the walls were the offerings. They were men and women in the prime of life, anointed in oils and scents, gold bands pulling their heads back to present their throats. Neferata felt the beat of their pulses, their rich blood a thin slice away from jetting into her mouth. Incense wafted from censors on either side of the divan. The atmosphere of the chamber was heady, luxurious. It was, Neferata thought, a most beautiful trap. If the opportunity arose, she must congratulate Ahalaset. She doubted Nagen had contributed much beyond his mere presence.

Neferata turned around slowly, her witchsight piercing the shadows. She did not think the attack would be that obvious, and she was right. The chamber was empty except for the slaves. She walked past the mortals, examining them closely but not touching any of them yet. They stared back at her, their pupils dilated. Their fear was mixed with a confused pleasure. Neferata inhaled the scent of their emotions, detecting the taste of a powerful opiate. She did not think it was poisonous. It seemed, to her senses, that its purpose was simply part of the flavouring of the blood.

Neferata's lips drew back over her fangs. The bait truly was irresistible. *Well done, Ahalaset. Well done.*

She circled the chamber again. Between the prisoners hung tapestries depicting the most sensual of atrocities. Neferata moved them aside until, to the left of one of the male slaves, she saw the barely discernible outline of a door in the wall. She located the keyhole and experimentally inserted the key Ahalaset had given her. It turned easily, and she heard the lock slide into place. It was curious, she thought, and therefore significant, that the same key opened both doors to the room.

She locked the entrance door too. She stood in the centre of the room for a few moments, waiting. Whatever the nature of the attack, she would adapt, and she would counter it. That was her most terrible strength – to see each moment for what it was, to discard a plan instantly, and form a new one, to flow across war like water.

The attack did not come.

'Very well,' she murmured. 'If we must play out this charade to the end, let us do so and have done with this.' She walked over to the slave directly in front of her and sank her fangs into his neck.

The blood was everything Ahalaset had promised. If the vintage in the ballroom represented the peak of the art of blending, here she encountered a rarefied purity of blood. These slaves had clearly been raised since birth for this purpose alone. The taste of life was intoxicating, and Neferata would have willingly gorged herself from this single slave, then waited before indulging in the next. But this was war, and she would not cede the battlefield to Ahalaset. She swallowed twice, then stepped back from the prisoner. He looked at her with bovine fear. His lips moved, but they were too sluggish to form words.

'You are a product of superb breeding,' Neferata told the slave. 'All of you are,' she announced to the chamber. 'Be proud of your destinies.'

With the flick of a clawed finger, she sliced the man's throat wide open. The enticing blood poured down his body and pooled onto the floor. Neferata moved on to the next slave, drank briefly from her neck, then slashed her throat too. And so she went on, taking just enough for a taste and then killing the mortals. The chamber filled with the smell of wasted blood. Neferata shook her head, feeling the rare moment of regret. To throw away such fine stock was a crime.

Still the attack did not come.

Neferata's senses were vibrating with tension. This had to be where she was most in danger. This had to be the trap. But the moments passed, and the slaves died, and nothing happened. The more time passed, the more she felt the temptation to relax her guard, and the more wary she became.

She had slaughtered two thirds of the slaves now. She bent down to the neck of the next one. As her teeth sank into his throat, he brought his arms up in a flash. His chains snapped, brittle as porcelain. His right forearm and hand were a leather sheath, its illusion perfectly crafted, and they slid to the ground, revealing the blade built out of his elbow. It was silver, etched in runes, and flashed with emerald light. The air crackled with its power, and the assassin stabbed the sword at Neferata's throat.

A moment's unwariness and the blade would have decapitated her. But she had not been unwary. Neferata leapt to one side and ducked. The sword passed over her head, flashing with the heat of an arcane sun. She reached out and grabbed the assassin's arm just below the elbow. He struggled to free himself, but he was held with a grip that could crush stone. Neferata pushed the arm back, holding it against the wall. The assassin struck at her with his other arm, but he might as well have been hitting steel.

'Very good,' she whispered. 'Very good.' She took the assassin by the throat and forced his head back. He began to whine in frustration and terror. 'Shhhhh,' she said. 'You did very well. You came closer to succeeding than you think. Your queen should be grateful to you. Or is it your lord?' Neferata cocked her head, breathing in the man's fear. 'No,' she decided, 'you are one of Ahalaset's playthings.' Nagen's role in all of this was the political ally, and the extra force inside the palace. 'Your queen decided to control all of the details of my assassination. She was correct to do so, even though she failed.'

The assassin squirmed in her grip. She lifted him off the ground, holding him in mid-air, depriving him of leverage. He groaned. 'Hush now, hush now,' Neferata said. 'Your part in the dance is not yet done. There is a great turn to make.' She yanked the assassin to her and bit into his neck. There was no time to savour the taste of his blood. There was only the attack. She drank his life. She drained him of his will, and of Ahalaset's, and she filled him with hers.

When she was done, she released the assassin. He stood before her, docile, a thrall waiting for the orders that would define his new purpose. She looked him up and down. He was clad only in a loincloth, unsuitable for his new task. 'You have robes elsewhere,' she said.

He nodded.

She unlocked the doors from the chamber, then handed the assassin the key he would have used had he been successful. 'Go and don your robes,' she said. Then she gave him Nagen's ring and issued her commands. He bowed and left the chamber through the hidden door. Neferata circled the room once more. She killed the remaining slaves quickly. Then, with sharp, rapid jerks, she tore the corpses apart and tossed the dismembered remains into a heap before the divan. In that hill of meat, discerning if there was a body that was missing would take time.

Neferata lifted the train of her dress. It was soaked in blood. She ran a hand over the silk, murmuring a soft incantation, and the blood pattered to the floor. Then she returned to the ballroom.

Nagen and Ahalaset were standing together at the feasting table when Neferata emerged from the chamber. Ahalaset hid her alarm well. Nagen looked rattled. Neferata smiled to them both, and ran a finger along her upper lip. 'Your gift was beyond expectations,' she said to Ahalaset. 'I can only hope that I will be able to offer you something half as delightful when next you come to Nulahmia. And you will visit me, won't you?'

'Of course I will,' said Ahalaset.

'As will you, Lord Nagen,' Neferata said.

He bowed, his composure returning. 'Nothing would please me more.'

The orchestra had stopped playing for a few moments, and now it began again. A celebrated chord sounded, slowly thrumming twelve times, summoning the celebrants for the Dance of the Skulls.

Neferata offered her hand to Nagen. 'I made you a promise,' she said. 'Now I shall keep it.'

His earlier rapture lighting up his eyes, Nagen took her hand and led her onto the ballroom floor. As they took their places, Neferata saw a handmaiden walk quickly from the chamber to Ahalaset and whisper to her. As careful as the queen of Mortannis had been when she was talking to Neferata, she could not disguise the relief that flashed over her features. She prowled the edge of the dance floor, her gaze on Neferata. Her look was of someone who had had a narrow escape, and now sought a new route to victory.

Satisfied, Neferata turned her full attention on Nagen as the dance began.

Vampires and human nobles faced each other in two lines. Servants gave each of the vampires an enthralled human slave with silver chains wrapped around the neck. Every mortal noble held an ivory bowl in the shape of a skull. The music played and the aristocratic dancers moved together in groups of four. Though the vampires and nobles faced each other, the true partners in each cluster were the undead. The humans were the subordinates. The only difference between the slaves and the bowls was that the slaves were able to support themselves for the first part of the dance.

The music hit its first crescendo, the dancers completed their first turn and, in time to a sudden, emphatic beat in the melody, the vampires cut the jugulars of the slaves. Now the dance proper began, where the skill of the participants was put to the test. The vampires controlled the jet of blood and as the humans whirled around them, they caught the blood in the bowls. At the start of each refrain, the humans bowed, presenting the bowls to the vampires, who drank, and then the bowls were filled again. Though the movements of the dancers slowed in time to the music, there were never any full stops. The motion was continuous, and it was forbidden for even a single drop of blood to fall to the floor. So the dance would go on until the slaves were exsanguinated and that, too, had to be timed perfectly so the victims did not die prematurely. At the final flourish, the vampires would decapitate the slaves and exchange skulls with the mortal nobles.

And all this time, the vampire partners never broke eye contact with each other. The letting of blood and the killing were performed as if unthought. The dance made the mortals unimportant, beneath notice. Blood flowed, people died, yet all that mattered was the contact between the partners, all the more intense because they never touched physically.

Neferata held Nagen's gaze in a grip of iron. Though he was her willing prisoner, her task as they danced remained delicate. She saw before her a vampire who was happy to play the fool for her, yet she had no doubt that his loyalty remained with Ahalaset. Nagen feared Neferata as much as he desired her, and he wanted that fear disposed of. But he was vain, too, and Neferata read the fatal weakness in his vanity. He believed that he could indulge in the pleasure of her company and the dance until the moment of the assassination. The trap had failed. Perhaps there was another plan, or perhaps he believed he could distance himself from association with it. Whatever he was thinking, he would be wary. He was enraptured, not enthralled. He was not without his own power. If Neferata was too forceful in an attempt to control his will, he would sense the attack, and all would be lost.

So Neferata was subtle. What she wanted from Nagen was a small thing, a very small thing, a thing so attuned to his natural inclinations that it should require only the tiniest push to make him take a single, brief action when and how Neferata commanded. As they spun about the dancefloor, rounding each other, bowing to each other, and drinking from the proffered skull bowls, she added subtle gestures to her arm flourishes. Her fingers played in the air for an extra moment, making patterns that were only for Nagen's eyes. Even he would not notice them, but they had their effect. Halfway through the Dance of the Skulls, his face hung a bit looser than it should, and his pupils were a bit wider. And as they leaned in towards each other after filling the bowls with blood yet again, the torn veins of the prisoners pumping out streams between their fingers, Neferata moved her lips, shaping a few inaudible words. She did not even whisper.

She did so little. She was sure she'd done enough.

She saw Mereneth watching from the sides as the Dance of the Skulls drew to its climax. With a light inclination of her head, Neferata directed Mereneth's gaze to the other side of the ballroom.

The exuberant finale of the dance came. The vampires snapped the heads off their slaves. The human nobles extended both hands, to receive and to give. The orchestra thundered a last, victorious chord, proclaiming the triumph of death.

And Ahalaset screamed.

All movement in the ballroom ceased. The assassin, clad now in the rich robes of a noble guest, unnoticed until he struck, stood behind Ahalaset, his blade arm through her back, her heart impaled on its point. The rune-enchanted silver glowed through a slick of gore. Ahalaset's shriek turned into a hacking choke. The assassin held her body up a few moments more, and then it slid off the blade.

The assassin stood motionless over the corpse of the queen. He did not look up, and barely reacted when Ahalaset's honour guard surged forward and cut him down with pikes and blades.

'Search him!' the captain of the guard commanded, and Neferata was pleased. It was much better that the idea come from one of Ahalaset's minions.

In the time it took for the guards to turn out the pockets of the assassin's robes, Neferata felt all eyes in the ballroom on her. This was the turning point of the larger dance, the one that only she had truly known everyone had been caught in this night. Right now, the two courts believed she was responsible for Ahalaset's death. There was no other reasonable conclusion to be drawn. It was also the truth.

But the truth was ephemeral. It was a tiny, weak thing compared to the armoured colossus of perception. And the moment turned.

'There's a ring,' said one of the guards.

'I have seen that before,' said the captain. After a pause, he said, 'It has the seal of the house of Nagen.' He sounded confused.

Now perception spread the fog of doubt throughout the ballroom, and truth retreated. It was time for her work during the Dance of the Skulls to bear fruit. Time for Nagen to do that single thing. To speak one sentence. A sentence that came easily, because it was the motto of his family. A sentence he took pride in, and believed in. It was his belief in that sentence, after all, that had led him to conspire against Neferata with Ahalaset.

He had simply never planned on uttering that sentence right now.

'Never bend the knee!' he shouted.

Neferata turned to look at Nagen with carefully crafted disgust. He was so shocked by what he had said that his mouth hung open, suddenly bereft of words.

Neferata raised her eyebrows in a show of anger calibrated so that only Nagen would be close enough to see that it was mockery. 'I will have no part of your conflict,' Neferata told him, and walked away.

'Wait!' Nagen called to her. 'Wait!' he shouted at Ahalaset's guards as they descended on him. He tried to protest his innocence, but his words were drowned out by the roar of anger from the warriors.

Neferata gestured to Mereneth and the rest of her retinue. They followed her up onto the dais where she elected to watch the final steps of the royal dance. The orchestra was silent, the musicians huddling together for protection, but Neferata could hear music all the same. It was the beat and melody of violence unleashed at her command.

The palace guard cut Nagen down, piercing him with a dozen spears before he could muster a defence. Too late, the soldiers of Nachtwache rushed to his aid, and then to avenge their lord. Soon the dais was the lone island of calm in the ballroom. Neferata and her handmaidens brushed away the warriors who staggered too close, and plucked stray arrows from the air.

The fighting spread through the ballroom, the nobles from both cities joining in the attacks or caught between the blades of the warring troops. Blood and fire swept through the hall and out the palace doors. Neferata listened to the greater clashes of blades from the courtyard and the streets beyond, and to the growing thunder of armies hurling themselves against each other. She tapped at the air with a finger, conducting the carnage. When the time came for her forces to enter the city, she did not think there would be much left for them to do.

Neferata turned to the orchestra master. The thin vampire was crouched beside his chair, trembling. 'My compliments,' she said, speaking quietly, though her voice rode effortlessly over the clamour of battle. 'Your music was most pleasing.' She would see the musicians were well rewarded. 'You played with exquisite skill.'

'So did you, my queen,' said Lady Mereneth.

Neferata smiled, accepting the compliment. 'Yes,' she said, 'I rather think I did.'

It had been a most excellent ball.

YOUR NEXT READ

NEFERATA - MORTARCH OF BLOOD
by David Annandale

When a threat to her realm of Nulahmia rises, the Mortarch Neferata must commit herself to a centuries-long battle if she is to save her kingdom and retain her position.

For these stories and more go to **blacklibrary.com, games-workshop.com**, Games Workshop and Warhammer stores, all good book stores or visit one of the thousands of independent retailers worldwide, which can be found at **games-workshop.com/storefinder**

SHIPRATS

C L Werner

Carefully, the heavy-set duardin warrior raised his weapon. His eyes narrowed, fixating on his victim. He appeared unfazed by the gloom of the darkened hold, his vision sharp enough to pick out a marrow-hawk soaring through a thunderstorm. The duardin judged the distance, allowed for the air currents that buffeted the moored aether-ship and estimated how much strength to bring to bear against his foe.

The shovel came cracking down, striking the deck with such force that a metallic ping was sent echoing through the hold. Drumark cursed as the target of the descending spade leapt upwards and squeaked in fright. The brown rat landed on his foot, squeaked again, then scampered off deeper into the hold.

Furious, Drumark turned and glowered at the other spade-carrying duardin gathered in the *Iron Dragon*'s hold. Arkanauts, endrin-riggers, aether-tenders and even a few of the ship's officers gave the angry sergeant anxious stares.

'Right! Now they are just begging to be shot! I am getting my decksweeper!' Drumark swore, not for the first time.

Brokrin, the *Iron Dragon*'s captain, stepped towards Drumark. 'You are not shooting holes in the bottom of my ship,' he snapped at him. 'We have enough problems with the rats. If you go shooting holes in the hull we won't be able to take on any aether-gold even if we do find a rich cloud-vein.'

Drumark jabbed a thumb down at his boot. 'It peed on my foot. Only respect for you, cap'n, keeps me from getting a good fire going and smoking the vermin out.'

'That is some sound thinking,' Horgarr, the *Iron Dragon*'s endrinmaster scoffed. He pressed his shovel against the deck and leaned against it as he turned towards Drumark. 'Start a fire in the ship's belly. Nothing bad could happen from that. Except the fifty-odd things that immediately come to mind.'

Brokrin shook his head as Drumark told Horgarr exactly what he thought of the endrinmaster's mind. No duardin had any affection for rats, but Drumark's hatred of them was almost a mania. His father had died fighting the pestiferous skaven and every time he looked at a rat he was reminded of their larger kin. It made him surly and quick to anger. This would be the third fight between the two he would have to break up since coming down into the *Iron Dragon*'s holds. Unable to find any aether-gold, the ironclad had put in at Greypeak, a walled human city with which Barak-Zilfin had a trading compact. The grain the city's farmers cultivated was well regarded by the Kharadron and would fetch a good price in the skyhold. Not as much as a good vein, but at least there would be something for the aether-ship's backers.

At least there would be if the rats that had embarked along with the grain left anything in good enough condition to sell. There were more than a few Kharadron who claimed that the

Iron Dragon was jinxed and that her captain was under a curse. Sometimes he found himself wondering if his detractors were right. This was not the first time Brokrin's ship had suffered an infestation of vermin, but he could not recall any that had been so tenacious as these. Whatever they did to try to protect their cargo, the rats found some way around it. They were too clever for the traps old Mortrimm set for them, too cunning to accept the poisoned biscuits Lodri made for them. Even the cat Gotramm had brought aboard had been useless – after its first tussle with one of the rats it had found itself a spot up in the main endrin's cuppola and would claw anyone who tried to send it below deck again.

'These swine must have iron teeth.' The bitter observation was given voice by Skaggi, the expedition's logisticator. Tasked with balancing profit against expense and safeguarding the investment of the expedition's backers, every ounce of grain despoiled by the rodents stung Skaggi to the quick. He held a heavy net of copper wire in his hands, extending it towards Brokrin so he could see the holes the rats had gnawed. 'So much for keeping them out of the grain. We will be lucky if they do not start in for the beer next.'

Skaggi's dour prediction made Drumark completely forget about his argument with Horgarr. He looked in horror at Skaggi. An instant later, he raised the shovel overhead and flung it to the floor.

'That is it!' Drumark declared. 'I am bringing my lads down here and we will settle these parasites here and now!' He turned to Brokrin, determination etched across his face. 'You tell Grundstok thunderers to hunt rats, then that is just what we will do. But we will do it the way we know best.'

Skaggi's eyes went wide with alarm, his mind turning over the expense of patching over the holes the thunderers would leave if they started blasting away at the rats. He swung around to Brokrin, his tone almost frantic. 'We will be ruined,' he groaned. 'No profit, barely enough to pay off the backers.'

Drumark reached out and took hold of the copper net Skaggi was holding. 'If they can chew through this, they can chew their way into the beer barrels. Me and my thunderers are not going dry while these rats get drunk!'

The sound of shovels slapping against the floor died down as the rest of the duardin in the hold paused in their efforts to hear what Drumark was shouting about. Many of them were from his Grundstok company and looked more than ready to side with their sergeant and trade spades for guns.

'The rats will not bother the beer while they still have grain to eat,' Brokrin stated, making sure his words were loud enough to carry to every crewman in the hold. How much truth there was in the statement, he did not know. He did know it was what Drumark and the others needed to hear right now.

'All due respect, cap'n,' Drumark said, 'but how long will that be? Swatting them with shovels just isn't enough and we have tried everything else except shooting them.'

Brokrin gave Drumark a stern look. 'I've said it before, and now I'm saying it again – you are not shooting holes in *my* ship.' The chastened sergeant held Brokrin's gaze for a moment, then averted his eyes. The point had been made.

'What are we going to do?' Gotramm asked. The youthful leader of the *Iron Dragon*'s arkanauts, he had watched with pointed interest the exchange between Brokrin and Drumark.

'I know one thing,' Horgarr said, pulling back his sleeve and showing the many scratches on his arm. 'That cat is staying right where it is.' The remark brought laughs from all who heard it, even cracking Drumark's sullen mood.

Brokrin was more pensive. Something Drumark had said

earlier had spurred a memory. It was only now that his recollection fell into place. 'The toads,' he finally said. The newer members of the crew glanced in confusion at their captain, but those who had served on the *Iron Dragon* before her escape from the monster Ghazul knew his meaning.

'Some years ago,' Brokrin explained to them, 'we sailed through a Grimesturm and a rain of toads fell on our decks. They were everywhere, even worse than these rats. You could not sit without squashing one or take a sip of ale without having one hop into your mug.

'To rid the ship of her infestation,' Brokrin continued, 'we put in at the lamasery of Kheitar. The lamas prepared a mixture of herbs, which we burned in smudge pots. The smoke vexed the toads so much that they jumped overboard of their own accord.'

'You think the lamas could whip up something to scare off rats?' Gotramm asked.

Brokrin nodded. 'Kheitar is not far out of our way. There would be little to lose by diverting our course and paying the lamasery a visit.'

'Kheitar is built into the side of a mountain,' Horgarr said. 'Certainly it will offer as good an anchorage as the peak we're moored to now.'

Skaggi's eyes lit up, an avaricious smile pulling at his beard. 'The lamas are renowned for their artistic tapestries as well as their herbalism. If we could bargain with them and get them to part with even one tapestry we could recover the loss of what the rats have already ruined.'

'Then it is decided,' Brokrin said. 'Our next port of call is Kheitar.'

The lamasery's reception hall was a stark contrast to the confined cabins and holds of the *Iron Dragon*. Great pillars of lacquered wood richly carved with elaborate glyphs soared up from the teak floor to clasp the vaulted roof with timber claws. Lavish hangings hung from the walls, each beautifully woven with scenes from legend and lore. Great urns flanked each doorway, their basins filled with a wondrously translucent sand in which tangles of incense sticks slowly smouldered. Perfumed smoke wafted sluggishly through the room, visible as a slight haze where it condensed around the great platform at the rear of the chamber. Upon that platform stood a gigantic joss, a golden statue beaten into the semblance of an immensely fat man, his mouth distorted by great tusks and his head adorned by a nest of horns. In one clawed hand the joss held forward a flower, his other resting across his lap with the remains of a broken sword in his palm.

Brokrin could never help feeling a tinge of revulsion when he looked at Kheitar's idol. Whoever had crafted it, their attention to detail had been morbid. The legend at the root of the lamas' faith spoke of a heinous daemon from the Age of Chaos that had set aside its evil ways to find enlightenment in the ways of purity and asceticism. Looking at the joss, Brokrin felt less a sense of evil redeemed than he did that of evil biding its time. The duardin with him looked similarly perturbed, all except Skaggi, who was already casting a greedy look at the tapestries on the walls.

The young initiate who guided the duardin into the hall stepped aside as Brokrin and his companions entered. He bowed his shaved head towards a bronze gong hanging just to the left of the entrance. He took the striker tethered to the gong's wooden stand and gave the instrument three solid hits, each blow sending a dull reverberation echoing through the chamber.

'Take it easy,' Brokrin whispered when he saw Gotramm

from the corner of his eye. The young arkanaut had reached for his pistol the moment the gong's notes were sounded. 'If we aggravate the lamas they might not help get rid of the rats.'

Gotramm let his hand drop away from the gun holstered on his belt. He nodded towards the joss at the other end of the hall. 'That gargoyle is not the sort of thing to make me feel at ease,' he said.

'The cap'n is not saying to close your eyes,' old Mortrimm the navigator told Gotramm. 'He is just saying do not be hasty drawing a weapon. Abide by the Code – be sure who you set your axe against, and why.'

Brokrin frowned. 'Let us hope it does not come to axes. Barak-Zilfin has a long history trading with the lamas.' Even as he said the words, they felt strangely hollow to him. Something had changed about Kheitar. What it was, he could not say. It was not something he could see or hear, but rather a faintly familiar smell. He turned his eyes again to the daemon-faced joss, wondering what secrets it was hiding inside that golden head.

Movement drew Brokrin's attention away from the joss. From behind one of the hangings at the far end of the hall, a tall and sparingly built human emerged. He wore the saffron robes of Kheitar's lamas, but to this was added a wide sash of green that swept down across his left shoulder before circling his waist. It was the symbol that denoted the high lama himself. The uneasy feeling Brokrin had intensified, given something solid upon which to focus. The man who came out from behind the tapestry was middle-aged, his features long and drawn. He certainly was not the fat, elderly Piu who had been high lama the last time the *Iron Dragon* visited Kheitar.

The lama walked towards the duardin, but did not acknowledge their presence until after he had reached the middle of the hall and turned towards the joss. Bowing and clapping his hands four times, he made obeisance to the idol. When he turned back towards the duardin, his expression was that of sincerity itself.

'Peace and wisdom upon your path,' the lama declared, clapping his hands together once more. A regretful smile drew at the corners of his mouth. 'Is it too much to hope that the Kharadron overlords have descended from the heavens to seek enlightenment?' He shook his head. 'But such, I sense, is not the path that has led you here. If it is not the comfort of wisdom you would take away from here, then what comfort is it that we can extend to you?'

Although Brokrin was the *Iron Dragon*'s captain, it was Skaggi who stepped forwards to address the lama. Of all the ship's crew, the logisticator had the glibbest tongue. 'Please forgive any intrusion, your eminence,' he said. 'It is only dire need which causes us to intrude upon your solitude. Our ship has been beset by an infestation of noxious pests. Terrible rats that seek…'

The lama's serenity faltered when Skaggi began to describe the situation. A regretful look crept into his eyes. 'We of Kheitar are a peaceful order. Neither meat nor milk may pass our lips. Our hands are not raised in violence, for like Zomoth-tulku, we have forsaken the sword. To smite any living thing is to stumble on the path to ascension.'

Brokrin came forwards to stand beside Skaggi. 'Your order helped us once before, when hail-toads plagued my ship. The high lama, Piu, understood the necessity of removing them.'

The lama closed his eyes. 'Piu-tulku was a wise and holy man. Cho cannot claim even a measure of his enlightenment.' Cho opened his eyes again and nodded to Brokrin. 'There are herbs which could be prepared. Rendered down they can be burned in smudge pots and used to fumigate your ship.' A deep sigh ran through him. 'The smoke will drive the rats to flee. Would it be too great an imposition to ask that you leave them a way to escape? Perhaps keep your vessel moored here so they can flee down the ropes and reach solid ground.'

Skaggi's eyes went wide in shock. 'That would cause the lamasery to become infested.' He pointed at the lavish hangings on the walls. 'Those filthy devils would ruin this place in a fortnight! Think of all that potential profit being lost!'

Cho placed a hand against his shoulder. 'It would remove a stain from my conscience if you would indulge my hopes. The death of even so small a creature would impair my own aspirations of transcendence.'

'My conscience would not permit me to cause such misery to my benefactors,' Brokrin stated. 'But upon my honour and my beard, I vow that I will not use whatever herbs you provide us without ensuring the rats can make landfall without undue hazard.'

'It pleases me to hear those words,' Cho said. 'I know the word of your people is etched in stone. I am content. It will take us a day to prepare the herbs. Your ship will be safe where it is moored?'

'We are tied to the tower above your western gate,' Mortrimm stated. He gestured with his thumb at Brokrin. 'The cap'n insisted we keep far enough away that the rats wouldn't smell food and come slinking down the guide ropes.'

'Such consideration and concern does you credit, captain,' Cho declared. He suddenly turned towards Skaggi. 'If it is not an imposition, would it be acceptable to inquire if the tapestries we weave here still find favour among your people?'

The question took Skaggi by such surprise that the logisticator allowed excitement to shine in his eyes before gaining control of himself and resuming an air of indifference. Brokrin could tell that he was about to undervalue the worth of Kheitar's artistry. It was a prudent tactic when considering profit but an abominable one when thinking in terms of honour.

'Your work is applauded in Barak-Zilfin,' Brokrin said before Skaggi could find his voice. The logisticator gave him an imploring look, but he continued just the same. 'There are many guildhalls that have used your tapestries to adorn their assemblies, and poor is the noble house that has not at least one hanging from Kheitar on its walls.'

With each word he spoke, Brokrin saw Skaggi grow more perturbed. Cho remained implacable, exhibiting no alteration in his demeanour. Then the high lama turned towards the wall from which he had emerged. Clapping his hands together in rapid succession, he looked aside at the duardin.

'I thank you for your forthrightness,' Cho said. 'Your honesty makes you someone we can trust.' There was more, but even Brokrin lost the flow of Cho's speech when the hangings on the walls were pushed aside and a group of ten lamas entered the hall. Each pair carried an immense tapestry rolled into a bundle across their shoulders. To bring only a few tapestries out of Kheitar was considered a rewarding voyage. Was Cho truly offering the duardin five of them?

Cho noted the disbelief that shone on the faces of his guests. He swung around to Skaggi. 'I have noticed that you admire our work. I will leave it to you to judge the value of the wares I would offer you.' At a gesture from the high lama, the foremost of his followers came near and unrolled their burden. Skaggi didn't quite stifle the gasp that bubbled up from his throat.

The background of the tapestry was a rich burgundy in colour and across its thirty-foot length vibrant images were woven from threads of sapphire blue, emerald green and amber yellow.

Geometric patterns that transfixed the eye formed a border around visions of opulent splendour and natural wonder. Soaring mountains with snowy peaks rose above wooded hills. Holy kings held court from gilded thrones, their crowns picked out with tiny slivers of jade wound between the threads. Through the centre of the tapestry a stream formed from crushed pearl flowed into a silver sea.

'Magnificent,' the logisticator sputtered before recovering his composure.

'It gladdens me that you are content with our poor offerings,' Cho told Skaggi. He looked back towards Brokrin. 'It is my hope that you would agree to take this cargo back to your city. Whatever price you gain from their sale, I only ask that you return half of that amount to the lamasery.'

'Well… there are our expenses to be taken into account…' Skaggi started. However good a deal seemed, the logisticator was quick to find a way to make it better.

'Of course you should be compensated for your labours,' Cho said, conceding the point without argument. 'Captain, are you agreeable to my offer?'

'It is very generous and I would be a fool to look askance at your offer,' Brokrin replied. 'It may be some months before we can return here with your share.'

'That is understood,' Cho said. He gestured again to the lamas carrying the tapestries. 'Pack the hangings for their journey. Then take them to the Kharadron ship.'

The unaccountable uneasiness that had been nagging at Brokrin asserted itself once more. 'I will send one of my crew to guide your people and show them the best place to put your wares.' He turned to Mortrimm. 'Go with them and keep your wits about you,' he whispered.

'You expect trouble?' Mortrimm asked.

Brokrin scratched his beard. 'No, but what is it the Chuitsek nomads say? "A gift horse sometimes bites." Just make sure all they do is put the tapestries aboard.'

Nodding his understanding, Mortrimm took his position at the head of the procession of lamas. Because of their heavy burdens, the navigator was easily able to match their pace despite one of his legs being in an aethyric brace. Brokrin and the other duardin watched as the tapestries were conducted out of the hall.

'Should I go with them, cap'n?' Skaggi asked. 'Make certain they do not mar the merchandise when they bring it aboard?'

'I think these lamas know their business,' Gotramm retorted. 'They are the ones who sweated to make the things and they have just as much to lose as we do if they get damaged.'

Unlike the banter between Drumark and Horgarr, there was a bitter edge to what passed between Gotramm and Skaggi. There was no respect between them, only a kind of tolerant contempt. Brokrin started to intercede when something Cho had said suddenly rose to mind. He turned towards the high lama. 'You called your predecessor Piu-tulku? Is not tulku your word for the revered dead?'

'The holy ascended,' Cho corrected him. 'Among the vulgar it is translated as "living god". You have yourself seen the ancient tulkus who have followed Zomoth-tulku's transcendence.'

Brokrin shuddered at the recollection. Deep within the lamasery there were halls filled with niches, each containing the mummified husk of a human. They were holy men who had gradually poisoned themselves, embalming their own bodies while they were still alive in a desperate search for immortality. The lamas considered each of the corpses to still be alive, tending their clothes and setting bowls of food and drink before them each morning. He thought of Piu and the last time he had seen the man. There had been no hint that he had been undergoing this ghastly process of self-mummification.

'I was unaware Piu had chosen such a path,' Brokrin apologised.

Cho smiled and shook his head. 'Piu-tulku did not choose the path. The path chose him. A wondrous miracle, for he has transcended the toils of mortality yet still permits his wisdom to be shared with those who have yet to ascend to a higher enlightenment.' His smile broadened. 'Perhaps if you were to see him, speak with him, you would understand the wisdom of our order.'

That warning feeling was even more persistent now, but Brokrin resisted the urge to play things safe. Something had changed at Kheitar and whatever it was, he would bet it had to do with Piu's unexpected ascension. Glancing over at Gotramm and then at Skaggi, he made his decision. 'We would like very much to meet with Piu-tulku.'

Cho motioned for the initiate by the door to come over to them. 'I am certain Piu-tulku will impart much wisdom to you, but to enter his august presence you must set aside your tools of death.' He pointed at the axes and swords the duardin carried. 'Leave those behind if you would see the tulku. I can allow no blades in his chambers.'

Brokrin nodded. 'You have nothing to fear, your grace. Our Code prohibits us from doing harm to any who are engaged in fair trade with us.' He slowly unbuckled his sword and proffered it to the initiate. 'We will follow your custom.'

Slowly the three duardin removed their blades, setting them on the floor. Gotramm started to do the same with his pistol, but Cho had already turned away. Brokrin set a restraining hand on Gotramm's.

'He said blades,' Brokrin whispered. 'Unless asked, keep your pistol.' He brushed his hand across the repeater holstered on his own belt. 'We will respect their custom, as far as they ask it of us.'

Brokrin gave a hard look at Cho's back as the high lama preceded them out of the hall. 'If he is being honest with us, it will make no difference. If he is not, it might make all the difference in the realms.'

Drumark escorted the lamas down into the *Iron Dragon*'s hold. He had tried to choose the cleanest compartment in which to put the precious cargo, but even here there was the fug of rat in the air. 'This is the best one,' he said. 'You can put them down here.'

'You think they will be safe?' asked Mortrimm. Like the sergeant, he could smell the stink of rat. He looked uneasily at the bamboo crates the lamas carried, wondering how long it would take a rat to gnaw its way through the boxes.

'As long as there is grain, the little devils will keep eating that,' Drumark spat, glowering at a fat brown body that went scooting behind a crate when the light from his lantern shone upon it. 'It will be a while before they start nibbling on this stuff.' He turned his light on the sallow-faced lamas as they carefully set down the crates and started to leave the hold. 'Tell your friends to get that poison ready on the quick. If we do not smoke out these vermin, your tapestries will be gnawed so badly we will have to sell them as thread.'

The warning put a certain haste in the lamas' step as they withdrew from the hold. Mortrimm started to follow them as the men made their way back onto the deck. He had only taken a few steps when he noticed that Drumark was still standing down near the tapestries.

'Are you coming?' Mortrimm asked.

'In a bit,' Drumark answered, waving him away. Mortrimm shook his head and left the hold.

Alone in the rat-infested hold, Drumark glowered at the shadows. The stink of vermin surrounded him, making his skin crawl. Instead of withdrawing from the stench, he let his revulsion swell, feeding into the hate that boiled deep inside him. Rats! Pestiferous, murderous fiends! Whatever size they came in, they had to be stamped out wherever they were found. He would happily do his part. He owed that much to his father, burned down by the foul magics of the loathsome skaven.

Drumark looked at the crates and then back at the noisy shadows. Despite his talk with Mortrimm and the lamas, he was anything but certain the rats would spare the tapestries. The vermin were perverse creatures and might gnaw on the precious hangings out of sheer spite. Well, if they did, they would find a very irritable duardin waiting for them.

Checking one last time to be certain Mortrimm was gone, Drumark walked over to a dark corner near the door and retrieved the object he had secreted there without Brokrin's knowledge. He patted the heavy stock of his decksweeper. 'Some work for you before too long,' he told it. Returning to his original position, he doused the lantern. Instantly the hold was plunged into darkness. Drumark could hear the creaking of the guide ropes as the ship swayed in its mooring, the groan of the engines that powered the ironclad's huge endrin, the scratch of little claws as they came creeping across the planks.

Gradually his eyes adjusted to the gloom and Drumark could see little shapes scurrying around the hold. Soon the shapes became more distinct as his eyes became accustomed to the dark. Rats, as fat and evil as he had ever seen. There must be a dozen of them, all scurrying about, crawling over barrels, peeping into boxes, even gnawing at the planks. He kept his eyes on the crates with the tapestries, all laid out in a nice little row. The moment one of the rats started to nibble at them he would start shooting.

But the rats did not nibble the crates. Indeed, Drumark began to appreciate that the animals were conspicuously avoiding them. At first he thought it was simply because they were new, a change in their environment that the vermin would have to become comfortable with first. Then one of the rats did stray towards the row, fleeing the ire of one of its larger kin. The wayward rodent paused in mid-retreat, rearing up and sniffing at the crates.

Drumark could not know what the rat smelled, but he did know whatever it was had given the rodent a fright. It went scampering off, squeaking like a thing possessed. The rest of the vermin were soon following it, scrambling to their bolt holes and scurrying away to other parts of the ship. Soon Drumark could not hear their scratching claws any more.

Keeping his decksweeper at the ready, Drumark sat down beside the door. He stayed silent as he watched the crated tapestries, his body as rigid as that of a statue. In the darkness, he waited.

The wait was not a long one. A flutter of motion spread through the rolled tapestry at the end of the row. Faint at first, it increased in its agitation, becoming a wild thrashing after a few moments, the cloth slapping against the bamboo that enclosed it. Someone – or something – was inside the rolled tapestry and trying to work its way out. Eyes riveted on the movement, Drumark rose and walked forwards. He aimed his decksweeper at the tapestry. Whatever had hidden itself inside, it would find a warm reception when it emerged.

The thrashing persisted, growing more wild but making no headway against the framework that surrounded the tapestry. Whatever was inside was unable to free itself. Or unwilling.

A horrible suspicion gripped Drumark. There were four more tapestries and while his attention was focused on this one, he was unable to watch the others.

Drumark swung around just as a dark shape came leaping at him from the shadows.

The decksweeper bellowed as he fired into his attacker. Drumark saw a furry body go spinning across the hold, slamming into the wall with a bone-crunching impact. He had only a vague impression of the thing he had shot. He got a better look at the creature that came lunging at him from one of the other crates.

Thin hands with clawed fingers scrabbled at Drumark as the creature leapt on him. Its filthy nails raked at his face, pulling hair from his beard. A rat-like face with hideous red eyes glared at him before snapping at his throat with chisel-like fangs. He could feel a long tail slapping at his legs, trying to hit his knees and knock him to the floor.

Drumark brought the hot barrel of his decksweeper cracking up into the monster's jaw, breaking its teeth. The creature whimpered and tried to wrest free from his grip, but he caught hold of its arm and gave it a brutal twist, popping it out of joint. The crippled creature twisted away, plunging back down on top of the crates.

Any sense of victory Drumark might have felt vanished when he raised his eyes from the enormous rat he had overcome. Six more of its kind had crawled out from their hiding places in the tapestries, and unlike the one he had already fought, these each had knives in their paw-like hands. They stood upright on their hind legs, chittering malignantly as they started towards the lone duardin.

'Skaven!'

The cry came from the doorway behind Drumark. The

discharge of his decksweeper had brought Horgarr and several others of the crew rushing into the hold, concerned that the sergeant had finally lost all restraint with the rats infesting the ship. Instead they found a far more infernal pestilence aboard.

The arrival of the other duardin dulled the confidence that shone in the eyes of the skaven infiltrators. The mocking squeaks took on an uncertain quality. Ready to pounce en masse on Drumark a moment before, now the creatures hesitated.

'What are you waiting for, lads!' Drumark shouted to Horgarr and the others. 'The bigger the rat, the more of our beer it will drink! Get the scum!'

The sergeant's shouts overcame the surprise that held the other duardin. Armed with shovels and axes, Horgarr led the crew charging across the hold. Their backs against the wall, the skaven had no choice but to make a fight of it.

As he rearmed his decksweeper and made ready to return to the fray, a terrible thought occurred to Drumark. The tapestries and their devious passengers had come from the lamasery. A place from which Captain Brokrin had not yet returned.

'Hold them here!' Drumark told Horgarr. 'I have to alert the rest of the ship and see if we can help the cap'n!'

The young initiate held the ornate door open for Cho and the duardin as they entered the shrine wherein Piu-tulku had been entombed after his ascension. The room was smaller than the grand reception hall, but even more opulently appointed. The hangings that covered its walls were adorned with glittering jewels, the pillars that supported its roof were carved from blackest ebony and highlighted with designs painted in gold. The varnished floor creaked with a musical cadence as the visitors crossed it, sending lyrical echoes wafting up into the vaulted heights of its arched ceiling.

Ensconced upon a great dais flanked by hangings that depicted the wingless dragon and the fiery phoenix, the living god of Kheitar reposed. Piu was still a fat man, but his flesh had lost its rich colour, fading to a parchment-like hue. He wore black robes with a sash of vivid blue – the same raiment that had been given to the mummies Brokrin had seen in the lamasery's vaults. Yet Piu was not content to remain in motionless silence. Just as the duardin had decided that the lamas were delusional and that their late leader was simply dead, the body seated atop the dais opened its eyes and spoke.

'Enter and welcome,' the thing on the dais said. The voice was dull and dry with a strange reverberation running through it. 'Duardin-friends always-ever welcome in Kheitar.' It moved its head, fixing its empty gaze in Cho's general direction. 'Have you given help-aid to our guests?'

'Yes, holy tulku!' Cho said, bowing before the dais. 'The tapestries have been sent to their ship, as you commanded.'

The thing swung its head back around, facing towards the duardin. It extended its hands in a supplicating gesture. The effect was marred by the jerky way in which the arms moved. Brokrin could hear a faint, unnatural sound as Piu moved its head and hands, something between a pop and a whir. He had seen such artificial motion before, heard similar mechanical sounds. The tulku was similar to an aethyric musician he'd seen in the great manor of Grand Admiral Thorgraad, a wondrous machine crafted in the semblance of a duardin bard. The only blight on the incredible automaton's music had been the sound of the pumps inside it sending fuel through its pipes and hoses.

Whatever the esoteric beliefs of Kheitar, what sat upon the dais was not an ascended holy man. It was only a machine.

Piu began to speak again. 'It is to be hope-prayed that we shall all profit-gain from...'

Brokrin stepped past Cho and glared at the thing on the dais. 'I do not know who you are, but I will not waste words with a puppet.' The outburst brought a gasp of horror from the initiate at the door. Cho raced forwards, prostrating himself before the dais and pleading with Piu to forgive him for such insult.

Brokrin gave the offended lamas small notice. His attention was fixed to the hangings behind Piu's dais. There was a ripple of motion from behind one of them. Pushing aside the snake-like dragon, a loathsome figure stalked into view. He was taller than the duardin but more leanly built, his wiry body covered in grey fur peppered with black. A rough sort of metal hauberk clung to his chest while a strange helm of copper encased most of his rodent-like head. Only the fanged muzzle and the angry red eyes were left uncovered. A crazed array of pouches and tools swung from belts and bandoliers, but across one shoulder the humanoid rat wore a brilliant blue sash – the same as that which adorned Piu.

'Now you may speak-beg,' the ratman growled as he stood beside Piu. His hairless tail lashed about in malicious amusement as he smelled the shock rising off the duardin.

'Mighty Kilvolt-tulku,' Cho cried out. 'Forgive me. I did not know they were such barbarians.'

Kilvolt waved aside the high lama's apology. He fixed his gruesome attention on Brokrin. 'No defiance, beard-thing,' he snarled, pointing a claw at either side of the room. From behind the hangings a pack of armoured skaven crept into view, each carrying a vicious halberd in his claws. 'Listen-hear. I know-learn about your port-nest. Your clan-kin make-build ships that fly-climb higher than any others. I want-demand that secret.'

'Even if I knew it,' Brokrin snapped at Kilvolt, 'I would not give it to you.'

The skaven bared his fangs, his tail lashing angrily from

side to side. 'Then I take-tear what I want-need! Already you let-bring my warriors into your ship.' He waved his paw at Cho. 'The tapestries this fool-meat gave you.' He gestured again with his paws, waving at the skaven guards that now surrounded the duardin. 'If they fail-fall, then I have hostages to buy the secret of your ship. Torture or ransom will give-bring what I...'

Kilvolt's fur suddenly stood on end, a sour odour rising from his glands. His eyes were fixed on the pistols hanging from the belts Brokrin and Gotramm wore. He swung around on Cho, wrenching a monstrous gun of his own from one of the bandoliers. 'I order-say take-fetch all-all weapons!' The skaven punctuated his words by pulling the trigger and exploding Cho's head in a burst of blood and bone.

The violent destruction of the lama spurred the duardin into action. With the skaven distracted by the murder on the dais, Brokrin and Gotramm drew their pistols. Before the ratmen could react, the arkanaut captain burned one down with a shot to its chest, the aethyric charge searing a hole through its armour. Brokrin turned towards Kilvolt, but the skaven took one glance at the multi-barrelled volley pistol and darted behind the seated Piu-tulku.

Instead Brokrin swung around and discharged his weapon into the skaven guards to his right. The volley dropped two of the rushing ratmen and sent another pair squeaking back to the doorways hidden behind the hangings, their fur dripping with blood. Gotramm was firing again, but the skaven were more wary of their foes now, ducking around the pillars and trying to use them as cover while they advanced.

'We are done for,' Skaggi groaned, keeping close to the other duardin. Alone among them, the logisticator really had come into the room unarmed. 'We have to negotiate!' he pleaded with Brokrin.

'The only things I have to say to skaven come out of here,' Brokrin told Skaggi, aiming his volley pistol at the guards trying to circle around him. The ratmen were unaware the weapon had no charge and seeing it aimed in their direction had them falling over themselves to gain cover.

A crackle from the dais presaged the grisly impact that sent an electric shock rushing through Brokrin. The armour on his back had been struck by a blast from Kilvolt himself. Feeling secure that the duardin were distracted by his henchrats, he had returned to the attack. The oversized rings that adorned one of his paws pulsated with a sickly green glow, a light that throbbed down to them via a series of hoses that wrapped around his arm before dipping down to a cannister on his belt.

The heavy armour Brokrin wore guarded him against the worst of the synthetic lightning. He turned his volley pistol towards the dais. Kilvolt flinched, ducking back behind the phony tulku. As he did, the ratman's eyes fixated on something behind the duardin captain.

'The boy-thing!' Kilvolt snarled from behind Piu. 'Stop-kill boy-thing, you fool-meat!'

Brokrin risked a glance towards the door. It had been flung open and the initiate was racing into the hall outside, screaming at the top of his lungs. Immediately half a dozen of the skaven were charging after him, determined to stop him from alerting the other lamas about what was happening in Piu's shrine.

The ratmen made it as far as the door before a duardin fusillade smashed into them. Skaven bodies were flung back into the shrine, battered and bloodied by a concentrated salvo of gunfire. Just behind them came their executioners, Drumark leading his Grundstok thunderers.

The surviving guards squeaked in fright at the unexpected

appearance of so many duardin and the vicious despatch of their comrades. The creatures turned and fled, scurrying back into their holes behind the wall hangings. A few shots from the thunderers encouraged them to keep running.

'The leader is up there!' Brokrin told his crew, waving his pistol at the dais. 'There are tunnels behind the tapestries. Keep him from reaching them.'

Even as Brokrin gave the command, Kilvolt came darting out from behind the dais. His retreat would have ended in disaster, but the skaven had one last trick to play. To cover his flight, he had sent a final pawn into the fray. Piu-tulku rose from its seat and came lurching towards the duardin. There was no doubting the mechanical nature of the thing now. Every jerky motion of its limbs was accompanied by a buzzing whirr and the sour smell of leaking lubricants. Its hands were curled into claws as it stumbled towards Brokrin, but the face of Piu still wore the same expression of contemplative serenity.

'Right! That is far enough!' Drumark cried out, levelling his decksweeper at the automaton. When the Piu-thing continued its mindless approach, he emptied every barrel into it. The shot ripped through the thing's shell of flesh and cloth. In crafting his 'tulku' Kilvolt had stitched the flayed skin of Piu over a metal armature. The armature was now exposed by Drumark's blast as well as the nest of hoses and wires that swirled through its body.

Despite the damage inflicted on it, the automaton staggered onwards. Drumark glared at it in silent fury, as though it were a personal affront that it remained on its feet. While the sergeant fumed, Brokrin took command. 'Thunderers!' he called out. 'Aim for its spine! Concentrate your shots there!'

The thunderers obeyed Brokrin's order, fixing their aim at the core of the Piu-thing. Shots echoed through the shrine as round after round struck the automaton. Under the vicious barrage, the thing was cut in half, its torso severed and sent crashing to the floor. The legs stumbled on for several steps before slopping over onto their side and kicking futilely at the floor.

'And stay down!' Drumark bellowed, spitting on the fallen automaton.

Gotramm seized hold of the sergeant's arm. 'We have to get back to the ship! There are more of them in the hold with those tapestries!'

'Already sorted out,' Drumark declared. 'By now Horgarr should be done tossing their carcasses overboard. I figured you might be having trouble over here so me and the lads grabbed one of the lamas and found out where you were.'

Brokrin felt a surge of relief sweep through him. The *Iron Dragon* was safe. At least for now. He turned his eyes to the dragon tapestry and the tunnel Kilvolt had escaped into. Even now the skaven were probably regrouping to make another attack.

'Everybody back to the ship,' Brokrin said. 'The sooner we are away from here the better.' He gave Skaggi an almost sympathetic look. 'When we get back we will have to dump the tapestries over the side as well. We can't take the chance the skaven put some kind of poison or pestilence on them.'

Skaggi clenched his fist and rushed to the wall. With a savage tug he brought one of the hangings crashing down to the floor. 'If we have to throw out the others then we had better grab some replacements on our way out!' Catching his intention, Gotramm and some of the thunderers helped Skaggi pull down the other tapestries. The hangings were quickly gathered up and slung across the shoulders of the duardin.

'What about the rat poison, cap'n?' Drumark asked as they hurried through halls that were empty of either lamas or skaven.

'We cannot trust that either,' Brokrin told him. 'We must do without it.' He gave the sergeant a grim smile. 'I hope you remember where you put your spade.'

Drumark sighed and shook his head. 'I remember, but overall I would rather stay here and shoot skaven than play whack-a-rat with a shovel.'

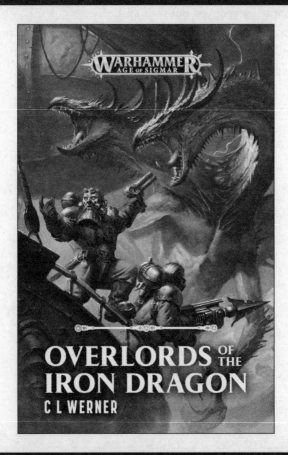

OVERLORDS OF THE IRON DRAGON
by C L Werner

Brokrin Ullissonn, a down on his luck duardin captain, has a change
in fortunes when he finds an untapped source of aether-gold – but is
the danger that awaits him and his crew worth the prize, or are they
doomed to further failure?

For these stories and more go to **blacklibrary.com, games-workshop.com**, Games Workshop
and Warhammer stores, all good book stores or visit one of the thousands of independent
retailers worldwide, which can be found at **games-workshop.com/storefinder**

AUCTION OF BLOOD

Josh Reynolds

At the stroke of seven on the arranged evening, Palem Bok found himself wandering the miasma-choked back alleys of Greywater Fastness. A bookseller and a spy, Bok was the epitome of neither. Tall and nondescript, he was all sharp angles and conservative colours. A grey man in a grey world. Despite the dull hues of his garments, however, they were of an expensive cut, tailored to his lean form. Bok was a man with standards, if nothing else.

As the evening wore on, he traversed the tangled rookery with no sign of fear, despite the hostile eyes he felt watching him from darkened doorways and the cracks in boarded-over windows. Greywater Fastness was a hard city, and its people unforgiving of weakness. Bok was not weak. There was death in his heart, and there was nothing stronger than death.

Even so, his pale gaze flickered warily from side to side, watching the shadows for some sign of the person he'd come to meet. His hand rested close to the edges of his frock coat and the slim, multi-chambered flintlock pistol holstered beneath his arm. The pistol was of duardin manufacture, and thus guaranteed to perform its function without incident. Much like Bok, it was a most dependable weapon. He smiled as the thought occurred to him. There were worse things to be than a weapon. And worse masters by far than the one who wielded him. Or, rather, mistresses.

It had its annoyances. For instance, his intent for the evening had been to meet with a certain contact. He wished to arrange the purchase of a rare duardin bead-book, purloined at no small expense from the libraries of the runemaster of the Hermdar lodge. There were any number of his usual clients who would dearly love to own such a rare volume on the art of fyresteel blending. Instead, he was now wandering this crooked labyrinth of back alleys, waiting for his mistress' servant to reveal themselves.

Laughter echoed from a side street, where a crowd tossed rotting food into a massive cage. Inside it, a serpentine cockatrice shrieked and slammed against the bars. Its avian skull was hooded in order to protect gawkers from its deadly gaze. The hulking beast's owner kept up a steady patter, trying to attract punters to come and see it up close. Bok felt a thrill of revulsion at the sight. He felt no sympathy for the creature. It was a foul thing, corrupt and twisted by sour magics into an abomination. He just hoped the cage was sturdy.

Loose metal rattled, somewhere out of sight. Bok paused, a fingerbreadth from drawing his pistol. Head cocked, he listened to the sounds of the city. Greywater Fastness was never silent. Its ironclad walls reverberated with the sounds of industry. The great furnaces roared day and night, and the sound of hammers ringing on metal filled the streets. A thick pall of soot and grime covered everything, blackening the walls of the buildings and obscuring the street. It was at its worst after a rain, and it was almost constantly raining.

Overhead, glowing spores drifted as they always did after a downpour, making strange patterns in the sooty air. Where they touched something solid, they took root and sprouted into shimmering fronds of iridescent greenery. Bok hurried into a covered alleyway, brushing some from his coat before they had a chance to blossom.

He heard muffled voices, echoing strangely through the cramped street. In the dim light of a sputtering oil lantern hanging above a nearby doorway, he caught a glimpse of shambling figures – beggars, seeking shelter, as he was. Night soil wagons creaked somewhere close to hand. The bells on Cathedral Hill tolled the hour, and a flock of crows hurtled skywards from the slum rooftops, croaking raucously, their feathers gleaming with spores.

Out of the smog lurched a beggar woman. She was small and hunched, wizened by hard living. She gazed at him through a veil of ratty hair, and her eyes lit up. She shuffled towards him across the filthy cobbles. 'Sir, good sir, alms, sir,' she wheezed. He could see bone gleaming through the pallid fuzz. Patches of leper-moss crawled across her skinny arms and marred her cheeks.

Bok's nose wrinkled at the stench of her. 'I have no alms, woman. No comets, no motes, no flinders for such as you.' He made a show of fumbling at his pockets. Despite his obvious disgust, she did not turn aside.

'Alms, sir. Alms for the poor.'

'Leave me in peace, wretch. I said I have no money.' Bok took a step back, as her stink enveloped him. His skin crawled at the thought of her touch. She caught the edge of his coat. Annoyed, he lowered a hand, and a thin blade slid from a concealed sheath into his waiting palm. One more body on the night soil carts would not be noticed.

'But you have red hands, brother, and they have performed black deeds,' the woman mumbled through rotting teeth. Arthritic fingers contorted themselves in a sign known only to a few. Bok relaxed somewhat, sliding the blade back into its sheath before making a similar gesture. This, then, was the person he'd come to this squalid alley to meet.

'The valley low, and the shadows long,' he said, completing the code-phrase. 'Hail and well met, sister. You bring some message from our lady of air and darkness?' He tried to keep the suspicion he felt out of his tone.

It wasn't unknown for agents of the Queen of Mysteries to practise their arts upon one another, in an attempt to rise in their mistress' esteem. Silent, swift wars occasionally broke out, between rival agents and their followers. Bok had taken part in his share of these altercations, though never without good cause. For her part, his mistress seemed unconcerned, even amused, by such internecine conflict.

'I do, I do, brother. Our queen is much impressed by your handling of that matter with the playwright, some months ago. You rise swiftly in her regard, bookseller. Continue to do so, and there is no limit to what a man of your calibre might achieve.'

'You may thank the great lady for me, but I am content with my lot. The life of a humble dealer in rare volumes suits me, I find. But I will serve her to the best of my meagre abilities, even so.' It was a practised speech. At once self-effacing and boastful. The beggar woman grinned, as if in shared jest.

'Just so, bookseller. What profits it a man to forget his station, eh?' She coughed phlegmily and wiped her mouth with the back of her hand. 'We all have our parts to play in the black game.'

Growing impatient, Bok leaned forwards. 'Get to it. What does she want of me?'

'What she always wants, bookseller… You are to procure her something. Tonight.'

'I have other business tonight.'

The beggar woman hissed, rheumy eyes narrowed in almost queenly disdain. She pulled herself erect. 'You have no business save that which our lady allows you, bookseller. And you would do well to remember that. The charnel grounds are full of those who forgot that her desires superseded their own petty yearnings.'

Bok smiled mirthlessly. 'I remember. What is it then? Another rare grimoire? A treatise on the architectural styling of Lantean Empire? A book of poetry, perhaps, or the journal of some forgotten explorer?'

'It is not a book at all, brother. It is something greater by far.' The beggar woman clutched at his coat. She leaned close, and he gagged at the smell of her. 'There is a certain house, near the Old Fen Gate, its shutters marked with the sign of the magpie…'

'I know it.' Everyone knew it. Everyone who was anyone, at least. The Magpie's Nest had played host to illicit dealings of all sorts, since the city's founding.

'An auction is to be held there, this very evening, for a select few. You will go and procure for our lady that which she desires.'

'Am I to guess, then, what that might be?'

The beggar woman licked her chapped and blistered lips. 'You will know it when you see it, bookseller. It is quite unlike anything else.' She fingered the buttons of his coat. 'Do not fail her, brother. Now give me an alm, sir. Give me an alm, lest someone mistake us for acquaintances.' She glanced around furtively. 'Hurry, brother.'

Grudgingly, he fumbled a coin from his coat and pressed it into her filthy hand. 'Here. Now be off with you, wretch.' He shoved her, for good measure. She scrambled away into the murk with a shriek he thought not a little overdone. He'd often heard it said that there was a frustrated thespian in every spy.

Bok sighed. An auction. He hated auctions, though he attended them often. At least this one was in the city, and close to hand. But he'd had no time to prepare. Then, that was likely the point. Neferata, Lady of Sorrow, was as cunning as she was powerful. The Queen of Mysteries gave her servants little warning of tasks they might resent, so as to ensure they did not waste time attempting to avoid them. Few tried to do so twice, in any event.

He turned his feet towards the Old Fen Gate. It seemed he would have to procure the bead-book another time. Such was the price one paid to serve the Mortarch of Blood. It was said by some that to serve Neferata was to serve death, and there was no master greater than death.

Bok had lived in death's shadow since his childhood. He had hunted rats in the alleys of Hammerhal, one more feral orphan among the teeming multitudes. His parents had been soldiers of the Freeguild, he thought, though he did not remember them with any true clarity. It had been another life, and in another realm besides.

From rats, he had graduated to men. Even in the most orderly of cities, there were criminals. And criminals, or at least those of a certain station, often required the assistance of a man of Bok's skills. He could balance a ledger and slit a throat with equal ease. Since he was a boy, he'd had a gift for sums and words, as well as blades. He had taught himself to read and write in his leaky lean-to, among the rubbish and vermin.

Now, he lived in a modest room above his little shop at the

end of a cul-de-sac. Even in a city like Greywater Fastness, there were those who appreciated books. Especially old books, with cracked bindings and yellowing pages, which enterprising booksellers could charge handsomely for.

He still wasn't certain how he had come to Neferata's attentions, or why she had chosen to take him into her service. He suspected that it had something to do with his previous life. He had sent many souls shrieking to the lands of the dead. It was not inconceivable that Neferata had heard of him from one of his victims, and saw in him some potential. She had many pawns, some human, some not. Ageless and deathless, Neferata regarded the Mortal Realms as a game board – and men like Bok were her pawns.

All he knew for sure was that he owed much of who he now was to her patronage. She paid well – better than his old criminal masters – and often. And all she asked in return were regular missives, reporting on the activities of certain individuals native to the city, or the acquisition of rare texts and items of minor interest. Sometimes those acquisitions turned bloody, it was true. But such was a bookseller's lot, and Palem Bok was a very good bookseller. Though there were days when he considered hiring an assistant. Someone to run errands, or commit the odd murder.

Upon leaving the tangled alleys of the rookery, he caught a rattletrap. The steel-rimmed carriage was an uncomfortable-looking vehicle, pulled by a steam-powered automaton wrought crudely in the shape of a horse. As he clambered into the battered conveyance, he held up a coin to the driver. 'There's an extra comet in it for you if you get me to the Old Fen Gate before the next tolling of the bells.' The driver, a retired Freeguild soldier by his look, saluted lazily with the hook that replaced his left hand and gave a gap-toothed grin. He wrenched on the levers that rose up around his bench, and an excess of steam flooded the artificial innards of the mechanical horse. It gave a creaking whinny and clattered forwards, the rattletrap swaying in its wake.

The streets of Greywater Fastness were narrow rivulets of stone and metal, lit by oil lanterns or lightning jars. The latter dangled from iron chains, their flickering radiance washing over buildings, and making the shadows dance. The rattletrap passed through these striations of crackling light, carrying Bok to the city's southern edge. Stone gave way to baked mud and thatch. The streets became wider, broken up by brick canals and wooden bridges. Turgid waters flowed slowly through these slimy corridors, diverted from the freshwater marshes beyond the walls.

Occasionally, marsh troggoths would haul themselves out of the canals, their flabby, scaly flesh encrusted with barnacles of ossified filth. The lumbering beasts would rampage through the slums, attacking anyone foolish enough not to seek shelter. They were almost always driven back by the soldiers of the Freeguild, and their bodies added to the great furnaces as fuel.

The marshes were smaller now than they had been when Bok first came to the city, and the walls farther out. Every season, the city grew and the wilderness shrank. Industry was ever the shield of civilisation, as an engineer of Bok's acquaintance put it. He gave little thought to such things himself, and rarely left the inner city if he could help it. Bok was a man of soot and solid streets. The wilds of Ghyran held little to interest him.

'Here we are then, sir,' the driver grunted. There was a harsh burr to his voice, marking him as an Azyrite. Bok had no issue with Azyrites, though he knew those who did. What realm a man was born in mattered less to Bok than whether he had coin to spend. Bok paid him, and climbed awkwardly to the street.

The Old Fen Gate rose tall and solid over one of the largest and oldest of the canals. It had been the first gate, when the city was new and the marshes wild. The walls of the city had bypassed the towering structure, leaving it to become the de facto centre of a neighbourhood. There were shops now, instead of barracks, and the sides of the canal were thick with clustered clapboard buildings.

The Magpie's Nest was one of those that crouched on the edge of the water. It bent over at an unsightly angle, faded bird-shapes daubed on its broken shutters. It looked as if one tremor would send all three stories sliding full into the canal. But looks could be deceiving. The building was sturdier than most, its foundations deep and its walls cleverly designed to fool the eyes of the uninvited.

He felt eyes on him as he made his way to the rear entrance, as was the tradition. The front door was for the Freeguild, or agents of the city's rulers. The door overlooking the canal was for those who'd come to conduct business. Entrance was normally by invitation only, though occasionally there were open auctions, for the less notable.

He had attended one of these open auctions before, but had left empty-handed. His resources, while substantial, were not infinite, and the bidding had been fierce. Then, given that it had been a rare copy of Kelaf's banned symphony, *The Mirror of Onyx*, perhaps not surprising. He wasn't sure what was required of one to receive an invitation. He hoped it wouldn't be an issue.

He knocked on the door, once and politely. It was always best to be polite, in these circumstances. It cut down on bloodshed. He heard the heavy rattle of a bar being withdrawn, and a moment later the door swung inwards. A slim figure was waiting for him. An aelf, he realised, taking in fine-boned features too perfect to belong to a human. Eyes like chips of obsidian met his own. She – and it was a she, though it was often hard to tell – was clad in loose robes of violet and a hauberk of black, jagged mail. A thick mane of white hair was swept back from her narrow face by a tiara of dark iron, and she had a curved falchion sheathed at her waist.

The aelf looked him up and down, an unpleasant smile crawling across her pale features. 'Invitation?' she purred, her fingers rubbing slowly against the pommel of her blade.

'I don't have one, I'm afraid.'

'That is a shame. But the canal is close, and it will be quick.' Her fingers tightened about the hilt and she made to draw her blade. Bok stepped back, ready to produce the blade hidden in his sleeve, though he disliked his chances. He'd fought aelves before. The experience had been unpleasant.

'Surely that I am here speaks to my character.'

'Not favourably,' she said, taking a quick step towards him.

Bok hesitated. Instinct said flee. But she hadn't drawn her blade yet. Maybe she was curious. Or bored. It must be dull, guarding a door. 'I've come for the auction.'

'No invitation, no auction.' She spoke serenely.

'How much to garner an invitation, then?'

'That depends entirely on who you represent, my friend.' The voice was a man's. The aelf turned, bowed and stepped back, though her eyes never left Bok. The newcomer took her place at the door. He was a small man. Fussy looking, but bedraggled. Like a scribe gone ever so slightly to seed. True to that image, he held an armful of scrolls, and his hands and the cuffs of his robes were stained with ink. 'Well?' he pressed, adjusting the battered pince-nez he wore. 'On whose behalf do you darken our doorway, sir?'

'A lady of some substance.'

'There are many ladies in Greywater Fastness. Shayl here, for instance.' The little man gestured to the aelf. 'I require a name.' The way he said it made Bok pause. It was as if the little man were trying to impart something.

'There we must part ways, sir. Her name is not mine to reveal.'

The little man shrugged and glanced at the aelf. She smiled and reached again for her blade. Bok, thinking quickly, said, 'Shadows and dust, sir.' Attempting the code phrase was a gamble, but he had little to lose.

The little man looked at him. He adjusted his pince-nez. 'Just and unjust alike,' he said, after a moment. 'You are one of hers, then.'

'I have that honour.' Bok relaxed slightly. He had guessed right. Neferata's influence stretched wide through the low places. All those who served her, even in the most minor capacity, recognised the code phrases of her agents. It was obvious to him now that she would have someone in the house, to alert her to the presence of certain items.

'That is a word for it, certainly. Very well. Shayl, he may enter.'

The aelf frowned, but made no attempt to argue. She ignored Bok as he stepped past her and entered the house. The entryway was a small, rounded chamber. A single corridor, out of sight of the door, extended deeper into the house. 'The auction is soon to begin. Come this way, Master…?'

'Bok. Palem Bok.' Bok followed the little man down the hall. Doorways lined its length, each draped with a thick, black curtain. Each curtain had sigils of warding and other, less recognisable magical symbols, woven into its folds. There would be illicit dealings going on in each of the rooms. Thieves laying plans, murderers plotting… The Magpie's Nest was a house of rogues.

The little man glanced at him. 'The bookseller?'

'You know me?'

'Of you. I am Pell. You are welcome here, sir. I trust you have come better prepared than your last visit. You were quite upset to lose that Kelaf symphony, I recall.'

'I am here on another's behalf, this time.' In truth, Bok had no idea how much Neferata expected him to pay for whatever it was she desired, or whether she was even planning to compensate him. Such were the perils of a whimsical mistress. Perhaps she expected him to simply steal whatever it was.

'Yes, I presumed so.'

'Last time I was here, you had someone friendlier on guard duty.'

'Shayl has her talents. Friendliness is not one of them.' Pell smiled. 'She serves well enough to keep things civil, among our patrons.'

Bok grunted noncommittally. Pell stopped before one of the doorways. 'You will notice that you have not been disarmed. We expect all patrons to show a certain level of decorum in repayment for our hospitality.'

'I remember.'

'Good. Through here, please.' Pell twitched the curtain aside, and Bok duly entered. The room beyond was not large. It was illuminated by half a dozen lanterns, scattered about and hanging from iron stanchions. The room itself was a plain square of wood and stone, barren save for several rows of hard benches, and a flat stage set at one end.

On the stage was a long table, and upon it were various objects of interest: a loose pile of thin volumes, obviously a set of some sort; a gruesome, bull-shaped icon that bore all the hallmarks of duardin craftsmanship; a bell jar, containing a night-blooming flower with amethyst petals; a small casket with brass hinges and a bear stamped on the lock; and a gilded skull with silver teeth.

But the most interesting of the lot was a curious whip-like weapon, consisting of eight jagged metal bars, joined together by thin rings, so as to form a chain of sorts. It had a handle made from a carved femur at one end, and a barbed dart at the other. The chain was coiled loosely, and rested in a circle of what appeared to be dust or salt. Protective sigils had been chalked into the surface of the table around it, and the air above them shimmered with an oily quality.

Something about the weapon unsettled him. There was a malign potency to it. It reminded him of a bog-viper, readying itself to strike. And even as the thought occurred to him, he knew that it was what he had been sent here to acquire. Neferata wanted it, whatever it was. And that meant he had little choice but to acquire it.

Bok took a seat, ignoring the glares of the other attendees. The benches were crowded. He surreptitiously studied the competition. Many of them were like him – intermediaries, acting on behalf of those too fearful or too well known to attend the auction in person. Others were more interesting.

One, sitting towards the front, was clearly a representative of the Collegiate Arcane, to judge by his ornate robes of white and gold, and the supercilious expression on his overfed features. He murmured softly to a small, dragon-like homunculus perched on his shoulder.

Another of the attendees was shrouded in all-concealing robes and a hood, with a strange, segmented mask hiding their face. The facets of the mask were marked with what might have been duardin runes, though not ones Bok recognised. The runes glowed dimly, and faint contrails of what might have been smoke or steam rose from them.

A woman dressed in crimson-dyed furs and leathers sat towards the back, her scarified features twisted in a frown.

Her head had been shaved, save for a single braid, bound with brass wire. A savage, from the wilds of Ghur, perhaps, given the ritualistic nature of her scarring. She caught his glance and smiled widely, as if in invitation. Her teeth were filed. Bok looked hurriedly away.

Any further study of the crowd was interrupted by the arrival of the auctioneer. A thin man, fox-lean and ginger-haired. Pell was with him, and took a seat near the stage. The scribe opened a heavy ledger on his lap and produced a writing quill from somewhere about his person. He dabbed it into a cup of ink hanging from around his neck, and began to write. The auctioneer took his place on stage, hands clasped behind his back.

'Greetings, gentles all. Welcome, and be at ease. My name is Ranaldsson, and I will be master of these ceremonies. Our first lot is the collected *Revelations of Necoho,* or the *Light of Doubt*, a fundamental text for an obscure sect of antitheists. Opening bid is one hundred comets, or the equivalent.'

Once begun, the auction progressed swiftly. One by one, the items were secured by eager bidders, and the losers were left to grumble and scowl. The stranger in the segmented mask claimed the grotesque, bull-shaped icon with a sizeable bid of two thousand comets. The gilded skull, revealed to be something called the Gelt Aurical, was decisively won by the Collegiate Arcanum representative, and a fat merchant from Hammerhal walked away with the amethyst blossom, after a winning bid of a hundred shards of shadeglass.

A pair of duardin almost came to blows over the casket, which proved to contain a single bottle of wine of ancient vintage. From the cut of their clothes and their harsh accents, Bok thought they might have been guilders, fresh from the Kharadron sky-ports.

Finally, the item he'd been waiting for came up for bid.

Ranaldsson seemed hesitant as he turned to the weapon. 'And our last item. A weapon of curious design, it has proven to be… unique, as were the circumstances of its… ah… its acquisition.' The auctioneer hurriedly looked away from the weapon. 'Through the diligent efforts of Master Pell and others of this house's staff, we have confirmed that this is, in fact, quite possibly Charu, the Soul-Lash – one of the infamous Eight Lamentations.'

A stunned murmur swept through the crowd. Bok stiffened. Neferata's desire for the weapon made sense, now. He'd heard the stories. Everyone in his profession had. Eight weapons, forged by the servants of the Blood God, Khorne, in the age before the storm of Chaos had washed over the Mortal Realms. The Eight Lamentations had been scattered and lost, appearing occasionally to wreak havoc before vanishing once more. Rumour had it that they had begun to resurface of late, and Neferata had directed her agents to keep their eyes and ears open for any hint of the weapons.

Bok had never thought to find one here, practically in his lap. From behind him, he heard the woman in red murmur, 'From fire, came heat. From heat, shape. And shape split into eight. And the eight became as death.'

Ranaldsson gestured for quiet, as the crowd's murmuring threatened to boil over. 'Please, gentles, please. Rest assured, we are certain of the item's provenance. All effort has been made to keep it contained safely. Though I hasten to add that we are not responsible for anything that may occur once it leaves these premises.' He gave a brittle smile. 'Opening bid is three thousand comets, or the equivalent.'

Bok grunted in consternation. A hefty sum, and one he couldn't go far beyond without emptying his coffers. It would be worth it, though, considering the rewards Neferata might bestow upon him for delivering such a prize to her.

But before he could make a bid, the woman in red called out, 'There will be no bids. The item is not for sale.' She stood, and a hostile muttering swept the benches. At her gesture, several other members of the crowd stood as well.

They all wore shades of red, Bok saw, though the garments of some were of a more expensive cut than others. Their faces were similarly scarred, some in less noticeable ways. But for all the barbarity of her appearance, it was clear the woman was in charge. She stepped into the aisle between the benches and strode towards the stage.

Ranaldsson cleared his throat. 'I beg your pardon, milady, but–'

'I am Kesh, and I do not give it. This weapon is not yours to sell, little man. It belongs to a god, and we have come to take it back, in the name of he who strides the red skies, wolf-fanged and mighty.' She swept back her furs, revealing a brass-banded belt, and a pair of crude hand axes hanging from it. The others threw off their cloaks or tore open coats to reveal similar axes, of varying craftsmanship.

'You will give it to us,' Kesh continued, 'or I will take your skull.' She unhooked an axe and pointed it at him. 'Khorne demands it, and you will not gainsay him.'

Ranaldsson spluttered. Bok had no doubt that the man had been threatened before, but perhaps never so bluntly. Others might have tried to win the bidding first, before threatening murder. But the servants of the Blood God were not known for their subtlety.

Pell chose that moment to lunge for a bell-pull hanging beside the doorway, but a thrown axe dashed his brains across the wall. As the scribe crumpled, Bok drew his pistol and fired. One of the cultists was punched off his feet, a red hole between his bulging eyes. With the echoes of the shot hanging on the air, the room exploded into violence. He saw the stranger in the segmented mask snatch a blood-cultist from his feet, and hurl him across the room in a display of inhuman strength.

A hurled axe sank deep into the bench behind Bok, narrowly missing him. He spun, but held his fire. Instead he cracked the blood-cultist across the skull, dropping her to the floor. The duardin pistol only had five shots. Bok was determined to waste none of them.

People were shoving and screaming, trying to escape the room. The blood-mad killers hacked and hewed at the crowd with furious intensity. Some among the patrons resisted, in their own fashion. The two Kharadron had drawn their cutlasses and fought back-to-back, their earlier argument forgotten. The Collegiate Arcane representative spoke a word of power, and turned a cultist into a living torch. The warrior screamed and fell across the benches, setting them alight. Somewhere, an alarm bell had begun to ring.

In the confusion, Kesh had reached the stage. Bok tried to take aim at the woman, but a cultist rose up before him, chanting the eighty-eight names of the Blood God as he chopped wildly at the panicking crowd. Bok shot him, but the cultist didn't fall. His axe slashed down, nearly taking Bok's arm off. A second shot punched his head back and dropped him to the floor. Desperate now, Bok forced his way through the crowd, determined to prevent Kesh from claiming the weapon.

As he reached the stage, he saw Ranaldsson leap to the floor with a panicked yell, clutching a bloody arm. He fled, screaming for help. Kesh laughed and reached for the chain-whip, a dripping axe clutched in her other hand. 'I think not,' Bok said. Kesh turned, teeth bared, axe raised. He fired his pistol as the axe left her hand.

She clapped a hand to her leg and shrieked. The axe pinned

his coat sleeve to the table, and knocked him off balance. The pistol clattered from his hand. He tore himself loose from the table as Kesh caught up her prize.

There was a crack, like stone splitting, as her fingers wrapped about the bone haft of the weapon. The links of the chain clattered, as if in welcome, and a shudder ran through it, and her. Her eyes flashed with red lightning, and as she turned, he saw that every scar on her face had opened anew and was bleeding.

'The Soul-Lash is mine, weakling,' she snarled, whirling the chain-whip about her. Bok threw himself aside, as the barbed tip snapped out with a silky hiss. It tore through the throat of an unfortunate man near the stage. There was a sound like tearing cloth, and a shimmer of greenish energy erupted from the dying man. It spun around the barb, and was almost instantly drawn into the weapon.

Kesh hissed in pleasure and leapt to the floor, whirling the chain-whip up and about her in a growing frenzy. It tore through the crowd and her followers alike. More surges of light were torn away from falling bodies – green, red, ochre, blue – and drawn into the links of the weapon. 'Yes, it is as the blood-seers claimed – Charu drinks the spirits of the fallen. I feel their strength within me.' She laughed wildly. 'Blood and skulls for my lord Khorne!'

The room was rapidly filling with smoke. The lanterns had been knocked over in the chaos, spilling burning oil everywhere, and the sorcerous fire started by the wizard leapt from bench to bench. There was a scrum at the doorway, as people tried to force their way out. Those left inside were either trying to stay out of Kesh's way, or brawling with her followers.

Kesh's form was limned with a sickly radiance. The chain-whip moved like a thing alive, rather than a weapon. Perhaps it was hungry, after its captivity. Bok pushed the unsettling thought aside as he found his pistol and scooped it up. He tried to line up a shot while she was distracted, but too late.

The chain-whip bent about her of its own volition and darted towards him. The barb tore flinders from the stage and forced him back a step. Kesh turned before he could recover, and the whip arrowed towards him again. He twisted aside, but not quickly enough. One of the metal bars caught him in the ribs and smashed him from the edge of the stage.

Pain flared through him as he hit the floor, and he felt as if something in him had torn loose. But luckily, the barb had missed him and his soul remained his own. He heard the crackle of magics and saw the Collegiate Arcane represent-ative fling aethereal lightning towards Kesh. She snarled and cracked the whip. The spell tore in two, and ragged motes of light danced across the air. Unhindered, the barbed tip caught the wizard in the chest and tore his soul scream-ing from him. The backlash of sundered magics howled through the chamber, overturning benches and smashing bodies against walls.

Bok lay still, eyes closed against the glare. When he opened them, the crowd was gone. Most had fled, but the rest had not managed to escape. And Kesh was nowhere in sight, though he could hear the clash of weapons somewhere out in the corri-dor. For a moment, he considered letting that be the end of it. He could slip out, with no one the wiser. But Neferata would know. And that thought was more frightening than any mys-tical soul-eater.

Wearily, he hauled himself to his feet and stumbled out into the hall, after retrieving his pistol. Smoke filled the space. The fire had spread. The corridor was littered with bodies. Some had been trampled, others bore bloody wounds. The unseen alarm bells were still ringing, and he heard the thump of running feet somewhere above him. He staggered down the hall, clutching his side.

Kesh had carved herself a path to the street. The marks of the chain-whip were evident on the walls and floor, as well as on many of the bodies. When he reached the entry hall, he saw that the heavy door had been smashed off its hinges. There was no sign of the aelf. From outside, he could hear the rattle of steel and the stamp of feet.

He reached the door and stopped. Outside, the aelf, Shayl, and Kesh spun and fought with a speed that defied description. The aelf moved with all the quicksilver grace of her kind, but Kesh matched her speed, driven to inhuman extremes by the power of the Soul-Lash. Shayl's blade deflected the chain-whip as it curled around her, sending the barb spinning away. Kesh parried the aelf's counter-stroke with her remaining axe. The two women stamped and whirled back and forth along the edge of the canal. The ragged remnants of stolen souls clung to Kesh like a smoky shroud, and her laughter boomed out over the waters as she fought.

Bok leaned against the doorframe, wheezing. His side ached where the chain had crunched against his ribs. Kesh's three surviving followers hadn't noticed him yet, enraptured as they were by the duel. He extended his pistol. One shot left. He would need to make it count. Time stretched unbearably. Smoke from the fire billowed past him, filling the street.

Then, it happened – Shayl lunged, but Kesh smashed her blow aside throwing her off balance. The barb of the chain-whip hissed down, smashing her sword from her hand and throwing her to the ground. Kesh gave a shout and swung the Soul-Lash up, ready to add the aelf's soul to her collection.

Bok fired.

Kesh stiffened. The side of her head was a red ruin. She

turned, wobbling on her feet, her remaining eye fixed on Bok as her warriors turned. Kesh took an unsteady step towards him. The Soul-Lash snapped and twisted like an angry viper. Her mouth worked, but no words came out. She made as if to raise the chain-whip, but instead pitched forwards with a disgruntled sigh and lay still.

Bok swung his pistol towards the remaining cultists. 'Stay back, or I'll fire.' The blood-cultists snarled as one and started towards him, axes raised. He tossed the empty pistol into the face of the closest, and drove a kick into the midsection of another. An axe bit the air dangerously close to his head, and he turned, punching its wielder. The haft of a weapon caught him in the side of the face and he staggered, the street spinning.

A second blow knocked him from his feet. He covered his head and rolled away. He heard a scream and glanced up. Shayl stood behind one of the cultists, her sword embedded in his back. She ripped it free and twisted, opening the jugular of a second. The third roared and leapt at her, axe raised. Bok snatched up a fallen axe and surged to his feet, catching the cultist in the abdomen. The man folded over with a gurgle and Bok released the axe, letting the dying man slump.

Shayl looked at him, eyebrow raised. 'I had him,' she said.

Bok shrugged. 'You're welcome to the credit.'

She frowned and studied him. 'You fight well. For a human. I am sorry we did not get to match blades earlier.'

'I'm not,' he said.

She laughed. 'No. It would have been a shame to kill you.'

Iron grated against the street. An ugly moan filled the air. Shayl turned, and past her, Bok saw Kesh struggling to her feet. Blood and brain matter dripped down the side of her face as her good eye fixed on them. Bok stared.

'A bullet to the head usually does the trick.'

Before Shayl could reply, the barbed head of the Soul-Lash rose up over Kesh's back like a scorpion's stinger. The links clicked like laughter as the woman took a step towards them, and he realised suddenly that Kesh was no longer in charge.

Whatever fell power lurked within the weapon, it had obviously decided that it wasn't finished with them yet. With an inhuman screech, Kesh jerked forwards, slashing at them with the chain-whip. Bok lurched aside and felt the air part before his face as the chain slashed down. Shayl attacked, driving her blade into Kesh's side. The woman ignored the blow and shoved the aelf aside.

'She's already dead,' Bok shouted.

'Then how do we kill her?' the aelf demanded, ducking beneath the arc of the chain-whip. She scrambled backwards.

Bok frowned, at a loss. Kesh laughed – there was nothing human in the sound. Broken spirits swirled about her, bound to the monstrous weapon. They moaned in what might have been pain, and the killing sigils hammered into the iron bars of the chain flared with unnatural heat. Kesh's wrist bulged oddly as she slashed the Soul-Lash out again, carving divots from the street.

'Her hand,' Bok snarled. Shayl looked at him, eyes narrowed. Bok flung his arm to the side. A twist of the wrist and the weight of his concealed blade slid into his waiting hand. A moment later, the blade was flying through the air. It sank into Kesh's remaining eye with a wet, hollow sound. She staggered, blind. 'Now,' he cried.

Thankfully, the aelf was quick on the uptake. Her blade chopped through Kesh's wrist. The Soul-Lash, and Kesh's hand, clattered to the ground with a petulant rasp of iron links. As soon as the weapon hit the ground, Kesh toppled backwards with a sigh.

Bok released a shaky breath. He approached the body carefully. But she seemed to have surrendered to the inevitable at last. He pried his blade free and wiped it clean on her ragged furs, before tearing them from her body. He nudged the chain-whip into the furs with his foot and wrapped it up. He could hear its links rasping in frustration.

'What an awful thing you are,' he said, as he tied the edges of the furs together. 'The Queen of Mysteries is welcome to you, and good riddance.'

'Is she dead?' the aelf asked, as he lifted the bundle and slung it over his shoulder. She held a hand pressed to her gashed arm, but was otherwise unharmed.

'For the moment.' He looked up. The Magpie's Nest was completely aflame now. It had burned before, and he had no doubt it would be rebuilt, in time. He looked at Shayl. 'You appear to be out of a job.'

She shrugged. 'It was boring.'

Bok hesitated. Then, he smiled.

'Have you ever considered a career in the book trade?'

EIGHT LAMENTATIONS: SPEAR OF SHADOWS
by Josh Reynolds

Eight mighty artefacts, crafted by the dark servants of Chaos, blight the Mortal Realms. The Ruinous Powers hunt them – and so do a group of heroes, chosen by Grungni for this dangerous and essential task.

For these stories and more go to **blacklibrary.com, games-workshop.com**, Games Workshop and Warhammer stores, all good book stores or visit one of the thousands of independent retailers worldwide, which can be found at **games-workshop.com/storefinder**

THE SANDS
OF GRIEF

Guy Haley

'I don't like it here, master. Please, let us go. Too much magic, hurts my bones.'

'Hush, Shattercap, they are nearly done, and then we can leave. Be patient.'

The second speaker was Maesa, a proud aelf prince in the bronze armour and green-and-grey clothing of the wayfarer peoples. The first was a vicious spite, a small, gangrel creature of ill intent. His appearance did nothing to disguise his nature. He was a clutch of bones and twiggy fingers, garbed in wizened green skin. From a small, apelike face, his button black eyes peered at the world with fearful malice, in marked contrast to the calm benevolence radiated by his keeper. But though a captive, Shattercap was more or less content to live among the folds of the prince's cloak.

Content, because the aelf offered a way out of wickedness, and Shattercap desired that in a half-grasped way. Less, because the prince and the spite were at that time within the shop of

Erasmus Throck and Durdek Grimmson, providers of the finest alchemical instruments in Glymmsforge in the Realm of Shyish, a place Shattercap feared greatly.

Throck and Grimmson were comical opposites. Grimmson was a stout duardin with a blue beard and bald head. Throck was a tall scrap of man with a shock of white hair and clean-shaven chin. The duardin rooted about behind the counter near the floor. The man was balanced upon rolling steps, searching cubbyholes high up by the ceiling.

Grimmson hauled out a leather-covered box and placed it on the glass counter top.

'This is it, aelfling, the soul glass you wished for.'

Throck tutted from the top of the steps at his colleague.

'Come now, Durdek! Prince Maesa is highborn and worthy of respect.'

Durdek's granitic face maintained its scowl. 'He's an aelf, and I call it as I see it, Erasmus.'

Throck shook his head, and pulled the wheeled ladder along to the next stack of cubbyholes.

'Don't worry, your worthiness,' said Grimmson to Maesa. 'I've outdone myself for you. Look at this.'

With a delicacy his massive fingers seemed incapable of, Grimmson took out a tiny hourglass. Its bulbs were no bigger than a child's clenched fists, decorated with delicate fretwork of silver and gold.

Durdek flicked open a lid in the glass' top. 'Life sand goes in here. Seal it. Tip it over when it's near run out. Keep on with that to prolong the life within. Away you go. Very simple concept, but simple usage is no reason for drab work.'

'We pride ourselves on the finest equipment,' said Throck. 'Durdek here makes the devices...'

'...and it's him as does the enchanting,' said Durdek.

'It is a beautiful piece,' said Maesa. He took the hourglass from Grimmson and turned it over in his hands. 'Such fine workmanship.'

Grimmson hooked his fingers into his belt, gave a loud sniff and pulled himself up proudly.

'We do what we can.'

'Aha! Here is the other item,' said Throck. He jumped from the ladder. From a soft velvet bag, he took out a complex compass. It too had a lid in the top, covering over a small compartment. 'A soul seeker. This should lead you to the realmstone deposit you seek.'

Grimmson took the glass and placed it carefully back into the box so Maesa could examine the compass.

Eight nested circles of gold, each free moving against the other, surrounded the central lidded well. On one side of the well was an indicator made in the shape of the hooked symbol of Shyish. Maesa pushed it with his finger. It spun silently through many revolutions at the gentlest touch.

'It floats on a bath of ghostsilver,' said Throck. 'Very good work.'

'Should be,' said Shattercap. 'For the money you are being paid.'

'You get what you pay for,' Grimmson growled. 'Quality. We are Glymmsforge's foremost makers of such devices.'

'We are expensive, I admit, but you will find none better,' said Throck.

'Indeed,' said Maesa. 'I have no issue with the cost. Ignore my servant, he has yet to learn manners.' He handed the compass back and produced a white leather pouch from his belt. 'Five hundred black diamond chips, from the Realm of Ulgu, as you required.'

Grimmson took the bag from Maesa's hand and tugged at the drawstring ready to count the contents.

Throck patted his partner's burly arm. 'That won't be necessary. I am sure the prince is good to his word.' Throck was awed by the prince's breeding, and couldn't help but give a short bow. Maesa returned the gesture with a graceful inclination of his head. Grimmson looked at them both fiercely.

'You best be careful out there,' the duardin said. 'We sell maybe eight or nine of these a year, but the folks that buy them don't always come to the best end. Most go out into the Sands of Grief, and vanish.'

'How do you know they work then?' said Shattercap, slinking around the back of Maesa's head from one shoulder to the other.

'Ahem,' Throck looked apologetic. 'Their ghosts come back to tell us.'

'Ghosts? Ghosts! Master!' squealed Shattercap. 'Why did we come here?'

'I trust you have supernatural means of sustenance?' said Throck amiably. 'I do not mean to pry into your business, but where you intend to go is no place for the living. There is no water, no food, no life of any kind, only the dead, and storms of wild magic. We can provide the necessary protections – amulets, enchanted vittles, all you would require – if you have none of your own.'

'Oh, no!' Shattercap shrieked again. Maesa ignored him.

'I have what I need. My kind have wandered in every place. This realm is no alien land to me. I shall return in person to inform you how well your goods performed.' Maesa bowed and picked up his packages. 'My thanks, and good day to you, sirs.'

The door of the shop banged closed behind the prince. Shattercap cowered from the strange sights of Glymmsforge. The sky was a bruised purple, forever brooding, its long night scattered with amethyst stars. Outside the walls were afterlives ruined by the war with Chaos, and haunted by broken souls. But the streets of the young city were full of life, bathed in the light of magical lanterns that held back the dark.

Throck and Grimmson's shop was located on Thaumaturgy Way, along with dozens of other purveyors of magical goods. Market stalls narrowed the street, leaving only a slender cobbled passage down the centre. Humans, aelfs, duardin and all manner of other creatures thronged the market, and not only the living, but the shades of the dead also, for Glymmsforge was situated in the afterlife of Lyria, where some vestiges of past glory still clung.

The crowd moved slowly. People browsed goods, creating hard knots in the flow that eddied irritably around each other. Maesa could pass through a thicket of brambles without disturbing a twig, but his aelven gifts were of no use in that place, and he was forced to shove through the crowd along with the rest.

'Market days, I hate market days!' hissed Shattercap. 'So many people. Where is the forest quiet? Where is the mossy silence?'

'You will yearn for their fellowship where we are going, small evil,' said Maesa. He slipped through a gaggle of ebon-skinned men of Ghur haggling over an imp imprisoned in a bottle, and reached the relative quiet of the main street.

Free of the overhanging eaves of Thaumaturgy Way, more of the city was visible. Concentric rings of walls soared to touch the sky. The innermost held within their compass the Shimmergate, a blue slash of light high up in the dark sky. Shattercap and Maesa were in the second district, thus close to the Stormkeep, the College of Amethyst and all the other wonders of the deepest ward.

Maesa turned his back on the central spires. His destination lay outside the city.

* * *

He returned to their lodgings in the fourth ward, and there arranged his equipment for the journey while Shattercap fretted in the corner. The spite could have bolted at any time, and for that reason Maesa had kept the thing chained for the first part of their association. As the days passed, a bond had grown between them. Besides, Shattercap was too cowardly to flee, so Maesa had abandoned the fetters.

Maesa packed his saddlebags with food, drink and sustenance of a less mundane kind. He stowed his unstrung bow into its case on the outside of his quiver. The compass from Throck and Grimmson he hung about his neck in its bag, and he stored the hourglass carefully in his packs. Lastly, he took from the table his most prized possession – the skull of his dead love, Ellamar – and placed it carefully into a light knapsack woven from the silk of forest spiders.

He called the house boy to take the bags to the stables, and followed him down.

The inn's stable block housed every sort of riding beast imaginable. At one end of the stalls was a mighty gryph-charger that rattled its beak in conversation with a pair of its lesser demi-gryph kin stabled next to it. Dozens of horses, flightless birds, great cats and more all whinnied, growled, squawked and screeched. As the air was a confusion of different calls, so the smell of the stables was a mighty animal reek composed of many bestial perfumes.

There was only a single great stag in the stable. His name was Aelphis and he was Maesa's mount. He waited for his master, aloofly enduring the clumsy efforts of the grooms to saddle him.

'Aelphis,' said Maesa softly.

The giant stag bowed his head and snorted gladly at the prince's greeting. He dropped to his knees to allow Maesa to load him with the baggage.

'I am sorry, my lord, but I do not think I have your saddle right,' said the head groom. 'I have never tacked up a creature like he before.'

'No matter,' said Maesa. Although the groom had made a poor job of it, he was genuinely apologetic. The prince adjusted the saddle while the groom looked on, and Maesa welcomed his desire to learn. When all was as it should be, Maesa leapt nimbly upon Aelphis' back. The stag let out a lusty bellow and rose up to his full, majestic height.

'We shall return,' said Maesa, and took his helm from a groom. Its spread of bronze antlers mirrored the magnificence of Aelphis' rack. Armoured, he and the beast were perfectly matched.

Maesa rode from the inn's yard. He would dearly have liked to give Aelphis his head, and let the beast break into its springing run, but the streets of the fourth ward were as crowded as those of the second. Beast and rider were forced to keep their patience until they reached the eastern outgate.

A permit was required to leave the walls at night. Maesa duly provided his papers to the gate captain, who scrutinised them carefully.

No one else was leaving.

'All is in order,' said the captain reluctantly.

At a shout from the captain, the gates swung wide. The road leading away from Glymmsforge was empty. Not one soul walked the level paving. A channel of purple salt cut through the road surface a hundred yards out, interrupting its journey into desert nowheres devoid of living souls.

The walls were patrolled by keen-eyed men armed with sorcerous guns. Two of them barred Maesa's exit.

'You must be an influential man to secure exit from the city at night,' said the captain, handing back the papers. 'I advise you to wait for the day.'

'I am eager to be away.'

'I have a suspicion where you are bound, prince,' said the captain. 'I've seen plenty of creatures with the same look you have in your eyes. They are not to be dissuaded, so I will not try. I will give you the warning that all free-thinking folk receive from me. At the line of salt out there, the protection of Sigmar ends. There are perils aplenty beyond these walls. This gate is the frontier of life. Out there is only death and undeath. Are you sure whatever reason you are going out there for is worth your soul?'

'It is a price I will gladly pay,' said Maesa.

'Then Sigmar watch over you. There are no others that can,' said the captain.

'Your warning is noted, captain,' said Maesa. 'But I have nothing to fear.'

The men stepped aside at a nod from the captain.

Maesa's trilling song set Aelphis bounding out into the empty desert, joyful to be free of the confines of the city.

The road entered the low hills some miles from Glymmsforge, and there it petered out at a half-finished cutting. Construction gear lay around, awaiting the day and the work gangs. Night-time was altogether too dangerous for mortal labour. As the stag left smooth paving for the sand, Maesa directed him up the slope and pulled him to a stop.

Dust kicked up by the stag's hooves blew away on a cold wind. Maesa turned back for one last look upon Glymmsforge. From the vantage of the hillside, it was set out like a model for him to examine.

The Shimmergate gleamed in the sky, surrounded by the gossamer traceries of the stairs leading to its threshold. The Realmgate reflected in the Glass Mere, the broad lake encompassed by the fortifications. Monumental buildings stretched spires skywards, taller even than the walls, all ablaze with fires and shining mage-light. Among the finest were the cathedral-like mausolea of the Celestial Saints, the relics of a dozen creatures whose holy power kept back evil, joined together by trenches of the purple salt. The twelve-pointed star the mausolea and the sand trench made was the reason for the city's survival, being a barrier to all wicked things.

Around this oasis city, the Zircona desert stretched its gloomy grey expanses. The haunting cries of tormented spirits blended with the fluting wind.

'Look back at the city, small evil,' Maesa said to Shattercap. 'It will be our last sight of life ere our task is done.'

Tiny, whistling snores answered. Shattercap was a relaxed weight in the bottom of Maesa's hood.

Quietly, so as not to disturb the slumbering spite, Maesa urged Aelphis into a run.

Zircona's desert ran for leagues. Aelphis covered its distances without tiring. He cut straight across the landscape, bounding as quickly over crags and shattered badlands as he ran over the flats. Day's watery light came and went, and Maesa did not pause. Every third night he would rest, for aelven kind are hardier than mortal men, and sleep rules their lives with a looser hand. Aelphis slept when the prince did while Shattercap kept watch. Trusting terror to keep the spite vigilant, aelf and stag rested without misgiving.

There were ruins in the wastes. Shattered cities dotted the lands, though whether raised by the living or the dead it was impossible to say. The metaphysics of Shyish were complicated. Before the Age of Chaos cast them into ruin, many lesser afterlives had occupied the desert. As time went on, the living had come into those places also, and lived alongside those who had been born and died in other places and come to Shyish for their reward. In the south of Glymmsforge, towards the heartlands of Shyish, there were mighty realms yet, but towards realm's edge where Maesa headed, only ruins remained, haunted by the shrieking gheists of the dispossessed.

None of these wandering shades dared come near him. To the sight of the dead, Prince Maesa shone with baleful power. His sword, the soul-drinking Song of Thorns, would bring their end with a single cut, and Maesa had other magical arts to command should it fail him.

They passed a great city whose walls were whole and aglow with corpse-light. No sound issued from the place. There was no sense of vitality, only an ominous watchfulness. The city filled the valley it occupied from side to side, and Maesa was forced to travel uneasily within the shadow of its fortifications.

A wail went up from the gatehouse as he approached, answered by others sounding from the towers in the curtain wall. Aelphis pranced and snorted at the din. Shattercap gibbered in miserable fright. Disturbed, Maesa spurred Aelphis on. The wailing harrowed their ears as they galloped by, but nothing came out from the city, not phantom nor spectral arrow, and as Maesa passed, the ghostly shrieks died one by one, until terrible silence fell.

They quickly left the city behind. Afterwards, the character of the land changed for the worse.

During the night that followed, they camped. All were weary, for the land took a toll on their spirits. Shattercap puled miserably and tugged at Maesa's hair.

'Master, master,' he whined. 'I feel so ill, not good at all.'

Maesa squatted at Aelphis' side. The giant stag was sleeping, its huge flanks pumping like bellows, gusting breaths whose warmth the bitter lands swiftly stole. Maesa took Shattercap from his shoulder and looked at him carefully. The spite's skin had gone dry and grey. Maesa too was ailing. His pale face had lost its alabaster sheen, becoming pasty. Dark rings shaded his almond eyes.

'It is the land. The nearer the edge we go, the less forgiving to mortal flesh it is, even to those like we, small evil, who are blessed with boundless lifespans.'

Shattercap coughed. Maesa cradled him in the crook of his arm like a sick lamb as he hunted through his bags with his free hand.

'It is time. For you especially, a creature born of the magic of life, this place is hard. I have something here for you to ensure your survival.'

He took out a round flask protected by a net of cord. Contained in the glass was a clear liquid that glowed faintly with yellow light. As Maesa uncorked it, it flared, lighting up the bones and veins in his fine hands. He held the bottle to Shattercap's lips.

'Water from the Lifewells of Ghyran,' Maesa explained. 'Drawn long before the Plague God's corruption. Take but one drop. Any more will change you, and we have but a little.'

Shattercap dipped his pink tongue into the glass. When it touched the blessed water, he let out a relieved sigh.

'It tastes of the forests. It tastes of the rivers and the seas. It tastes of home!'

Maesa set Shattercap down and wet his own lips with the water. His skin tingled. His face glowed with renewed life, and the dark rings faded. He dabbed a little on his forefinger, to rub on the gums of the sleeping stag, then corked the flask and put it away.

A miserable moaning sang out of the night.

'Best keep this out of sight,' Maesa said. 'The dead here are cold, and will seek out a source of life such as this.'

They went further edgewards, heading away from the heartlands of Shyish. At night, the dark was full of desperate howls. Cold winds blew, carrying whispers that chilled the marrow. Thunderous storms cracked the sky with displays of purple lightning. No rain fell. Nothing lived. The days grew shorter with every league they went, the sun paler, until they passed some fateful meridian, and went into lands clothed perpetually in shadow.

Where the light died, the sky changed. Beneath amethyst chips of stars a new desert began. Zircona was a wasteland, but it was part of a living world. This new desert was wholly a dead place.

Maesa slipped from Aelphis' saddle.

'We have reached the Sands of Grief. Now is the time for the magic of Throck and Grimmson,' he said. He took out the gold compass, and set it on a stone. From a velvet bag he removed the skull of Ellamar and unwound its wrappings, set it on the ground, and knelt beside it.

'Forgive me, my love,' he said. Delicately, he took up the brown skull, and pinched a tooth between forefinger and thumb. 'I apologise for this insult to your remains. I shall replace it with the brightest silver.'

Grimacing at what he must do, he drew the tooth. It came free with a dry scraping.

He set the tooth aside, rewrapped his precious relic, and returned it to the back of his saddle. Then he opened up the lid of the compass-box and placed the tooth within.

'Let us see if it works.'

He held the compass up to his face.

Slowly, the pointer swung about, left, then right, then left, before coming to a stop. Maesa moved the compass. The pointer remained fixed unwaveringly on the desert.

'Success?' said Shattercap.

'Success,' said Maesa in relief.

Daylight receded from recollection. Shifting dunes crowded the mind as much as the landscape, and Maesa put all his formidable will into remembering who he was, and why he was there. Had he not, his sanity would have faded, and he would have wandered the desert forever.

Time without day loses meaning. The compass did not move from its position. Hours or lifetimes could have gone by. The desert landscape changed slowly, but it did change. Maesa came out of his fugue to find himself looking down into a gorge where shapes marched in two lines from one horizon to another. One line headed deeper into the desert and the realm's edge, the other oppositely towards the heartlands of Shyish.

The sight was enough to shake Maesa from his torpor. Shattercap stirred.

'What is it?' asked Shattercap. His voice was weak.

'Skeletons. Animate remains of the dead,' said Maesa. The percussive click of dry joints and the whisper of fleshless feet echoed from the gorge's sides. Purple starlight glinted from ancient bone.

'What are they doing?' said Shattercap.

'I have no idea,' said Maesa. 'But we must cross their march.'

'Master!' said Shattercap. 'Please, no. This is too much.'

Maesa urged Aelphis on. The great stag was weary, and stumbled upon the scree. Stones loosened by his feet sent a shower of rock before him that barged through the lines of skeletons and took two down with a hollow clatter. The skin of magic holding the skeletons together burst. Bones scattered. Like ants on their way to their nest, the animates stepped around the scene of the catastrophe, and continued on their silent way.

'Oh, no,' whimpered Shattercap.

'Be not afraid,' said Maesa. 'They see nothing. They are set upon a single task. They will not harm us.' He drew Aelphis up alongside the line, and rode against its direction. The skeletons heading outwards marched with their arms at their sides, but those going inwards each held one hand high in front of eyeless sockets, thumb and forefinger pinched upon an invisible burden.

Shattercap snuffled at them. 'Oh, I see! I see! They carry realmstone, such small motes of power I can hardly perceive them. Why, master, why?'

'I know not,' said Maesa, though the revelation filled him with unease. Nervously, he checked his compass, in case the undead carried off that which he sought, but the compass arrow remained pointing the same direction as always. 'I have no wish to discover why. Few beings could animate so many of the dead. We should be away from here.'

They left the name unsaid, but it was to Nagash, Lord of Undeath, Maesa referred. To whisper his name would call his attention onto them, and in that place Maesa had no power to oppose him.

'Come, Aelphis, through the line.'

The king of stags bounded through a gap. The skeletons were blind to the aelven prince. With exaggerated, mechanical care, they trooped through the endless night, bearing their tiny cargoes onwards.

They passed several skeleton columns over the coming days. Always, they marched in two directions, one corewards, the other to the edge. They followed the lie of the land and, like water, wore it away with their feet where they passed, forming a branching of dry tributaries carrying flows of bone. Not once did the skeletons notice them, and soon the companions' crossing of the lines became routine. The compass turned gradually away from their current path. By then notions of edgewards and corewards had lost all meaning. They knew the direction changed simply because they found themselves coming against the skeleton columns diagonally, then, as the compass shifted again, walking alongside them to the deeper desert. For safety's sake, Maesa withdrew a little from the column the compass demanded he follow, shadowing it at a mile's distance. Time ran on. The line of skeletons did not break or waver, but stamped on, on, on towards Shyish's centre, each step a progression of the one behind, so the skeletons were like so many drawings pulled from a child's zoetrope.

Some time later – neither Maesa nor Shattercap knew how long – they witnessed a new sight. In a lonely hollow they spied a figure. On impulse Maesa turned Aelphis away from their route to investigate.

A human male squatted in the dust, a prospector's pan in one hand. From the other he let a slow trickle of sand patter into the pan, then sifted it carefully around the pan while croaking minor words of power. Sometimes he would take a speck of sand out and put it into something near his feet. More often he would tip the load aside.

'Good evening,' said Maesa. It was dangerous approaching anyone in the wastes, but even the prince, who had spent solitary decades in his wandering, felt the need for company.

'Eh, eh? Evening? Always night time. What do you want?' said the man. He did not look up from his work.

Maesa saw no reason to lie. 'I seek the life sands of my lost love. I hope to bring her back, and be with her again.'

'Mmm, hmmm, yes. Many come here for the realm sand, the crystallised essence of mortal years,' said the necromancer, pawing at the ground. He mumbled something unintelligible, then suddenly looked around, eyes wide. His skin was pallid. A peculiar smell rose from him. 'You must be a great practitioner of the arts of necromancy to attempt to find a particular vein, though I doubt it. I never met an aelf with a knack for the wind of Shyish. But I, Qualos the Astute, necromancer supreme, I will have my own life soon bottled in this glass! By reversing it, I shall live forever. I alone have the art to exploit the Sands of Grief, whereas you shall fail!' He chuckled madly. 'What do you think of that?'

'It is most impressive,' said Maesa.

The smile dropped from Qualos' face, his eyes widened. 'Oh, you best be careful! He doesn't like it when souls are taken! You take the one you're looking for, even a part, and he'll come for you. He'll not let you be until your bones march in his legions and your spirit shrieks in his host.' He looked about, then whispered. 'I speak of Nagash.'

The whisper streamed from his lips and away over the dunes, growing louder the further it travelled. Thunder boomed far away. Aelphis shied.

'Not I, though. I have this! Within is my life! My soul is none but my own.' He held up the bottom bulb of an hourglass. The neck was snapped, the top lost. The glass was scratched to the point of opacity. No sand would run in that vessel, unless it was to fall out.

'I see,' said Maesa neutrally.

'The man is mad!' hissed Shattercap.

'Just a few grains more, then I will be heading back,' said Qualos. 'All the peoples of Eska will marvel at my feat!' he said. He licked his lips with a tongue dry and black as old leather.

'I don't think you can do it, not like me.' He cradled his broken glass to his chest.

'We shall see,' said Maesa.

'Well, on your way!' said the necromancer, his face transformed by a snarl. 'You distract me from my task. Get ye gone.'

Aelphis plodded slowly by the man. As they passed him, Maesa glimpsed white shining inside his open robes. Shattercap growled.

Qualos' ribs poked through desiccated flesh. Splintered bone trapped a dark hole where his heart had beaten, now gone.

'He is dead!' whispered Shattercap.

'Yes,' said Maesa.

Shattercap scrambled across Maesa's shoulders to look behind. 'You knew?'

'Only when he spoke,' admitted Maesa. 'I thought him alive, at first.'

'Should we not tell him?' asked Shattercap.

'I do not think it would make any difference, and it may put us in danger. His fate is not our business. The Lord of Undeath has him in his thrall. A cruel joke.'

Maesa directed Aelphis back upon their course and rode for a while. When he was sure they were out of sight of Qualos, Maesa pulled out Ghyran's bottled life and regarded it critically.

'The lack of this, however, is a cause for concern. There is enough for a few more days,' he said. He looked towards the centre of Shyish, estimating the ride to more hospitable lands. 'No more than that.'

'What do we do when we run out?' whimpered Shattercap.

Maesa would not answer.

Maesa and his companions were dying. Not a sharp blade-cut end, but the slow drip of souls weeping from broken hearts.

Grey dunes rolled away to chill eternities. Aelphis stumbled up slopes and down slip faces, his antlers drooped to his feet. Maesa swayed listlessly in the saddle. Shattercap was silent. A few drops of Ghyran's life-giving waters remained to sustain them. They would have to return soon, or they would die.

At the same time, they grew hopeful. Increasingly in the dust they saw glittering streams of coarse grains of green, black, amethyst and other gemstone colours. These were realmstones of Shyish – life sands, each streak on the dunes the crystallised essence of a life, a grain for every week or so. Maesa looked at his compass often, hoping against hope that the needle would turn and point to one of the deposits, but he was disappointed. The needle aimed towards the horizon always. None of the coloured streaks were Ellamar's mortal days.

And then, the miraculous occurred. After what felt like years, and could have been, the needle on the compass twitched. Maesa stared dumbly at the device cupped in his hands. The needle was moving, swinging away from their line of travel.

'Shattercap!' said Maesa, his voice cracked from days of disuse.

'Master?' replied the spite, a breath of words no louder than the whisper of the windblown sand.

'We approach! We are near!'

Maesa spurred Aelphis into life. Huffing wearily, the king of stags lumbered into a trot.

'To the right, Aelphis! There!' said Maesa, intent upon the dial.

Their path took them closer to the line of skeletons. At last, the source of the animates' burdens became apparent. Where realmstone gathered most thickly, a depression had been carved.

Within the bowl of a great quarry, the two lines of skeletons joined into one. They entered, looped round, bent without slowing to peck at the sand, then walked around the back of the bowl and thence out again, carrying their dot of treasure away to their master. In the dim starlight, Maesa spied many such pits, some worked out, some alive with the flash of dead bones.

A moment of horror gripped him. If Ellamar's sands were in one of those pits…

Relief came from the compass. It span a little to the left, then as Aelphis followed, to the right. The compass rotated slowly around and around. Maesa brought Aelphis to a halt and slid from his back.

Sand shifted under his feet. Rivulets of it ran from the dunes' sides to fill his footsteps. The grey dust comprised the lesser part of it, much was realmstone. Many colours were mingled there. Many lives blended.

The prince stooped low, the compass held to the sand. By lifting individual grains to the compass rose and watching its spin, he ascertained that Ellamar's life was of an indigo hue. One grain set the compass twirling sharply. A handful made it blur.

'Fitting,' he said. 'Indigo was her favourite colour.' He took out the last of the life water, and roused the spite. 'Shattercap.'

'Good prince?'

'We shall finish this. We shall need all our strength. The servants of Nagash will come.' He took a sip, gave a drink to Shattercap, and then tipped the last of the water into Aelphis' mouth. The stag huffed and stood taller as vitality returned.

'Help me. Pluck up this indigo sand.' He drew out the hourglass from his saddlebags and placed it on the desert floor. He opened up the lid. 'Fill it up. Carefully. Not one other grain, only hers.'

When lowered to the sand, Shattercap mewled. 'It burns me, master!'

'Bear the pain, and you shall be four steps closer to freedom,' said the prince sternly. 'Hurry!'

Together the aelf and spite worked, fastidiously plucking single grains of the glittering sand from the dust and depositing them in the hourglass.

The bottom bulb was almost full, and the grains becoming harder to sift from the rest, when a piercing shriek rose over the desert.

Shattercap's head whipped up. His hands opened and closed nervously.

'Master…' he whimpered. 'We are noticed.'

Another shriek sounded, then a third, each one nearer than the last. The ceaseless, gentle wind of the desert gusted fiercely.

'Fill it, spite!' commanded Maesa. He drew the Song of Thorns. The woody edge of the living sword sparked with starlight. 'Get it all. I shall hold them back.'

Howling with outrage, a wraith came flying over the ridge of a nearby dune. It had no legs, but trailed streamers of magic from black robes in place of lower limbs. Its face was a skull locked into a permanent roar. Its hands bore a scythe. This, unlike the aethereal bearer, was solid enough, a shaft of worm-eaten wood and a blade of rusted metal with a terrible bite. Other wraiths came skimming over the sands, their corpse-light shining from the tiny jewels of other creatures' lives.

The first wraith raised its weapon, and bore down on the prince. Moving with the grace native to all aelves, Maesa sidestepped and with a single precise cut, sliced the spirit in two. It screamed its last, the shreds of its soul sucked within the Song of Thorns. Another came, swooping around and around Aelphis and Maesa before plunging arrow-swift at the prince. Maesa was faster, and ended it. The Song of Thorns glowed with the power of the stolen spirits.

More wraiths were coming. A chorus of shrieks sounded from every direction. The undead burst from the sand, they swooped down from the sky. The watchdogs of Nagash were alert for thieves taking their master's property, and responded to the alarm with alacrity.

'Quickly, Shattercap!'

Maesa slew another, and another. The Song of Thorns was anathema to things such as the wraiths, but there were hundreds of them gathering in a tempest of phantoms. The spite scrabbled at the ground, his earlier finesse gone as he shovelled Ellamar's life sands into the glass.

'Be careful not to mix the grains!' the prince shouted, cleaving the head of another wraith from its owner.

'I am trying!' squeaked the spite.

'I cannot fight all these things,' said Maesa. He was right. Now the wraiths saw the danger the Song of Thorns posed, they turned their attacks against Aelphis and Shattercap, and it took all of Maesa's skill to keep them from harm. Aelphis reared and pawed at the wraiths, but all he could do was deflect their weapons from his hide. When his hooves hit their bodies, they passed through, leaving wakes of glowing mist.

'I have it all!' said Shattercap, ducking the raking hand of a wraith. He slammed closed the lid atop the hourglass.

'You are sure? You have checked the compass?'

'Yes!' squealed Shattercap.

The prince danced around the stag, snatching up hourglass and compass in one hand while killing with the other. Shattercap leapt from the sand to the prince's arm. Maesa jumped onto the back of the stag, cutting away the head of a scythe in mid-air, then reversing his stroke as he landed in the saddle to render another phantom into shreds of ectoplasm.

Aelphis reared. Maesa slashed from left to right. Braying loudly, the stag leapt forward.

Invigorated by Ghyran's waters of life, Aelphis ran as fast as the wind. The wraiths set up pursuit, and more streamed from the depths of the desert to join them. Maesa slew all that came against him. He cried out when a scythe blade nicked his arm, numbing it with the grave's chill. The wraiths screeched to see his discomfort and they closed in for the kill, but Maesa yelled the war cries of his ancestors and fought on.

It seemed as if the great stag flew. The wraiths were outpaced. Their dark shapes were left behind. No more came from the wastes.

Aelphis ran on. Light grew ahead. The vastness of the Sands of Grief were coming to an end. Desert of a more ordinary sort blended into its edges. At last, Maesa came to a place where dawn stood still upon the edge of the world, and pale sun lit upon his face. At the margins of a wadi, dry grasses rattled in the wind – life had returned. They had gone far from the lines of skeletons and their ghoulish mines. Maesa brought Aelphis to a stop.

The stag snorted. Froth lathered his skin. He shuddered from antlers to tail, spraying foam across the rocks, then settled, and blared out his throaty call in pleasure at their escape.

Maesa held up the hourglass. He looked with wonder at the indigo sand within.

'The first part of the task is done,' he said. 'With this, when Ellamar returns, she will not age. She will be forever at my side.'

'Yes, my master,' said Shattercap. 'But the Lord of Undeath will not rest until he has brought you to account for your crime, and we must find a way to steal her back from whatever place she languishes within first.'

'Let Nagash's servants come,' said Maesa. He sheathed the

Song of Thorns. It vibrated with strange warmth from its feast, passing its strength into him. 'I will be ready. You did well, Shattercap. You are learning.'

'Learning to be good?'

'Learning to be useful. Goodness comes later.'

'Thank you, kind prince,' said the spite. He snuggled down into Maesa's hood. But though his words were fawning, his heart retained a little flinty wickedness. His tiny fist was clenched. In it he held a single grain of Ellamar's soul dust, kept for himself.

Unaware of his companion's thievery, Maesa set his joyous face into the dawn, and rode out full of hope.

SHADESPIRE: THE MIRRORED CITY
by Josh Reynolds

Amidst the ruins of the once-great Mirrored City, ex-Freeguild soldier
Seguin Rayner and his allies seek secrets – but even if they retrieve
them, can they ever escape Shadespire?

For these stories and more go to **blacklibrary.com**, **games-workshop.com**, Games Workshop
and Warhammer stores, all good book stores or visit one of the thousands of independent
retailers worldwide, which can be found at **games-workshop.com/storefinder**

THE WITCH
TAKERS

C L Werner

Mangled bodies lay stretched under the blazing desert sun. Puddles of blood glistened in the light. The gory litter lay scattered in a patch of carnage dozens of yards wide, broken weapons and severed limbs half buried in the scale-like metal sands of Droost.

In the very midst of the havoc, an ugly pit yawned. The piles of sand and broken stone marked it as a recent excavation. The jumble of old bones and rusted armour strewn about the opening served as silent testament to the callous looting of the uncovered tomb.

'Tal, is there anything down there?' The question was voiced by a tall and powerfully built woman. Long locks of deep golden hair peaked out from under the hood of the white cloak Esselt wore. There was an expression of deep concern on her well-defined features. Her gloved hands kept a firm grip on the immense silver-bladed greatsword she held at her side.

In response to Esselt's query, a man emerged from the

shadowy tomb. He was more compactly built, wolfish in form and a few inches shorter. He, too, wore a white cloak, though it was now greyed with the dust and grit of an ancient grave. His face had a pinched, almost hungry look to it, his moustached lip drawn back in irritation. Keen eyes studied the broken stones where robbers had smashed their way into the crypt. With a sigh, Talorcan shook his head.

'Nothing, Esselt,' he declared. He waved his gloved hand at the bodies strewn all around them. 'Vulture scum they may have been, but they were very thorough. I don't think there is so much as a strand of hair they didn't drag out of there.' He stepped over to one of the corpses, a body more complete than some of its mutilated companions. With the edge of his boot he kicked it onto its side. As it rolled over, a brand on the dead man's forehead was revealed. A single hieroglyph depicting the slouching figure of a hyena.

'The brand of thieves,' Esselt observed. 'The same as the man we found in Skra Voln.' A hardness swept into her voice. 'This is where the murderers came from.'

Talorcan inspected the ground, carefully noting the disturbances in the sand. 'Only one set of tracks lead away from here. From here to Skra Voln... and the massacre.' As he made his study of the bodies, he began removing objects from them. A bronze breastplate, a jewelled dagger, rings and necklaces. From one man's fingers he pried away a vicious-looking sword.

'Grave robbers who argued over their plunder,' Esselt growled. 'After murdering their comrades, the rest must have gone to Skra Voln to slake their bloodlust.'

'Only one set of tracks,' Talorcan reminded her. 'When we reached Skra Voln, except for the herdsman who discovered the massacre, there was only one set of tracks going into the village.' He turned the sword around so that Esselt could see what he had discovered. The grip of the sword was formed from a gnarled curl of bone, but its pommel was fashioned from blackened steel.

Instinctively, Esselt drew back, alarm shining in her eyes. She recognised the grisly symbol the pommel had been shaped into. None of the witch takers of the Order of Azyr were unaware of the Skull Rune, emblem of the Chaos God, Khorne.

'Grace of Sigmar, Tal!' Esselt cursed.

'This is the madness of the Blood God,' Talorcan said, gesturing at the carnage around them. 'Looks like this tomb was something more than the robbers bargained for. The grave of some champion of the Dark Gods. When they broke in here, they unleashed something. Some infernal force that provoked them to... this.'

Esselt shook her head. 'And the victor carried his murdering frenzy with him to Skra Voln. Praise the God-King the evil died with him.'

Talorcan was looking at the collection of grave goods he had removed from the thieves. Every body had yielded up something. 'When we examined the branded corpse in Skra Voln, there was nothing that was remarkable about him. No treasure that could have come from this tomb.'

'No,' Esselt said. 'There was nothing. Only the tattered rags he was wearing.' She looked at the pile of loot Talorcan had gathered. 'Every man had his share. The thief at the oasis should have had something.'

'But he didn't,' Talorcan stated, a haunted look stealing into his eyes. He suddenly dashed across the sands to where they had hobbled their animals. The demi-gryphs squawked in protest as he rummaged through the saddle bags. Finally, he found what he was looking for: a big metal flask with a dragonhide stopper. He returned hurriedly, removing the stopper from the flask and dousing the pile of grave goods with its contents. Metal and jewels began to smoke and bubble as the alchemical concoction spilled onto them.

'We will destroy this filth,' Talorcan said. 'Then we must make haste back to Skra Voln.' He gave Esselt a grim look. 'I fear I followed the wrong trail. I wanted to see where the killer came from. I did not think to follow any trail leading away from Skra Voln.'

'You believe someone survived the massacre?' Esselt asked.

'A survivor or someone who came upon the scene before the herdsmen did,' Talorcan said. 'Either way, whoever it was took something.'

'The killer's share of the treasure,' Esselt stated, watching as the other plunder was swiftly reduced to a molten puddle. 'Some cursed relic from a heretic's tomb.'

Talorcan nodded, looking across the havoc around them. 'Something from the grave of a champion of the Blood God. Something damned by the filth of Chaos. Something that could possess a man and make him ferocious enough to commit such atrocities. Something that may pass its curse along to whoever carries it.'

Esselt shaded her eyes as she looked across the vast dunes of Droost. To her it was like watching a sea of crawling silver. The blazing sun shimmered across the thin scales of metal that composed the sand. Despite the heat, a chill swept through her as she watched the wispy haze that rose from the hot ground.

'It looks like water,' she said, leaning around in her saddle to speak with Talorcan.

'Many a traveller has thought so,' Talorcan said. 'Drawn on by the mirage. Parched brains imagining the illusion of rivers and lakes just beyond their reach.' He shook his head. 'A terrible end for anyone.'

'And if I were to get lost out here?' Esselt nudged him in the arm. 'Don't say you couldn't find me, Tal. You're almost as much a part of the desert as the dust-vipers.'

Talorcan was pensive a moment. 'I might find you,' he said. 'But it would have to wait until the Order's business is finished.' He drew back as Esselt tried to swat him. 'I'm only warning you to stay close until our work is done,' he laughed.

'When our work is done, you won't have much to laugh about,' Esselt promised, patting the greatsword sheathed along the side of the saddle.

Talorcan smiled. 'An assignation then,' he said. 'I'll hold you to it. You might have the advantage with that gargant-sticker of yours, but never forget that I fight dirty.'

Esselt gave him a sharp look. 'You also cheat at cards. But if we're going to discuss all of your faults we'll be out here until the rainy season.'

Talorcan bowed in defeat and turned his eyes back to the landscape before them. From atop the summit of a scaly dune, he gazed out across the crawling desert and the rippling haze. They were no strangers to the great wasteland that encompassed the Khanate of Arlk. The cloaks that covered them were fashioned from the porous hide of the dune-jackal and bleached to a brilliant white to better defy the sun's heat. The talons of the demi-gryphs they rode were swathed in thick moccasins to keep them from sinking into the scaly sands. A third demi-gryph followed close behind them, the creature's beak muzzled by a mask of steel chain so that it could not twist its long neck around and snap at the burden lashed across its back – a keg of stout Varthian blackoak filled with water from the River Chael.

The witch hunters were silent for a time, intent upon their study of the surroundings. When the silence was broken, it was Esselt who spoke, her voice edged with frustration. The tomb of the Chaos chieftain and the massacre of Skra Voln were many days behind them, yet still their quarry was beyond their reach. 'They cannot have gone much farther, Tal,' she declared. 'By the Light of Azyr, we should have come upon them already.'

Talorcan kept his eyes roving across the dunes, watching the rippling heat rising from the scaly sands. 'By the Light of Azyr, we will find them,' he said. 'Skill and determination can lead a hunter only so far. After that it becomes a test of faith.' One of his hands released its hold on his demi-gryph's reins and pointed across the dunes. 'There. Do you see? Where the mirage falters?'

Esselt followed Talorcan's gesture, her own eyes narrowing as she spotted the disruption of the heatwaves. There was only one thing that could distort the sun's effect upon the dunes, and that was some object blocking its rays from the metallic sands. There were some nomads who could track a hare by the faintest chink in the haze.

'Your observation, as ever, surpasses my own. If you say there is some sign, I believe you, my love,' Esselt said. Her face dropped into an expression of gravity. 'Please to Sigmar God-King we have found our quarry.'

Talorcan nodded his head, his voice taking a sombre turn. 'We do Sigmar's work. He is always with us.' He reached to the hammer-shaped amulet that hung from the clasp of his cloak. 'But there are other powers and they are in opposition to our work. Where faith is weak, the Dark Gods prevail.'

'Our faith is as sharp as our blades.' Esselt once again patted the immense sword hanging from the saddle sheath beside her. A flicker of a smile crossed her face as she peered intently at Talorcan. 'Or do you question my sincerity?'

'I would not dare,' Talorcan said, looking to Esselt and returning her smile. For a fleeting instant, the grim duty ahead of them was forgotten. Then his demi-gryph started down the incline of the dune and the onerous nature of their task resumed its primacy.

They could not know what they would find at the end of the trail, but of one thing Esselt and Talorcan were certain: there would be death. That was the one constant in the work of witch hunters.

He was dying. Perhaps he should be dead already. He wanted to die. He wanted to just lie down and let Black Nagash have him.

But to live or die was no longer his choice. A burning, snarling compulsion drove him on. His breath was a reedy rasp that seared his lungs, yet still he persisted. His muscles felt like they would rip through his skin, yet still he kept walking. Blood, yes, blood. It dripped and trickled, oozing from his wounds. So much blood. How could there be any left in his veins? How could there be enough to keep his heart pumping?

The demand that roared inside him would not let him stop. He could not pull out the spear-shaft that was lodged in his chest. He could not tie off the sword-slash that left his back open from shoulder to hip. He could not see from the eye that had been crushed when a mace had caved in the side of his head. Still, it would not let him die.

There was a terrible imperative that forced him onwards. Only when it was satisfied could he relent. Until then, he would stumble on through the dunes, lost and damned.

Tears glistened in his remaining eye. He wanted to die so badly. He deserved to die. The things he had done... atrocity! He had no right to draw that next breath.

But draw it he did. And the next. And the one after that. The compulsion kept him moving. Up and down the crawling dunes, defying the desert heat and the ghastly wounds.

Through the desolation, at last a sight greeted him. The force driving him on became ferocious. Hungrily it urged him to greater effort, compelling him towards... something? No. Some*one*.

He tried to stop himself when he understood. He tried to throw the damned treasure away, to cast it out among the dunes where it should never be found. He didn't have that kind of strength now. He only had the strength his destroyer allowed him to have.

The nomad spotted him. He saw the robed man draw a sword and watch him with wary eyes. The force driving him onwards exulted. It had no need of him now. The strength it had been dragging out of him evaporated and he crumpled. Almost lifeless, he slid down the dune towards the stranger.

His vision was already fading. He didn't see the nomad, but he felt the boot that prodded his side. A moment later he felt the hands roving across his body. Frantically, he tried to warn the nomad, but all that escaped his lips was a gargled rasp.

The last thing he heard as his life drained from him was the nomad walking away. Death, so long denied, closed around him, conveying his spirit not to the morbid halls of Nagash but to a realm of blood and skulls.

Everywhere Talorcan looked the sand-like metal scales were stained a dull crimson, blotting out both their shine and the eerie animation that set the dunes of Droost crawling across the wastes. The unblemished scales about the blighted region shivered their way over the gory spectacle, creeping around the destruction.

'Massacre,' Esselt declared the site as she gazed down upon it. Boxes and bundles lay scattered about the depression between two dunes, strewn as though by a petulant gargant. The tatters of tents and pavilions fluttered in the hot desert breeze. Carcasses of immense draft-lizards quivered on their backs, their sluggish nerves still tugging at the muscles of their slaughtered bodies. Smaller bodies were littered about the scene, so covered in their own gore that it was impossible to tell simple drover from wealthy caravaneer.

'By the Hammer, we are too late,' Talorcan growled. He tried to urge his steed down into the depression, but the demi-gryph balked at his commands. The creature threw back its head and crackled an anxious cry. Annoyed, he dismounted and trudged down the crawling slope to reach the grisly scene. Throwing back his hood, Talorcan kneeled beside a small body, carefully folding what was left of its hands across its breast.

Esselt followed Talorcan down, leaving her own steed with the other animals. In her hands she carried the massive greatsword she had taken from her saddle. The silver blade glistened in the afternoon light, the sacred runes etched across its length shining like golden flames. The holy sword had been forged by the armourers of the Order of Azyr and thrice-blessed by no less than High Priest Crautreic himself. She had used the weapon many times to strike down the obscene daemons and mutated monsters of Chaos, but as she looked across the massacred caravan, the desire to visit justice and judgement with the edge of her sword burned more fiercely in her heart than ever before.

'How many?' Talorcan shook his head and looked up at Esselt. His face was lean and hard, browned by the desert sun, weathered by the horrors he had unearthed and combated for so long.

'Three nomad camps, one village, and now this caravan.' Esselt stepped to Talorcan's side and laid her hand on his shoulder. 'I've been with you a long time, Tal. I know whatever atrocities you've been confronted by have not caused you to waver. You have never failed to see Sigmar's justice meted out. It doesn't matter how many it has claimed.' An edge crept into her voice, a tone of menace that promised vengeance for the fiend they sought. 'All that matters is we keep it from taking any more.'

Talorcan closed his hand around Esselt's, drawing comfort from her reassurance and her determination. 'I will track this fiend to the gates of Shadowfell if needs must,' he vowed.

'Perhaps it is dead already,' Esselt said. She drew Talorcan's attention to one of the bodies lying nearby, a corpse wearing the mail hauberk of a mercenary. Clenched in his hand was a bloodied scimitar. A little further on, another armoured body gripped a spear with its head snapped off. 'The killer didn't find such helpless victims this time. These people fought back.'

'No,' Talorcan stated, releasing her hand and rising to his feet. 'It isn't here. If it was, we would know it. The Order of Azyr has trained us to sense the corruption of Chaos. We would sense its taint, feel it crying out for new victims. The evil is gone. It has gone to seek new prey. To lurk unsuspected until its hunger is aroused.' He stood and began stalking about the scene. Crouched over, his face peering intently at the ground, his hand brushing across the scaly sands. He looked at the footprints scattered about the havoc, trying to pick from the marks left by victims and killer. At length he found a track that steered away from the murder site. As he pursued it towards the farther dunes, he shouted to Esselt.

'The trail will be easy to follow,' Talorcan declared. 'The ground on the slope of the dune bears similar discolourations. Faint, but obvious enough if you know what you are looking for.'

Esselt stood above the small body Talorcan had first inspected. She repressed the empathy the corpse evoked, her mind processing the sight with the cold practicality demanded of all witch hunters. 'No vultures have been around,' she observed. 'Not even a hint of bloat-moths sucking at the wounds.'

Talorcan managed a smile. Despite the grim circumstances, he was proud Esselt had learned so much from his teaching. 'Bloat-moths would already have laid eggs if they were here. That means these bodies have not been here overnight. At best this happened in the morning. The killer cannot have gone far.'

Esselt's fingers tightened on the grip of her sword. Her eyes roved across the carnage. 'I ask few favours of you, Tal, but I ask for one now. When we find this thing, I want to be the one who brings it the doom it has earned.'

Three hours riding across the crawling dunes of Droost brought the witch hunters to yet another morbid scene. From the crest of one dune, a dark shape sprawled in the sand. Crimson-stained blemishes along the slope of the dune gave vivid evidence of where the body had initially fallen and rolled its way downwards.

Cautiously the witch hunters dismounted and approached the gore-spattered body. Talorcan threw back the folds of his cloak, drawing sword and pistol from his weapon belt. The blade he bore was smaller and slighter than the one Esselt carried, a weapon made for finesse and speed. The pistol was a silver-barrelled device fitted to a frame of sacred shimmerwood. The charge within was derived from an alchemical powder, the shot itself a ball of silver bathed in the holy unguents of Sigmar's temple. Talorcan kept his sword held out to one side and aimed the pistol at the body's head.

Esselt stepped closer, both hands locked on her weapon. Her

strength, the brutal impact of the silver greatsword she carried, the heavy armour she wore under her cloak, drove her to investigate the grisly carcass. Talorcan's forte was the quickness of his reflexes. Coupled with the reach of his pistol, it made sense for him to provide cover for Esselt.

The wounds that afflicted the body were almost beyond measure. Esselt could count at least five that should have been mortal blows. The caravan had fought hard, even if their efforts had not been enough to save them. Keeping a wary eye on the body, she kicked it over onto its side. For a moment she watched it, waiting for some kind of reaction. She was about to dismiss the thing as nothing but a corpse when a sanguine glow filled the empty eyes.

In a heartbeat the thing sprang onto its feet. It rushed at Esselt with outstretched hands. Long talons were emerging from them and the clawed fingers raked across her breastplate, scraping the metal surface.

The next instant there was a cracking boom as Talorcan fired his pistol into the cadaverous thing. The shot caught the fiend in its shoulder, shattering bone and shredding flesh. A spray of dark blood and gleaming ichor flashed from the wound. The creature swung around, glaring at its new attacker. Its head was distorted beyond the vicious injuries the body had suffered in life. Great black horns were tearing their way up from beneath the scalp. Long yellow fangs pushed up from the jaws.

Talorcan readied himself for the fiend's charge, but before it could rush him it was served a violent reminder of the foe it had left behind. In a shining arc of silver, Esselt brought her sword slicing down upon the monster's neck, all but cleaving its head from its body. Smoke sizzled from the mutilating wound, ichor vaporising as it encountered the blessed residue left behind by the slashing blade. It swung back around, clashing its fangs together as it glared at Esselt. Then it collapsed against the scaly sands, the impact tearing its head free from the flap of skin that held it.

'Receive Sigmar's judgement, horror of Old Night,' Esselt recited as she stared down at the desiccated remains. The horns and other daemonic manifestations were rapidly fading into a crusty residue, leaving behind only a mangled corpse.

'A minor daemon of the Blood God,' Talorcan said as he observed the dissolution. 'I should think it took possession of this body only after the soul was gone. The flesh was seeped in the energies of Khorne, enough to act as a temporary host. Without the life-force to sustain it, the thing could not have lingered long in Chamon.'

Esselt shook her head and pointed at the bullet wound in the corpse's shoulder. 'It had vitality enough to endure being shot. The one we found outside the village withered as soon as it was struck.'

'And the host bodies we found outside the nomad camps were simply corpses,' Talorcan expanded. 'Time is the explanation to that riddle. We were farther back on the trail when we found the others.'

'Then the strength of this possession means we are close,' Esselt stated. A hard glint came into her eyes; a coldness settled upon her face.

Talorcan stepped past her and inspected the corpse. 'It isn't here,' he declared. 'Whatever damn thing was brought up from that tomb, it isn't here.'

'Someone else has it,' Esselt said. 'Like every other time, it found someone else to take it before relinquishing its previous owner.'

'Someone else has it,' Talorcan agreed. 'But we can be thankful the evil is dormant now. It lacks even the power to make its new owner cover his tracks.' He waved his empty pistol at a line of footprints that stretched out across the dunes. Already some of them had been covered by the crawling sands, but enough remained to betray a general direction.

'It is my belief that whatever devilry is within this cursed relic,' Talorcan said, 'lies dormant until something serves to provoke it. The robbers outside the cairn can be assumed to have argued over their spoils. In Skra Voln it looked as though the village had started to butcher an old draft-lizard for a feast. At every site there was some sign that violence occurred before the massacre started. The relic must be empowered by the malignity of the Blood God, and once it senses bloodshed, it uses whoever carries it to create even more to sate its hunger.'

Esselt caught at Talorcan's arm. 'How long will it remain dormant? Can we catch the new owner before the evil is aroused?'

Talorcan placed a rough hand over hers. Wrapping his fingers around her wrist, he drew her close. 'Sigmar knows we must,' he said in a sombre whisper. 'Otherwise the trail will lead us to another massacre.'

The oasis of Tora Grae was one of dozens scattered across the vast desert of Droost. Shielded from the crawling dunes by great outcroppings of copper-hued rock, Tora Grae offered succour from the blazing sun. Great stands of frond-leafed trees grew around a large pool of dark water. Tough shrubs and hardy desert grass formed an outer layer that ringed the trees, stretching to the very periphery of the rocks.

Where there was water to be found in the desert, so too would the society of man be found. Built within the outer ring of grass and shrubs, a small village had persisted for many generations. Huts woven from palm-fronds and reinforced with bartered cloth lay clustered together in a confused huddle.

Beyond the huts, herds of wiry antelope nuzzled the grass within their fenced enclosures. Huge draft-lizards basked on the tops of rocks, soaking in the warmth of the day until, sated, they crawled into the shadows of their burrows. Demi-gryphs milled about, each animal tethered by a ring fastened to its beak and fixed to a stout wooden post. Dogs and poultry roamed freely through the village, doing their best to avoid the rambunctious children who raced around the huts. The older inhabitants of the village lounged in the shade of the trees. Early morning and early evening were their hours of labour, when they would see to their flocks and gather water from the pool. The middle of the day, with the hot sun blaring down on the world, was a time for rest and repose. Only children and fools bestirred themselves at such an hour.

Scattered about the rocky outcroppings, sentries maintained a lazy watch upon the desert around Tora Grae. Their main concern was the withering scalestorms that would reach down and rip away at the dunes, driving a blinding wall of shimmering sand across the desert to smother anything in its path. A lesser but still serious worry were the raider bands who prowled the wastes. Their usual prey were the caravans, but sometimes a gang would become large and bold enough to attack a village.

When one of the sentries spotted movement through the shimmering haze, his first inclination was to dip his fingers into the water jug resting beside him and moisten his eyes. After a few blinks, he looked again. There could be no doubt, there was someone riding through the desert in the very worst of the day. Two riders leading a third animal. The sentry hesitated only long enough to assure himself there weren't others who had evaded his first sighting, then he scrambled down from his shaded perch and hurried into the village to alert his people.

* * *

As Talorcan and Esselt rode through a winding cut between the coppery rocks and onto the grassy expanse that surrounded Tora Grae, the witch hunters found themselves the centre of attention for hundreds of villagers. All the able-bodied inhabitants of the village were gathered together, hands locked around the hefts of axes and spears, the grips of swords and lizard-goads. Behind them, from the edge of the settlement itself, the very old and very young watched with anxious gazes as the strangers approached.

Talorcan looked across the assembled villagers, studying them with cold eyes, meeting the mute hostility of their own scrutiny. With a flourish he threw back the white cloak, displaying the weapons holstered on his belt, but more importantly revealing the heavy pectoral that hung across his chest. The surface of the metal plate was adorned in gold, displaying the image of a hammer centred above a pair of crossed lightning bolts. It was the mark of his chapter, the Witch Takers of Azyr.

Even in so remote a place as Tora Grae, the symbol of the witch hunters was recognised. An instant before and the villagers had been ready to fight these intruders. Now they shrank back, eyes wide with fright.

'Who is headman here?' Talorcan called out. 'I would have words with your leader.'

The crowd was silent. Though they maintained their distance, none of them had lowered their weapons. Esselt shifted around in her saddle, slowly drawing her silver-bladed greatsword. An awed murmur rose from the villagers and they withdrew several paces back, some of them stumbling as they bumped into huts and fences.

'We are the Hunters of Sigmar,' Esselt declared, letting her words linger in the air. 'We will speak with your headman,' she added as she set her sword across the front of her saddle, its bright edge glistening in the sun. 'Let him come forwards.'

An old man emerged from the midst of the crowd, his wrinkled brown body wrapped in a yellow burnoose bound about the waist by a heavy lizard-hide belt. The elder's thin fingers were closed around a wooden hammer icon, and as he came towards the witch hunters, he held the holy image out to them.

'Peace and rest be yours,' the headman said, bowing low before the riders. 'I am Morleo, leader of this community. Excuse the antagonism of my people. We did not recognise you for who you are.' He drew the icon to his lips, kissing it reverently. 'Tora Grae is dutiful in its faith. The God-King's shrine is never neglected and I myself lead the morning devotions to Great Sigmar. We embrace and abide by the sacred teachings of his strictures–'

'Into the halls of paradise the serpent of Chaos may slither,' Talorcan interrupted, warningly. His gaze roved once more across the villagers. 'We would have private conference with you. Then you will appreciate our purpose here.' His tone dropped to a low whisper that barely reached the headman's ears. 'Then you will understand the danger your people are in.'

Talorcan and Esselt followed Morleo through his village. The shrine of Sigmar stood some small way from the huts, raised up on a log platform. Only a little larger than the huts themselves, the space within the shrine allowed enough room for a small altar with a stone hammer fastened to the wall behind it. A basin of water rested to one side of the altar while on the other side was an open box with a litter of coloured stones. The blues of lapis lazuli and turquoise clustered with the yellows of amber and the greens of malachite.

'Offerings to Mighty Sigmar,' Morleo explained when he

noticed Esselt staring at the box. 'My people are not wealthy, but such small treasure as they do find they bring here to render up in gratitude to the God-King.'

Esselt turned from the box. 'Has anyone made an offering today?'

'Not that I am aware,' Morleo said. 'It is possible someone may have come without my knowing. The shrine is open to all.' An expression of almost painful regret replaced the worry that had been on his face. 'Has something been stolen? Do you think one of my people to be a thief?'

'Something has been taken,' Talorcan said, slowly walking around the shrine, 'but not from here. A foul relic from an unholy grave.'

'Our problem is twofold,' Esselt added. 'We do not know who has it, nor do we know what it is.'

Morleo scratched at his chin in confusion. 'If you do not know these things, then how do you know there is anything to look for?'

'A string of massacres that has left red sand almost to your own threshold,' Esselt growled, smacking her fist into her palm in frustration.

Talorcan glanced at her and frowned. Arriving too late to stop the slaughters was taking a toll on them both. He wished there was some comfort he could offer Esselt that wouldn't seem a mere platitude.

'Twenty days,' Talorcan told the headman. 'Twenty days we have been on the trail of this horror. It began with the grave of some chief of the Chaos hordes that once threatened the Khanate. Robbers took something from that tomb. Something saturated in the evil and madness of the Dark Gods.'

Morleo's face took on a sickly hue. 'You say that the trail has led you to Tora Grae? That a thief has brought this unclean thing here?'

'Someone has brought it here,' Talorcan said. 'The relic has a way of abandoning its owners.' His eyes were like slivers of steel as he met Morleo's gaze. 'It takes possession of them before the end and uses the one who carries it to further its evil.'

Morleo wrung his hands in despair. 'It is horrible! Monstrous! If you do not know what this thing looks like, if you do not know who carries it, then how can you find it? I cannot even lead my people away from Tora Grae for, if you are right, we would be taking the curse with us!'

Esselt stepped beside the old man, grabbing him by the shoulder. 'You will achieve nothing if you surrender to fear. Keep faith with Sigmar. Know that he has sent us here before this evil could be set loose. If you keep faith, then we will prevail.'

'This is the only settlement near the place we found the body of the last man to carry this obscene relic,' Talorcan told Morleo. 'Whoever took it from him, this is where they went. I need to see anyone who was away from the village today. Man, woman or child. We must interrogate and examine them all.'

Morleo rang the bell that hung outside the shrine, summoning the people of Tora Grae. It took little time for a crowd to gather for most of the villagers had kept nearby, both intrigued and frightened by the headman's visitors. The elder stood atop the log platform flanked by the two witch hunters as he addressed his people.

'As many of you have heard, our visitors are from Sigmar's Order of Azyr,' the old man said. 'They wish to speak with anyone who was away from Tora Grae today.' Morleo waited while the hunters and herdsmen who had left the oasis stepped out from the crowd. Some of them, intimidated by the presence of the witch hunters, needed the encouragement of family and neighbours to admit that they had been away.

Talorcan stepped down from the platform and began speaking with each villager. He watched each of them with a piercing gaze, studying their faces for any trace of duplicity. His questions were simple. Had any of them found a dead man in the desert? Had someone taken something from the body?

Still upon the platform, Esselt was able to see more of the villagers than Talorcan. The questions he posed to the hunters and herdsmen were heard by those further away. At the very fringe of the group who had left the oasis, one of the hunters showed increasing signs of agitation. He kept looking at Talorcan, then hastily averting his eyes. Sweat beaded his brow and he kept fidgeting, kicking his feet in the dirt.

Esselt knew guilt when she saw it, and the simple hunter wasn't crafty enough to hide his. Carrying her sword with her, she dropped down and pushed her way through the crowd. 'Talorcan,' she called to her partner. 'No need for more questions. The one we want is here.' The hunter's face went pale as the armoured woman strode towards him.

'I think you have something to tell us,' Esselt said as she closed upon the hunter. She held her greatsword over one shoulder, her stern gaze boring down upon the man.

'I didn't kill him,' the hunter sputtered. 'By the Hammer, he was dead already!'

Talorcan circled around to one side of the hunter. He threw back the folds of his cloak, keeping his weapons in easy reach. 'The man you found is of less concern to us than what he was carrying,' he said, his words quick and sharp. 'We want what you took from him.'

'He was dead,' the hunter insisted. 'What good would it have done to just leave something so pretty to be lost in the sand?'

'Fool,' Esselt snapped. 'Do you have any idea what you are trifling with? What did you take?'

Talorcan was studying the hunter closely, but his eyes suddenly shifted from him to the crowd watching them from the village. He saw a woman, lissom and youthful, with an almost frantic expression on her face. He saw something more. Something that was out of place in a simple village like Tora Grae. Around her arm was a bronze armlet adorned with an immense girasol. The red opal was bigger than any he had seen in the courts of Arlk, bigger than the diamond that adorned the khan's turban.

'Esselt,' Talorcan hissed. 'He doesn't have it. He gave it away!'

Before Talorcan could move towards the woman wearing the armlet, the hunter dashed ahead of him. 'Please!' he cried. 'Leave her alone. I will get it for you.'

Reaching the woman, the hunter begged her to hand over the armlet before there was further trouble. She drew back from him, one hand closing protectively around the armband. Seeing her resistance, Esselt and Talorcan drew nearer.

'Stay calm,' Talorcan said. 'We only want the relic.'

The woman either didn't hear or didn't believe Talorcan's words. Her efforts to pull away became more desperate. The hunter tried to soothe his lover's fright, but his words, too, went ignored. The woman grew more panicked the closer Esselt and Talorcan came towards her. Her attempts to flee only made the hunter more frantic to get the armlet away from her. The other villagers retreated from her vicinity, alarmed by the conflict but more frightened by the attention the witch takers were showing in the woman.

'Get away from her,' Esselt warned the hunter. 'The relic is dangerous.' The greatsword was no longer resting across her shoulder but was clutched tightly in both hands as she took another step towards the woman.

'Please! I'll get it for you! Don't hurt her!' the hunter pleaded.

Desperation made his effort to get the armlet away from his lover violent. In his move to wrest the armband free, the rough edge of the bronze ripped open the palm of his hand. Blood gushed from the wound, streaming down the woman's arm.

The huge girasol began to glow with a hellish light. A hideous chill swept through the village. Grass wilted. Breath turned to frost. A charnel stink filled the air, the stench of busy abattoirs and old battlefields.

'Get away from her!' Esselt shouted a second time. The warning came too late. Even if the hunter had intended to listen to her, the hand of his lover closed around his arm in a steely grip. He looked into the woman's face, screaming when he found her eyes vanishing beneath a glaze of blood. Crimson tears ran down her face as her mouth curled back and long fangs sprouted from her gums. The cursed woman's other arm drew back, slamming her fist into his chest with such colossal force that it erupted from his back in a spray of blood and splintered bone.

Terror raced through the village. The crowd parted, scattering in every direction. Morleo cried in horror and fled into the Sigmarite shrine. Animals bleated and howled in their pens, trying to trample through their enclosures. Dogs and chickens fled out into the desert, yelping and shrieking. Even the trees of the oasis seemed to shudder as the profane power of Khorne was unleashed.

The possessed woman moved with ghastly speed and power. In one swift motion she peeled her dead hunter from her clawed hand, casting the carcass aside like an old glove. Bones could be seen shifting and changing beneath her skin and clothes, a fringe of spikes stabbing out from her shoulders and spine. Hideous knots of muscle swelled around her arms and bulged from her legs while her face elongated into a lupine muzzle.

'Butcher of Khorne!' Talorcan shouted, firing his pistol

into the monster. 'By Sigmar, you will kill no more!' The shot smashed against the thing's breast, burrowing through to the heart. The shot alone would have finished a mortal, the blessings on the bullet should have vanquished a daemon. The awful power of the thing the witch hunters faced was that it was neither mortal nor daemon, but rather the murderous legacy of the ancient chieftain made flesh.

With steaming ichor spilling from the bullet wound, the abomination turned on Talorcan. It sprang at him like a rabid jackal, crimson froth dripping from its fangs. One clawed hand slashed for his face. Talorcan matched the incredible speed of his foe, bringing his sword licking across the mutated arm. A deep furrow was gouged into the corrupted flesh; bestial fingers were hewn from the gnarled hand. Yet the beast was oblivious to its hurt and its attack did not falter. Talorcan was thrown back as the maimed limb smashed into him. Unable to penetrate his armour, the blow still had enough force to send him flying. He crashed down on his back, almost cracking his skull against the edge of the log platform.

'Leave him!' Esselt's cry rang through the air, so fierce it rose even above the screams of the villagers. She charged at the possessed creature, bringing her greatsword chopping down in a vicious arc. The thing snarled in fury of its own as the silvered sword chewed through its neck and sent its head slopping to the ground.

Esselt turned away from the mangled thing as it slumped to its knees. She looked for Talorcan, alarm in her eyes. He managed to sit up, making a dismissive wave of his arm to allay her concerns. Esselt was hardly reassured. She knew he would conceal the gravity of any injury from her in order to calm her fears. Slinging her greatsword up onto her shoulder, she started towards Talorcan.

It was Talorcan's face that suddenly became twisted with fear. Eyes wide with horror, he thrust his hand and pointed. 'Esselt – behind!' he shouted.

Even as Esselt turned, the headless fiend attacked. Far from vanquished, its claws came sweeping down, scratching across her vambrace and tearing away her pauldron. She dived to the ground to avoid the vicious talons. She struck hard against the earth, kicking up a cloud of dust. She scuttled back as the dust settled and found herself staring into the grisly eyes of the fiend's severed head. The monster noticed her, rolling its eyes and gnashing its fangs as it tried vainly to strike at her. Then a feral grin contorted its visage. The eyes stared upwards. It was warning enough for Esselt. Rolling across the ground she avoided the slashing claws of the thing's body by the narrowest margin. Strips of shredded cloak fluttered upon the beast's talons when it stalked after her.

Esselt had no intention of running from the possessed monster. Once she was clear of its reach, she regained her feet and waited for her opportunity. Removing the beast's head had not killed it, but at least it had slowed the creature down, made its movements less agile. When it failed to strike her with another sweep of its claws, she lunged at its body. Esselt drove her sword deep into the thing's side. With a brutal wrenching motion, she tore the blade free, tearing open a great gash from sternum to flank. A confusion of entrails spilled from the wound, flopping against the monster's legs in a welter of gore.

Still the fiend would not fall. The back of its hand slammed into Esselt, sending her reeling. The headless horror came after her, relentless as a juggernaut.

At the base of the platform, Talorcan rallied. His head ringing from his violent impact, all pain was banished when he saw Esselt. A wave of dread seized him. Snatching up his sword from the ground, he staggered to where the decapitated head lay. The thing glared at him, clacking its fangs together in a display of mute fury. Then he brought his sword crunching down into the mutated skull. Twisting the blade, he bisected the head, the two halves sizzling as the ichor within them steamed away.

Unlike the discarded hosts they had found before, destroying the head was not enough to end the monster's rampage. Talorcan saw the headless body lunge at Esselt once again, its claws just missing her face. Then he spotted the armlet still fastened around the beast's arm, the girasol still ablaze with hellish light.

'The relic!' Talorcan shouted. 'That is its power!'

Esselt gave no sign of hearing Talorcan's cry, but her actions showed that she understood. When the monster came at her again, she ducked beneath its talons and attacked it from the side. The cleaving edge of her silvered sword smashed down on the thing's shoulder, cutting through bone, muscle and tendon. The arm went rolling across the ground. Esselt was sent spinning through the dirt as the monster's remaining hand caught hold of her cloak and flung her backwards.

Talorcan hurried towards the severed arm. The fingers were scratching at the earth, trying to flip the limb over so it could drag itself back into the fray. He stamped down on its palm, pinning it in place. His eyes stared down at the armlet locked about the bicep, the ghastly girasol still aglow with infernal power. Taking his sword in both hands, he brought it chopping down, striking the ancient bronze in which the gem was set.

A mighty howl roared across Tora Grae as the armlet was severed and the girasol was sent tumbling away from its host. At once the unnatural cold and gory scent that had descended upon the oasis was banished. The headless monster that only a moment before had been ready to attack Esselt now slumped to its knees. Esselt prodded it with her sword and it fell onto its side, already losing its monstrous proportions. Soon it wilted into the maimed body of a young woman.

Talorcan reached to his belt and removed a strip of golden cloth from one of its pouches. Carefully he set the cloth over the loosened girasol, noting with some dismay the way the cloth darkened when it came into contact with the gem. He didn't ponder the phenomenon for long. Turning from the cursed relic, he staggered over to where Esselt stood above the carcass of their late enemy.

'Are you harmed?' Talorcan asked, his voice heavy with concern.

Esselt gave her companion an appraising look and raised an eyebrow. 'I think I should be asking you that question, Tal,' she told him.

'Nothing that won't heal,' Talorcan said. He tried to smile, but the effort was ruined by a wince of pain. 'I am more ashamed than hurt. I thought I had some idea of what we were up against, but the first thing you should never forget is that Chaos obeys few rules in its manifestations.'

Esselt removed what was left of her cloak and draped it across the mangled remains of the woman's body. 'What matters is that our faith in Sigmar brought us victory,' she said. 'How many times have we visited judgement on the filth of the Dark Gods? It will need more than a cursed bauble to overcome us.'

Talorcan looked back at the cloth he'd set over the girasol. The golden colour had turned a deep scarlet, almost the colour of clotted blood. 'It still has power and I am not sure it is safe to carry back to the temple for disposal.'

'What do we do with it then?' Esselt asked. 'We can't just leave it.'

'No, we can't,' Talorcan agreed. His gaze turned to the little shrine of Sigmar. 'But maybe we won't need to take it away with us.'

* * *

It was late the next day when the witch hunters left Tora Grae. The cool of dusk would soon descend upon the desert of Droost and the keen-eyed demi-gryphs would be able to pick their way across the dunes by moonlight as easily as they could by sunlight. With a long journey between themselves and the temple complex of Vorthion, Esselt and Talorcan were eager to avoid as much of the daytime heat as they could.

The villagers watched them ride away from the tops of the barrier rocks. They had seen enough of the fight to know the peril they had been saved from. The witch hunters had their gratitude if not their adoration. Even for simple desert folk it was difficult to be at ease knowing the Order of Azyr was watching.

Old Morleo didn't join his people on the rocks. Instead he was crouched inside the shrine, bowing his head before the altar and praying to Sigmar that Talorcan and Esselt would have a safe journey. The basin to one side of the altar was empty now and on the morrow he would have to bring up a new supply from the pool to bless in Sigmar's holy name.

The box of offerings at the other side of the shrine was a little fuller than it had been before. There was a new stone there, a plain and withered-looking thing. All that remained of the brilliant girasol after it had been drowned in holy water and offered up to Sigmar.

All that was left of Khorne's obscene relic once the Blood God's malice was removed.

THE TAINTED HEART
by C L Werner

Amidst a deadly blight that has engulfed the Realm of Metal, witch
hunters Talocarn and Esselt pursue a cultist whose bloody trail leads
them into danger – and a possible solution, if they can survive…

For these stories and more go to **blacklibrary.com**, **games-workshop.com**, Games Workshop
and Warhammer stores, all good book stores or visit one of the thousands of independent
retailers worldwide, which can be found at **games-workshop.com/storefinder**

THE PRISONER OF
THE BLACK SUN

Josh Reynolds

I still endure.

I still stand.

This realm is mine.

Spiders have spun their webs across my eyes, and worms burrow in my chest. But I still live. I yet stand against my enemies. I shall always do so, for I can do naught else. My will gutters and flares, like a fire newly stoked. The Great Necromancer awakens.

I still endure.

The Three-Eyed King crushed the ranks of my servants. His daemon-blade shattered my bones, and cleaved my heart in two. My rites and magics were torn asunder, my power broken on the altar of fate. My body was left to the dust, and to the dust I returned. My soul fell shrieking into the darkness as a black comet, streaking across the underworld, and the impact of it cracked the roots of this world.

I still endure.

Nagashizzar is toppled. Its great towers and basalt pillars are dust. Where it once stood, there is now only broken earth; in the streets where a thousand warriors marched, the only sound to be heard is the wailing of jackals.

Yet I still endure.

I have pulled down the sun, cracking the seals of the underworld, and dried the seas and burned the grasses. I have humbled my enemies and cast the earth into the sky, walking to and fro in the deep places, and still I am returned.

Nagash has risen.

Something stirs in the wild places of all that which is mine. Some power, stinking of the storm, comes slinking into my demesnes. I sit upon my throne in starless Stygxx and feel it rising all about me, drawing to it that which is mine. Souls slip my grasp, spirits flee my voice. Thieves and invaders stalk my realm. They think me gone.

I still endure.

Heed me. Listen to my words, those of you who have the wit to hear. The Realm of Death is my body. Its caverns are my bones, its peaks my crown. The realm is as large as my word, as small as my wish. I bestride the seas of the east, and shatter the mountains of the west. My throne is in the north, and my shadow in the south. Wherever you so seek, I am there. Wherever you make worship, so Nagash strides.

Whosoever believes in me, whosoever follows my will, the will of Nagash, shall prosper. I have awakened, and my enemies shall know my name again. Seek out my foes, and make them yours. Seek out these thieves, and take from them as they have taken from me.

Hear me. Heed me.

Listen, and be joyful.

Nagash is all, and all are one in Nagash.

Nagash has risen.

* * *

Tarsus, Lord-Celestant of the Hallowed Knights, gave voice to a full-throated bellow. He brought his hammer down on the crimson helm of a howling bloodreaver and the warrior fell, its skull split in two. Tarsus whirled to open the belly of a second opponent, the sword he held in his other hand slashing in a deadly arc. His weapons crackled with holy lightning as he struck out left and right, dropping foemen with every blow.

'Who will be victorious?' he roared.

'Only the faithful,' came the reply, from the small host of Stormcasts that streamed in his wake. Liberators, Prosecutors, Judicators and Retributors – all were clad in star-forged sigmarite, and bearing weapons of the same material. Their panoply of war gleamed silver where it was not rich gold. Their shoulder guards bore their sigil – the curling white slashes of a bull's horns – and, like their heavy shields, were of deepest regal blue. The weapons they carried shimmered with holy fire. Now, they swept them out to smash down any enemy who managed to avoid the attention of their Lord-Celestant.

He stepped over the body of a bloodreaver and looked ahead. Through the ranks of the enemy, the path they had been following since they had arrived some days previous was visible. Sigmar had cast his lightning down upon the shattered husk of a once-proud citadel, now overgrown with grey lichen and nodding, vast-rooted trees. A carpet of yellowing grass had clung to the cracked stones of the courtyard, obscuring the heaps of bones that clustered thickly throughout. The thunderous arrival of the Stormcasts in the Vale of Sorrows had set thousands of crows to flight, and a black cloud of the croaking birds had followed them ever since.

The path ahead had previously been a road, but was now mostly overgrown with the stiff, yellow grasses that seemed to cover this region. Ancient ruins and shattered hovels stretched out across the landscape to either side of the path. At one time there had been a city here. Now it was only a howling wilderness full of enemies and carrion birds.

'Who shall win Sigmar's favour?' Tarsus cried, swinging his hammer over his head. He brought it down on a bloodreaver with bone-shattering force. With his sword, he chopped through the deplorable icon the blood-cultist had borne and trampled it beneath his feet.

'Only the faithful,' the Stormcasts around him shouted, as one.

'Only the faithful,' Tarsus echoed as he whipped his sword around in a deadly pattern, splitting the gullets of the enemy who pressed close. He smashed the dying bloodreavers aside, using his greater weight to grind them under.

Tarsus' warriors called him the Bull-Heart, a name earned at the Battle of the Cerulean Shore, when Tarsus had crashed in amongst the enemy ranks with a ferocity few could equal. It was a fitting war-name for both he and his Warrior Chamber, and they bore it with pride. Their swords were as horns, their hammers were as hooves, and they employed both against the enemies of Sigmar in equal measure.

'Smash them,' he bellowed. 'Grind them under, in the name of Sigmar and the Realm Celestial!'

Bodies littered his path as he drove forwards, into the very teeth of the foe. The bloodreavers were maniacs, but mortal, and none who were such could stand before Tarsus. He was a Stormcast Eternal, and in him flowed the might of Sigmar Heldenhammer. He roared and stamped, battering opponents from his path as he led the way towards the knot of heavily armoured Blood Warriors that formed the raging heart of the enemy battle line. The latter charged to meet him, chanting the name of the Blood God as they smashed aside their own followers in their eagerness to come to grips with the Hallowed Knights.

'Who will be remembered?' Tarsus cried.

'Only the faithful,' thundered his Stormcasts as the leading retinues of Liberators came to grips with the Blood Warriors. Spread out in a line, they closely followed the vanguard of Retributors and Decimators led by their Lord-Celestant.

Tarsus caught one of the Blood Warriors in the belly with his shoulder, and flipped the frothing berserker over his back even as he plunged on without slowing. The hammer of a Retributor from one of the retinues marching behind him slammed down, ensuring that the Blood Warrior remained where he'd fallen. Tarsus caught a second across the head with his hammer, and rammed his sword into the belly of a third, plunging it all the way to the hilt. His blade became lodged in the baroque plates of the Blood Warrior's armour, forcing him to spend precious moments wrenching it free. Even as he did so, a saw-toothed axe crashed down on his shoulder plate.

The force of the blow drove him to one knee. A second blow clipped his head, and he teetered off balance. Brass and crimson shapes surrounded him, and axes covered in daemonic sigils chopped down. For every one he turned aside two caught him, drawing sparks from the sigmarite plates. No blow had yet pierced his armour, but it was only a matter of time.

'Hold fast, Bull-Heart,' a voice thundered.

Lightning speared down, washing over Tarsus and his attackers. He grinned fiercely as the Blood Warriors shuddered and jerked in the clutches of the storm. Smoke boiled from their mouths and eye sockets, and what flesh was visible beneath their armour was charred black.

Tarsus surged to his feet and caught one of the smoke-wreathed Blood Warriors beneath the chin with his hammer. The warrior pitched backwards and then lay still. Tarsus hacked another down and turned to greet his rescuer. 'Nicely done, Ramus,' he said. 'A few more moments and I might have been sorely pressed indeed.'

'Think on that, the next time you find yourself so eager to meet the foe that you outpace the rest of us,' the Lord-Relictor of the Bull-Hearts said. 'There are not so many of us that we can spare you, Tarsus.'

Like all those of his rank, Ramus of the Shadowed Soul bore weapons and armour replete with icons of faith, death and the storm. It fell to him to keep the souls of the Hallowed Knights of his Warrior Chamber from the gloom of the underworld with words and fire.

Tarsus nodded. 'I shall. But for now – show them your power, my friend.'

Ramus raised his reliquary and murmured a soft prayer, his words lost amidst the clangour of battle. The sky overhead was already dark, and roiled and jagged as spears of lightning struck the enemy, burning them to ash or reducing them to stumbling, screaming torches. Tarsus raised his hammer, bringing his Stormcasts to a halt as the lightning continued to strike again and again, until all was silent, save for the soft crackle of flames.

'Who will be victorious?' Tarsus murmured, as he gently tapped his Lord-Relictor on the shoulder with his hammer.

'Only the faithful,' Ramus intoned, glancing at Tarsus. 'The road ahead is clear, Lord-Celestant. We are free to continue our march.'

'Indeed, and we shouldn't tarry,' Tarsus said, as he signalled for his retinues to fall into a proper marching order.

The Stormcasts swung fluidly into position with an ease born of centuries of training. Liberators moved to the fore and flanks, encircling the Judicators, while the Prosecutors swooped overhead. The retinues of the winged warriors would range ahead of the host as it marched, keeping a keen eye out for any more would-be ambushers.

Not that such a tactic had succeeded yet, and nor would it if Tarsus had anything to say about it. Had he been anything other than a Stormcast Eternal, he might have taken the continued attacks for an omen, but fear had been burned out of him long ago and left only faith in its wake. He and his warriors were heroes, their valour proven in battles all but forgotten in the haze of their reforging. The Hallowed Knights had been the fourth Stormhost to be founded, the ranks of their Warrior Chambers filled with the faithful of the Mortal Realms. Their only commonality was that each had called upon Sigmar's name in battle – and been heard – and that each had shed his mortal flesh in the name of a righteous cause.

Tarsus could but dimly recall the days of his own mortality. He remembered the weight of his sword and armour, and the rustle of a war cloak of deepest purple. He remembered screaming himself hoarse on the stone battlements of a burning citadel as red, lean-limbed daemons scrambled up the walls and across the causeways towards him and those he led. He remembered a name – *Tarsem* – and a word – *Helstone* – and the moment a monstrous shadow had fallen across him and the air had writhed beneath the beat of great wings. Then a roar, and… nothing. Nothing until he'd awoken in Sigmaron, forged anew.

That was the way of it, and Tarsus was glad. His enemies had not changed, but now he had the power to meet them, and break them. He was Stormcast, and they would learn to fear that name, before the end. His reverie was soon broken by Ramus.

'This is a fell place,' Ramus said, as he and Tarsus led the host.

'Parts of it, yes,' Tarsus said. He thought of the things they'd seen since arriving: strange hourglass-shaped mountains that rose along the far horizon, and clumps of pale flowers that softly sighed when one walked past them.

'A land of endings and silent decay,' the Lord-Relictor said. 'This is a place of whispers, where forgotten ghosts wander roads and paths that lead nowhere. A place where mountains crumble only to be raised anew with the sun, and birds and beasts are born and die in the same day. All is in decline here, though I know not whether it is the doing of our foes or the dread master of this realm.' He looked at Tarsus. 'Do you think he will listen?'

'I do not know,' Tarsus said. 'Nagash betrayed Sigmar once. Mayhap he will do so again. But that is not for us to worry over... Our concern is to gain audience with him and make common cause, so that we might begin to wrest this realm from the enemy.'

'But first we have to find him in this wilderness,' Ramus said.

They had been searching for a way into the underworld since their arrival – one of the legendary Nine Gates into the underworld of Stygxx. The Great Necromancer had vanished, disappeared into the depths where none could find him. But Sigmar had set his scribes the centuries-long task of scouring the ancient records, compiled long before the Allpoints War, for any hint of where the Nine Gates might be. That knowledge had been passed on to the Stormcasts charged with seeking out Nagash. The Nine Gates had been housed in nine citadels, some massive and well-defended, and others so small as to be forever hidden from the eyes of the enemy. Nine Warrior Chambers had been despatched to find these structures and the gates secreted within their walls.

So far the gates had proven elusive, but Tarsus had hope; Sigmar would not have sent them to this place were victory not achievable. A gate was within reach, somewhere. And they would find it.

The trail grew rougher and steeper as the Stormcasts marched on, leaving the detritus of battle far behind them, winding through verdant fields that withered in the moonlight only to flourish once more as the sun rose, and trees that shuddered and sighed in the slightest of breezes. The sky overhead was pale and dim, even in the middle of the day, as if the sun feared to show its face in the Realm of Death. The crows were still overhead, circling and wheeling amongst the Prosecutors as they swooped above on wings of lightning.

'Aye,' Tarsus said. 'And we will do so, even if we must fight our way across this land to do it.' They had come into conflict with the deranged servants of the Ruinous Powers more than once since their arrival. The worshippers of the Blood God were as thick as fleas in the crags around them. The Realm of Death was under siege, and every peak and valley was infested with the followers of the Dark Gods. He shook his head. 'Though I'd not turn down aid in that regard, if it were offered.'

A cry from above caught his attention, and Tarsus looked up. One of the Prosecutors swooped low and pointed towards a rocky outcrop that rose abruptly from the surrounding landscape, towering over the bare trees.

'Something ahead – a structure of some sort at the top,' he cried. Tarsus waved them forwards, the winged warriors hurtling into the distance, towards the dome-roofed ruin that occupied the summit of the tor.

'Another ruin,' Ramus said.

'And perhaps a way into the underworld,' Tarsus said. He raised his hammer, signalling to his retinues. 'Liberators to the flanks, shields out,' he said, his voice carrying over the gleaming ranks of his Warrior Chamber.

Liberator retinues moved to the flanks of the formation, shields at the ready, in case there was an ambush in the offing. If it was the place they sought, it could be defended and such a place might well provide refuge for warbands like the ones that had relentlessly attacked them since their arrival. With a single gesture from Tarsus, shields raised over the heads of the Stormcasts and to the sides, transforming the Stormhost into a veritable serpent of sigmarite. Their protection allowed them to weather arrows, rocks and even sorcery as they moved. Satisfied, Tarsus swung his hammer towards the ruin.

'Forwards,' he bellowed.

A wide path wound around the outcrop and led to the top. Tarsus led the way, and saw that the path ahead was lined with skulls as he rounded the slope. Mounted on spikes of brass and iron, the skulls twitched and champed yellow, cracked teeth, as if in protestation of their fate. Bones were scattered below them, mixed with bits of rusty armour and broken weapons, and piled up in drifts alongside the path. Tarsus stared at the skulls, pity warring with disgust. 'They still live,' Tarsus murmured. 'Even now.'

'No, Tarsus,' Ramus said. 'They do not. And that is the horror of it. Nothing in this realm ever truly dies, even now,' he said, looking at the skulls. 'Their souls are bound here, in chains of magic of the darkest sort.'

Tarsus shook his head. 'Keep moving,' he called over his shoulder.

More bones awaited them at the summit of the tor. They were scattered and in piles – some whole, though most cracked and broken. Crows hopped among the heaps, cawing to one another. Everywhere dolorous icons and foul standards, marked with sigils of murder and slaughter, had been stabbed into the rocky slope. Jawbones and finger bones hung from many of these, softly clattering in the breeze.

'We are not the first to come here,' Ramus said.

'No,' Tarsus replied.

The structure crouched ahead of them, partially built into the massive fang-like crag of rock that topped the outcrop, and resembled nothing so much as a dome. Its walls curved outwards in an immense semicircle from the crag, dominating the slope below despite the ragged gaps in their length. A curved roof surmounted the walls, resting in the crook of the crag, crows circling it in great numbers. Vast symbols had been carved into the outer walls – symbols representing the sun, moon, stars and other, more esoteric shapes.

'It's as large as any citadel I've seen,' Tarsus said. 'Though in worse condition than most.' Despite the state of it, he could see that it had taken great skill to shape the stone. Sundials and dry fountains decorated the courtyard, and Tarsus thought that it might once have been a beautiful place before the occurrence of whatever evil had befallen it. As Tarsus studied it, he felt a pang of something – sadness, perhaps, or the twitch of some long forgotten memory, newly stirred – and his hands tightened on his weapons.

'I have seen this place before,' he murmured.

'Lord-Celestant?' Ramus asked.

Tarsus shook his head, irritated. 'I'm fine. This place – there is something about it.' Overhead, the Prosecutors had dropped onto the dome, scattering the crows, who croaked in agitation. The Stormcasts moved into the ruins and through the remains of what had once been an outer wall, collapsed for many years into irregular piles of stones and shattered columns.

Tarsus left several retinues of Judicators and Liberators on guard in the courtyard and led the rest of his warriors into the ruin. More bones greeted them inside the gargantuan entrance hall: crushed, splintered and scattered about at random. The entrance itself was composed of heavy stone slabs, marked by more symbols – suns and moons, comets and falling stars, all carefully carved into the rock face.

Tarsus traced one of the latter with his fingers as he passed, wondering why it all seemed so familiar.

'What was this place?' he asked, as he gazed up at the faded mural that had been painted on the curve of the roof above, depicting a vast field of stars and a black-cloaked scythe-wielding figure hard at work, reaping a cosmic crop.

'An observatory, perhaps,' Ramus said, looking around. 'There are places in the Nihiliad Mountains that this reminds me of. They were places of contemplation, for stargazers and sky-worshippers, maybe this is one. This outcrop is the highest point in the vale – a perfect place to watch the night sky.'

'Perhaps, but watch it for what?' Tarsus said. 'The stars in this realm are all askew, and the night sky is in upheaval.'

'It was not always so,' Ramus said. He gestured to the strange carvings that marked the walls. Tarsus thought they resembled the star-fields depicted in the mural above. 'I suspect that these are the patterns of the stars as they were, before the coming of Chaos.'

'As they could be again,' Tarsus replied. He pointed down the corridor with his hammer. 'There. The central chamber.' He moved through the archway at the end of the hall and into the heart of the observatory. Despite its outward facade, the observatory was, in reality, merely a single, immense room.

The central chamber was massive – easily large enough to accommodate a hundred men – with high vaulted ceilings that curved upwards to meet at a central open skylight of stone.

Crows clustered about the circumference of the skylight, staring down at the Stormcasts below. A massive dais occupied the centre of the chamber, directly beneath the stone. Sloped, circular steps led upwards to an enormous wheel-like orrery, crafted from black iron and made in the shape of a sun. The orrery was larger than three men, and its colossal rings were spread outwards, so that the dull light from above streamed down through the holes in them, casting weird shadows upon the walls and floor of the chamber.

Ramus gazed at the orrery. 'More stars,' he said, his voice echoing through the chamber. 'The holes in the iron correspond to the patterns on the walls. This used to be a place of study and contemplation.' He sounded almost wistful.

'Now it is nothing save a curiosity,' Tarsus said, looking around.

As with the rocky slopes outside, the floor of the chamber was obscured by broken bones and scattered pieces of armour. All the walls were covered in faded murals and tenacious lichen, except one that was occupied solely by a basket-hilted sword, wedged deep into the stone. Dead clumps of the lichen marked the floor beneath the blade, and the steel had turned cracked and powdery where it had touched the stone. Something about the blade bothered him. He felt a chill, though he could not say why.

'We should go. I was wrong, there is nothing for us here,' he said.

'Tarsus, wait. Look at the orrery,' Ramus called out. Tarsus turned towards the great dais and peered at the orrery. He blinked, startled. There was something caught in the rings. No, not caught, he realised; *trapped*. He hadn't seen it before, because it had been hidden by the rings. But now, he could see it clearly.

Quickly he climbed the dais, Ramus one step behind him. 'It's a man,' Tarsus said.

'Alive?' Ramus asked. Around the dais, the Stormcasts spread throughout the chamber. Though they were wary, they were curious about this realm and all it held. Many of them, after all, might have stood in this very chamber in centuries past. They might even have died in its defence, or in defence of any one of the great and shattered citadels thrust up from the dry sod of these lands like scattered tombstones.

'I do not think so,' Tarsus said, softly. The orrery moved, albeit very slowly, clicking and creaking along its runnel, and allowed the sunlight to flow through the holes in the iron. The man's body was held aloft by brass spikes hammered through his wrists and into the curve of one of the orrery's rings, leaving him to dangle within a makeshift cage. Dried blood coated the marble flesh of his bare arms and head, staining the ornate armour he wore on his torso and legs. Wounds marked his arms and face. His armour too was marked, and by many weapons. A tattered crimson cloak was pooled on the ground at his feet, as if it had been ripped from him and then summarily discarded. The body stank of blood and death, and the aquiline features were slack.

Something about the dead man's face held Tarsus' attention. It was not familiar, and yet… was. Were you there, in that final battle when I proved my worth to Sigmar? But how could that be, for that was centuries ago, the Lord-Celestant thought.

'Help me move these rings.' Tarsus caught hold of the outer ring and began to push it back, so that the others folded into it. The metal squealed as rusted joints and hinges were propelled into motion. 'We must release him,' he said, looking at Ramus. 'Whoever he was, no man deserves such a fate.'

Ramus did not question him, and together the two Stormcast

Eternals managed to move the ancient mechanism so that the body was no longer trapped out of reach.

Ramus caught hold of the dead man's jaw and looked to Tarsus. 'These wounds on his flesh – the followers of the Blood God are known for their brutality to those taken in battle. Perhaps he had the ill luck to be taken alive...'

'Come... closer... and mayhap... I shall tell you.'

Tarsus drew his sword as the stink of old blood washed over them. 'Ramus, beware,' he said.

The body twitched in its bonds. Metal scraped metal, and the battered head rose, eyes red and alight with a terrible need. Quicker than either Stormcast could react, the thing's feet suddenly slid up to brace against the curve of the ring, and the body lunged forwards, held in check only by its pinned wrists.

Bones popped and shifted hideously as it snapped long fangs together, just shy of Ramus' face. The Lord-Relictor stepped back, hammer ready, as the thing thrashed wildly, biting at the air in a frenzy. Around the dais Stormcasts snapped to attention, weapons raised. A retinue of Decimators began to move towards the dais, axes ready to chop the creature apart. Tarsus waved them back.

'Hold,' he rumbled. 'Stand fast.' Whatever this thing was, he was confident that he and the Lord-Relictor would be enough to handle it.

'Enough,' Ramus said. His hammer snapped out, catching the thing in the stomach, and knocking it from its perch. It squalled as it fell and the spikes tore its flesh. It dangled, shuddering, then coughed and looked up.

'Haaaa...' The vulpine jaws sagged, and a bloody stink swept over Tarsus again. The red eyes faded to orange, then yellow, and the tension drained from the dangling shape. 'Do... do forgive me, I am... I am not at my best,' the thing croaked.

Tarsus extended his hammer and used it to lift the creature's head. 'What are you?'

Even as he asked the question, he realised that he knew the answer. *Vampire.* The word was jostled loose from the depths of his memory. Had he encountered such creatures before, in his previous life?

Withered lips peeled back from long fangs, and the vampire gave a rattling laugh. 'A better question might be… what are you?' One sunken eye narrowed. 'I smell… storms and clean water. You are not mortal men.'

'Not for a long time,' Tarsus said.

'The same might be said of me, I suppose,' the vampire rasped.

'What is your name?'

'What use is a name, when one is bound thus?' The creature twitched its thin fingers, causing the brass spikes to screech against the iron rim of the orrery. It winced, in obvious pain. 'If you release me, perhaps I shall tell you, eh? How curious are you?'

'Not enough to release a monster,' Tarsus said, lowering his hammer. 'Vampires are not to be trusted. They lie as easily as other men breathe, and treachery festers in their veins.' Even as he spoke, he wondered where the words came from. They felt familiar on his tongue, as if he'd spoken them before. *Helstone* – the word floated to the surface of his mind.

'Then kill me,' the vampire croaked. 'I would be free of this place one way or another.' The creature peered at Tarsus, and then gave a harsh chuckle. 'Unless you lack the fortitude to do so, Stormcast?'

Tarsus' eyes narrowed. The old, faded memories receded, as suspicion flared. He traded a glance with Ramus, and then replied, 'I thought you didn't know what we were.'

'Did I say that?' the vampire said. 'I merely asked a question.

The implications thereof were of your creation.' He showed his fangs. 'I know what you are, well enough.'

'Why were you here?' Tarsus demanded. 'Speak plainly, or I will leave you here for the carrion birds,' he said, gesturing to the crows gathered above.

'Implying... what? That if I answer truthfully you'll free me?'

'Enough of this,' Ramus said. He looked at Tarsus. 'We have wasted enough time here, bandying words with a talkative corpse. Let us leave this place, Bull-Heart.' He started down the steps. Tarsus turned to follow.

'Wait.'

Tarsus turned.

'I was looking for something.' The vampire grimaced. 'A gateway into Stygxx.' He smiled, though there was little humour in the expression. 'I was looking for a way... home.' His hands twitched, and the smile twisted into a snarl of pain.

'Where is it?' Ramus demanded.

'Why do you care?'

'We seek an audience with the Great Necromancer,' Tarsus said.

The vampire blinked.

'With *Nagash*?' he hissed, in evident disbelief. 'Are you mad?'

Tarsus frowned. 'No. But we have a duty, and we will fulfil it or die in the attempt.'

'Yes, one or the other is quite likely. Both, even more so,' the vampire said. He shook his head. 'I was right. You *are* mad. Leave me, madmen. Let me rot in peace.'

'Did you find the gate?' Tarsus demanded.

The vampire snorted and closed his eyes. 'No,' the vampire said. 'Before I could do so, I was set upon by a servant of the Blood God calling himself the Woebringer. He and that pack of beasts he calls a warband cast down my servants, and bound me here. They thought it amusing, given my nature, to imprison me inside a sun, black iron or otherwise.'

'Why not simply kill you?'

The vampire's smile widened. 'How can you kill what is already dead?' The smile faded. 'In truth, I think they took my durability as a challenge...'

Tarsus' eyes strayed to the many wounds that covered the vampire's exposed flesh and the blood that stained the dais. 'They tortured you,' he said.

'They *are* torturing me,' the vampire hissed. 'Every few days. The sunlight, weak as it is, and a lack of blood have kept me dangling here – a prisoner of mindless brutes. I have no doubt you've encountered the Woebringer's foraging parties – he sends them out, looking for worthy prey, while the rest of the warband wanders about these hills, fighting anyone and anything they come across, including others of their ilk. When that gets boring, he comes here and carves his name on my flesh.' The vampire grinned suddenly, and his eyes flashed with amusement. 'In fact, he's due any moment now, I'd say.'

The sound of horns suddenly echoed through the chamber.

'Lord-Celestant, the enemy approaches,' one of the Prosecutors called from the dome above.

'How many?' Tarsus asked. Inwardly, he cursed his inattention to priorities. He'd failed to send the Prosecutors to scout the area around them, and now the enemy was almost upon them.

'Twice our number, easily,' came the reply. 'They're climbing the eastern slope, and with war-beasts.'

'Khorgoraths,' the vampire hissed. 'Ugly brutes, and hard to kill. The Woebringer quite likes his pets. Dotes on the beasts.'

'Then we shall make ready for them. Ramus, fortify this chamber for war. It is no keep, but it must do,' Tarsus said.

'And what of you, Lord-Celestant?' Ramus asked.

'I wish to see the enemy's strength and disposition for myself,' Tarsus said, striding towards the largest of the gaps in the wall. As he did so, the Stormcasts he had left outside streamed into the observatory, as their training dictated. The enemy outnumbered them, and only proper discipline would ensure the Bull-Hearts' victory.

'Hold,' Tarsus said, casting his voice to carry over the clatter of sigmarite plates. 'Shields to the vanguard. Sigmar has provided the room, let us make use of it. Who will hold, when the daemon-winds rage?'

'Only the faithful,' his Stormcasts cried. Liberators turned and sank to one knee in the gaps until a low hedge of shields lined each one. Soon more retinues joined them, dropping the bottom rims of their shields atop those of their brethren, creating an improvised wall. Tarsus stepped forwards into an opening the Stormcasts provided for him and surveyed the approaching enemy.

'By the Realm Celestial,' Tarsus muttered, as he looked out over the brawling horde. Foul standards rose over seething ranks of howling barbarians and armoured Blood Warriors. Their numbers dwarfed the small warbands they'd encountered earlier in their travels. This was a horde, in the truest sense of the word. Worst of all were the chained monsters – the khorgoraths – that bellowed and thrashed amidst the mortal warriors, including those who prodded and whipped their charges, driving them into a frenzy.

Despite the clamour of these monstrosities, Tarsus found his eye drawn to a lean, loping shape. The creature was made not of flesh, but of dark metal and other, less identifiable things. Its bat-like features were twisted in an expression of inhuman agony, and he could see that it was held in check by brass chains and festooned with ruinous icons. A febrile steam rose from its twitching, catlike form as it stalked forwards, goaded by a number of bloodstokers who continuously slashed its flanks with barbed whips and prods.

'What in the name of the great drake is that?' he murmured.

'Its name is Ashigaroth,' the vampire called out, weakly. He had overheard him, somehow.

Tarsus glanced over his shoulder. The vampire wasn't looking at him, but he noted something in the voice. 'What is it?' he asked Ramus.

'Mine,' the vampire hissed.

'A dread abyssal,' Ramus said, as he joined Tarsus at the wall. 'They are things of darkness, bound by necromancy.' He looked at the vampire. 'He is no mere pilgrim.'

'No, but I can be of service to you… Free me and I shall aid you,' the vampire said.

'We do not need your aid,' Ramus began. Tarsus waved him to silence, and looked back out over the slope of the tor. The ranks of the enemy stirred, and a broad, muscular shape pushed its way through, dragging a screeching khorgorath in its wake. The warrior was no mere bloodreaver, Tarsus knew. No, he was of the elite – a champion of the Ruinous Powers. His skull was surmounted by great, curling horns and his thick chest, where the armour did not cover his flesh, was branded with the sigils of the Blood God. He carried a wide-bladed axe in his free hand, and the arm that held the monster's chains was protected by a heavy gauntlet topped by claw-like blades.

'I am Tarka Woebringer,' the Chaos champion roared. 'Exalted amongst all deathbringers, and master of a hundred beasts.' The khorgorath whose chains he held slavered and gnashed at the air. The champion hauled back on the chains, fighting to keep the beast from breaking loose. 'This is my place, earned with the red coin of crushed shield and splintered spear. Who are you to walk these stones without my permission?'

'He's a talkative one,' Ramus said, one foot braced on the broken wall, the haft of his hammer resting across his knee.

'The more he talks, the more time we have to make ready,' Tarsus said.

'I know you, for you reek of lightning, and word travels quickly on the roads of ruin,' the Woebringer continued. 'The Blood God will smile on me for delivering up your skulls. Aye, and the skull of my slave as well, for I've grown tired of cutting his ever-healing flesh.' The khorgorath roared and shuffled forwards, dragging Tarka a few steps. The champion laughed. 'Bloodswiller is eager to sup on your entrails, silver-skins. He and his brothers did for the vampire's bony servants, and they'll do for you as well – go, Bloodswiller!' Tarka released the chains and stepped back, as the monster surged forwards.

It was not alone in its mad charge across the broken courtyard that separated the Stormcasts from their foes. From behind the Woebringer, several more of the beasts plunged past, freed from their chains by Tarka's oncoming warriors. The khorgoraths bounded through the rubble, covering the distance more swiftly than any man or Stormcast. Tarsus' Prosecutors hurtled down, hammers whirling from their hands to strike with meteoric force. One of the khorgoraths stumbled and fell, its crimson flesh puckered by smoking impact craters.

'Shields up,' Tarsus roared, as the first of the monsters thundered towards the gaps in the observatory wall, smashing aside a sundial in its haste.

Liberators were thrown back as the khorgorath barrelled into them. Hammers thudded into its flesh, and warblades bit at its flanks, but it refused to fall. The shield wall disintegrated into flying bodies as the rest of the monsters tore at their foes.

'Ramus,' Tarsus said.

'At your command, Lord-Celestant,' Ramus cried, as he thrust his reliquary forwards. Lightning crackled about the standard, and then sprang forth in a blinding flash to strike the beast in the chest. The khorgorath stiffened and shrieked.

'Judicators,' Tarsus roared. Boltstorm crossbows hummed, and explosive bolts peppered the monster, dropping it to its knees. Liberators swarmed over it, hammers rising and falling in deadly rhythm. Tarsus looked around. Two more of the beasts were locked in combat with the Decimator and Retributor retinues just inside the chamber, and a third was still outside of the observatory, swiping blindly at the swooping forms of the Prosecutors who were holding its attention. But the last, the beast the Woebringer had named Bloodswiller, was charging across the observatory floor towards Ramus, whose attention was on the creatures fighting his Decimator bodyguards.

Tarsus moved to intercept the beast. Hearing the monster's approach, Ramus turned, but not quickly enough. Bloodswiller's talons smashed down, knocking the Stormcast Eternal from his feet, his reliquary clattering from his grip. Ramus rolled aside as the khorgorath stomped down, but even as he came to his feet, hammer raised, the monster caught him and lifted him up.

'Unhand him, beast,' Tarsus snarled, as he reached them.

His hammer crashed against Bloodswiller's back, but before he could strike a second blow, the creature backhanded him hard enough to rattle his armour. He was sent flying backwards and crashed down on the dais, cracking the stone. As a Decimator tried to hack through the wrist of the claw holding Ramus, Bloodswiller screeched and tore the unlucky Stormcast apart. It slung the Lord-Relictor down, battering him against the floor and wall.

Ramus' struggles grew weaker, and none of the nearby warriors could land a telling blow against the frenzied beast to free him. Blue bursts of lightning, spearing upwards towards the heavens, attested to the fate of those who tried. The monster was faster than it looked, and stronger than its kindred.

Tarsus pulled himself to his feet, and readied himself to lunge back into the fray.

'I can save him,' he heard someone say. He looked up to see the unsmiling vampire gazing down at him from where he hung.

'I am faster than you, even now, and stronger,' the vampire said. 'You will not get close to it before it kills either you or your friend. More, I owe that particular beast for the blow that landed me here, in such a humiliating state. I can save him, Stormcast – free me. Or die. It matters not to me.'

Tarsus did not hesitate. He spun and brought his sword down, slicing through the rings of the orrery. It toppled forwards, and as it did so Tarsus dropped his weapons and caught it with a grunt of effort. Swiftly, he wrenched the brass spikes free of the vampire's flesh, and the creature fell to the dais in a crouch as Tarsus chucked the orrery aside. The vampire glanced up at him. Then, with an eyeblink, he was suddenly at the far wall where the sword Tarsus had seen earlier was embedded.

As swift as lightning, the vampire tore the blade free of the wall and sprang towards Bloodswiller. The great crimson brute roared and swung a thickly muscled arm, but the vampire dodged the blow, and, with two hands, drove his blade down into the flesh between the beast's shoulder and neck. The sword's blade flared with unholy power, and a crimson steam spurted from the wound. The khorgorath shrieked and flailed, trying to fling the vampire loose. It dropped Ramus and Tarsus charged forwards, weapons at the ready.

'Well, what are you waiting for, fools?' the vampire snarled. 'Help me kill this thing.'

Tarsus lunged forwards. His hammer crashed against one of the Bloodswiller's bone-studded knees, splintering it. The beast shrilled and sank down, still clawing futilely at the vampire, who held tight to his perch on its shoulder. The vampire hissed and gave the hilt of his sword a vicious twist. Then he tore it free in a welter of gore and leapt away. The khorgorath fell forwards, its talons gouging the ancient marble floor of the observatory.

'Now, Stormcast – strike now!' the vampire said.

Tarsus drove his hammer down on the exposed crown of the Bloodswiller's skull, cracking it. Ramus, having regained his feet and his hammer, joined him. Together, they struck it again and again, until black ichor spilled across the floor, and the beast fell still. Tarsus looked around – the other khorgoraths had met similar fates, brought down by the weapons and divine fury of the Stormcasts. Already, his warriors were reorganising their lines, and readying themselves for whatever might come next. He looked at the vampire, who said, 'What now?'

'Now? Now we finish this.' Tarsus turned towards the gap and extended his sword towards the distant shape of the Woebringer. 'Is that the best you can muster?' he shouted, clashing his weapons. 'We are still here. Who will stand?' he bellowed.

'Only the faithful,' the Hallowed Knights roared in response. Hammers crashed against shields. 'Only the faithful!'

Tarka threw back his head and screamed in rage. The Woebringer sliced the air with his axe and his warriors surged forwards – a snarling horde, clad in the colours of blood and brass – bloodreavers, Blood Warriors and worse things bounding in the wake of the mortals.

Tarsus stepped back from the gap. 'Stand fast, Bull-Hearts,' he said. 'We have won a short reprieve, but they come again, in strength. Judicators, thin their ranks. Fall back when they reach the gaps. It'll be close work then. Hammer and shield work, eh, my friends?' he said, swatting a nearby Liberator's shield with the flat of his sword. 'Who will be triumphant?'

'Only the faithful,' came the reply. Tarsus nodded.

'Only the faithful,' he said firmly. 'Stand fast, and fight as if Sigmar himself were watching. Or as if Ramus were watching, for he's closer.'

The air throbbed with the hum of boltstorm crossbows firing and men screaming. Tarsus glanced quickly towards the gaps in the wall where the Judicators had formed two firing ranks: one kneeling, one standing. Together they fired into the disorganised mass of foes climbing towards them. The Prosecutors harried the enemy as they charged, adding to the tally claimed by the Judicators. They had earned a few moments of peace before the battle would be well and truly joined. Nevertheless the enemy pressed on, and soon they would be spilling into the observatory.

Tarsus caught Ramus staring at the vampire. 'You do not trust him.'

'You said it yourself – he cannot be trusted.'

'He saved you,' Tarsus said.

'He saved himself. My fate was incidental,' Ramus countered.

'Indeed it was,' the vampire said, striding towards them. 'But, for the moment, our paths align. They have my beast. I would have him back. He is… precious to me.'

Tarsus nodded. 'So be it. But if you turn on us, know that it will be my hand that strikes you down.' He raised his hammer for emphasis. The vampire smirked.

'Duly noted,' he said, as he laid his sword across his shoulder.

There was a clatter of sigmarite as the Judicators fell back, and the Liberator retinues moved to take their place in the vanguard. 'Shields up,' Tarsus said, his voice carrying throughout the chamber. Shields rose, and then slammed together, rim to rim, forming a wall of sigmarite.

'Hold the line,' Tarsus continued. He tightened his grip on the hafts of his weapons. 'Move on my order.'

'Where do you wish me to go?' the vampire said, bowing shallowly. 'Shall I take my place in line and fight alongside your warriors?'

'Fight as it pleases you,' Tarsus said, watching the approach of the enemy. 'You are no longer a prisoner.' He glanced at the vampire. 'You are free.'

The vampire blinked. Then, he inclined his head. 'As you say.' He turned towards the broken wall as the howls of the blood-worshippers filled the air. The first bloodreaver burst through the gap at a run – an axe in either hand – and more followed. Soon a wave of murderous fury swept towards the waiting Liberators, who continued their war-rhythm, waiting for their Lord-Celestant's order.

Tarsus stepped off the dais, arms spread and weapons ready. 'Hold, Bull-Hearts. Hold,' he rumbled. 'Ramus, call the storm.'

Ramus lifted his reliquary and slammed the haft down so that the sound quavered through the air like the peal of a bell. Outside the observatory, a heavy rain began to fall. Thunder rumbled, and the blood-worshippers still outside screamed as crackling streamers of lightning slashed through their ranks, speeding along armour and edges of weapons to lance into branded flesh. Men died in droves, cooked in their armour, or else set aflame as they ran. Confusion swept throughout the enemy.

'Lower your horns,' Tarsus roared, pushing through the ranks to the front. Liberators bent, their shields thrust to the fore and hammers held low. 'And… forwards.' As one, the Liberator retinues began to march on. Tarsus led the way, picking up speed with every step. His warriors kept pace and, with a thunderous crash, the shield wall met the front rank of the bloodreavers. Shields locked as the Liberators pushed against the enemy, driving them back. Tarsus fought at the fore, making room for his warriors to move forwards with every blow.

More enemy warriors continued to press through the gaps, even as the front ranks were forced back. Frenzied Blood Warriors tore through their own fellows as the crush of battle intensified. The Liberators fought efficiently, using their foe's numbers against them. Hammers cracked against knees and shot forwards to crush chests. In other such encounters, it had been enough. The Stormcasts were as relentless in their own way as the servants of the Blood God were in theirs, and when they marched no enemy could stand against them.

But soon, numbers began to tell against discipline. Howling Blood Warriors hooked shields and arms with their axes, dragging the Stormcasts into the depths of the mob and ripping them asunder in explosions of blue light. The hulking shapes of khorgoraths lurked outside the observatory and tore at the remaining walls in a frenzy, trying to widen the gaps. Debris sifted down from above as cracks raced across the roof and walls of the structure. A section collapsed with a roar, crushing Stormcasts and bloodreavers alike.

'Fall back,' Tarsus shouted as he blocked an axe blow. 'Tighten the line and fall back from the walls.'

Those Liberators who could began to back away, shields still locked. Others could not break away from their opponents and were swiftly surrounded and brought low. More explosions of searing blue light streaked skyward, and Tarsus cursed. He looked around, watching Ramus organise the Retributors and Decimators for a counter-charge.

It wasn't going to be enough. They were outnumbered ten to one and the enemy wasn't afraid of death. They didn't care if they were crushed, mangled or pierced. They kept coming regardless. He needed a new strategy.

'Lock shields,' he cried, setting his feet. Around him, Liberator retinues stopped their retreat and did as he ordered, forming up around the wide steps of the dais. 'We hold here. Not one step farther.'

As he spoke, the Prosecutors hurtled into the chamber, striking like lightning and retreating swiftly, trying to take some of the pressure off their comrades. Celestial hammers crashed into the closely packed mobs of bloodreavers, hurling broken bodies into the air. But the remainder pressed on. Tarsus waved the Judicators forwards. Several of the retinues had made the dais defensible, moving the heavy bookshelves and stone biers into place like barricades. Those who were not firing from behind their improvised ramparts moved quickly to take up position behind the Liberators.

Lightning flickered across the ranks of the enemy, blinding and burning them. A section of the shield wall opened, and Ramus led his Paladin brotherhoods forwards. The great two-handed axes of the Decimators chopped through crimson armour with ease, as the lightning hammers of the Retributors smashed the strongest Chaos champions from their feet. But the enemy pressed close about them, and even the heavily armoured Paladins could not stand alone against such a tide. Still too many of them, he thought. He'd hoped the observatory would provide some defence against numbers, but it wasn't enough.

Over the heads of his warriors and the heaving ranks of the

enemy, Tarsus saw the Woebringer fighting his way through his own followers, dragging the creature the vampire had named Ashigaroth in his wake and striking down anyone too slow to get out of his way. The dread abyssal came unwillingly, continuously fighting its chains.

As Tarsus took a step towards them, he caught sight of the vampire crouched atop the shattered dome of the observatory with arms spread and body angled so that he leaned over the chamber below. A guttural chant rose from his lips as he threw back his head. The dread abyssal began to buck and scream in its bindings. The bloodstoker struck the creature with his lash again and again, but the beast only grew more agitated. A weird purple light played across the piles of bones scattered on the floor and in the corners of the great chamber. They began to shiver and rustle, and Tarsus felt his hair stand on end.

'Stop him,' Tarka howled, motioning towards the vampire with his axe as he stepped into the observatory, hauling Ashigaroth after him by its chains. The bloodstoker followed him and struck the dread abyssal again before smashing off the chains that bound it, gesturing at the vampire with his blade. But rather than lunging immediately towards its former master, the creature twisted about and snapped its ebony jaws shut on the bloodstoker's head. Tarka lashed out at Ashigaroth with his axe, and the monster struck at him with its talons, scraping his armour and knocking him back a step as it bounded over him and towards a nearby Stormcast. The latter was crushed to the ground, his body evaporating into blue light. The dread abyssal screeched and flung itself into the melee, ravaging all those it could reach, without distinction. Blood warrior and Stormcasts alike fell to its frenzy.

Tarsus charged towards the Woebringer, bulling aside any bloodreaver foolish enough to get in his way. Behind him, he heard the vampire's chant growing louder, but the Woebringer was his only concern. Even as Tarsus closed with his foe, the Chaos champion staggered to his feet and sent his axe slicing out. Hammer, sword and axe clashed in a whirring dance of death as the Bull-Heart and the Woebringer traded blows.

'I will take your armour and mount it upon my lodge-pole, warrior. Your skull will be my drinking cup, and your weapons I will give to my slaves,' the Woebringer growled, as the clawed gauntlet he wore tore Tarsus' warcloak. 'After I am finished with you, I shall peel the flesh from the bones of a dead man, and wear it as my cloak!' He sliced at Tarsus' gut.

'Are you here to talk, or to fight?' Tarsus said, as he avoided the blow. His hammer thudded down, cracking the red armour that covered Tarka's shoulder. The Chaos champion howled and reversed his axe, digging it upwards in a mighty blow. Tarsus stepped back, but not quickly enough, as the edge of the axe drew a spray of sparks from his chest plate and sent him staggering back. The Woebringer crashed into him, driving an elbow into the side of the Lord-Celestant's head. His opponent was strong, stronger than any Tarsus had yet faced.

Tarsus fell, and only narrowly managed to avoid his opponent's axe as it crashed down where his head had been. Before the Woebringer could launch another blow, however, a broken sword crashed against him. Tarsus looked up and saw the fleshless limbs of several skeletons gathered about him protectively. The undead warriors attacked the Woebringer, jabbing at him with splintered spears and hacking with blunt, chipped swords. More clung to him, grabbing his arms or the great horns that topped his bestial head. He roared wordlessly, lashing out to shatter a skeleton. The dead thing fell, but crawled back towards him.

Khorgoraths screamed in agony as they were swarmed by skeletons and dragged down through sheer weight of numbers.

The dead rose up amidst the press of the melee and fell upon the Woebringer's warriors with silent savagery, cutting them down even as they fought the Stormcasts. Everywhere, the silent legions hurled themselves into the fray, compelled by the vampire's will and sorcery.

Tarsus got to his feet as the Woebringer whirled towards him, bleeding from a dozen wounds, but showing no signs of weakness.

'I defeated the dead before, and I will do so again. But first, I will take your skull, silver-skin,' the Chaos leader shrieked as he charged towards Tarsus, smashing aside the skeletons in his path. Tarsus raised his hammer, ready to meet his foe's charge, when a black shadow spread over them both.

The Woebringer looked up. Tarsus took advantage of his opponent's distraction and caught the Woebringer with a blow that rocked him off his feet. As he fell, the dread abyssal dropped out of the air and onto the Chaos champion with a cry. The vampire sat astride the creature, and laughed as Ashigaroth's claws tore the life from the fallen warrior. As the creature tore at the body, the vampire looked down at Tarsus.

'I do apologise, my friend, but... debts of blood were owed to both Ashigaroth and myself,' he said. He smiled thinly.

Tarsus shook his head and looked around. The battle was over. And now, the living and the dead stared at each other warily across the bodies of their common foe. He looked up at the vampire.

'You have my thanks,' Tarsus said, careful to keep his weapons lowered, reminding himself that *the dead could not be trusted*. The vampire chuckled, as if reading his thoughts.

'Mannfred,' the vampire said. 'I am Mannfred.'

'Mannfred, then,' Tarsus said. He hesitated, then extended his hand. Mannfred stared at it for a moment, as if puzzled, then he clasped Tarsus' forearm. 'I am Tarsus, Lord-Celestant of these warriors.'

'And I am Mannfred von Carstein, Count of the Hanging Wood,' Mannfred said, bowing deeply. As he straightened, he said, 'Do you still wish to find a way into the underworld, friend Tarsus?'

'Then you did find a gate here,' Tarsus said.

'No,' Mannfred said. His smile widened. 'Not here.' He slid from the back of his monstrous steed. 'But I know of one, and can lead you there.'

'Why?'

'Call it a debt of honour,' Mannfred said. 'I owe you, for freeing me, Tarsus of the Stormcasts.' He paused, as if thinking, before adding, 'Perhaps for more than just that.' He extended his hand. 'And as you've seen, I pay my debts.'

Tarsus hesitated. He looked up, into Mannfred's unblinking yellow eyes, judging. Somehow, he felt as if he had lived through this before, and wondered if it had turned out for the best then. Somehow, he didn't think so.

But he had a mission to complete. And live or die, he would see it done.

Tarsus clasped Mannfred's hand.

'Lead on then, Mannfred von Carstein. Where you go, the Stormcasts will follow.'

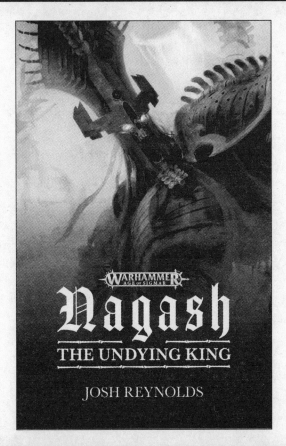

NAGASH: THE UNDYING KING
by Josh Reynolds

In the Realm of Death, the Rictus clans face their most relentless enemy ever, and even the intervention of two of the Great Necromancer's Mortarchs might not be enough to turn back the lumbering minions of the Plague God. Where is Nagash, the Undying King, when the people of Shyish need him most?

For these stories and more go to **blacklibrary.com, games-workshop.com**, Games Workshop and Warhammer stores, all good book stores or visit one of the thousands of independent retailers worldwide, which can be found at **games-workshop.com/storefinder**

GREAT RED

David Guymer

Forwards, thought Ramus, as though it were sheer will rather than Azyr-forged muscle that thumped his boot into the dust and dragged the other past it.

He could see nothing through the swirl of dust beyond the spitting candle flare of his reliquary staff, hear nothing but howling and the nail-like rap of fine grains of weathered bone hitting his black plate. He did not pity himself the loss of his senses. If there was anything that could be felt anywhere on the Sea of Bones then it was dust and sand and endless wind.

On, his mind intoned, and his body responded to the word as though it were a rod across his back. I will cover every grain of this accursed desert if that is what it takes to have Mann-fred von Carstein's neck between my hands, he swore silently.

The shield, Sigmar's Gift, clanked against his back. The skull of the ogor, Skraggtuff, swung out and in and banged against his thigh. And he pushed on, forwards.

'We should ride this storm out, brother,' yelled Vandalus.

The Knight-Azyros was to Ramus' left and half a dozen paces behind, walking bent into the wind, the skeletal frame of his wings tugged back. Wind-whipped totems of feathers, leaves and bits of bone swirled around his maroon armour, partially obscuring the depictions of stars, storms and wild beasts in gold. 'My Prosecutors saw a huge number of Ironjawz orruks moving ahead of us. We could be on top of them already. The dust will give us no warning.'

Ramus snorted. 'I thought men once called you the King of Dust.'

'An easy title to claim and an easier one to give to another, but the dust respects me no more for it.'

'We go on. Our guide is insistent that this is the Betrayer's path.'

'An ogor, and a dead one at that. The dead cannot be trusted.'

There was a dull pain in Ramus' chest. Lord-Celestant Tarsus had used to say that. He shook his head and ploughed on.

He touched his fingers to the shield banging against his shoulders. There was a sudden hiss of burning metal and he snatched his fingers back. He smiled a grim smile as he shook off the sting. Sigmar's Gift had delivered unto the Betrayer the God-King's fire, and it remembered. The closer they drew the hotter it burned, and Ramus ardently prayed that the same would be true for Mannfred von Carstein's undying flesh.

The ogor skull butted his thigh plate and bounced, out, in, and banged again. Skraggtuff had initially been part of a trap left for them by the Betrayer, but Mannfred was not the only one with talents.

Was he not Ramus of the Shadowed Soul, Lord-Relictor of the Fourth-Forged Host, the Hallowed Knights? His will was a conduit for the divine storm. Life and death were his to go between.

Splaying his fingers over the skull's broad features so that they scratched in the sand over its eyes and mouth, he closed his eyes, and bent his mind towards the soul-eternal. He could see it still, a dull ember bound by the Betrayer's dark necromancy to the ogor's bones.

'Awake, Skraggtuff.' His spirit voice darted in and around his flesh like a sibilant, quicksilver tongue.

The sepulchral echoes that rang back from the storm brought an animal growl from Vandalus' mask. He raised his lantern and readied his starblade, warily. 'I still don't like this, brother.'

Ramus ignored him. He did not like it either, but Sigmar demanded much of those to whom much was given, and the ogor was what Ramus had been given. If he was to recapture Mannfred, and in so doing atone for the failure of his embassy to the Great Necromancer and the loss of the Hallowed Knights' Lord-Celestant, then he could ill afford to dismiss such gifts from his enemies.

'Awake, Skraggtuff. It is I, Ramus, your brother in vengeance.'

Frost rimed the weathered metal of Ramus' gauntlet where it covered the skull's mouth. A spark of blueish light took up deep within the dead thing's eyes.

'*Ungh. You.*' A pause. They were creeping in more often, growing longer. '*Are we there yet?*'

'You tell me.'

'*He's near. I can smell him. Can't you?*'

Ramus pulled his hand away. He felt the tenuous bridge between them snap and the light guttered and died. The frost on his palm needled to nothing, scoured to bare metal by the wind.

'What did it say?' Vandalus shouted after a moment.

'He is near.'

'That still leaves the problem of the Ironjawz.'

To the left and right, haggard-looking Hallowed Knights marched, draped in dust cloaks so heavy that only the meanest sliver of gold or silver glinted through the storm. Nodding in thought, Ramus forced himself on into the wind.

Were the Ironjawz a problem? Or were they just another gift from his enemies?

'Sigmar has seen us this far, my friend. Have faith that he will not let us stray now.'

The broad axe hit Ramus' shield with the weight of a felled tree. It scratched, snarled, squealed for purchase, but the shield held firm. Sigmarite was more miracle than metal, able to take many colours and forms, and this part of his mortis armour was far tougher than the mirrored silver it appeared to be. All that force had to go somewhere though, and if the shield did not yield, then it would go through Ramus.

He grunted with effort and the throbbing pain. His arm yielded, and the back of his shield struck his skull helm, twisted his face in, and drove his shoulder remorselessly down towards his bent knees. Metal scraped over metal. The crushing weight lifted, dragged back for a final, cleaving blow. Ramus imagined it scuffing along the dusty ground and looping up, up, glinting at arm's length above his assailant's monstrous head. The moment.

With a roar, he uncoiled and slammed his shield through the brute's unguarded jaw.

The big orruk grunted. It was an ugly mound of muscle, sinew and scar tissue encased in armour plates, impractically thick. Sand-worn spikes thrust out from shoulders, forearms and thighs. Another set curved up from the collar, so long they almost doubled as a visor and forced the orruk to squint between the notched edges. There were no conventional 'joints' or obvious points of weakness. There were no buckles or straps. Rather, the plates had been *bent* into one another as if by hand.

It swayed back maybe half a foot, braced its back leg, then drove a knee that sliced the lower rim of Ramus' shield into his groin and knocked the Lord-Relictor's legs from under him.

Not the reaction he had been hoping for.

'Tough, these Ironjawz,' he muttered as he rolled sideways.

He caught a glimpse of silver and blue where a Retributor and something hunched and dusty tussled in the wind, and then the orruk stomped down a boot.

Ramus came up onto his haunches, grey sand spraying from his hammer as he smashed aside the orruk's axe. This was not a duel. Neither axe nor hammer was a weapon of refinement. Each was designed for smashing and killing, as the orruks and Sigmar's Stormcast Eternals had themselves been so designed.

A lot of blood had been shed since Ramus had last crossed an opponent he could not overpower with the simple virtues of smashing and killing.

They crossed hafts and strained, beast versus divine. The orruk's nose flapped wetly where Ramus' shield had broken it, green-black blood and snot bubbling out with every breath, but it concerned the brute not at all. Ramus felt the desert dust sink around his boots. His arm began to burn with the effort.

'We are not... your... enemy!'

Putting all his remaining strength into it, Ramus levered his haft up, turned the locked weapons like two halves of a wheel and forced the orruk to be turned with it or let go. It chose wrong. Ramus guessed right.

'Hah!'

The orruk folded after its weapon, its nose cracking against the headbutt coming the other way. Ramus heard the crunch and splatter of a half job being messily finished. The orruk bent across him, off balance, axe blade in the dust. Ramus rammed his shoulder into its ribs, this time sending it stumbling away, then lashed his shield back across its jaw with a sound like an iron pot being smashed through a wall.

The blow actually straightened the orruk up. Its head snapped almost fully around, but it did not seem to feel a bit of it below the neck. It stuck out an arm and grabbed his throat.

Ramus felt his feet kick away from the ground as the Ironjaw hauled him to the level of its spiked grille. It glared at him with scrunched up red eyes. The visible bit of its dark face, wedged in tight, was scabbed with tough stubble. Its breath stank of leaf mulch and mushrooms.

Metal squealed as the Ironjaw tightened its grip, seeking to shape Ramus' armour with its bare hands as it had presumably shaped its own. Like his shield, the armour held. It would take more even than the grip of an Ironjaw to make sigmarite bend. It still felt as though his eyeballs were going to burst out of his face.

He smashed his hammer into the orruk's grille, but could not deliver force enough to break it. At the same time he drove his boot into its gut, but could not hit anything more vulnerable than muscle and iron. He managed to hook a finger up the orruk's nose and dragged it up towards him. The creature twisted irritably and snapped at his hand, spraying his faceplate with spittle.

His vision began to blur. Bent, disjointed figures stumbled through the beating dust into his peripheral view and then faded to black. His ears, however, seemed to grow keener to compensate. The rasp of sand on dead throats, the pop of old joints.

'Not... your... enemy.'

There was a hiss, a string of metallic *thunks* and a row of foot-long sigmarite-tipped bolts stitched up the Ironjaw's side. It grunted, in surprise rather than pain, and glanced down at the striking line of starmetal piercings running from hip to armpit. Ramus swung his boot up onto the lowest bolt. The sigmarite shaft held true, blessed be, his kick twisting the bolt sharply and driving it deeper into the orruk's guts.

And that, by almighty Sigmar, it felt.

Ramus had his feet on the ground and dry, dusty air in his lungs before the orruk had thought to let rip a howl. Letting his shield hang from the wrist strap, he took his hammer two-handed like a mallet and cracked it across the side of the Ironjaw's head. Moving around behind it, Ramus hammered his weapon into its back and shoved it down onto its face. It struggled to push itself up only for its arms to sink into the sand and Ramus' boot to step on the back of its neck.

He ground in his heel until its spine finally snapped. The Ironjaw went limp, and Ramus made sure with a last hammer blow that cratered the back of its head and stippled his black greaves with gore.

'Tough, these Ironjawz.' He glanced sideways and nodded. The Judicator lowered his boltstorm crossbow, his dusty armour silver and blue. 'My thanks, Sagittus.'

The Judicator-Prime gave a quick nod, redressed his aim to a point just above Ramus' shoulder and fired again. Bolts fizzed past, and punched into the shambling corpses until there was no longer enough meat left on them to stand.

'Only the faithful, Lord-Relictor.'

'Only the faithful.'

With another tilt of the helm, the Judicator turned back to the fight.

Ramus did the same. He spotted his reliquary where he had left it, plunged into the shifting bone sands, both a battle standard and a waypoint should any of his knights become lost in the swirl. A fuzz of Azyric power spread into the grey around it, illuminating the morbid imagery of faith, death and the storm depicted thereon, in fits and snatches. Big, hulking shadows brawled around it, tusks, blades and iron plates glinting blue, on the ground and in the sky above.

As Vandalus had predicted, the dust had allowed the Stormcasts to walk right into the Ironjawz and given neither side warning. Finding the orruks themselves beset was something neither had anticipated. Mannfred had been wily enough to avoid an encounter with the warclans of the Great Red thus far.

If Ramus had expected the orruks to be grateful for his aid – and in that initial flush of self-righteous glory in which he had almost *felt* his breath upon the vampire's back, he had expected it – then he should have expected too his disappointment.

It was impossible at a glance to tell who had the edge. Sigmar's Stormhosts excelled in close combat, as they had been forged to excel in all things, but the Ironjawz took a savage delight in it, as if they had been purposefully bred to go toe to toe with the mightiest warriors in the realms, and some of the largest carried twice the weight in muscle and half again the breadth.

Ramus stowed his shield and ran for his reliquary. He snatched it up, feet sliding in the shifting dust before he regained his footing, boot wedged under a sand pile of long, partially buried bones.

'You!' came the grunted, straightforward challenge, from a veritable behemoth of armour plate mounted on a seething, boar-like beast veering from the churn of bodies. 'You're mine! The Great Red's gonna be the first over the Bone Sea, and I'll be there with 'im.'

Its iron frame was so massive that it was almost as thick

across the shoulders as it was tall. Each pauldron looked to have been remade from a complete anvil, and its elbows struck out like the two points of an upended diamond. Its mount was itself dressed in knotted sheets of mail that abraded its grizzled fur with every step and no doubt accounted for a measure of its wild-eyed ill temper.

The beast swept itself a path through the dust with long, saw-edged tusks, snorted, and thundered into a charge.

Ramus drew back his reliquary, lowered it as though it were a spear and the orruk a charging juggernaut. He growled the opening bars of a prayer. Lightning played around the metal haft. He felt a static tickle under his gauntleted fingers.

Before he could unleash it, the orruk was gone.

There was a creak, then a groan, as the Ironjaw's hands flapped up despairingly, and it sank rapidly into the ground. Ramus backed up quickly, his own feet sinking into the sudden flow of dust.

'Grindworm!' he roared, biceps bulging as he pushed back with his staff against the swelling current. He sought out Sagittus and his other Primes, couldn't see them in the confusion, but waved his arm back anyway. 'Stay clear!'

The ground flexed like a muscle and an Astral Templar Liberator disappeared in a plume of dust. There was a trembling deep underfoot. Stratified layers shuffled and restacked, the subterranean flows of sand shifting to accommodate the approach of some kraken of the desert sands, and then a terrific explosion carried the lot of it sky high, bones and debris blasted like grapeshot around the bolt of lightning that jagged up in search of the sky.

Ramus swore as his body plunged a foot deeper into the sand. Knuckles and teeth and weathered nubs of bone he could not identify swirled around him like the surface manifestation of a developing whirlpool. Everywhere, fissures opened to drink in the desert dust and the shambling undead, while Stormcasts and Ironjawz wrestled for the skeletal islands the retreating sands laid bare, carcasses so vast that entire armies could have fought over them unnoticed.

And then the Ironjaw leader and his boar mount reappeared.

Thrashing about under six feet of dust, both orruk and beast were trapped in a hellish, faceless orifice large enough to swallow both whole with room to spare. Dust spouted around the struggling orruk and a segmented body that seemed to be made wholly of sand reared up out of the desert floor.

Ramus scowled, trying to draw further away from the rising worm, but the suction on his legs was tremendous.

He did not know whether the creatures were truly living predators or a natural phenomenon of the Sea of Bones. The Astral Templars, however, had dubbed them grindworms, for the screeching, sand-scratching roar they made as they appeared and killed. Their attacks seemed random, drawn by fighting or the movement of large numbers on the surface, but Ramus could not with certainty say that there was not some malign will driving this monster onto *him* before all others.

He forced his staff into the sand, not deep enough to arrest his downward slide, but enough to slow it. He clamped his hammer to his belt and took the reliquary in both hands. Overhead, storm clouds boiled through the gravel-white sky. 'If you hear this, Mannfred, if you see it, then pray tell me how this feels.'

A bolt of lightning tore through the sandstorm and detonated the grindworm's emerging head. Clods of sand and tiny pieces of glass rained over the desert. The Ironjaw, torso blackened, legs gone, hit the ground with a muffled clank.

Ramus gave a roar of defiance as the headless sand-beast

thumped to the ground not far from where he was caught. Every muscle heaved in the direction of one last gargantuan pull towards freedom. There was some give. He felt his legs beginning to slide out of the dust, could see the weathered black plate of his thigh. He bared his teeth for the coming effort.

'Can I help you, Ramus?' Vandalus called down. 'Or do you mean to climb out yourself for a greater tale?' The armoured angel beat his wings, dust fizzling and popping as it was blown through his lightning feathers. His attention was down, pointing at Ramus with his sword, clearly blind to the gaunt shape flapping furiously towards him.

'Attend yourself, Azyros.'

Vandalus turned his head, lifted and unshuttered his lantern in the same moment it must have taken him to recognise the threat, and burned the ghoul from the sky with a searing shaft of celestial light. The ghoul simply evaporated. By the time he had closed his lantern again and looked down, Ramus had dragged his body out and onto more stable ground.

He looked around. The grindworm was sinking into the desert, the dust it had disturbed beginning to resettle into new formations, burying titanic skeletons greater than dragons and lifting still more from the depths. Already a whole new landscape, utterly alien to what had been before, lay about them. The surviving Ironjawz were withdrawing – and it was a *withdrawal* – into the storm. The remaining undead were being methodically hacked apart by the Astral Templars and Hallowed Knights. Ramus counted exactly two dozen of the former and about double that of the latter.

More losses.

Vandalus touched down on the sand and walked towards him, blade pointed accusingly at Ramus' hip. 'I told you that the dead cannot be trusted, brother. That *thing* you carry led us right into that battle.'

'It took us on Mannfred's trail, which is all it can be expected to do. The battle is on us.'

The Knight-Azyros snorted and stowed his weapons. 'As it should be. And with the Ironjawz occupied with the dead it was a battle we had every chance to avoid. Astral Templars will never grieve over a pointless exercise in killing, but I know you saw it too.'

'I had believed that if the Ironjawz could see us fight alongside them then they might be persuaded to aid us in our quest. The Sea of Bones is vast. Even I am not so proud as to deny that we could use their aid if we are to search it fully.'

'What you could use, brother, is ten full Stormhosts scouring this wasteland west to east, and driving your vampire into the desert sun. We should focus our energies on seeking out the Celestial Realmgate.'

'No!' Ramus snapped, startling himself with his vehemence. 'No,' he growled, more softly, but with teeth still. 'This path has been set before me by Sigmar himself and I will not veer from it one inch.'

'Peace.' Vandalus clasped Ramus' forearm and with the other hand gripped his pauldron plate. Some barbarian embrace from the Azyros' mortal heritage. 'My Chamber has enough bad blood with Mannfred to follow you, you know that, but did the black-skinned orruk we captured on the Marrow Delta not tell us it was the Great Red himself who took the Realmgate from my brother Lord-Castellant in the first place?'

'A Realmgate you cannot now find.'

Vandalus flung out an arm. 'Light of Sigmar I may be, but I defy anyone to find their way in a landscape that changes from moment to moment.'

'And was it not also you who once spoke to me of the reasonableness of orruks? That all one needs to earn their trust is to win their respect?'

'The orruks I knew,' Vandalus muttered darkly. 'These Ironjawz are another breed entirely. I don't know what you would have to do to earn the respect of such foes.'

Ramus shook his head, his hand drifting to the skull at his hip, a faint but reassuring whisper occupying the darker corners at the back of his mind that might otherwise provide a purchase for doubt. 'I am resolved. If the Great Red can be convinced that Mannfred is the threat he surely is, if he can be won around by our strength...'

He clenched his gauntlet and Vandalus took a step back. The look Ramus felt from behind that gilded, implacable mask was searching. The Knight-Azyros shook his head and raised his hands. 'As you want it, brother. I had my Prosecutors follow the Ironjawz retreat. I heard one of them speak of a fort not far from here.'

'Then gather the host, Azyros. We march the moment they return.'

The Ironjawz had erected their fortress on what must have been the only example of static geography for a thousand leagues. It was certainly the first that Ramus had seen since crossing the Junkar Mountains.

It was a skeleton, the mountain-sized remains of a Titan of the Age of Myth, and cold proof, were it needed, that Mannfred von Carstein could *never* be allowed to possess the Sea of Bones. The skull was buried under a massive dune, vertebrae arching high up into the dusty sky where a scrap heap of rust-brown walls, towers and metal gangways vied for height and space. Ribs that had been weathered smooth by aeons of wind curled beneath it like a dead spider's legs. Sand devils whipped and swirled around the half-buried bones. Partially sheltered under the gargantuan cavity, a fleet of ironclad war-junks – ships of all things – creaked and listed and banged together.

Vandalus had told him that orruks liked to build high, that the size and towering nature of a boss' stronghold spoke directly to his status. The Ironjawz seemed even more itinerant and warlike than the orruks of Ramus' experience, but they were every bit as territorial. Whatever warboss ruled from this structure was surely very high indeed.

Perhaps even the legendary Great Red himself.

Green shapes cavorted over the distant walls, jeering. The scrap fort's windswept turrets clattered and clanged with gongs, cymbals and pans.

'Rank up, shields ready, weapons high, Prosecutors in formation,' Ramus barked.

He looked left, seeing the two lines of Hallowed Knights, mixed Paladins front, Judicators back, glittering silver and blue, as straight as statues in the wind. To his right were the Liberators of the Astral Templars, their battered maroon and gold decked out in eclectic war paint and charms that wagged about them like animals' tails. Above, Astral Templars Prosecutors hung in the sky like baubles of light. The harsh wind tugged at their fur cloaks and the strips of scripture stuck to their war-plate. It had even managed to tease some of the hair from under their sealed helms and whipped it giddily about them as though triumphant at what it had done. They had been beaten hard, but they were all the more magnificent for it. By Sigmar, they stood yet.

'Let them see what the strength of the finest two chambers in Sigmar's host looks like. Who shines with his light?'

'Only the faithful!' shouted the Hallowed Knights, and even a handful of the Astral Templars, gamely attempting to out-shout their brothers-in-arms.

Bursting with pride in them all, Ramus returned his attention to the fort.

'Three of its sides overhang the monster's ribs,' observed Vandalus, pointing them out. 'An aerial assault on that quarter would almost certainly find the orruks' defences unprepared.'

'You have not the numbers to carry out such an attack,' Ramus returned.

Vandalus clapped his shoulder. 'Which is why I'll need my brother to relieve me.'

Ramus shifted his gaze to the gate. According to millennia of military theory, it should have been the weakest point. The Ironjawz were clearly unfamiliar with this theory. Their gate was a lump of iron that, at first glance, actually looked fractionally too large for the frame it had been wedged into. It would take a monstrous application of force simply to get it open, much less to knock it down.

The approach to the gate however was the first, and arguably greater, obstacle. An uncertain-looking stairway of iron planks, not all of them flat, zig-zagged up the titan's spine towards the fortress. It was presumably stable enough to bear the tremendous weight of an Ironjaw but it was a challenging path, and every second that the Stormcasts' attention was on not falling to the desert floor was a second in which the wall's defenders would be showering them with missiles.

'Restrain yourself, Azyros. We do not need to take their position outright, just impress upon their leader our strength as allies.'

Vandalus waved a clenched gauntlet in the direction of the fort. 'What did you think I was proposing?'

'But first,' muttered Ramus. 'To get their attention.'

Ramus raised his reliquary and muttered a grim prayer. The sky began to bruise, deeper, blacker, and a sudden wind blew against Ramus' back and swept the dust off it to leave the smell of thunder and fresh rain. Sheet lightning flashed. The thunderhead folded and churned, the wind whipped into a howling cyclone with Ramus the eye of the storm.

'I am Ramus of the Shadowed Soul,' he roared. The wind stole his voice from his mouth, but it rumbled from the black clouds like the anger of the storm itself. Rain lashed the scrap fort, deadening the chaotic clangour. 'I am Lord-Relictor of the Hallowed Knights, the Fourth-Forged of Sigmar's Eternal Host. I seek embassy with your leader. The one that calls himself the Great Red.'

'That should do it,' Vandalus yelled.

Thunder rolled, unappeased, and the rain picked up. Ramus saw several of the Astral Templars turning their faces towards it, letting the water rinse the dust from their faceplates. The Hallowed Knights stood still, statues come rain or storm. From the fortress however, something moved.

A horn was blasted, a set of deep drums enthusiastically pounded, and in a tooth-aching squeal of metal along bone, the scrap fort's great gate began to grind open.

As Ramus watched, a huge orruk in garb garish enough to be seen even through the downpour danced through the opening gate. It was clad in a spiked and heavily decorated half-plate of mismatched iron scraps and painted bone that clapped as it dropped, leapt and spun down the stairway. It was unarmed in the conventional sense, but carried a club-like length of bone in each hand, using them to slap its thighs, its wrists, its iron garb and each other, in a frantic, strangely thrilling rhythm.

A mob of black-skinned orruks in conventionally wrought

heavy armour, full helms and shields stomped out behind the weird warchanter.

Following them with a swagger came the true Ironjawz themselves. Ironclad behemoths, each one clanked inside a personal battle-frame that made the black-skinned orruks look like whelps, wrapped for their own safety in foil. They nodded metal-encased heads to the warchanter's rhythm, bashed axes, maces and articulated fist-claws to the beat.

'I'd say they weren't impressed,' shouted Vandalus, wings shrieking into energetic life as he lifted himself off the ground.

'Lines of battle,' Ramus snapped.

The Astral Templars clumped forwards and locked shields. His own Exemplar Chamber bore no shields – wielding instead a deadly blend of two-handed thunderaxes, stormstrike glaives and lightning hammers – and simply took a forward step to maintain a perfect line with their more eager Astral Templar counterparts.

As they positioned themselves, the first of the greenskins reached the rain-packed desert floor. There they spread themselves into battle lines that mirrored those of the Stormcasts, except for being half again as long and several ranks deep. Ramus estimated that they were outnumbered at least three to one. The big Ironjawz brutes held the centre, flanked by disciplined detachments of the sober black orruks. On the left flank, opposing the Astral Templars, was a vast and unruly mob of grots, armed with anything that was going and cursing shrilly across the rain-driven gulf. On the opposite flank, two full ranks of boar cavalry drew themselves into a roughly unified mob and snorted impatiently for the signal to go.

'No flyers,' Ramus muttered, choosing to focus on that advantage, however small.

The Protector, Cassos, scoffed at his Lord-Relictor's attempted optimism. He was the last of that particular calling left. Ramus had never seen a man more adamant in avoiding his return to Sigmar's keep.

Ramus thrust his reliquary above his head and looked down the line. 'Who fights with Sigmar by his side?'

'Only the faithful!' sang the Hallowed Knights.

'Who will be victorious?'

'Only the faithful!'

The warchanter took the last few steps in a leap and began to flap about in the sand, hunched over as he danced up and down the greenskin line, sticks a blur, huffing and grunting in a singsong growl. Faster, louder. The orruk sank to his knees in front of the Ironjawz brutes in an ecstatic crescendo, bone sticks drumming on his thighs. The rain lashed his upturned face as he roared, and the entire greenskin line erupted with him.

First to break forwards were the brutes, then the black orruks. The boar cavalry, for all their impatience, got themselves together last but quickly pulled ahead as the vicious beasts thundered into a gallop. Only the grots held back, loosing a volley of arrows that sucked wet sand well shy of the Astral Templars.

'Hold,' Ramus muttered, conscious of the Astral Templars edging forwards, then turned to glance over his left pauldron. 'Judicators, loose.'

A rattling volley of sigmarite-tipped war-bolts fizzed towards their distant targets, arcing up, up into the rain, and droning down, their accuracy and potency far superior to the missiles fired by their greenskin counterparts. The bolts fell amongst the boar cavalry, thunking into heavy armour. One boar-beast slammed to the ground with a foot-long bolt in its shoulder and crushed its rider. The beast behind barged it out of the way on its tusks without slowing down. The rest rode on, armour bristling with shafts and crackling with Azyrite power.

'Again. Loose.'

Another volley shot across the distance. This time there was no need to correct their aim for range. The boar cavalry were a wall of scrap iron and bludgeoning power. The ground shook. Another Ironjaw rider took an impaling hit in the belly, grunted, but did not fall. To the right, an Astral Templar in shining bright maroon and gold, called only recently from Sigmaron to Vandalus' beacon, aimed high, and drew back on his enormous shockbolt bow. There was a rush of charged air as the giant arrow twanged from the bowstring. It looped over the running black-skinned orruks, fizzing like a firework, and exploded amongst the grots in a storm of lightning.

The boars picked up speed. Wet sand flew from thundering, iron-shod trotters. They were now just moments away – close enough for Ramus to see the red of their slathering mouths. Grasping his reliquary, Ramus closed his eyes. He could hear their grunting breaths, feel the shaking of the ground, but he set it aside to focus his senses on the rampant energies of the divine storm that raged around him. It was untouched, as wild as Azyr's Eternal Winterlands.

'There is no shaman here,' he muttered as he opened his eyes.

'That will level the field,' said Cassos.

'Yes, it will.'

Feeling his power rise to fill him, Ramus lifted his reliquary. He felt its unsubtle pull, as though it would lift him from the ground and make him as one with the broiling storm clouds if he did not fight to control it.

'Sigmar, lord of lightning!' he roared. 'Bare their flesh to Azyr's fire.'

He blasted a lightning bolt into the onrushing cavalry,

reducing orruks to ash and turning their brutish mounts into running meat. Teeth bared, he unleashed his power again and again until his body glowed. Lightning blitzed the terrified beasts, bolt after searing bolt, until armour bubbled over scorched flesh, and hulking warriors squealed like pigs as they rolled in sand to quench the flames.

'Sigmar!' he cried, breaking into a charge with his steaming reliquary held aloft. 'He fights beside us!'

The two armoured blocks slammed together in a splintering squeal of shields and blades and split pig-flesh. A thunderaxe hacked off an Ironjaw's arm at the elbow in a clap of noise. A riderless boar impaled a Retributor on a tusk. Bolts whistled from behind. An orruk bellowed a curse, and a moment later was spit through. Weapons hummed with Azyric charge. Two Ironjawz shoved towards Ramus, barding grinding until it shrieked. There was a snap of energy, a crimson blur that cut left to right, and both orruks slumped headless from their mounts. Cassos swept in front as the boars pulled apart and galloped past, stormglaive whirling with such venom it looked as though he must be holding two of them. It threw a barrier of spattered red between Ramus and the press of Ironjawz, and flicked the desultory shower of grot arrows waspishly from the air.

The Retributors and Decimators surged into the break, the Astral Templars a yard ahead as always. Ramus heard the Stormcasts' savage howls and the ring of starmetal as the Liberators crashed into the black orruks and through to the brutish Ironjawz behind. Smashing and killing. War as the God-King had always meant it to be.

Vandalus lanced overhead, beams of light from his lantern punching golden holes through the orruk ranks, then rolled left while the Prosecutors that followed peeled right.

Flight alone was a mighty task for these angels in armour, and to do it with grace demanded not only a fluidity of body, but a finesse of mind and will that transcended even the super-human. Wielding javelins like lances and celestial hammers two-handed, they thumped into the terrified grots like comets. Bodies flew, and to a cacophony of ululating war cries, the Stormcast barbarians set about tearing the light skirmishers apart.

The grots were broken almost as the first Prosecutor fell to earth amongst them, and they were already fleeing for their weird ironclad paddle ships.

'Ardboyz!' bawled the heaviest brute in the block of Ironjawz ranks, clacking a big, clunky grabber claw, all rivets and red paint, at the second mob of black orruks. 'I has this. Go sort out those ones with wings.'

The second mob wheeled one hundred and eighty degrees and tramped back towards the grounded Prosecutors.

'The centre holds,' called Sagittus from somewhere nearby.

'Judicators to the flanks!' shouted another Stormcast.

Ramus drove his boot heel into the face of an Ironjaw that was trapped under his dead boar. Cassos' stormglaive hummed around him like an angry guardian spirit. Somewhere amidst the smoking remains and the iron clamour, Ramus could hear the orruk warchanter pounding away with his bone sticks. A vicious tempo that the orruks strove to match with their weapons.

'The brutes rally to him,' growled Cassos. 'See how they shield him.'

An Ironjaw rose up in front of Ramus like a wall. It was the claw-toting boss, and the brute alone occupied the width of two others. Ramus dropped his shoulder and slammed into the Ironjaw's pectoral before he had the chance to turn his weapons on him. Air woofed out of him, but he did not yield an inch. The grabber claw champed shut inches in front of Ramus' neck. The Lord-Relictor swayed back, whipped up his hammer and deflected the moon-shaped axe that had been scything for the crown of his helm.

A crackling stormglaive spat across its turned shoulders. The Ironjaw bent out of reach, swatting the blade gruffly aside on the back of its claw. It was a split-second distraction and Ramus took it. His hammer dented the iron cladding on the Ironjaw's right side and drove all the brute's weight onto its left. It gave a threatening growl and paddled its arms for balance, but had nothing free to stop Cassos punting his stormglaive into its throat and tipping it onto its back.

Ramus knelt over the big boss and smashed the brute's helm open with a blow from his hammer.

'Sagittus!' he roared, as Cassos moved protectively in front of him. The warchanter's tempo had picked up, and it seemed to thump out of the bloody air. Ramus caught glimpses as the rest of the Ironjawz mob pressed forwards to defend the performer. Its eyes shut, mouth open, it played through the grip of some wild, degenerate rapture. 'Take him down, Sagittus.'

Heavy bolts hammered into the Ironjawz but they held firm, too thickly packed for the missile fire to get through. Even the Prosecutors that had managed to retake to the skies before the black orruks' charge had hit home found their javelins and thrown hammers blocked or knocked out of the air. And driving it all to ever greater heights of aggression and fury, was that drumming beat.

'I have him, brother.'

Vandalus swooped in behind the block of brutish heavy infantry, and there executed a barrel roll that dragged him across the rear of their formation. He unshuttered his golden lantern. Ironjawz howled as the wondrous light of Azyrheim burned across their backs, bled through cracks too slight for any boltstorm bolt or stormcall javelin to reach, and even tightly shut as they were, brought green smoke from the warchanter's eyes.

The orruk's demented chant bubbled off in a rabid scream.

Ramus saw the Ironjawz waver, enough for him to barge through the heavier orruk warriors and put the warchanter out of his torment with a hammer blow to the temple.

That was enough for the remaining black orruks, who immediately began to break off and run after the scattered grots. The Ironjawz however, outnumbered and surrounded, fought on.

Vandalus flung out his wings and speared upwards into the rain. The pall around him thickened. Lightning flashed. Ramus felt the hairs on his body respond to the rising charge, and sparks danced along the points of his reliquary's sigmarite halo. The Knight-Azyros slid his lantern's aperture to its widest setting and the full force of its illumination seared the dark of the storm away. For a moment, for one divine moment, Ramus felt the eyes of the God-King upon them all.

The throaty screams that greeted his gaze were affirming – the sudden, burning blindness of the apostate. The sky cracked open and lightning jabbed again and again into the desert floor like a chisel against a tooth, until the rain-soaked ground was cloaked in bone dust and all Ramus could see were the flashes.

Cassos laughed as cries of 'Sigmar!' greeted the Azyros' display of might.

The cloud began to settle, thinning as it did to reveal the glitter of maroon and gold, perfect as gemstones. Two dozen Stormcast Eternals, fresh from the barracks of Sigmaron and perfect to the finest facet of their war-plate, gave voice to a thunderous cheer and charged the Ironjawz' rear.

Breathing heavily, Vandalus landed beside Ramus.

'Difficult to win an audience when everyone's dead.'

Ramus smiled grimly. 'The Astral Templars were not part of the embassy to Shyish, were they, my friend?' With an amused snort, he pointed over the determinedly fighting Ironjawz to the scrap fortress, seemingly abandoned on its lonely, bone-top promontory. 'A day or two of rest will serve us well. We will regroup, resupply and recover the Betrayer's trail. And maybe someone will show up to reclaim it.'

The Ironjawz' clan hall was cold. Air came in through a pair of iron-grilled fireplaces in the long side walls and ruffled the dyed skin hangings. A long feasting table filled most of the floor space, a mishmash of metals so beaten, rumpled and chewed on there was not flat space enough to set a jug.

Ramus took it all in with a cursory sweep of his gaze. He stood with the open door behind him where it was coldest, dust circling, the big fireplaces either side, the table extending before him to a large, bloody iron throne. A hide banner covered the whole wall behind it, depicting two crudely drawn glyphs on a red background. He knew little of the orrukish languages, less of their written forms, but these he had seen everywhere.

Great. Red.

'We have searched the compound thoroughly, Lord-Relictor.' Sagittus stepped in from outside, letting in the dull clangour of pots and pans, strung up wherever they might catch the wind. Mist clung to his grim-faced silver mask. His boltstorm crossbow hung by his side in one heavy gauntlet. 'It is empty.'

'Very good,' Ramus murmured. In his mind he pulled those two symbols apart, turned them over, searching for the hidden complexity that was so jarringly absent.

'Lord-Relictor?'

'Look again.'

'My lord, I assure you.'

Ramus turned his head towards his second, the deep sockets of his skull helm boring in. 'When I feel assured, I can guarantee that none will know of it before you.'

The Judicator gave a stiff bow from the neck. 'Very well, my lord. Once more.' His boots clicked on the metal floor as he walked back outside.

Ramus returned to his contemplation of the fluttering banner. Sagittus had not been part of the Warrior Chamber at the Bridge of Seven Sorrows and had not experienced the Reforging. He had not been given the time to reflect on the consequences of that quest's failure. Tarsus was Sigmar's and he had been *stolen*. To Ramus' exhaustive knowledge of the histories, such a violation had never befallen another Stormhost and the shame of his participation in it seared. And if he should fail to recover the Lord-Celestant now...

The Hallowed Knights were a company of immortals. There was no precedent for the elevation of one of their number to leader.

He touched his fingers to Skraggtuff's skull and closed his eyes, giving himself to the cold. His lips parted in a wisp of vapour. They were numb and pinched.

'Awake, Skraggtuff.'

'*Mmmmm*,' came the answering echo, the dull murmur of a dreamer.

'How much ground has Mannfred gained on us? You are connected through the aether, Skraggtuff.'

'*Mmmm.*' Ramus felt the impression of a wretched spirit, tossing and turning, eyes flickering between sleep and wakefulness. '*Not far. Time to sleep maybe. Just for a bit.*'

Ramus withdrew his fingers with a start and opened his eyes, his perceptions suddenly, jarringly normal. He blinked a few times, licked his lips, worked his fingers to restore them to some kind of warmth, and as he did so a door clicked open at the far end of the hall where there had been none. It put a ruck into the banner that had been draped over it and blew dust in underneath. A golden gauntlet felt under the fabric, swept it up and back over the top of the thick metal door. Vandalus peered around, looking slightly lost, then turned to Ramus and pointed to the ceiling.

'I came in from the roof. Don't be too harsh on Sagittus, it was bolted from this side.'

'Did you–'

'No,' Vandalus sighed. 'I did find a grot hiding back here, but I suspect it was his duty to open the door for whoever sat in that throne.' He pointed to it and gave a dead-eyed smile. 'Orruk bosses prefer high spots. It shows everyone else how important they are, and lets them see everything that's theirs.'

'See how far?'

'The dust covers everything. Not far.'

'Show me.'

White, as deep as the eye could show. The one thing from his experience that Ramus could compare it to was being trapped in mist. It looked like mist, superficially perhaps, but to stand within it was to know what deceptive devils appearances could be. It was bone dry and bitingly cold. The wind hissed. Bone shards tinked against his armour and further out where he could not see, all around, the chitter of bone whispering across bone was constant. If the dead were to converse away from the ears of the living, then Ramus knew by the chill in his soul that this was how it would sound.

He moved to the spiked metal rampart, set his gauntlets on

the sharpened edge, and peered down. White. All the way. He could not even see the spiral stair any more.

The wind moaned against his helm's frozen sides. Sound moved strangely in the Sea of Bones. It hung in the air, making it seem sometimes more like being under water than on a desert. The dull mutterings he heard could have been an army passing under his nose, a lone beast trumpeting a thousand leagues away, or even the tectonic wars of the Junkar, far, far behind them.

Something on the rampart beside him blew its nose and he turned his scowl upon it. He had reasonably assumed that 'found a grot' meant 'killed a grot' but now the wretch was looking up at him with wide wet eyes, ears flat back against its head, Ramus had to concede that the mood was not exactly on him either.

Gorkamorka had once been part of Sigmar's great pantheon, he reasoned. It was belligerence, rather than fundamental theistic differences, that set the two powers at odds.

'We are looking for the Great Red,' he said, speaking firmly. 'Where is he?'

''s not here,' the grot squeaked.

'I see that. I asked where he was.'

'Gone.' The grot swallowed, the big lump in its throat bobbing up and down. 'Gone to fight at the thunder door.'

The scrawny greenskin nodded vigorously.

'Why?' asked Ramus.

'To fight.'

'But *why?*'

'To be first over the Bone Sea. Think of the fame. Even the old Junkar never did that.'

Ramus turned to Vandalus, over by the door onto the stairwell.

'The desert nomads that greeted us on our first arrival

believed the Sea of Bones went on to the edge of the world. In Cartha's libraries, we found texts describing distant lands, so far across the lifeless plain that even the Age of Chaos had yet to reach them.'

Ramus snorted. 'Stories told to give hope to children.'

''s true,' piped the grot. 'And the Great Red was all about to head off too. Had his boats loaded and everything, before the dead one snuck in and took his thunder gate.'

Ramus' jaw clenched. His chest had gone suddenly cold.

Mannfred.

'He means the Celestial Realmgate,' said Vandalus, moving across.

'There's another fort there,' said the grot quickly, warming to its theme. ''s very important. The Great was gonna use it to bring in stuff and store it. 's a long way over the Bone Sea.'

'Tell me about the dead one,' Ramus demanded, dropping down beside the grot and eliciting a terrified squawk. 'Tell me everything you know about Mannfred.'

'Wait,' said Vandalus, turning to the deep white view and cocking a gold-helmeted ear. 'Do you hear that?'

Ramus gave an irritated wave, but as soon as he did it he realised that the distant susurrus had changed. It was no longer so distant, for one. Drums. It was scores and scores of big, deep drums. The cracked chant of guttural voices. The tramp of armoured feet.

'Clear the skies,' said Vandalus urgently. 'As you did before.'

Though he ached body and soul from his efforts in the battle, Ramus raised his reliquary and gave voice to a doleful prayer. The wind picked up and the dust pall began to thin, the sky so cleared blackening and producing a rumble of distant thunder.

'There!' Vandalus shouted.

Wearily, Ramus looked in the direction the Knight-Azyros

pointed. The stamp and clank of massed ranks rolled in from the desert plain towards the scrap fort. Several score of the damnable warchanters cavorted ahead of armoured columns, each a thousand strong, beating out a marching rhythm that held little in common with their neighbours' to create a raucous banging. Steaming between the formations, vast ironclad paddleboats, top heavy with crowded siege decks and bristling with artillery, chugged through the sand. Energy coursed through them and occasionally arced off. Ramus could see one of the strange Ironjaw shamans enthroned on the main deck of each monstrous vessel. He could sense their power, swollen to near god-like proportions by the weight and vibrancy of their greenskin kith around them, and somehow understood that these vessels served equally as troop transports, shock weapons, and amplifiers to ward off the grindworms.

The Great Red had planned his warclan's migration well.

Searching the marching files, Ramus saw him at last.

'There he is. The Great Red.'

A dark shape, a knot of ill-defined aggression, hung over the front ranks, mounted on a lumpen monstrosity of a creature that beat furiously at the surrounding air as though to physically subdue it with its small but muscular wings.

Ramus was aware of Sagittus shouting from under the iron floor beneath him, Judicators charging for the walls and priming crossbows.

'So many,' Ramus muttered.

'Too late to worry about that now,' Vandalus snapped. 'You wanted to impress the Great Red and I'd wager that's him right there. Impress him. Be strong, show no fear, and if he doesn't kill us both then *maybe* he'll be intrigued enough to hear your piece.'

Nodding his understanding, Ramus turned back and channelled his voice into the storm. 'I am Ramus of the Hallowed Knights, orruk, and I have been waiting for you. Come to me, and let us settle this as equals.'

He strained to catch the Great Red's reaction as the wind failed and cloaked the space between them in dust. The last thing Ramus saw was the Ironjaw's beast pulling ahead of his army and striving for height.

'A maw-krusha,' said Vandalus. 'I saw one in the Carthic Oldwoods once. The native ogors used to leave living prey in the forest to keep the monster from their tribes.'

Ramus caught the grot staring at him in open-mouthed, wide-eyed and flat-eared horror. He grunted and turned to Vandalus. 'Will he come?'

'He will. No orruk would let a challenge like that go unan–'

The Azyros looked sharply up. Ramus heard it at the same time. It sounded like–

'Waaaaaagh!'

Ramus pushed himself back against the spiked battlement as an armour-plated boulder smashed into the centre of the rampart.

The structure tilted sharply and squealed. Ramus clung grimly onto the rampart spike with one hand, arm hooked behind it and grinding on the metal. He saw the grot tumble past him, smack once against the wall, again on the skeletal structure, coming apart like a ball of yarn and disappearing into the pall.

Unconcerned by the swaying tower and the alarmed clangour of chimes and bells, the maw-krusha unfolded arms and legs and rose up onto knuckles the size of Ramus' fists. Forelimbs covered in hard scales, some of them carrying faded red paint, opened out like a pair of shield walls to reveal a head that was almost all mouth. A massive underbite, made even more pronounced by a muzzle of huge prosthetic fangs, chomped up over its small red eyes.

Stooped under a mass of wargear with ironclad thighs around the monster's neck and toes scraping the ground, was the largest greenskin Ramus had ever seen.

He had had cause to say that many times over the past months, but he doubted he would ever have another. The brute was gigantic, clad in thick armour daubed half and half in red paint and black, with massive, clawed gauntlets and spiky boots, dull red with old blood. Only its head was exposed, the black and red pattern reversed with a slash of red paint over its brutalised, dark hide. One eye was nailed shut with an iron plate, a wandering green eye crudely drawn over it. The megaboss grinned down at the Stormcasts, a slow, ape-like drawing in of muscles to reveal a mouth full of sharp, oversized metal teeth, bloody where they must have bitten into the roof of its own mouth.

If Ramus and Vandalus had stood together and been clad in a single piece of armour, they could not have been as large.

'I'm da Great Red,' the megaboss bellowed, voice so deep it seemed to come up out of the ground. The beast snorted and dragged its knuckles over the floor in an agonising screech. The Ironjaw glared at Ramus with his one eye, then twisted to mark Vandalus with a squeal of metal plates. He turned back to Ramus. 'Kill my boyz, take my stuff, you fink you're big enough to take Korruk da Great Red?' He dropped his heavy jaw and roared with laughter.

Ramus planted his reliquary into the metal between them. 'This land has been claimed. From the Celestial Realmgate to the Junkar Mountains and beyond the forests of Cartha, this land is Sigmar's.'

At the name 'Sigmar' power lashed from his staff and stung the hulking Ironjaw a blow to the shoulder. Korruk jerked back, bellowed in pain and shock, electric spasms forcing out a grunt of annoyance as he involuntarily yanked on the chain attached to his mount's spiked collar and locked his thighs down on its neck. It choked out a growl and instinctively threw out a battering-ram punch that smashed Ramus in the gut and off his feet.

His legs flipped over his head. Light to dark. Sky to metal. His face plate smashed the top of the crenel spike, a crack spidering from the left eye socket of his helm. Dark to light, the sky above him. He flung out a hand and caught the spike. His arm snapped taut and jerked him back, slammed his body hard against the fort's metal wall. Ramus' feet slid across the wall without getting any kind of purchase.

'Haha!' roared the Great Red. 'Maybe you should both have a go. Hah! Take turns, maybe.'

A flash of light burned like forked lightning through Ramus' shattered orbit as Vandalus explosively took wing. There was another bark of pain from the Ironjaw, and the clash of blades.

With a grimace, Ramus tested his bicep against his weight and heaved. He began to lift, bellowed as his shoulder passed his elbow, and then tossed his reliquary back inside and hauled himself after it. He collected his staff and rose, lightning pouring into him until the metal beneath him turned blue.

Vandalus and the Great Red were fighting high up above the fort's roof. The Azyros flitted agilely around the Ironjaw's monstrous axes, leaving a glowing trail where he passed as though it were a net, cleverly lain to trap the brute in his own savagery.

The megaboss' metal teeth glinted hungrily, one booming growl rising from his vast jaw without any apparent need for breath. He was a green storm, destruction made manifest, his brute physicality merely the solid housing for a force of nature. His axes flashed down together, forcing Vandalus into a parry that sent the Azyros spinning. The maw-krusha's claws clenched as though taking the air in its grip and then lunged out. A paw like a gargant's spiked mace smacked the careening Azyros, and hammered him back down.

Vandalus hit the roof in a blaze of spinning pinions and rolled until he hit the inside of the parapet. Ramus could hear armoured boots pounding up the staircase below. It would be Cassos.

'Sigmar is the true lord here, beast!'

Lightning stabbed from Ramus' staff and coursed through the megaboss and his monster. The Ironjaw sprayed Vandalus in phlegm before he could grind his metal jaws shut. Blood ran down his chin as his enormous body seized. Howling, flapping with erratic fury, the maw-krusha crashed back down. Exhausted, Ramus recalled the flow of current and turned to check on Vandalus.

The Knight-Azyros stood up, almost fell right back over, but steadied himself with a widened stance and shook out his light wings, creating a dazzling show of might and colour, as if to ward off a rival or a predator. To Ramus' surprise, Korruk gave a rumbling chuckle. The Ironjaw dismounted with a gravely structural *clang* and kicked his war-beast out of the way.

'You fight good for thunder men. Better than the big boss I killed at the thunder door.'

Vandalus started forwards, only for Ramus to hold him back.

'*Take him,*' hissed Skraggtuff, down by his hip. '*While his guard's down.*'

Of their own volition, Ramus' muscles tensed to lift his reliquary, but then he frowned. 'I did not summon you.'

'*He's too strong. He doesn't need you. He won't listen. End him while you have the chance.*'

Ramus lowered his staff. 'That is Skraggtuff's voice. But those are not his words.'

A sepulchral chuckle issued from the skull. Not one, in fact, but two, an eerie echoing effect as though he were being laughed at from both sides. The first was gruff and breathy, recognisably Skraggtuff, while the other was the sound of courteous good humour. Korruk ground his thickly armoured slab of neck around, one eye narrowed in annoyance. It was that, rather than the voices from the other side, that turned Ramus' insides colder than the desert wind.

Ramus was the conduit for the divine storm, the beacon for the soul-eternal.

Only *he* could speak with the dead.

'*Awake, Skraggtuff,*' whined the skull in a wheedling falsetto. The ogor's voice was gone, replaced entirely by the urbane imposter that Ramus recognised all too well. '*So tediously stentorian. Where is Mannfred, Skraggtuff? You are connected through the aether, Skraggtuff.*'

Now that it was presented to him, it was clear that the voice had always been there behind the ogor's words. How had he not heard it before?

'That voice,' breathed Vandalus.

'The Betrayer.'

'*Here, O conduit of the tepid squall, beacon of arrogance eternal. Tell me, are the Stormcast Eternals prone to delusions or is it just you? Imagine, believing that your quaint, half-mastered talents could begin to rival mine.*'

The voice tutted, and Ramus realised that it was no longer coming from the skull. A hazy human figure had appeared, wavering about a foot above the rampart. His black, ridged armour was dented and scratched from countless battles, and the red cloak he wore, though magisterial still, was tattered.

The wind blew through him, his long dark hair fluttering in some other breeze. His hair was wilder than Ramus remembered, his teeth longer, his eyes redder. His patrician features were horribly burned. Sigmar's gaze was not so swiftly healed.

'*Poor, pathetic hero.*'

'You brought me here,' Ramus yelled, fury making his voice crack. 'You led me by the damned nose. Why?'

'*Temper, temper, Lord-Relictor. What kind of example does that set the peasants?*'

'Why!'

Mannfred laughed. '*I think we demonstrated back in Cartha that I have little to fear from you.*' He half turned towards Korruk, one melted, hairless eyebrow suggestively raised, like a school master trying to goad the proper answer from a well-intentioned but slow-witted pupil.

'Me?' rumbled the Great Red, scrunching up his face in thought.

'*Where have you just been?*' Mannfred prodded.

'The thunder door.'

Vandalus' face dropped in understanding. '*Just think, my friend. Had you gone straight to your Realmgate as you suggested then I might never have been able to get by the Ironjawz to take it.*' The megaboss drew up at that. '*Of course, Great Red here would have killed you out of hand, but we can't have everything can we, and as he's likely going to do that anyway, that would have come at no real cost to you.*'

The apparition turned to Ramus and bowed. '*Of all the Stormcasts I have encountered, dear friend, you are the most rigid.*' He grinned, teeth sharp and somehow brighter for their transparency. '*I appreciate rigidity in my friends. It makes them so much easier to bend.*'

'I am no friend to you, Betrayer,' Ramus spat, but Mannfred

continued as though he had not heard, and turned to the glowering Ironjaw with a long, low bow, cloak falling to a floor that was not there.

'*It will be I, not you, who will be the first to cross the Sea of Bones. The march of my horde will be felt in the Realm of Death.*' With an elaborate flourish, he rose and turned back to Ramus. '*I will hold our mutual friend Tarsus with affection, when he is my prisoner instead of Nagash's.*'

With a spluttering cry, Ramus thrust his reliquary into Mannfred's wavering face and cried out to Sigmar for lightning. His staff pulsed blue-white and sprayed power in indiscriminate, arcing forks that carved through the apparition without effect. The vampire replied with a tolerant smile, swept his cloak across him and became a cloud of red that disintegrated on the wind.

'*Dwell upon your failures, Stormcast,*' came the disembodied voice, '*as I make the Sea of Bones mine.*'

Korruk's sudden howl of fury struck Ramus from any fixation on his own boiling blood. Stomping around without another intelligible word, the Ironjaw jumped onto his maw-krusha's back and kicked the beast into the air. It gave a bellow, flung out its vestigial, leathery wing-flaps and leapt from the parapet. It dropped into the pall like a stone.

Ramus listened as the megaboss' livid cries receded. He bowed his head as though in prayer. His eyes stung. It was impossible to hear the Ironjaw and not be reminded of the same unthinking rage that had driven him to this place. Despite it, his heart hammered for further vengeance.

If only his own intemperance could be soothed away as readily as the bone cloud took the Ironjaw's.

'Vandalus. Brother, I–'

'What's done is done, brother. Sigmar will judge you, but not I.'

Ramus hung his head. Such a covenant should have been reassuring, but for some reason the prospect of receiving Sigmar's judgement gave him a flutter of apprehension.

The Knight-Azyros spread his wings, stowed his starblade and offered Ramus his hand. 'What are we waiting for, brother? Would you leave all the fighting to the Ironjawz?'

Ramus lifted his face to the golden light of the Azyros and felt an icy peace quell his heart – the peace that only a certainty of purpose could bring. The Hallowed Knights had departed Azyrheim to renew old alliances, and perhaps a truce with the warriors of Gorkamorka had always been Sigmar's will.

'They will have all the fight that they please,' he said as he clasped the Azyros' gauntleted hand. 'But Mannfred is mine.'

FURY OF GORK
by Josh Reynolds

Still in search of allies for their war against Chaos, the Stormcasts brave the Ghurlands... but someone else is there, a champion of Tzeentch seeking a mighty weapon. Only a dangerous mission into the Howling Labyrinth can stop the sorcerer before it's too late.

For these stories and more go to **blacklibrary.com**, **games-workshop.com**, Games Workshop and Warhammer stores, all good book stores or visit one of the thousands of independent retailers worldwide, which can be found at **games-workshop.com/storefinder**

WRATHSPRING

Gav Thorpe

Something noisome carried on the wind. The reek was born of blood and rotten offal and rodent droppings. It was a harbinger, the vanguard of a thoroughly loathsome tide. Not just the air carried the taint. The Wrathwaters knew what was coming. Even the springsfed surge churning down from the peaks of the White Stair could not clear the pollution from the winding waterways and rising pools. The trees drew in their roots, sickened by the presence of the corruption. Fish lay gut-to-sky, rotting amongst withered leaves and decaying rushes.

In the heartwaters below the rivers and lakes, deeper than the delving of millennia-old trees, the miasma of decay spread through the veins of the forests. The font of wyldmagic – the essence of life, the meltwater of souls – thickened into sluggish swells, bloated and bubble-ridden like a stream choked with noxious gasses and rank sludge.

Diraceth, Leafmaster of Clan Arleath, felt all of these changes – upon his bark, in his sap, on the tips of his taproots.

The cloying, stifling Chaos taint was like a fungus on his spirit, leeching his essence, spreading fibrous tendrils through the lands of the Wrathwaters into every part of him.

It was hard to rouse himself, even with the strength of the long-awaited blooming forcing rivulets of life energy into his body. All of the worldwood sickened – it was folly to believe that the Wrathwaters could hold out. Better to succumb, to give up the last clinging vestige of life. Oblivion was preferable to further torture, the never-ending gnawing of soul and strength.

'Lord!' Callicaith, the branchwych, had climbed into his upper limbs and was dragging her wood talons against his rough bark – insistent but not painful, nor deep enough to draw sap. Her heartsong was a distressed twittering like the alarm of a bird. On her shoulder, a glimmersilk grub twitched with agitation. 'Lord Diraceth! The ratmen, they come at last. They come for the lamentiri!'

He opened deep green eyes and looked at the slender tree maiden.

'The soulpod groves?' His voice was sonorous, as deep as the earth into which his roots ran. He quivered at the thought. Diraceth's drooping branches scattered leaves onto the surface of the lake. Around him the bloodwillows responded, straightening their trunks, pulling up ruddy-leafed limbs.

Beyond his copse, other spirits were answering the growing strength of the clan-song. His fellow treelords rumbled echoes in their diminishing slumber. Sylvaneth warriors stirred in the dappled gloom at the water's edge. Polished wood and firestone of bared blades caught the scant sunlight, scattering glints like water droplets.

'No more pestilence, no more sickness,' Callicaith continued. 'Ratmen with blades, with spears. Creatures we can fight. Creatures we can kill!'

The thought brought Diraceth further from his slumber, drawing up an influx of the essence of Ghyran, the magic of the Realm of Life streaming through his sap.

'A poor move,' he growled. He let his roots fall away and drew up a foot. 'Skaven, always impatient. Another hundred seasons and we would be quite beyond resistance.'

'There are many, lord.'

'There always are, my glade-daughter.' Diraceth levered his other foot out of the sodden lakeside bank and took a step, his sap continuing to rise. It felt good to move again. 'Rouse the clan. We go to war!'

The wailing of trees competed with the deafening chitter of rats. Arboreal screeches and thrashing leaves beset the river glades of the Wrathwaters as the skaven advanced within a bank of burning mist. Tainted by warpstone, the deathfog of Pestilens scorched leaves and blistered bark. Droplets of warp-touched acid settled on the pools and meres, sinking slowly into the waters with greenish trails.

Diraceth waited, ignoring the pulses of pain that ran through him from the wickedly deep cut across his trunk – a wound that still seeped with the corrupted taint from the blade of the plague priest that had struck him. He wept streams of thick sap, the agony of his body nothing compared to the injuries inflicted upon his domains. The treelord ancient could feel a shudder of misery throbbing through the pools and rivers every time the filth-ridden missiles of the catapults crashed through the canopy. A dozen of the accursed engines had pounded the last scraps of territory for two days, littering the banks and water with heaps of steaming, disease-ridden offal and corrupting shards of warpstone.

Most of the trees were dead, and the rest had retreated with the sylvaneth. Beyond the painfully slender ring of forest sheltering Clan Arleath, the Wrathwaters had been turned into a steaming mire, a wasteland of sucking marsh and drifting, suffocating clouds.

They waited, the last Wrathwater scions of Glade Winterleaf. They waited without hope. At their backs lay the lifepool, the last vestige of their home. Heartseeds covered the surface, but the replenishing waters did not rouse the spirits within. The taint of the skaven came before them, quelling the life force that sustained the lake of the sacred grove. Even more faintly luminescent heartseeds gleamed beyond the perimeter of the clan's remaining realm – lost in the fog, overrun by the skaven, beyond reclaiming by the branchwyches.

As the last of the warp-wounded trees succumbed to the deadly miasma, the Wrathwaters fell silent. The impenetrable mists surrounded the dell, obscuring everything beyond a bowshot of the water's edge, revealing only dim silhouettes of trees bowing beneath the effect of the toxic cloud, curling like parched leaves. Diraceth shifted, sensing that something approached through the mist.

Drums. Slow-beating drums. The death fog muted the sound, every percussive rumble seeming to come from all directions. The distant crack of catapults had stopped too. Diraceth could hear the rustling of his glade-daughters and the creak of the other treefolk as they shifted, turning to and fro to watch the closing mists.

'We die here,' the Leafmaster told his glade-kin. He looked down at Callicaith. Like all of them, the branchwych bore the injuries of furious battle against the Chaos ratmen. Her leaf-limbs were snapped, her arms scored by deep marks from notched, rusted blades. 'On the shore of our life-grove, we fight to the last. No more retreats. Without our soulpods, there can be no Clan Arleath.'

The sap in his veins felt clammy and cold. The last of the Wrathwaters were succumbing to the encroachment of Pestilens. Diraceth could feel it like claws dragging at his spirit, trying to pull him down into the ground to suffocate him.

'There!' hissed Callicaith, pointing a talon towards the fog.

Others were calling out, indicating a growing darkness in the mists, the approach of the plague monks. Along with the sombre beat of the drums drifted the sound of feet splashing through the swamp.

Screeches split the air a few moments before individual shapes solidified and burst from the fog bank. Fanatics bearing fog-spouting censers sprinted towards the line of sylvaneth, faces flecked with saliva, thick tongues lolling, eyes wild. They swung their censer-maces in wide arcs, surrounding themselves with wreathing spirals of poisonous fumes.

Diraceth let his will flow back into the sustaining pool. He pushed his essence out into the remnants of the Wrathwaters, tapping into what little life magic remained. He felt a reciprocal force, as the Wrathwaters themselves sought a response to the invaders.

''Tis the last time your feet shall sully these lands, children of the Horned Rat!' bellowed Diraceth, letting his rage flow free in a torrent of magic.

The ground beneath the onrushing censer bearers erupted with the Leafmaster's power. Tiny rootlets sprang into full-grown rushes that speared up through the skaven, spitting them as surely as any lance strike. Grasses with blades like swords slashed through others, turning ragged robes and flesh to red tatters, gizzards hanging like blossoms on the tips of their rapidly growing stalks.

The spattering of running feet heralded the final rush of the plague monks. Hooded and robed, the ratmen advanced out of the fog bank, rank after rank of snarling, spitting vermin. With them, they brought a great wheeled altar, on which was hung a giant censer of burning warpstone. The fumes from this infernal engine streamed over the coming horde, roiling and bubbling with a life of their own.

The sylvaneth did not wait for the skaven to charge, but counter-attacked at a signal from their lord. Dryads and tree-revenants fell upon the Chaos vermin with sweeping branches and shredding claws, their war-song like the cawing of crows and shriek of hunting hawks. The plague monks fought with serrated daggers and warpstone-tipped staffs, their own cries every bit as strident as the calls of Clan Arleath.

The greater treefolk, Diraceth's glade-cousins, were about to move forwards to support their smaller kin but the Leafmaster halted their long strides. Callicaith glanced up at him, feeling it too. The Leafmaster pointed into the fog.

'Await, kin of the glades! Do you feel its presence? A greater darkness comes upon us this eve.'

As he spoke, the sensation grew stronger. It was like a deeper pit in the darkness that was the Pestilens horde. The magic of Ghyran swirled as it approached, turned away like dead leaves before a gale, scattering and burning at its touch.

In the fog, something as large as Diraceth loomed through the withered remains of the trees. The Leafmaster drew in all the life magic that he could, expelling it as storm of sharp, glittering kernels that parted the encroaching deathfog.

As the miasma billowed back, it revealed the daemonic master of the skaven.

A crown of curling, twisted horns framed its huge, rattish head. Its tail was like a barbed whip longer than it was tall, tipped with rusted blades. Pink-grey flesh was draped in a ragged brown tunic, over which sat overlapping plates of serrated oil-black armour. A helm with long cheek-guards protected its skull. A huge book hung on its waist, chained to a thick belt of hide, and an unnatural breeze fluttered the pages, spilling forth seeping tendrils of sorcerous mist. The dark magic of the grimoire was like a heavy weight in Diraceth's thoughts, an artefact of corruption and decay wholly anathema to the Leafmaster and the life-giving magic that had given birth to him.

Bellowing wordless hatred for the greater daemon, the Leafmaster's tree-cousins stomped forth, whipping lacerating limbs against the Verminlord's armour, thrusting penetrating branches towards its flesh.

The creature reeled back, allowing more of its underlings to stream forwards, hurling themselves at the treelords and tree-revenants. While the arboreal giants crushed these attackers beneath root-splayed feet and pulverised them with hammering fists, the rat-daemon belched forth a noxious cloud of vile fumes. The treefolk retreated from this poisonous mist, their bark withering and drying at its touch, blighted sap erupting from widening skin-cracks and splitting knotholes. At the touch of the sorcerous fumes, their leaves shrivelled to blackened wisps. Low moans of pain made the earth shake.

All around the ancient, the song of his kin was falling in volume, as spirit after spirit fell silent. He tried to rouse them with bass urgings of his own, infusing them with his renewed desire to fight.

Snarling, glittering spites erupted from Diraceth's canopy as he stormed forwards, surrounding him with a whirling shield of biting, spitting spirits. He hardened his limbs into lance-points and drew his arm back, ready to strike.

The daemon creature turned, as swift as any of its rapacious minions, its tail whipping around Diraceth's arm. The two titanic beings braced against each other, pulling, each trying to tear the appendage from their foe.

Fog swirled and lightning crackled around the daemon's free hand. It coalesced into a four-tined spear. Stepping closer, allowing Diraceth to drag it forwards, the greater daemon of the Horned Rat plunged the weapon into the trunk of the Leafmaster, the points opening up the wound already marking his bark.

Chaos power flared through the injury, a thousand tiny bites engulfing Diraceth. He lashed out, throwing dagger-needles into the face of his foe. Ripping the spear free with a spray of golden sap, the skaven-beast stepped back, its tail unwrapping from Diraceth's arm.

The treelord ancient staggered away, life fluid spurting in thick fountains from the gash in his torso. He thrust a hand into the wound, growing branch-fingers to bind it together. The ancient felt the burn of the Chaos magic, tiny flecks of corrupted rust burrowing through his exposed heartwood.

Even as he stumbled and almost fell, Diraceth let forth a retort. Vines burst from the broken ground at the monster's feet, snaking around its legs, seeking its throat and eyes.

The Verminlord took a step closer, spear raised for the kill. Diraceth looked up into its red eyes, undaunted by its horrific majesty.

The Verminlord hesitated.

As it was about to strike the blow, it shifted, cocking its head to one side. A moment later a breeze rippled through Diraceth's leaves. Fresh, restorative. The fogs were swirling, becoming ragged tufts on the gusts of a new wind. The darkness beyond was diminishing, overpowered by a burgeoning yellow gleam.

Sunlight.

Warmth touched Diraceth. The heat of the sun. The power of Ghyran.

With it came a new spirit-song. It was like nothing he could remember, swelling up from the heartrock of the ground and cascading down from the sky, melodic and subtle, but dramatic and discordant all at once. Fuelled anew, the wound in his chest sealed by the magical touch, the Leafmaster surged to his feet. His hands crooked into wicked blades as he advanced towards his enemy with renewed purpose.

The daemon thrust its spear into one of its own followers, spitting the mewling plague monk upon the points. Sorcerous lightning crackled again, forming an arc that pulled the skaven apart, its scattered body forming a swirling circle of green fog that flickered with Chaos power. Through the miasma Diraceth felt a yawning chasm, a deep shaft that dropped away between the physical realms.

The daemon stepped into the fresh gnawhole with a last look at the Leafmaster. Though its expression was impossible to read, the spear thrust towards the ancient was a clear threat – this would not be their last encounter.

With a wet sucking noise the portal closed, the remnants of the sacrificed plague monk splashing to the mulch-covered ground.

Diraceth's attention was drawn back to the strange sunrise. The fogs were almost completely dissipated now, taking on more of the cast of mountain lake mists at dawn.

The plague monks felt it too, and having been abandoned by their immortal master did not take flight but threw themselves upon the sylvaneth with frenetic desperation.

Where the gold light touched, the Wrathwaters responded. The blackened, withered morass burst into renewed life, saplings and bushes springing forth from the groundwaters, blossoming into full growth as Diraceth watched.

The rush of magic flowed around and over and beneath him, through air and water and ground. Heartseeds thought lost in the mire crackled with energy amongst the fronds and strands of fresh growth. He heard the tremulous strains of their nascent soul-songs quivering into life, ready to grow into fresh generations of sylvaneth.

Behind him the waters of the lifepool glimmered with the magic of birth. Sylvaneth souls that had long been repressed by the noxious flow of skaven corruption suddenly burst into full bloom, brought to fruition by the influx of life essence. Out of the heartseeds his clan had salvaged from the incessant skaven encroachment burst forth a fresh surge of dryads, branchwraiths and tree-revenants. These newborns splashed out of the waters, their birth-songs tainted by rage and bloodthirst, and they fell upon the skaven with vengeful cries and haunting moans.

And then it was as though the sun itself entered the sacred grove.

The presence was blinding, both in light and as a spring of the energy of Ghyran. Diraceth could not quite comprehend what was in their midst, all senses both physical and spiritual overwhelmed by the force of the entity that had arrived. The sound of thrumming wings made the air and ground vibrate. Heat prickled on his bark, like fingers caressing the folds and cracks, bringing forth green buds where they passed.

As the wave of life magic seeped into the earth of the grove, its power restoring tree and spirit alike, the Leafmaster looked upon their saviour.

Her wings were feathery streamers of dawn light, luminescent and hot. Her face was serene, her eyes a rich leaf-green. Diraceth met that godly gaze and felt a moment of connection, from root to branch, spreading out across the entire Realm of Life. Here was the font, the spring of creation, the mother of his people.

Alarielle, Everqueen of the sylvaneth.

His gaze moved away, freeing him from the trance. It was now that he saw that his goddess was not as he remembered, in robes of autumnal growth. She wore armour, her body clad in shimmering plates of birch-silver edged with ironbark and studded with firestones. The apparition held a spear as tall as she was, its head shimmering with destructive magic. The Leafmaster watched as she turned her attention to the skaven. Alarielle's tranquil expression changed, and the light of her presence changed with it. Ire twisted her features. The dawn light aura became a crackling halo of incarnate fury that burned with the fire of an unrelenting noon sun.

'Kill them all,' she commanded in the voice of a burgeoning storm.

As her children eradicated the stain of the ratmen from her realm, Alarielle's anger faded. It did not disappear completely, for how could she not feel rage whilst her children teetered on the edge of extinction? She could not rest while her people in the Realm of Life and far beyond suffered from the malignance of Chaos. But for the moment, in this place and at this time, her vengeance was temporarily sated.

She held up a hand and the heavens opened at her command, bringing rain as sweet as nectar. The Wrathwaters responded to her call, swelling in a spume-topped mass over the shores of the lakes to wash away every vestige of the skaven. Her tree-kin set down their roots as the deluge swirled past them, making sanctuary for the smaller sylvaneth in their branches. A glorious wind swept down from the Laureneth Peaks, driving away the last of the rat-must. The rustle of green leaves and the creak of swaying canopy was a song in her ears after the thunder of the skaven drums.

While the floodwaters drained, a carpet of new grass and flowers in their wake, Alarielle turned her attention to the deeper wounds, the taint laid upon the souls of the Wrathwaters. She settled, furling her nebulous wings, letting her armour fade so that she could feel cool breeze on her flesh. Its touch brought flashes of recollection, scattered images of her previous lives.

She held the pain at bay, a mortal memory not suited to an immortal spirit.

Alarielle purged the taint of Chaos from the Wrathwaters, using her magic as she had used the Wrathwaters, driving out the corruption from the lowest earth. She became part of the Realm of Life, splitting again and again, allowing her essence to be one with the land and water and air.

She tumbled over rocks, her cleansing current bringing freshwater to algae-swathed pools where rat corpses bobbed. Her essence eased through cracks, nourishing the broken-stemmed plants, the pressure of her spirit forcing the magic of life into the deepest roots of the maligned forests. She lapped against the banks and gurgled over the rapids, reed beds and rushes growing fulsome in her light. Lilies rippled on the pools amidst the crackle of life magic shimmering in the waters. She nestled with the crabs in the sands of the Scarlet Sea, into which the vast delta of the Wrathwaters flowed.

All that lived felt her coming, renewed by the Everqueen's magic.

Even as she danced on waves as sparkles of sunlight, she spiralled along high branches. Blossom erupted in her wake. Snapped limbs healed and trunks marked by welts and rot were made anew.

Winds carried the Everqueen's spirit far over the swamps that had engulfed the Wrathwaters. From murky pools sprang every variety of marsh flower in a profusion of rainbow colours. Even in the darkest regions she could not be denied. Grubs and beetles, worms burrowing through the dark mud, acted as a conduit for her power.

Bringing together her energies, Alarielle ascended, leaping skywards from one drop of falling rain to another. She reached the clouds and looked down upon the great rivers and winding streams of Clan Arleath's territory. Renewed, it stretched in vibrant greens down to the white sands of the coast, and was lost in the haze of the mountains.

Higher still she climbed, into the stars bordering the Celestial Realm. She could feel Ghyran, the Realm of Life, pulsing and changing, awakened by her return.

Yet it was only the start, the first breaking of bud through hardened frost. All across her lands, Chaos lay like a choking clot, stifling and repugnant. Even to touch upon it in thought revolted the Everqueen. The pollution made her soul sicken.

They had come so close to ruin. Chaos had almost overrun everything. Though the enclaves of the sylvaneth were like bright sparks, they were almost lost in the darkness – here and in other realms. Even the great glades where Alarielle had arisen as the war maiden seemed like a pinprick against the vast pustulant expanse.

And through the decay, on the far side of the rot and destruction, she could feel the thunderous heartbeat and ponderous breaths of the power that desired dominion over her. Life perverted, built upon death. The tendrils of Nurgle's Garden stretched far and deep into the Jade Kingdoms, coursing with vile purpose, throbbing with vigorous intent. And the gnawholes of the skaven ran like maggot trails through rotten meat.

So close to utter destruction, so much to reclaim.

It seemed not so long ago, to her immortal reckoning, that

she had conquered all, that victory over Chaos had seemed but a breath away.

Yet it had been lost, and the darkness had prevailed again.

Alarielle woke, returning to her physical shell. In her absence, her council had gathered – mighty treelords and ancients from across the Royal Glades and woodland clans. The Old King of Winterleaf conversed with Leafmaster Diraceth, newly reacquainted with his clan-cousins. Their senior, the High King of Oakenbrow, noticed first the return of the queen. Rippling his leaves, he pushed silence out into the song of his clan, quietening both it and their boisterous mood.

'The Wrathwaters run fresh once more, Jade Mother,' the High King intoned solemnly. 'Clan Arleath returns its strength to Winterleaf, and your reach extends once more. Whither now shall the attention of your host fall?'

She ignored the question for the moment and beckoned to the Winterleaf conclave.

'Attend me for a moment, lords and ladies of Winterleaf.'

The tree-beings approached, their silver bark and leaves pale in the sunlight. A procession of branchwraiths followed, wearing long coats of golden leaves, each accompanied by a tree-revenant – spirits of the forest clad in the guise of wood-dwellers from an older age. In stately accord they arrayed themselves behind the treelords, bowing before their queen.

Diraceth was ushered forwards by the High King. The ancient approached with eyes cast down, his long strides slow and purposeful. Callicaith and a few branchwyches nestled in his limbs. They averted their gaze from the Everqueen.

'Look upon me,' Alarielle instructed. 'See your queen as she is now.'

Diraceth looked up, almost flinching. He met her gaze for a moment and then looked away, branches trembling with shame.

'I am thankful, bounteous goddess, but unworthy. I have failed you and the Winterleaf clan. But for your miraculous presence the Wrathwaters would be lost forever. Our guard was not strong enough.'

'You are not alone in such tribulation, and I do not absolve you of blame. But know this, Leafmaster. Clan Arleath held when others did not. The Wrathwaters, though tainted, remained a part of my domain.' She held out a hand and stroked his bark, comforting the troubled spirit. 'You resisted a long time. Long enough.'

'Thank you, queen of the forests. Clan Arleath shall repay the debt in whatever fashion is required. We owe our existence to you, mother of hope.'

'Mother of hope no more,' Alarielle replied, her expression turning grim. 'The avenger, the scourge, the cleansing sun I have become. None failed the Jade Kingdoms more than I, and none has more for which to atone.'

'No, my queen, that is not so...'

'It was not the lords of the clans that turned back at the very brink of victory. It was not my ancient warriors that lacked the heart to finish what had been begun.'

Diraceth said nothing, not understanding what she meant. Even he, an age old as he was, could not remember the first wars against Chaos, when the Realm of Life had been wrested from their grip and the sylvaneth first born.

Alarielle remembered well enough, and too well the part she failed to play. How could she judge any of her children harshly, who had done more than she to resist the encroachment of Nurgle's touch, who had battled daily against the incursions of the skaven? While she had slumbered, afraid and spent, her people had died without hope.

'I have returned, but I cannot bring hope,' she told the treelord ancient. 'We stand upon the brink of oblivion and have only taken a single step from the edge. My return will herald not hope, but war, and suffering on a scale none but the immortals have known. I am strife-bringer, woe-seeder. Look not to me for hope, Diraceth, for I have none.'

'Then why...?'

'Because we must fight or surrender. Victory is so far away that even I cannot see it, but it is not victory for which we strive at the moment. This is a war to survive, to push back from the precipice, to claw our lands free of the grip of darkness and corruption.' Alarielle stepped back, her canopy-wings turning to golden streamers behind her. 'I guarantee nothing, Leafmaster, but bloodshed, misery and death. I am clothed in the light of the sun, but I cast the shadow of the grave. Without hope, without even hope of hope, will you fight beside me?'

The Leafmaster lowered himself to one knee, a lengthy process accompanied by much creaking and swaying of his branches.

'You fight without hope, majestic sunqueen, but I cannot deny mine at your return. In the mire of despair I almost succumbed. With the great lords and ladies of the Royal Glades to stand witness, I swear I will not show such weakness again.'

Alarielle gestured for him to rise. He retreated to the company of his clan-kin as the Everqueen addressed her entire council. Her voice carried without effort, as thunderous as a waterfall and yet like the sigh of a playful breeze.

'There was greater purpose in coming to the Wrathwaters than freeing Diraceth and his kin. The path to the Vale of Winternight has been opened.'

A fractious rustling disturbed the council. The Willowqueen of Harvestboon voiced the discontent.

'We are not yet strong enough to reclaim the Vale of Winternight, dawnqueen. And little will its liberation add to our cause.'

'What of the besieged clans of the Verdant Cliffs?' suggested the Archduke of Ironbark.

'Or the Mooncrags?' added the Oakenbrow High King. 'My bud-brother holds still against Foulslug and his corrupted host. A brave ally.'

'We owe it to those that stayed loyal, my queen,' said the Willowqueen. 'More allies will bring greater strength.'

'The bargain has already been struck!' The voice was a whip crack like snapping limbs, silencing the others. The members of the Royal Moot turned like a forest bending in a new wind, directing their glares to the speaker – the Keeper of Dreadwood. Bark blackened along one side by recent battle, the scarred ancient stepped forward. Fanged and clawed spite-revenants swung through his limbs, whispering angrily to their master.

'The Dreadwood fight no less than any other Royal Glade,' the Keeper snarled. He thrust an accusing limb at the councillors, fingers stained dark with the blood of humans and skaven – and the sap of other sylvaneth, if the dark rumours were true. 'At the Emerald Moors my kin and folk fought beside you, Everqueen, for promise that my forest-kin of the Winternight would be freed from captivity.'

'A fortress holds them,' said the Oakenbrow ancient. 'Many heartseeds will be scattered to take it from the enemy.'

'No fortress can stand against the will of the forest,' countered the Keeper. He looked at the Everqueen. 'And the Royal Moot does not stand against the will of its ruler. What say you, Alarielle the warrior-reborn?'

'They did not answer our call for aid,' said Diraceth before Alarielle replied. 'We offered aid when the Rotbringers came, but they did not want us. When Pestilens beset the Wrathwaters, they turned a deaf ear upon our pleas for help. Ancient Holodrin cares nothing for others. Clan Faech are traitors to their own, corrupted seeds that fell far from their mother-tree!'

'Recant your accusations!' roared the Dreadwood Keeper. 'Vile lies!'

'The truth burns deeper than flame,' retorted the Willowqueen, moving to stand between the Dreadwood entourage and the lords of Winterleaf. Her branchwraiths jeered and snarled at their counterparts in the Dreadwood, and tree-revenants looked on with glowering stares.

'My word is the law,' declared Alarielle, drawing herself up to her full battle-aspect. The Spear of Kurnoth appeared in her right hand. Her other manifested as the Talon of the Dwindling, flaking dead wood falling from her fingers as glittering dust. 'I have spoken and so it shall be. Clan Faech live on, trapped within the festering walls, hiding in the deepest shadows. But they are not yet lost. Not to death and not to darkness. I feel them, their pain and suffering. We shall free them. Go now, spread the word, ready your armies.'

The Keeper of Dreadwood withdrew, bowing in deference to the Everqueen. The others followed in turn, their leaves rustling with murmured apologies. Only Diraceth remained, trembling with sorrow and rage.

'You will find nothing but rot in the heart of the Vale of Winternight, my queen,' he said quietly. He uprooted and turned away, following the trail of rucked earth left by his clan-kin.

Alarielle diffused her power again and sighed. She no more wanted to travel to the Winternight than any of the others, but the Keeper was right. A bargain had been made, and it needed the alliance of all the Royal Groves, including the Dreadwood. If she was to reclaim the Jade Kingdoms from Chaos, she would have to win back the loyalty of the Outcasts, the dark and broken spirits she had denied.

There had been a time when the Vale of Winternight might justifiably have been called a jewel of the Jade Kingdoms. Though an age had passed during her slumber, Alarielle could still recall the white-and-silver trees, the sparkling mists that rose from the tarns each morning, the threads of streams that glittered on the walls of the deep valley.

Dark rock and bright ice, that was how she remembered this place, how it had come by its name. The twin peaks that stood as sentries to the valley were steep-sided, their white-clad summits lost in the haze of cloud above the vale. The Sisters of Serenity they were called, but there was little peace to be found on their slopes since the coming of Chaos.

A bastion had been raised across the mouth of the Vale of Winternight, running from one Sister to the other in an uneven line. She could feel the wall like scar tissue on her flesh. It was not a thing merely built, but constructed from the spirit-stuff of the lands, warped by corrupted magic into something far more hideous than a simple fortification. It was a mortuary-thing, made of corpses and tree-carcasses, heaped between with black rock and baked earth, a core of dead roots binding its foundation. Thornweave grew along its length, spines as long as swords, seeping toxic sap that would slay even the sylvaneth.

In three places the wall was broken by broad arches, through which flowed the great rivers of the vale. Gone were the bright waters. Now the banks brought forth bile, blood and seeping ichor. Their pollution stained the groves into which they flowed, carrying the taint of Chaos into the Jade Kingdoms and towards the shores shared by the Wrathwaters.

The bastion was broken irregularly by seven towers, each grown from an immense tree with branches of bone and fumaroles where knotholes should be, spewing a dark smog along the entire wall. Cadavers hung from the branches like fruit, and on the dead flesh puckered fungal growths and bright moulds.

The stench of death lay on the vale as surely as the fog-mire of the towers. The corruption was near total. Alarielle could scarce stand to be so close, as though she walked on the borders of Nurgle's Garden itself. She shuddered at the prospect of wandering into such accursed territory, but it was for this reason that she had come. Here, the grip of decay was so great that the Realm of Chaos and the Realm of Life were almost indistinguishable. From this vile sanctuary, the warriors and daemons of Nurgle could march with impunity to conquer and despoil.

Just as sight could not penetrate the fog shrouding the valley past the wall, so the Chaos magic held at bay the questing tendrils of the realmroots sent forth by Alarielle. Linked to all the parts of the Jade Kingdoms, the realmroots allowed her and her children to pass from one glade to the next without effort. In such fashion had they come upon many foes unaware of their approach, and encircled even enemies that were.

The Everqueen was baulked by the corruption. There would be no infiltration from without, and so heavy lay the hand of Nurgle she could scarce detect the tiniest flutter of spirits within. But they were there, she was certain of it. She heard their lamentations and felt their despair. As much as the other Royal Glades despised the Dreadwood, they were all her children, wayward or not. She bore the suffering of them all with equal sorrow.

The ground trembled and the realmroots quivered as Alarielle sent the summons to her Royal Moot. Life force swelled like a springsfed tide, pulsing along the arteries of the Jade Kingdoms, each flutter the spirit of one of her children. Along the realmroots surged the power of the Wyldwoods, animated by the will of the queen, root and branch responding to her demand as surely as the clansfolk of the glades.

The Wyldwoods ploughed towards the wall of decay, bush and tree and grass flowing like an incoming sea, until it reached the extent of her power just a bowshot from the wall. There the grip of Nurgle was too great for her to push through. Only when the plague bastion had been broken, when her children entered the valley, would she be able to thrust her power deep into the heart of the enemy and tear it out from within.

With the Wyldwoods came the glade hosts. From Oakenbrow and Harvestboon, Ironbark and Winterleaf, Gnarlroot and Heartwood. Dryad tree-maids and ancient treelords, tree-revenants in arboreal likeness of the ancient dwellers of the world-that-was. From each Royal Glade, from their clan groves spread across the reclaimed realms they came.

And like the touch of first frost creeping along a stem, the army of Dreadwood heeded her call. Led by their Keeper they came into the Wyldwoods – tree spirits and forestkin that had dwelt long in the shadow of Chaos. Vicious and bitter spite-revenants accompanied them, and branchwraiths and dryads that had been cast from their clans for their disruptive behaviour and bloodthirsty ways.

In the near-forgotten time of reconquest, when Alarielle had required alliance with Sigmar and his kind, such creatures had been a liability, preying on allies as well as foes. Now the Everqueen needed them back, and was willing to deal with whatever consequences that might bring.

'Break it,' she told her children, pointing at the wall. Her voice rippled through the realmroots, touching the spirit of every sylvaneth that had gathered. 'Tear it asunder and make bloody mulch of its defenders. Open up the vale for me, my children, and become the vengeance we all crave.'

Diraceth advanced with his clan elders, proud to stride amongst the great army of the Winterleaf Glade. His loremasters walked beside him, two ancients called Drudoth and Ceddial, and behind came the lesser nobles and forest folk of Clan Arleath.

Each stride that took him closer to the looming wall made his sap rise in ire. Through his roots he could feel the death and decay woven into the barrier, seeping into the good earth of the Jade Kingdoms. It was a deeper, more malignant curse than the gnaw-wounds of the skaven. He felt his leaves shrivelling at its touch.

The sylvaneth host pushed out from the sanctuary of the Wyldwoods, a gathering of spirits such as Diraceth had never witnessed before. Treelords and ancients by the score led their clans, following the stern warriors of the Royal Glade households. Hundreds of tree-revenants and thousands of dryads flowed from the mystical forest, thorn-fingered and bright-eyed.

And on the periphery, from the darkest patches beneath the boughs, the Outcasts came. Like shadows they lingered near their clans, spite-revenants that lusted after mortal flesh, whose wickedness had earned them exile in ages past. Diraceth noticed that more than half the host of the Dreadwood was made up of these dispossessed spirits and wondered what manner of clan they marched to liberate. Ancient Holodrin and his folk had always kept to their own glades, but it had been a shock when messenger-spites of Diraceth had returned with tidings that Clan Arleath would stand alone against the skaven.

The forest host passed into the thick smog. It smeared along Diraceth's leaves and bark, slicking his twigs and buds with its oily, noisome touch. The branchwyches and branchwraiths spat and cursed, and flicked droplets of the foul vapour from their talons. By his side, Callicaith adjusted her grip on the long greenwood scythe she carried. Her glimmersilk grub wriggled back and forth across her shoulders, reacting to the tension.

'I can see nothing,' she said.

It was true, the smog was as thick as marsh water. It felt as though Diraceth waded through a mire as much as pushed through the dank fog. He could barely see the branchwyches and ancient treelords to either side. The armies of his fellow Winterleaf clans were lost from view.

'Press on,' he told them, sensing the unease of his folk. Their spirit-song was quiet and flat. Diraceth set free his own song, a martial beat that resounded through the thoughts of his followers. He quickened the pace of his stride and the tempo of his war-song.

It was then that he felt the glade-voice of the Old King, calling him on, adding its weight to the harmony of Clan Arleath. And the other houses around him, each clan-song different but called from the same source, creating a growing chorus, making his sap rise further. Like an echo rebounding, the booming of the ancients was returned by the heart-songs of the lesser folk, a staccato of expectation and fury over the deliberate percussion of their leaders, the intensity growing as they continued through the smog.

Diraceth was taken aback as they broke through the fog and came upon the wall itself. The mists were still thick, but the great darkness of the edifice rose up before the ancient, more than twice as high as his topmost branches.

The spirit-song reached a crescendo as Diraceth and the

treefolk charged the bastion. It sang in his heartwood, filling him with strength and purpose. He raised his own voice, urging his clan to prevail.

Thorny tentacles lashed from the wall, and a storm of projectiles flew down from above. Dryads were snared by the bloodvines and crushed, tree-revenants pierced by the spines. Bloodsap fell in glimmering rain, showers of light in the dark fog.

Bellowing his rage, Diraceth hurled himself at the wall, sinking branch-claws deep into the blackened mud. Forming rootlets from his fingers, he pushed deeper, feeling the bone and sinew of dead animals parting, trickles of ichor dribbling down his arms as though blood from a living thing.

He ignored the slash of the thorn-vines against his bark, leaning close to the filthy wall to penetrate deeper and deeper with his thrusting attack. Callicaith and the other branchwyches led the clan maidens up his back and across his upper limbs, leaping from branch to branch to reach higher up the wall. They ascended through the bodies of the other treelords and ancients, and set about with scythe and claw to hew at the pseudo-tentacles.

Spreading rootlet-fingers wide, Diraceth pulled back, wrenching the guts from the wall. Like intestines splayed from a wounded animal, ropes of rotting flesh and sodden wood erupted from the bastion. Hurling the vegetative offal aside, the Leafmaster attacked again, tearing and ripping, splitting foundation roots and ribcages, engulfed by spores from exploding fungi.

Around him the other Noble Spirits tore at the skin of the bastion, severed roots flopping like eels on the ground, broken pustules spewing ichor over limb and trunk, matting their canopies with greenish-yellow gobbets.

With a sound of snapping bone and branch, a portion of the wall collapsed into a rotten heap. Armoured warriors toppled into the morass, crashing into the piles of steaming mulch. They struggled to their feet, reaching for rusted axes and serrated blades. Their armour was pitted with corrosion, the plates covered with a film of filth that leaked from rents and breaks in the metal. Some were bloated creatures, their guts barely contained by their armour. Others were skeletal-thin, rusted mail hanging loosely over famine-wasted frames.

The dryads shrieked in triumph and leapt upon the Nurgle warriors, their claws seeking visors, piercing chainmail at the joints of their armour, pulling the warriors apart.

Other foes, more lightly armoured, leapt down onto Diraceth. They sawed at his limbs with their blades and jabbed spears into his knotholes and cracks.

'Begone, minions of the decaying one,' rumbled the treelord, plucking a tribesman from his branches. He crushed the human in his fist, splitting him like overripened fruit. Lance-claws speared another, piercing him from belly to throat. Diraceth flung the corpse away and turned swiftly, shaking another three of his assailants from his canopy.

Widening the gap in the wall, the ancient stepped into the barrier while more branchwraiths and dryads scaled the breach to spill along the rampart above. Pulling up the last vestiges of the wall, Diraceth broke through into the valley proper.

Elsewhere the bastion was breached too, the sylvaneth flowing into the Vale of Winternight like water through a broken dam.

'For the Everqueen and the Jade Kingdoms!' rose the roar of the treelords.

Spite-revenants flowed around Diraceth, snarling, eager to be at the enemy. He recognised spirits he had banished from the clan long ago, but they paid him little heed, their hatred now focussed on a mutual foe. Their enraged howls were quickly joined by the cries of dying Chaos followers.

Seeing that the wall had fallen in many places, her subjects pouring through the breaches, Alarielle sent the summons to her own grove-host. Her song carried the furthest of all, light and lilting, rippling through the Wyldwoods and the rootways to all parts of the reclaimed kingdom.

She held out a hand to one of the nearby Wyldwood trees. Its trunk shuddered and a knothole parted, disgorging a bulbous grub. Though but a larva, it was as long as her forearm. It crawled over the leaf-carpeted ground and burrowed into the magic-rich dirt at her feet. A few moments passed before the ground under her feet started to tremble. Leaf and earth parted as an immense swarm of glinting fireflies erupted around her. Swirling like sparks, they coalesced into a single creature. The massive wardroth beetle bore up the Everqueen, its carapace glistening like oil, antlers gleaming in the light of Alarielle's aura.

She added a fresh melody to her call, the long note of a horn that echoed through the trees. Haunting, distant replies drifted back to her, rebounding and growing in volume. She felt the flow of magic changing, becoming a stream and then a river, converging on her location from many directions.

From the trees came forth her Kurnoth Hunters, each taller than any warrior of Chaos, with bark stronger than metal armour. Some carried long, straight swords, others bore scythes that could slay the largest mortal monster with a single blow. The rest were armed with greatbows, accompanied by scurrying quiverlings – spites that grew fresh missiles from their backs.

Their leader, Raldorath the Huntmaster, came forwards and bowed low. He looked at the broken bastion, wooden brow furrowing.

'A harsh task, my queen,' he said. 'Though the wall be broken, the Vale of Winternight holds an army of foes.'

'Yet not enough to hold back my ire,' said the queen. 'With me, Hunters of Kurnoth – your prey awaits.'

High upon the hunched back of the wardroth beetle, her wings of light flowing behind her, the Everqueen advanced quickly through the Wyldwoods. The Kurnoth Hunters spread around her, loping strides carrying them as swiftly as their queen. More treelords and ancients answered her call as she moved. Among them marched the mightiest of the old nobles – the Spirits of Durthu.

The fog had all but dissipated, and as Alarielle emerged from the Wyldwoods she saw that two of the seven towers had fallen. Yet from the upper reaches of those remaining, missiles and fire cascaded down upon the spirits surging through the breaches.

'Break the towers, bring them down!' she commanded. The Spirits of Durthu responded to her command, breaking away to fall upon the nearest fortification.

She felt the swirl of magic as the revered treelords summoned the energy of the Jade Kingdoms, letting it pass through their bodies. It erupted from outstretched limbs in gusts of emerald energy, scouring the armoured warriors from the higher limbs and platforms of the tower. The treelords smashed against the blackened trunk with their fists and stomped upon the ground to break open its foundations, root-claws driving deep into the earth. Throwing their weight against the tower while others dragged at the upper limbs, three of the huge forest spirits sent the entire tree-edifice crashing down. More armoured warriors plummeted to their doom as it fell, and those that picked their way out of the splintered, black-leafed foliage were swiftly crushed by the raging Spirits of Durthu.

The wall was shattered, more towers falling as the sylvaneth ascended into the heights and tore at their roots. Alarielle could feel the Vale of Winternight responding. She let her essence gush free into the land beyond, bracing herself against the clammy touch of decay that still lingered within.

She searched back and forth, seeking the slightest trace of Clan Faech, steeling herself against the cold darkness as she plunged deeper into the Chaos-tainted magic permeating the vale. Her song became a strident call, ringing clear through the wash of wyldmagic flowing into the valley.

The flutter of an answering spirit-song drew her into the heart of the vale, the loathsome power of Nurgle like a cold corpse hand pawing at her body. Pressing past, she looked for the tiniest glimmer of the song's source.

She found it ringed with Chaos power, a cornered animal panting and whining with fear. Anger replaced Alarielle's distaste and she forged on, fuelled by ire. At the approach of the Everqueen's presence the corruption parted, scattered like leaves in a gale, but swiftly the taint returned, pressing hard against her soulform.

The grim surroundings nearly silenced her voice. The crushing stench of Chaos energy was overpowering, endless waves of decrepitude and corruption crashing over her. Her light was no star, nothing more than a guttering spark in everlasting darkness. Timidity all but stilled the tongue of her spirit-song.

Gathering her nerve, ignoring the fear that she would draw unwanted attention upon herself, Alarielle sang loud and clear, calling to the quivering spirits of Clan Faech. She pushed back the darkness as it encroached on the path she had made behind her. The Everqueen beckoned and cajoled, tried to soothe away the primal dread that trapped the sylvaneth as surely as the warriors of the Plague God.

'Fight it!' she insisted, bursting forth with fresh soulsong. Alarielle could almost touch them, could almost make the magic flow into the spirits to rouse them from their terrified stupor. 'Reach out to me. Break free!'

But they did not. Not only dread quelled them. Bitterness spat back from the renegade forest spirits.

Recoiling, Alarielle could do nothing as the grip of Nurgle tightened again, a black sludge that filled the space around Clan Faech as tar bubbling up from its pit. It hardened, seizing them fast once more. Their song was muted and deathly silence engulfed Alarielle.

The Everqueen realised she was alone in the great sea of darkness. She fought back panic, searching for the rivers of life-essence that had brought her here, desperate as a ship's crew tossed on a tempestuous sea.

She caught upon a glimmering trail and started to follow it, but in her agitation did not sense the approach of something else. It was too late that she detected another presence in the mystical strata – a triumvirate entity. A three-spawn fly of Nurgle made into bodily form somewhere in the vale. A sting strike, a spine of pure Chaos, pierced her spirit, pumping darkness into her soul. Like a toxin in the blood of a mortal, the Chaos energy flowed through her, trying to drag the Everqueen into the mire of death that surrounded her.

She fled.

Returning to her body, Alarielle gasped, suppressing the scream of horror that wanted to break free – her subjects had to fight on, could not know anything was amiss.

The Chaos taint was still in her. She could see it now, like a blackness in her veins, darkening her skin, dimming the light of her presence. It worked fast, weakening her, trying to consume her with burning pain.

Horror gripped her. All that she had feared, all that had cowed her for those long years of slumber, was coming to pass. The touch of Nurgle was in her. Beneath the surface of her being, raw wyldmagic and Chaos power thrashed against each other, their conflict sending agonising stabs through her.

'My queen?' A Spirit of Durthu stood over her, its spirit-song a sombre throb of concern. She realised a single crystal tear marked her cheek, a sign of the struggle within.

She took in a shuddering breath but dared not speak of what had happened. The Everqueen mastered her fear and urged the tree spirit to leave her.

Unprompted, the Spirit of Durthu lay a twig-fingered hand upon Alarielle's arm. At his touch she felt the foul magic burst forth, engulfing both of them. The spirit's branches shuddered and its soulsong became a low moan of age-old aching.

She felt the spirit drawing forth the blight. Alarielle tried to fight it, to hold the poison in herself. But the spirit would not be deterred, placing another leaf-limb on her to bring forth more of the taint.

'It is not... yours to... take...' she gasped, but the spirit silently looked at her with deep emerald eyes as the corruption flowed into its heartsap.

When it had siphoned away the last of the dark power, the Spirit of Durthu reared up, taking a step back from the Everqueen. Already its leaves were wilting, branches drooping with the weight of the poison in them. Its spirit-song was little more than a few whimpering notes as wood turned to dust and sloughed away, revealing blistered greenwood beneath.

'My queen, everlasting font of life,' croaked the spirit, sinking down. Threads of mould spread over its splintering, disintegrating form. 'Lead our people to fresh life. Fear nothing more. Let the wrath of the sylvaneth carry you to victory.'

The spirit slumped, degenerating into scattering motes and spores that drifted away, leaving nothing but a blackened heartseed. The last vestiges of its song died away with its body.

She had almost failed her people again. Freed of the taint, Alarielle calmed herself, her sorrow short-lived. In the past she had allowed fear to rule her, to break her resolve. Not this time. Not now.

The fire of her wrath flared from her body like a fresh dawn. Where its light touched, Alarielle's presence filled the sylvaneth with a deep rage. She drove the wardroth beetle forwards with a thought, weapon held high. Her spirit-song called to her glade-warriors to follow.

Incandescent with fury, the Spear of Kurnoth singing its own bloodthirsty hymn in her thoughts, the Everqueen passed into the Vale of Winternight.

If the breaking of the wall was a dam bursting, the coming of Alarielle was an ocean rising to engulf the Vale of Winternight. With her came the Wyldwoods, limbs and leaves angrily swaying, creepers and thorn bushes advancing beneath their shadowed canopies. Ahead of her life magic streamed. The gale of her approach washed away the thick fog, revealing the parched lands of the Vale of Winternight.

All had been drained of vitality, the cracked earth like the dry skin of an ancient mortal. Scrubby bushes with blood-red thorns grew out of split heartseeds, and fungal fronds played in colourful profusion from the corpses of animals. Such trees as had survived were twisted, stunted things with flies as big as birds buzzing in their limbs. More insects fluttered in thick swarms, fighting against the rush of air that heralded the Everqueen's arrival.

At the heart of the valley, where once had stood the lifetree of Clan Faech, a tower now rose at the centre of a soulpod-studded grove that had become a thick mire of bubbling mud. Three-fold were its bastions, winding about each other like vines, becoming one at the pinnacle. It seemed to have grown of tumorous bone, split and blistered, cracked and flaking. No windows broke its surface, but a single fracture formed a jagged door at its root.

The warriors of Nurgle were arrayed about this fortress, grotesque and bloated, cadaverous and vile. In ranks of rusted mail and blood-spattered plate they awaited the attack of the sylvaneth.

They did not have to wait long.

The earth erupted with choking, snaring vines, and the spirits of the worldwood descended upon the Nurgle army. Branch and root vied against hammer and spear, talon versus blade. Whipping leaf-limbs crashed against shields marked with the fly rune of the Plague God. Ensorcelled iron bit deep into spirit-folk flesh. Blood and phlegm, bark and sap flew.

The trembling ground beneath the stride of the wardroth beetle set the beat of the battle-song that rose from Alarielle. From her heart poured out a rhythm of defiance and death. It drove the sylvaneth, enriching their hatred as mulch fertilises soil, filling their limbs with vigour and growth. Where Alarielle fought, the followers of Chaos died.

A dozen armoured warriors set themselves against her advance, their axes flaking rust and dried blood. Alarielle did not hesitate, but met them head-on. Their blades broke on the carapace of her wardroth beetle, and other blows went astray in the blinding light of her presence. The beetle charged without pause, trampling foes and spearing another on its antlers. The Spear of Kurnoth whirled and plunged, lancing through the bodies of the survivors, foetid blood streaming from the mortal wounds left by its touch.

The Wyldwoods enveloped the fighting, dragging tribesmen and beasts into the foliage where birds and spites plucked at eyes and clawing twigs lacerated flesh. The screams of the dying were accompanied by the patter of blood falling like rain form the canopy. Roots quested for the pools of life fluid, drinking deep of the Chaos followers' suffering.

The Outcasts were a nightmare to behold, led by the ancients of the Dreadwood glade. Though fire and axe were set against them, the bitter forest spirits would not be stayed by the shield walls and warped spawn of the Chaos army. Armoured plate was no obstacle to piercing talons powered by magical sinew. With banshee howls of glee, dryads tore the limbs from their foes, glorying in the sprays of blood. Flesh and bone parted under the razor-strikes of the branchwyches, strips of gory flesh flung into the air. So vengeful was their aspect that even as lumbering beasts crushed them underfoot the Outcasts bit and clawed with their last strength. Spite-revenants leapt into their foes without regard, happy to tear down an armoured warrior even if in turn they were battered and slashed by the corroded weapons of their enemies.

As a root prises apart a rock, the sylvaneth drove through the corrupting host to within striking distance of the tower. Alarielle's magic washed up to the perimeter of the fortress, unable to penetrate it but still gathering strength. The spirits of Clan Faech murmured beyond her reach, trapped. Alarielle urged them to rise up, to tear down their captors from within. She was greeted with a quiet echo of spite and dread.

The gate of the tower widened with a terrible tearing of wood, and from the dark interior emerged a trio of bloated figures. The three sorcerers let free swarms of biting flies and choking mists, stalling the sylvaneth attack. Whirring, buzzing things beset Alarielle, flying into her eyes, trying to crawl into her mouth. She choked and spat, fighting back the memory of the cloying power of Chaos that had nearly taken her.

Out of the swarm lumbered an immense gargant, its skin falling away in strips to reveal bloody fat and muscle. Its shadow fell over Alarielle, bathing her in a sudden chill.

Her beetle hissed its anger. At her command it dashed forwards, but its antlers simply sloughed away rotten flesh from its enemy's shins and thighs. The gargant seized up the wardroth, trying to tip the Everqueen from its back. The beetle sank its antlers deep into the sore-ridden flesh of the gargant's hand and arm, fixing itself there while blood streamed over its head, bathing Alarielle in thick crimson fluid.

Though repelled by its stench, Alarielle took the pouring vital fluid as a libation, as refreshing to her as the cascade of a waterfall. Blood-masked, she reached out with the Talon of the Dwindling and drove a claw into the gargant's arm. At her bidding, dire power flowed. Not the magic of life, but the turning of seasons, years, centuries.

In a few heartbeats the monstrous creature's flesh fell in dried scraps and its bones turned to dust, pitching the wardroth and its rider back to the blood-soaked earth. A triumphant melody erupted from Alarielle, sweeping her warriors into the enemy.

A great moan of despair erupted from the Nurgle host at the loss of the gargant. Surrounded and pushed back, they were forced into a semicircle about their sorcerous masters, battered and torn but not yet broken.

Alarielle pulsed a warning note to her servants as she felt a surge of Chaos power flow from the dark tower. It bubbled up into the three sorcerers, filling them with unnatural energy. The trio of warlocks swelled, metaphysically and literally, their robed bodies distending, skin stretching further and further until it split with cascades of blood. Each Chaos wizard bloated beyond possibility until they formed a single quivering mass of plague-ridden flesh.

With a final influx of power, the sorcerers burst, showering pus and ichor, flesh-gobbets and organs over a wide area, their scattered entrails forming a triple-sided sigil of Nurgle. Within the unholy pattern, the air seethed and the skein of reality stretched just as the skin of the wizards had done.

Daemonic things pressed against the thinning barrier, their power seeping through the sundered gap. Alarielle knew that in moments a host of the Plague God's daemons would break through, summoned by the destruction, for Nurgle found life in all death.

At the heart of the flesh-icon, the sorcerers remained – small mounds of sentient meat no bigger than a fist, forming porcine eyes and fanged mouths. Yet for all she urged her spirit-warriors to attack, the line of Chaos followers held amidst the bellows of ancients and the crash of blades.

Alarielle summoned the depths of her hatred and with it fuelled her courage. She dared one more time to send her spirit into the quagmire of Nurgle that filled the tower. Holding tight to the threads of magic that sustained her, the Everqueen dived into the spirit-morass.

Ignoring the slithering, sliding things that were breaking through into her realm, she drove directly for the final remnants of Ancient Holodrin and Clan Faech. This time she would not be repulsed. Like a bolt she sped into their midst with the full glory of her battle-song.

We are afraid! You abandoned us! You will desert us again.

Their plaintive wails did not sway her. Whatever wrong had been done to these spirits in the past, whatever transgressions she and they had committed against their own people, the sylvaneth fought and died as one.

'I am the Everqueen – the font of life, the despairing storm, the wrathspring. I do not command your loyalty, I demand it!' She reached out as though with her hand and seized up the guttering remnants of the sylvaneth souls. 'Your fear counts for nothing. You will fight!'

The ground shuddered, and a moment later the dark tower split asunder, dividing into its three parts in a shower of offal and rotten wood. The great tree of the Vale of Winternight, silver-barked and white-leaved, erupted from the falling ruin, its branches gleaming with soulpods.

Alarielle's essence raced along the branches, liberating trapped spirits even as the first daemons tore their way into the Realm of Life. Heartseeds fell like rain, and where each landed a sylvaneth sprang forth – branchwyches and branchwraiths, treelords and dryads, tree-revenants and ancients. And with them was unleashed wrathful Ancient Holodrin, a towering pine-lord with silver needles and claws like scimitars.

The lord of Clan Faech brought down a foot onto the mewling flesh-pile that was the sorcerer trio. Grinding them under his roots, the ancient tore the heart out of the Nurgle sigil, blood and mud and daemon becoming a single bubbling cataract of dissipating power. His booming roar crashed as a wave over the fighting, swelling the war-song of the sylvaneth.

'The Vale of Winternight belongs to us! Obliterate the defilers!'

Screaming, bellowing and howling, the freed spirits of Clan Faech hurled themselves at the beset Chaos warriors.

'Would that I had felt such courage sooner, great queen,' said Ancient Holodrin, making obeisance to his ruler. The taint of Nurgle was already seeping away, fresh tufts of grass and red blooms consuming the bodies of the Plague God's mortal followers.

'There are none of my folk that are strangers to fear,' Alarielle replied. 'When all is nearly lost, one thinks only to cling to what is left. I am not guiltless in such regard. The ages have turned and a different season is upon us. We cannot seek to simply resist our inevitable decline. A new power is coming, and we must allow ourselves to be borne up on the fresh tide or be washed away forever.'

'What new power, Everqueen?' asked Holodrin.

She looked up to the skies. Against any natural wind, clouds were gathering, tinged with azure light. Lightning flickered, not of any mortal origin.

'We are not alone,' she said. Sadness marred her divine features for a moment. 'It was only fear that made me think that we ever were.'

WARDENS OF THE EVERQUEEN
by C L Werner

The War of Life rages on, as Torglug the Despised and the forces of Nurgle seek to destroy the Everqueen. But with their new Stormcast allies, the beleaguered sylvaneth at last have a hope of victory...

For these stories and more go to **blacklibrary.com**, **games-workshop.com**, Games Workshop and Warhammer stores, all good book stores or visit one of the thousands of independent retailers worldwide, which can be found at **games-workshop.com/storefinder**

THE VOLTURUNG ROAD

Guy Haley

I

They always came for the Hardgate.

To one side of the volcano, its flanks sloped more gently, allowing the Slaaneshi to gather in larger numbers than elsewhere. After one hundred years of siege, the ground was a mess of bones and old armour, the remains of men and titanic monsters tangled with the broken remnants of great siege engines. Time after time, the forces of the daemon prince Qualar Vo threw themselves at the gates with ecstatic abandon. They laughed as they died, revelling in the sensation of death. Time after time, the Fyreslayers of the Ulgaen lodges cast them back.

Today was different. When the Slaaneshi assailed the gate, they broke into the hold from below.

'Stop them!' roared Ulgathern, twelfth runeson of the lord of Ulgaen-ar. 'Kill the breaching worms!'

Hideous, pallid things thrashed as Vulkite Berzerkers buried their axes in rubbery flesh. Petal mouths gaped and snapped, but the duardin were too swift. Their ur-gold runes lent them speed and strength, and the worms could not land a blow. Other Fyreslayers battled with the human tribesmen coming up the tunnels that had been chewed through the rock by their monsters. The south passage was a disorienting racket of clashing arms and screams.

Ulgathern sliced through the body of a worm behind its head. The creatures were massively thick, and it took several blows to sever its head completely. The body did not cease thrashing, but yanked back into the tunnel keening shrilly, leaving a slick of clear blood on the floor.

The sounds of battle receded. All around the tunnel were heaped the bodies of Slaaneshi marauders. Their gaudily coloured skins were smeared with blood. The last fell with a defiant yell.

'Ha! Chaos filth!' roared Mangulnar, third and oldest surviving runeson of Karadrakk-Grimnir. He slapped Ulgathern hard on the shoulder and flicked the gore from his moustaches with a grin. Both of them were covered in the stinking fluids of the worms. 'When I'm runefather, little brother, we'll run out after them and kill the lot, not skulk in these caverns waiting to die.'

Ulgathern looked sidelong at his elder sibling. Sometimes, Mangulnar enjoyed fighting a little too much.

'That would be the best way to lose the war,' he said.

'You sound like father. Where's your hunger for the fight? There's pleasure in war, and we should embrace it. Fear brings no ur-gold to our lodge.'

'Be careful what you wish for. The thirst for pleasure is what drives our enemies at us.'

Mangulnar spat. 'Their pleasure makes them weak. Battle joy makes us strong, it's completely different.'

'These are not their best warriors. I sense a ruse. Their attacks are getting bolder, more inventive. The worms are new. It is nearly one hundred and one years since the siege began. Storms fill the skies, and we should be wary.'

'Are you talking about that bloody prophecy of Drokki's again?' said Mangulnar harshly. 'You should be careful whose words you heed. As withered in mind as he is in arm, that friend of yours. Listening to the likes of him is why you'll never be a runefather, but if you're fortunate, I might let you serve me when I am lord of Ulgaen-ar.' Mangulnar stalked away, looking for something else to kill.

Ulgathern stared after his brother. Mangulnar and he rarely saw eye to eye.

'You there!' shouted Ulgathern to one of his warriors. 'Report back to my father that the third deeping is clear.' The warrior nodded and ran off. Ulgathern looked to the holes. The walls of the burrows were slick with the worms' secretions. 'And get a building team here, plug these up. I don't want anything else coming through.'

'Are you to join your father, my lord?' asked Grokkenkir, Ulgathern's favoured karl and leader of his Vulkite Berzerkers.

'The runefather ordered me to the Hardgate once done. My brothers and father will stop the other breaches soon enough without my help, you can be sure of that.'

Ulgathern took the steps up to the gate parapet three at a time, his muscles hot with Grimnir's power. Well before the thin daylight penetrated the gloom of the stairwell, he heard the enemy: a frenzied roaring as repetitive as the booming of the sea. On the wallwalk over the gate stood the auric hearthguard, firing their magmapikes into the packed hordes a hundred feet below. Ulgavost, thirteenth runeson of Karadrakk-Grimnir, watched the enemy die from a step behind the battlement. Ulgathern went to join his brother, and looked out over the mountain slope.

The Hornteeth Mountains were in Ghur, but they might well have been in the Realm of Fire: a long chain of sharp-peaked volcanoes stretching sunward and nightward across the continent, dividing the prairies from the Darkdeep Ocean. The mountains were all black ash and young rock, cut through by chasms that often filled with torrents of lava. Precious little grew around the Ulmount. The skies were choked with clouds of dust that glowed orange when the mountains spoke to one another. Blue skies were a rarity; more so recently, for strange storms raged daily.

The Slaaneshi tribesmen had occupied the lands below the Hardgate for so long they had constructed their own town there. Ulgathern looked over the screaming masses to the fortress occupying the settlement's middle. It was a hideous thing, the blocks hewn from the side of Ulmount itself and carved with repulsive images.

Around the fortress was a sea of tents. Darkness ruled down there, away from the ember-glows of the volcano, and the bright silk banners of the Chaos worshippers appeared muddy in the shadows.

Most of the horde must have marched out from their twisted township, for they were arrayed before the Hardgate in numberless multitude. A pair of gargants with striped blue skin battered at the gates. Endless ranks of warriors and tribesmen surged around them, roaring out praises to their unclean deity.

'If they think they're getting in here, they're going to be disappointed,' said Ulgavost. 'Nobody's coming to open the gates for them today.'

'You sealed your breach?'

Ulgavost sniffed. His perpetually dour expression lifted a moment in a display of modesty. 'Nothing to it, there were only a hundred or so of them.'

'I don't like the look of this. There are more of them all the time,' said Ulgathern.

'Think they'd just give up and leave us be? Chaos won't be done here until we're all dead. It's just a matter of time,' said Ulgavost.

'Aye,' said Ulgathern. 'I fear that time is coming soon.'

'Have you been talking to Drokki again?' said Ulgavost. 'That rhyme he's always trotting out has the runefather dead before the hold falls, if I recall, and I don't see our father laying down his life just yet.'

'There are the storms, Ulgavost. How do you explain them?'

'It's just a rhyme, Ulgathern.'

They stopped talking as hissing streams of molten rock poured out of the statues lining the wall below the crenellations. The heat of it hit them like a blow, but they were unperturbed; fire ran in their blood.

The gargants were not impervious. The lava hit them both, crushing them with its weight and setting them ablaze. They bellowed in pain and died quickly. The smell of roasting meat wafted up over the battlement and the horde bowed back.

'See? We're not going anywhere,' said Ulgavost. He looked to the sky, where storms had played for over a month. For the moment, they flickered with occasional lightning, but banks of black clouds were building to the sunset horizon. 'Looks like it's going to rain again. That usually has them leaving off for a while.'

Ulgathern watched the clouds gather. 'I still don't like this.'

Just then the sound of running feet echoed up the stair to the parapet. A puffing runner burst from the darkness. Ulgathern grinned in relief, certain the messenger was about to deliver news of their imminent victory, but the runner's expression quickly wiped the smile from his face.

'My lords, you must come swiftly,' he said. 'Runefather Karadrakk-Grimnir is dead.'

Upon the Isle of Arrak, deep under the Ulmount, two brother lodges stood. The duardin of Ulgaen-ar stood to the left of the island, while those of Ulgaen-zumar stood on the right, and each lodge was arranged around the end of the bridge leading to its respective delving.

The wrights and the warriors, matrons and maidens faced the Cages of Loss in respectful silence. Youngflames had their heads bowed, their youthful boisterousness doused by sorrow. The twin magma streams that made the rock an island ran dim and ruby. The very mountain mourned the passing of its mightiest son.

Over the Fyreslayers' heads the Ulmount opened its throat. Five hundred feet high and more, the uneven sides of the central chimney had been crafted into a straight, octagonal shaft by the duardin. Four-foot high ur-gold runes spiralled up the walls, their magic stabilising the volcano and holding back its eruptions. At the top the stern faces of Grimnir looked down. In the centre of their leaning heads the shaft opened at the base of the caldera, and the sky could be seen. The storm had broken and thrashed the heavens, flashing lightning the like of which none had seen before. The thunder was so loud it was as if Grimnir waged war upon Vulcatrix once again. The rain that fell on the Ulmount's cupped peak was gathered by cunning channels and sent deep into the hold. Smiths and artisans teased out its load of dissolved elements, before sending it on to water crops and the duardin themselves. The rain that fell into the vent could not be caught, and dropped down into the centre of the mountain. The water heated rapidly as it fell, and the duardin under the opening steamed.

Karadrakk-Grimnir lay in one of twenty funerary cages. These were wrought of fyresteel fixed to the brink of the cliff, and mounted upon axles. Two burly hearthguard stood at the wheels, ready to send their lord to his final rest. The runefather was swaddled tightly from head to foot in broad strips of troggoth leather, leaving only his face exposed and hiding the places where his body had been stripped of its ur-gold runes. His magnificent orange beard and crest had been washed free of blood, combed and laid carefully upon his wrappings. The deep gash in the side of his skull was covered over with a plate of gold that could not quite hide the lividity of his flesh. Gold coins stamped with the image of Grimnir-in-sorrow covered his eyes, while between Karadrakk-Grimnir's broad teeth was clamped an ingot of fyresteel, carefully crafted to fit his mouth perfectly – the gold because he was the master of gold and ur-gold, the steel because he was a warrior.

Karadrakk-Grimnir did not sleep alone. Twelve other cages on the Ulgaen-ar side cradled their own sad burdens, each attended by pairs of auric hearthguard. Ulgaen-zumar's funeral apparatus was set on the cliff opposite, the cages equal in number, though not so many were occupied. The fallen of Ulgaen-zumar lodge may have been fewer in number, but the blow to the hearts of all the Fyreslayers by the loss of Karadrakk-Grimnir was grievous.

A clank of gold pendants and the soft tread of many duardin feet came from the far side of the bridge arching over the lava to Ulgaen-ar's deepings. A low, rumbling song struck up, audible between the bangs and booms of the storms above. Runemaster Tulkingafar came over the bridge. His staff was visible first, burning hot with the borrowed fires of Ulgaen-ar's sacred forge. Then his crest, then his face, grim with the duty he must carry out, and painted white with the bone ashes of mourning. His hair was dark red, his upper lip shaved. Ten runesmiters walked in his train, eyes downcast as they sang, their skin coloured charcoal black.

The Ulgaen-ar lodge parted silently to let the zharrgrim priesthood through, and the procession came slowly to the centre of the Isle of Arrak, where it halted in the rain. From the other side, where the bridge to Ulgaen-zumar was situated, came a similar song, and another procession of the priests of the zharrgrim wended its sorrowful way forward, headed by Runemaster Marag-Or the Golden Eye.

Marag-Or, older, scarred, one eye replaced by a featureless orb of gold, came to a halt before Tulkingafar.

'Runemaster,' he said.

'Runemaster,' responded Tulkingafar. The hot water streaming down their faces made their mourning colours run.

They turned sharply, leading their processions out from under the volcano's vent to their respective lodge's cages. Tulkingafar had the graver duty today and so would begin. Marag-Or took his followers to the side of Runefather Briknir-Grimnir, Karadrakk's brother.

Marag-Or looked sidelong at Briknir. The runefather's expression was set hard as a mountain's, no indication of what he thought or felt, but that he mourned his brother was clear to one as wise as Marag-Or. Briknir-Grimnir's beard showed fresh strands of grey within its fiery bunches, and his eyes were hollow as cave mouths.

Tulkingafar left his runesmiters and went to the side of his master's last resting place. He rested his broad hands on the fyresteel a moment, and looked at the dead lord and his funeral goods.

'Our runefather is slain!' he said. His voice was loud, and carried well over the constant rumbling of the twin lava rivers and the crackling boom of the storm. 'For three hundred years he led us. No longer!' He stared over the heads of his congregation, speaking directly to the heart of the mountain. 'He and twenty other good duardin were slain as they drove the enemy out of our hold.' He dropped his gaze to meet the eyes of his fellows. 'The runefather was not fond of long speeches.' There was scattered laughter at this. 'Who needs talk? He was brave! He refused defeat each time it was so generously offered to him by our besiegers. He was noble! He was the most generous of ring-givers.' He paused. 'And he was my friend.'

More than a few voices rumbled *aye* to that. Karadrakk-Grimnir had been well loved.

'We will not be broken. *Burukaz Ulgaen-ar*!' called Tulkingafar.

'Ulgaen-ar burukaz!' the others responded.

Tulkingafar nodded at the hearthguard manning the cage machinery. They turned the wheels reverently, the ratchets on the axle clacking one tooth at a time.

'From fire we were born, to fire we return,' Tulkingafar intoned. 'Burn brightly in the furnaces of Grimnir, Karadrakk-Grimnir Ulgaen, and be forged anew. May the heat of your soul never cool, and its flames never dim.'

The cage reached a near-vertical position and the hearthguard ceased their turning. One pulled a lever. A gate opened at the foot of the cage, and Karadrakk-Grimnir slid from its confines and fell into the Ulgaen-ar magma river. A bright flash of fire marked his passage from one world to the next, lighting up the faces of the mourning lodge members, showing many tugging at their beards with sorrow.

The mountain rumbled. The cracking of stone sounded deep in the ground. Short-lived geysers in the rivers sent shadows leaping across the craggy stone, and teased starbursts from the veins of minerals in the rock. The cavern returned to its sombre ruby.

'The Ulmount mourns the loss of a good master,' said Tulk-ingafar. 'Grimnir has taken him to his forge.'

A battlesmith went to the empty cradle. In a droning chant he began to recount the many deeds of Karadrakk's long life as Marag-Or and Tulkingafar went down the row of occupied cages and immolated their dead.

However, one priest-smith present had his mind on other things. Drokki of the Withered Arm looked up the tall chimney of the Ulmount's throat. The faces of Grimnir looked down at him reproachfully at this stinting of duty, but he was not interested in their disapproval. He stared at the lightning flashing across the sky, and he worried.

'In a week's time, the Ulgahold will have been under siege for one hundred and one years. We come here to discuss the wishes of Karadrakk-Grimnir Ulgaen, and who among you, the seven surviving sons of Karadrakk-Grimnir, will assume the heavy burden of responsibility for leadership of Lodge Ulgaen-ar.'

Tulkingafar gave the seven sons a steely look. They stared back with varying amounts of defiance, hope, sorrow and fear.

Get on with it, you pompous ass, thought Ulgathern. He bridled at Tulkingafar's superior manner, his ponderous delivery. Ulgathern was eager to be done; he itched to avenge his father, and he needed to talk to Drokki. At first he had dismissed Drokki's talk of the Great Omen, but since the storms he had come to half-believe him. And now this...

The auric regalia he had to wear was heavy, a wide poncho of gold plates sewn to thick leather, and a huge, ceremonial helm. Fyreslayers as a rule rarely wore much. Their holds were warmed by the blood of the earth, while their own Grimnir-given fires kept them heated in the most inhospitable of environments. To wear too many clothes or, Grimnir forfend, too much *armour,* was an affront to their shattered god. Ulgathern found the gear uncomfortable. The zharrgrim temple was nigh to the forge, where streams of lava were harvested for their metals and channelled into the fyresteel foundry. The grumbling of hot stone bottled up behind its sluices was as oppressive as the heat. But borne the heat must be, and he stood there sweltering and stiff with all the stoicism expected of a duardin.

Ulgathern did not like or trust Tulkingafar. He was too invested in politicking, always seeking to exert his temple's pre-eminence in the hold over that of Magar-Or's, and he was the worst of Drokki's persecutors. Too often the intention of Tulkingafar's actions appeared not to be to increase reverence of Grimnir, but to consolidate his own power. To have risen to so lofty a rank within the zharrgrim at such a young age spoke of a certain ruthlessness.

Behind Ulgathern were his six brothers, gathered before the great statue of Grimnir in their coats of gold. Behind them were the guildmasters of both lodges. The stout matrons and males of the Mining and Gleaning Fellowships, the Kin-gather Matrons, the battlesmiths and loremasters and brewmistresses and a dozen others. The leadership of each lodge occupied the chequered floor on either side of the temple's central aisle in strict orders of hierarchy, in most respects mirror images of each other, save one.

Ulgathern's uncle, Briknir-Grimnir Ulgaen, stood at the head of his lodge. The space Ulgathern's father should have occupied was empty. By the time Tulkingafar stopped blowing hot air, it would be occupied again.

'A number of you have been chosen for honour,' said Tulkingafar. 'Only one was deemed worthy by Karadrakk-Grimnir to assume leadership of Lodge Ulgaen-ar.' The runemaster gestured. A chest was brought from an alcove to the side by his acolytes, and placed at his feet. The venerable battlesmith Loremaster Garrik came forth with an elaborate key, and fitted it to the lock.

'The legacy chest of Karadrakk-Grimnir. Within is his truth,' intoned Garrik.

The chest was opened. Tulkingafar's acolytes took out plaques stamped with the names of those Karadrakk-Grimnir deemed worthy, and handed them to the runemaster. The number caused the brothers to shift. Four were to be chosen, a high number. They waited tensely for their fates.

Tulkingafar played it out as long as he could. The bastard, thought Ulgathern.

'Ulgamaen, ninth son of Karadrakk-Grimnir. You are to be runefather of the lodge of Ulgaen-ar.' He tossed the plaque at Ulgamaen's feet. Ulgamaen looked serious as he retrieved it, but that was him through and through. Probably why Father chose him, thought Ulgathern. Anyone who could crack a smile of delight at landing that role isn't up to the job.

'Come forward, Ulgamaen-Grimnir Ulgaen!' sang Tulkingafar. He took Karadrakk's latchkey grandaxe from an attendant and presented it to the new runefather. 'By your father's command, you are to unlock the great vault of Ulgaen-ar, and take out three-sixteenths of the lodge ur-gold.'

'Yes, runemaster,' said Ulgamaen-Grimnir. 'I shall instruct the hoardtalliers that it be done immediately.'

Mangulnar shot his brother Ulgamaen a poisonous look. He was furious – his beard bristled and face glowed red. The heat of his anger was palpable to Ulgathern.

'Ranganak! Fourteenth son of Karadrakk.' The runemaster tossed the second plaque at Ranganak's feet. 'You are to receive one of these sixteenths. The quiet halls of the Sunward Deeps are yours, Ranganak-Grimnir. You have leave to forge your latchkey, construct a vault of your own, and establish a new lodge there, for the protection and betterment of all within the Ulmount.'

'Thank you, runemaster, thank you,' said Ranganak-Grimnir with a hasty bow, and retrieved his own plaque. He looked at it lovingly.

'To Tulgamar, twentieth son of Karadrakk, the same,' said Tulkingafar, tossing the third plaque toward Karadrakk-Grimnir's youngest son. Tulgamar caught it. 'The lost halls of the Far Delvings are yours, if you can take them from the beasts that dwell there, Tulgamar-Grimnir.'

Tulgamar nodded once, fingering his token of office thoughtfully. His gift was a hard one.

One portion remained. The four other sons of Karadrakk waited with bated breath. Mangulnar's hands were clenched so tightly his knuckles were white.

Tulkingafar drew it out, surveying the eager runesons with a crafty look. Ulgathern thought he might explode. Or punch Tulkingafar in the face.

Tulkingafar's round eyes swung to look upon him. 'And lastly, Ulgathern, twelfth son of Karadrakk-Grimnir. One sixteenth of the lodge ur-gold.'

The plaque clunked onto the floor at Ulgathern's feet. He could not keep the grin off his face as he retrieved it. The three disinherited runesons glowered, their dreams of wealth and honour gone.

'For you, Ulgathern-Grimnir, a choice is given. You are to aid whichever of your brothers you choose, and request of them a right to settle.'

The old sod, thought Ulgathern. His father had often berated him for forging his own path and not thinking of the future. It looked like he had one final lesson for his son; cooperation, or exile.

'You are charged with these responsibilities on one condition,' Tulkingfar went on. 'That you forsake the leaving of the hold, and work with your kin to strengthen it against incursion. Keep the Ulgahold free of the servants of Slaanesh, and you shall forever be honoured in the records of all the Ulgaen lodges.'

Ulgathern accepted claps upon the back from his newly elevated brothers and returned them. Of the three who had received nothing, Grankak and Ulgavost gave grudging respect, though their faces were sunk deep into their beards. Mangulnar held himself apart. He watched from the side for a moment before losing his temper completely.

'Outrage! Perfidy! I am eldest! I am runefather by right!' He moved toward Ulgamaen. The new runefather's auric hearthguard stepped forwards, crossed magmapikes barring his path.

'You have no right to leadership, runeson,' said Tulkingafar. 'Karadrakk-Grimnir's last wishes have been read. They are inviolate.'

When Mangulnar spoke again, his breath shimmered on the air, and smoke curled from his nostrils. 'You will all regret this. All of you!' He stormed out, his few followers hot on his heels.

A shocked silence followed this grievous breach of tradition, until a few minutes later, when hogsheads of magmalt ale were brought in and breached. After the first dozen tankards, they forgot about Mangulnar's outburst completely.

The Hall of Memory was unusually cool and peaceful. For those reasons, Drokki liked it there. The remembrance beads made long rows of gold that glimmered ruddily in the hall's low light. So big was the library that a duardin could lose themselves there. Drokki wandered down the aisles between the books dangling on their iron frames. The smell of hot gold and an occasional clatter and hiss drifted over the racks from the die rooms at the rear, where battlesmiths cast new books. From a nearby aisle he could hear hushed conversation. When the battlesmiths were in training, the Hall of Memory was altogether noisier, each basso profundo duardin voice competing with the next in volume and complexity of rhythm as they recited the lodge's history. But today it was quiet.

The remembrance bead books were arranged by reigning runefather and year. He knew he shouldn't, but Drokki let his good hand trail lightly along the records, setting off tiny, leaden clacks as the beads swayed on their thongs and knocked one another. He loved the slippery, cool feel of the gold, the random snatches of knowledge he read as his fingers touched upon the books' runes.

His other arm was small and stick-like and lacking strength. He had lost count of the number of times Tulkingafar had said he should have been cast into the magma at birth. Some had taken the defect as a mark of Chaos. The Matrons of the Kin-gather had stood their ground, insisting that it was nothing of the sort and that the fires of his spirit burned true. Drokki might have been allowed to live, but he was reminded daily that it was upon sufferance.

Drokki habitually kept his withered arm pressed against his side. It wasn't the most comfortable position – that was to have it up against his chest. But when nestled into his chest his little claw of a hand adopted a form that made it look like it was about to dart forward and snatch at purses, or it gave him a sinister, calculating air, as if he were raking his bent fingers through his beard. The worst of it was that when he held it across his chest, everyone could see. So he had taught himself to hold it straight, and many hours of pain it had cost him.

With it forced down by his side, Drokki half-convinced himself that no one noticed.

Everyone always noticed.

Friends did not care, that was the important thing. To them he had been Drokki, and now he was Runesmiter Drokki, not Drokki of the Withered Arm – or worse. He was becoming respected, in his own small way; he had to remind himself of that often. The truth was that twenty friendly faces could not counterbalance one hateful comment, not in his heart.

'Drokki! What are you doing skulking about back there?'

Battlesmith Loremaster Kaharagun Whitebeard came huffing up an intersection in the aisles, a half-dozen heavy remembrance bead books looped over a soft cloth wrapped around one arm, a slender, hooked staff in the other. Whitebeard was stout, almost as broad as he was tall, with a belly to match.

Drokki darted him a shy look. He found it hard to hold the eyes of others, and he kept having to force his gaze to meet that of Kaharagun. 'Oh, you know. Looking, um, reading. Are you not at the calling?'

'No, I'm not. I have given Loremaster Garrik the honour of performing that duty. He's still got the knees for all that bowing and scraping.'

Garrik was at most six months younger than Kaharagun. Drokki hid a smile.

The loremaster looked back down the way Drokki had come. The swaying of the beads was minute, but Kaharagun noticed. 'You've been up to mischief, again! Have you been disturbing the lore?'

'Er. Well, I have. Yes. Sorry,' admitted Drokki.

Kaharagun huffed. 'Drokki! You're no youngflame now, you're a runesmiter! I expect better of you. Eighty-nine and still poking the beads like a bare-faced child.'

'Sorry.'

'You know it wears the gold. What's the first rule of the beads?'

'Touch them for reading, otherwise never.'

'Right. Now, can I help you?' Kaharagun's scolding was gentle. Still, Drokki found it hard to look him in the face.

'Um, yes. I was looking for the records from Gaenagrik Hold.'

Kaharagun sucked at his beard and rearranged his belly. 'Gaenagrik eh? What do you want the beads of the ur-lodge for?'

'There's something I need to check on,' said Drokki. He dared not share his unease yet, not until he was sure. 'The prophecies of Hulgar Farseeing.'

'I'd leave all that alone, young one. He was regarded mad, you know.'

'Yes. Yes, I did know,' said Drokki softly.

The duardin looked at each other for a moment.

'Can you show me?' prompted Drokki. 'The records from the old hold aren't arranged the same way as the new, and there is something I need to check.'

'They're perfectly easy to negotiate if you know what you are doing,' said Whitebeard sharply. 'They're this way. If you'll keep me company while I return these books to the racks, I'll show you.' He jabbed out a gnarled finger. 'But no more touching the beads!'

Drokki followed the old loresmith down the lanes of cast gold. Each book was made up of triangular beads threaded onto orruk hide thongs. They were written in the high runes, three to a face, ideograms depicting entire words or discrete concepts. Not many could read them, partly because the information they conveyed was dependent on context and fiendishly dense.

'I lived in Gaenagrik when I was a lad,' Kaharagun said as they walked. 'Fine hold. I was ten years old when Marthung-Grimnir Ulgaen, Grimnir warm his soul, set this place up. Ten! Can you imagine?'

Drokki could not. Kaharagun was already ancient when Drokki was born.

They stopped at a space in the rack. Kaharagun carried on talking as he unwound a bead book from his arm. 'I'd never have thought I'd end up living here. Funny how life turns out.' His face set. 'Not that there was anything funny about the ur-lodge falling. Five thousand years the hold stood, and in two nights it was gone. Half the Ulgaen lodges wiped out.' He fitted the book's loop onto the hook on the end of his staff, using it to reach up to the top of the racks and put it back onto its numbered hook on the racks. The book swayed as he replaced it. There were eight strands of beads to it, six feet long when hung. 'It's a wonder we survived.'

They passed towards the very far end of the hall. Kaharagun replaced his last book, folded up the cloth on his arm, kissed it reverently, and stowed it under his robe. 'Right then. This way. Past here are the Gaenagrik records, what we saved of them.'

He led Drokki further in. The torches in the sconces at the end of the racks were unlit and it was dark there. The careful ordering of the younger Ulgahold records gave way to a more chaotic system, if there was any system at all. The books were very old, the gold dark with age and the runes round-edged with touch-reading.

Kaharagun passed a fire iron to Drokki. Drokki spoke to the device, and the runes on it glowed then the end shone with heat. He pressed it to two torches, the pitch spluttering as it ignited. Drokki smelled burning dust. No one had been down there for a long time.

'Hulgar, Hulgar, Hulgar...' muttered Kaharagun. He ran his

fingers along the beads. 'Aha! Here we are. What was it you were after?'

'His *Telling of Great Omens*.'

Kaharagun snorted. 'Child's stories.' He unhooked a book of six strands with his staff, inspected it briefly and passed it to Drokki. 'Volume one. Careful with it. The hide is brittle. I keep meaning to get the thongs replaced, but there's been a shortage of orruks about since the siege began. Some might say troggoth or ogor hide works just as well, but I won't use anything else. Can't take the weight.'

Drokki took the book. He draped it over one shoulder rather than over his arm in the proper manner. Kaharagun frowned, but it was the only way he could read it. Drokki ran the beads through the fingers of his good hand. It was an introduction, written in Hulgar's portentous manner. The first half of the string was a long list of thanks to various patrons.

The beads ran out. A knot had been tied in the thong to keep them from falling off, the end of it scorched hard.

'Is there any more?'

'Of that volume? No. Melted. There's twenty more volumes though.'

'I need to see them. All of them.'

'Very well,' grumbled Kaharagun.

Drokki and Kaharagun spent the next hour reading. There was a good deal missing from the book. One volume had come apart and been threaded back together without care for its content, and was unreadable without checking the tiny order numbers stamped into the base of each bead. Two more stopped abruptly, another started in the middle of a passage.

Volume number twelve, string four, had what Drokki needed, and what he had dreaded. His heart beat faster as he read. It was all there. Everything. The lightning, the siege, the death of the runefather. It was all there in solid gold, not a half-remembered rhyme, but a real prophecy.

Kaharagun leaned in, his old face creased in concern at the look on Drokki's face.

'Drokki?' he asked. 'Is everything alright?'

'I very much need to borrow this,' said Drokki.

Ulgathern-Grimnir returned to his chambers lost in thought. He was a runefather now, something he had wanted all his life, but now he had it, he felt strangely hollow inside. All that responsibility, all those people relying on him – if he could convince them to join his lodge in the first place. The plates of his robe caught on his muscles as he struggled out of it, and with relief he tossed it onto his bed. There was so much to do! He needed to appoint a runemaster, and he needed to marry...

He was so preoccupied he did not notice his visitor until she gave out a gentle cough. 'A runefather's greed's worth of gold, and you toss it on the bed.'

'Amsaralka?'

'I should think so,' she scolded. 'I hope there aren't any other maidens frequenting your chambers.'

Amsaralka stepped forward fully into the runelight. At the sight of her Ulgathern forgot the events of the last two days. Amsaralka was breathtakingly beautiful. He took in her massive shoulders, her strong, heavy miner's arms. Her feet were delightfully huge, and he suspected the toes (he often dreamt of her toes, when life was slow) hidden behind her steel toe-caps to be exquisitely blunt. Her hair was gathered into two tresses, thick as an ogor's golden torcs, and as lustrous. Her face was wide and square, her eyes attractively far apart. She had a broad mouth and full lips, behind which hid white teeth as evenly placed as bricks.

'What are you mooning at?' she said, and embraced him, then stood back and gripped his upper arms. Her hands were vices on his biceps. 'What did they say? What is Karadrakk-Grimnir's legacy, who will be the next runefather of Ulgaen-ar?'

Ulgathern reached up a broad finger and gently traced the downy hair on Amsaralka's jawline. Fine hair, softer than spun gold.

'Not I,' he said.

She wrinkled her nose in disappointment. 'Oh, Ulgathern.'

'Such a pretty nose,' he murmured. 'Like a rock chip.'

She punched his arm. 'This is important!' she said. 'Ulgathern, I don't know what to say. You were your father's favourite.'

'I was his favoured,' said Ulgathern. 'Not favourite to lead Ulgaen-ar. He always thought me a little too frivolous.' He toyed with the end of her tress.

She slapped his hand. 'Leave that alone! We're not married. And if you're not runefather we won't ever be,' she said glumly. She pushed herself away from him.

'A runeson's not good enough for your darling mother?'

'Runesons end up dead. You know what she says. I'm the daughter of the Chief of the Mining Fellowship, mother won't let me.'

'Who says I'm a runeson?'

A brief moment of confusion flitted across her face. When her smile broke through, it was like the sun bursting out of the clouds.

'You mean..?'

'Yes! Father divided up the ur-gold. Ulgamaen is to be the new runefather of Ulgean-ar. Tulgamar, Ranganak and I have been given portions. We're to establish our own lodges in the old halls.'

Amsaralka clapped her hands. 'We can marry!'

'Perhaps,' he said worriedly. He couldn't get Drokki's blathering out of his mind. He shook it away and said wolfishly, 'maybe I should have a look at those toes first?'

They both glanced down at her heavy boots.

'Not before our wedding night!' she said sternly, then smiled, 'which will be soon, Ulgathern-*Grimnir.*' She added the honorific to his name with delight. 'Grimnir put much fire into my belly, Ulgathern. I promise to bear you many fine sons.'

'If you're half as good a mother as a miner, I'd expect at least a score,' he said.

They closed their eyes and touched noses. They held each other, happy for a moment, all the concerns of the outside world shut out.

'Oh good, you're in,' Drokki said.

Ulgathern turned round to see the Runesmiter in the doorway, his withered arm held rigidly by his side.

'Ring the bloody gong next time, Drokki!' said Ulgathern, his face flushing crimson. 'Can't you see I'm busy here?'

'Ah yes, right. Uh, hello, Amsaralka,' said Drokki absentmindedly. 'What I've got to show you is important. Er, congratulations by the way. I suppose I have to call you Ulgathern-Grimnir now, or, or my lord?'

'Go *away*, Drokki. Whatever it is can wait until morning. We've got a wedding to plan.' He grinned at Amsaralka, and reached for her hand, but she slipped away.

'I've got to go,' she said quietly. She left with her eyes downcast.

Ulgathern narrowed his eyes at his friend. 'Now look what you've done.'

'Er, what have I done?'

'Don't you have any sense of common decency? You've shamed her, you catching us cuddling like that! Think of the gossip.'

'I'm sorry. But, but you have to listen, or it's not going to matter. Records. You're not going to want to see, but you have to.'

'Drokki, I am not going tramping down to the Hall of Memory with you at this hour.'

'You don't have to.' Drokki whistled. Two strapping young battlesmiths trooped in, carrying a rack dangling dozens of records strings. The gold clacked and slapped as they trotted in. 'It was important enough that Kaharagun let me take the book. Put it there,' said Drokki.

'Don't! Stop!' said Ulgathern. But it was too late, the young duardin had put the rack down and were bowing their way backwards out of the door.

'Really. Sorry, I am, I mean. But you have to read this.'

Ulgathern sighed and pulled at his moustache. 'Clearly you're not leaving. What is it?'

Drokki bared his teeth nervously. 'The end, the end of everything. Ulgathern, we have to abandon the Ulmount.'

'What?'

'Hulgar's *The Great Omen*! I know! You keep saying it is another of his bad prophecies, that it's just a rhyme. But I know you're worried too. When we were at the funeral I was watching the storm, and I got thinking. It's happening, Ulgathern. Next week is the one hundred and first anniversary of the beginning of the siege. The runefather is dead "by stealth and surprise", just like in Hulgar's poem. The storm is not like anything we've seen before, it's...'

'*Salvation and disaster, the end of a hold, where once was two is now one, but even that will be undone?*' quoted Ulgathern. 'Grimnir's fires, Drokki, you can't put any faith in that doggerel. Hulgar was a fat fool.'

Drokki held up the beads. 'The original is more detailed. It's all here! Hulgar was certain of it. Look!'

'You know I don't read the high runes.'

Drokki blinked. His face was white and sweaty in a way unnatural for a Fyreslayer. 'You have to believe me, Ulgathern. The Ulgahold, it's going to fall.'

Ulgathern sighed through his teeth. 'All right. Show me.'

'You expect me to believe this, nephew?' said Briknir-Grimnir.

'Drokki says it's all there in plain gold,' said Ulgathern. Ulgathern-Grimnir, he had to keep reminding himself. He tried to stand taller in his uncle's imperious stare. He really should, now he was a runefather himself, but the older Fyreslayer intimidated him. A sixteenth share of Ulgaen-ar's ur-gold seemed nothing when he stood before so great a lord. 'I didn't want to believe him either but–'

'Drokki of the Withered Arm!' sneered Tulkingafar. 'A know-nothing fool.'

Ulgamaen-Grimnir held up his hand and gave Tulkingafar a nervous look, unsure as yet of his authority over his father's runemaster. Tulkingafar snorted and fell silent.

'Well,' said Briknir-Grimnir. 'Well!' He slapped the golden arms of his high throne. The duardin of Ulgaen-ar and the three new, as-yet-unnamed lodges were guests of Ulgaen-zumar and met in their High Seat. The Ulgahold was a modest place compared to some, but even its throne halls were vast and lofty, the ceilings of gleaming stone so tall that the eight-foot high runes around the frieze at the top looked no bigger than a babe's fingernails.

'It is Hulgar, isn't it?' said Marag-Or of the Golden Eye. He sat in his runemaster's chair, dwarfed by the huge carvings of Grimnir surrounding him. 'It is said he caused a lot of trouble in Gaenagrik in the old days, predicting this and that. It is also a matter of history that his record of accuracy was somewhat patchy.'

'But some of his prophecies were right,' said Ulgathern.

'And a lot of them were wrong,' said Marag-Or. '*The war of a hundred and one years will come to an end, as lightning cleaves the sky, salvation comes late for those that see no sense, greed overcomes virtue and the lodge-line shall be broken,*' said Marag-Or. 'That's the one that's got Drokki all in a lather, isn't it?' He leaned forward, the beads in his grey-shot orange beard clacking together. 'Drokki, Drokki. What's to be done?'

'What are you suggesting, Ulgathern-Grimnir?' said Briknir-Grimnir.

'That we head for the Broken Plains of Aqshy and the Volturung. They're our ancestral kin. They will take us in.'

'For the love of Grimnir,' muttered Briknir-Grimnir. 'We've not had any contact with them for a hundred years!'

'We've not had contact with anyone for a hundred years,' said Ulgathern-Grimnir. 'We've been under siege for over a century. Qualar Vo is not–'

'Do not utter that name in my throne hall!' yelled Briknir-Grimnir. An uncomfortable silence fell. The new runefathers looked uneasily at one another.

Ulgathern-Grimnir swallowed. 'He is not going to give up. There are more of the Slaaneshi out there than ever. It's only a matter of time. Volturung were always the strongest among our kin lodges. They're the most likely to still be there.'

'If you don't die on the way, which you will,' said Briknir-Grimnir. 'Can you have a word with Drokki?' said Briknir-Grimnir to Marag-Or. 'Get this nonsense out of his head?'

'I will, runefather. As soon as we're done here.'

'He should never have been accepted into the temple,' said Tulkingafar.

Marag-Or turned his sole good eye on the younger rune-master. 'Aye, but he was. By me. Drokki's a good lad. Only the one arm, and he draws the cleanest runes out of the ur-gold I've seen for a long time. He's better than you were when I trained you, runemaster. Bear that in mind when you're bad-mouthing him.'

Tulkingafar's lips curled. Sparks sprang up in his eyes. He tried to hide it, but the fires of his heart were stoked by his hatred of Drokki.

'That's that then,' said Briknir-Grimnir.

'With all reverence, uncle, it is not!' Ulgathern-Grimnir said.

Briknir opened his mouth and shut it again, setting it firm. 'What then?'

'I have a very bad feeling about it, here, in my fires.' He pat-ted his stomach and hurried on before he could be interrupted. 'Next week it'll be one hundred and one years since the siege began. We've suffered some setbacks recently.' He did not cite his father's death. 'There's this storm… We should go.'

'Lad, runefather,' said Marag-or, 'that prophecy could apply to anyone, anywhere in any realm at any time. How many hundred-year sieges have there been since Chaos came to the realms? It's not one or two, let me tell you.'

Briknir-Grimnir grumbled and his big orange beard shook. 'Feelings now is it lad? That's no way to run a lodge! Do your feelings know how to bypass the siege? Get down off the mountain into the Howling Waste? We can't chance the Ulmount's Realmgate, I'll tell you that much, nephew. That's under my protection, and it will not be opened. It cannot be opened, not since that perfumed libertine out there did his business on it.'

'I know it's tainted,' said Ulgathern-Grimnir. 'I'm not a fool, uncle.'

'Well then, looks like you're stuck here with us,' said Briknir-Grimnir.

'Drokki says he has an idea. He won't tell me what it is until he's sure it will work, you know what he's like.'

'Runefathers Tulgamar-Grimnir, Ulgamaen-Grimnir, Ranganak-Grimnir. What say you? You are the masters of your own lodges now, this concerns us all.'

Ranganak-Grimnir shook his head. 'I say we stay.'

Tulgamar-Grimnir held up his hands and shrugged.

'I'll not be going. Unlike my brother, I'll be obeying my father's dying wish,' said Ulgamaen-Grimnir. 'Ulgaen-ar's home is here.'

'*Baharun, baharar!*' said Ulgamaen-Grimnir's hearthguard, clashing their wristbands together. Many were young, newly elevated from the lower ranks of Ulgaen-ar lodge, and greater in number than those sworn to the other runefathers.

'There you are,' said Briknir-Grimnir. 'I'm sorry, lad, we'll not be abandoning the Ulgahold. It might've been your great-grandfather founded this place, but it was your father and me built it up from nothing. When the ur-lodge fell, we stood strong. Gaenagrik's a ruin. Last time I looked we're still here. We'll not be leaving. Now stop this nonsense. One hundred and one years'll come and go like every other anniversary. The Slaaneshi scum outside have been getting complacent of late, we'll see them off.'

'This is a time for celebration, and you scaremonger,' said Tulkingafar coldly.

'No one agrees with me?' said Ulgathern-Grimnir.

'No lad,' said Briknir. 'I thought I made that quite clear.'

Ulgathern-Grimnir looked around the semi-circle of Ulgaen-zumar's seated elders. Their faces were hostile. He looked to Marag-Or, but he shook his head. His brothers would not meet his eyes, all but Tulgamar-Grimnir, who mouthed an apology.

Ulgathern-Grimnir sighed. 'Then firstly I appoint Drokki

of the Withered Arm to be my runemaster, with all the rights and responsibilities thereunto.'

'He's not ready!' snapped Tulkingafar.

'Quiet!' said Ulgamaen-Grimnir from the corner of his mouth. 'Let my brother have his moment of infamy. If he's going to cut off his own head with his axe, let's not help him.'

'Is he ready?' asked Briknir-Grimnir.

'In some ways, yes, in others, no,' said Marag-Or. 'He's got the rune gift, and he can sniff out ur-gold better than most. But he's yet to gain wisdom.'

'Can't teach that, Marag-Or.'

'No, got to earn it,' said Marag-Or. 'Being runemaster will do that, or he'll die.'

'Alright then, Marag-Or releases Drokki from his service.'

'He has his permission to found his own temple,' said Marag-Or.

'And good luck to him,' said Briknir-Grimnir. 'Will that stop all this crazy talk?'

'No.' Ulgathern spread his hands. 'I invoke the right of far-wandering. I will take my people with me, and I will go. We shall found a new hold of our own, somewhere safe, for our lodge to occupy.'

'The stipulation on your runefatherhood was that you stay,' said Briknir-Grimnir.

'It's not binding. It was my father's wish, but it can't be a command. The right of a runeson gifted with ur-gold as runefather to found his own hold is paramount.' Ulgathern-Grimnir swallowed his guilt. 'I checked.'

Briknir-Grimnir's face hardened. 'There's a reason your father didn't tap you for the runefatherhood of Ulgaen-ar. Too full of bloody stupid ideas, that head of yours is. Leave us? You'll be stripping our defence mighty thin, lad. Your father wanted you to open up the old halls, strengthen the Ulgahold from the inside out, not tear it apart.'

'My father is dead!' said Ulgathern-Grimnir. 'And I am a runefather in my own right. It is my command that my portion of the folk of Ulgaen-ar leave.' He choked on his own words, and became quiet. 'Before it is too late.'

Briknir-Grimnir's lips thinned. 'You're strong-headed. I have to respect that. I can't stop you. It's your right to go if you want it. But you've a touch too much fire in your brain if you reckon on this being a good idea.'

'Thank you, uncle.' Ulgathern-Grimnir bowed.

'Two things, nephew. You don't have to bow to me any more, you're a runefather now.'

'Right,' said Ulgathern.

'And the other is this, you try to take any of my folk with you, or tell them what you told me to get their bellows pumping and the iron in them soft enough that you can beat your daft ideas into them, then I'll take that as an act against me, and I won't hold back.'

Ulgavost stepped forward from the throng of Ulgaen-ar's representatives. 'I'll come with you brother, more for the adventure than anything else. There's not much here for me now.'

Ulgathern-Grimnir nodded at Ulgavost gratefully. Encouraged, he looked to the others. They looked away.

'Tulgamar?' said Ulgathern-Grimnir. 'I know you're torn. Come with me. Your magmadroth would be mighty handy.'

'I…' said Tulgamar. 'I can't.'

'Your brother can make up his own mind!' snapped Briknir-Grimnir. 'Now get gone if you're going. I won't wish you luck, because you'll need more than there is in all this realm. I only hope you don't get us all killed and that your ur-gold isn't lost for all time.'

'Ur-gold is never lost, runefather,' said Marag-Or.

'So you keep saying,' Briknir-Grimnir slumped into his throne. 'But if this *kahuz-bahan* has his way, some will be. Go on Ulgathern-Grimnir. Audience is over. Get out.'

Drokki emerged from a hidden door low down the Ulmount. The underway between the ruined hold of Gaenagrik and the Ulgahold was blocked for a way, and he was forced to venture over ground. He consulted the map in his hand, an ancient artefact made of etched brass. It showed the many ways that had once existed to Gaenagrik. Only one existed now.

Gaenagrik would be dangerous, unstable after so many years uninhabited. The moulding runes that held its stone together would have failed, leaving it at the mercy of the Hornteeth Mountains' rumblings. He could find his way to the city easily enough, but he did not know the safe way through to the hold's Realmgate. In point of fact, he did not know if the gate were still accessible. He needed a guide, and it was to look for one that he ventured outside the safety of the duardin city.

Drokki followed a path along the cliffs over the Hardgate. He looked down often onto the Chaos camp, nervous he would be seen. Cries of ecstasy and agony drifted up from the town and wild music played from many quarters, clashing discordantly. Under the harsh, acrid smell of ash and burning rock, there was the cloying stink of daemonic perfume. Bat-winged creatures sported in the sky over the camp, showering it with their excrement and fluids. It was these that Drokki feared the most. If they spotted him, they would be on him in moments, and would tear him to pieces. But they were absorbed with their games and they did not see him. Luckily, he did not have far to go.

A black hole opened in the mountainside. Drokki scrambled

gratefully towards it, steadying himself with his good arm as he skidded down the loose material into the welcome dark.

The angry red sky was reduced to a ragged patch that flickered with distant lightning. He was back in the underway to Gaenagrik, and he hurried down out of sight.

A few hundred steps from the opening, the tunnel broadened. The raw rubble of rockfalls was replaced by carefully laid blocks of granite. Smooth setts, so artfully laid that the joins were almost invisible, paved the floor. He held up his lantern and ignited it with a word.

The old road to Gaenagrik stretched ahead into the black.

This is it then, he thought, and set off at a hurried pace.

Signs of war were visible here and there – the bones of an overlooked duardin, or shattered remnants of enemy armour. The underway was otherwise free of debris and in good condition. The realms were filled with ruins, but 'duardin-made, eternally stays' went the old saying, and here that was evident.

The underway sloped downwards. Gaenagrik Mountain was lower than the Ulmount. He went as fast as he dared, trying to make his footfalls as light as possible, painfully aware that this was the route his own ancestors had fled along when Gaenagrik had fallen, and that to all objective sense he was heading the wrong way.

He went unchallenged. Bones were the only things he saw.

After a time a pair of richly carved gates materialised in his lantern light. They were ajar, the gap between them an impenetrable black. The drafts of the tunnel were forced into sighing winds by the narrowness of the gap, and Drokki smelled slow decay.

He squeezed between them, and came into the outskirts of Gaenagrik. The road split, half going upward, half down. Doorways to deserted guardrooms showed as dark holes. Nervously he sniffed the air, his zharrgrim-trained nose searching for ur-gold. The smell of ur-gold was like no other, a tingle at the back of the sinuses, like before a good sneeze. It didn't take him long to find it. That would help him find the duardin he sought. Doing so would either save his life, or end it. He patted the pouch of fresh ur-gold runes at his belt, hoping that they would be enough.

Glancing around, he set off on the upward path.

Once in the hold, Drokki had no concern about encountering the enemy. This was the renegade Grimwrath Berzerker Brokkengird's territory, and that made Drokki very nervous, more nervous than if he were facing a horde of pleasure-worshippers. Never mind that Drokki had come to find the Grimwrath; Brokkengird was insane.

Not the best of allies, but Drokki could see no other way. Only Brokkengird knew the safe route to Gaenagrik's Realmgate.

Drokki followed his nose. The road continued upwards at an unvarying incline. A canyon, carved straight by duardin picks, opened up to his side. On the far side roads switched back and forth up the cliff, leading to the open mouths of mines. Lava glow came from the bottom of the crevasse, so faint it must have been hundreds of feet down. Strange sounds came out of the dark, louder and odder the further in he walked.

When Drokki reached the top of the canyon road, the smell of ur-gold had the back of his nose tickling. He held up his runic lantern, playing the bright yellow cone of light over a wide plaza, its walls carved with friezes showing the daily life of duardin centuries dead.

Something barged into Drokki's back, sending him flying. He rolled over and over, coming to a halt face down over the precipice. His lamp flew from his hand, clattering from the canyon walls before spinning away. The light of it dwindled to nothing. He did not hear it hit the bottom.

A hard hand gripped him by the scruff of the neck and threw him backwards as if he weighed nothing. He flew across the plaza into the carved walls. Stone met his back, bruising his ribs and driving the wind from him, and he slid to the floor, gaping like a landed fish for breath as a figure advanced on him from the dark. He saw only the gold at first, glowing runes studded into skin in such numbers they should have torn the bearer apart with their magic. The smell of ur-gold was maddeningly strong, almost strong enough to overcome the powerful stink of unwashed duardin.

Brokkengird had found him.

'Ur-gold for Brokkengird!' said the duardin gleefully, aiming his axe at Drokki's head. The runemaster rolled out of the way as he swung. Rock chips stung his cheek as the axe blade bit into the pavement.

Drokki kicked out in desperation, his feet meeting a body as yielding as rock. The priest wriggled back, but Brokkengird grabbed his ankle and yanked hard, dragging Drokki right towards him. The berzerker jumped onto the runemaster's chest, laid his axe haft across his neck, and began to throttle.

'Ur-gold! Ur-gold! Brokkengird kill, Brokkengird keep!' He laughed madly.

Drokki pushed at the axe haft, but Brokkengird burned with the might of Grimnir, and his strength was terrifying.

'Stop, stop!' gasped out Drokki. 'I can bring you more, much more.'

'They all say that to Brokkengird when Brokkengird comes for them,' said Brokkengird, and pressed down on his axe harder. The haft closed Drokki's airway.

'Pouch!' he squeaked. 'Ur-gold I brought for you! It's… in…

my… pouch…' He flapped at his belt helplessly. A roaring filled his head. Blackness spotted with dancing colour crowded his vision.

Brokkengird removed his axe.

'Ur-gold in pouch? No promise to go away and come back and never return? Many try to bribe Brokkengird, to keep their worthless beards.'

'I have it, in truth!'

'Then show Brokkengird.'

Drokki drew in a great wheezing breath and clutched at his neck.

'Go on then,' said Brokkengird. He grinned nastily. Even his teeth were made of ur-gold, haphazardly hammered into his gums. 'Show me what you have.'

Drokki sat up. Still gasping, he undid the strings of his pouch and tipped out three new runes. 'These are freshly forged,' he croaked. 'Warm from the forge and full of Grimnir's might.'

Brokkengird reached out and took one of the runes reverently. He fingered it, and his face lit up with greed. 'Good. Now Brokkengird will kill you.'

'I can get you more!' said Drokki hurriedly, holding out the other two.

'How much more?'

'Lots.'

'You won't come back, they never do,' said Brokkengird. He stood up and lifted his axe. 'No. Brokkengird kill you now, if it's all the same to you.'

'I will come back!' protested Drokki. 'I need to. I need you.'

Brokkengird lowered his axe a touch. 'It's a long time since anyone needed Brokkengird, longer since anyone wanted him. Why?'

'I need a guide through Gaenagrik. I want to get to the Realmgate.'

'Got a little message to deliver?' said Brokkengird. 'Going to see his mother?'

Drokki shook his head. He reached out for Brokkengird's hand. Brokkengird looked at it, then back at Drokki's face.

Drokki pulled his hand back, and got heavily to his feet. His chest burned, and his throat felt like it was clogged with hot rocks.

'We're leaving, to found a new lodge.'

'Nowhere to go. Nothing to see. Only Chaos. Chaos everywhere,' said Brokkengird. 'Stay home, little priest.'

'The end is coming,' said Drokki. 'And you can either kill me now and die with everyone who won't leave, or you can take us to the Realmgate, be handsomely paid for it, and live.'

Brokkengird cocked his head on one side. His filthy, stinking crest flopped sideways. 'Forty runes.'

'Twenty.'

'Thirty-five,' said Brokkengird.

'Twenty-seven...' said Drokki.

'Done,' interrupted Brokkengird.

'...and an oath,' continued Drokki.

Brokkengird snarled. 'No oaths!'

'Brokkengird better swear not to harm me, and to lead the lodge to the Gaenagrik Realmgate, or Brokkengird won't get anything,' said Drokki. For one awful second he thought Brokkengird would strike him down, but the renegade berzerker let his axe head thump to the floor, and reached out one hand. He spat on it. His spittle sizzled in his palm.

'Brokkengird swear.'

Drokki spat in his own hand and shook. 'Be here in one week.'

'Brokkengird here. Brokkengird swore!' shouted Brokkengird.

Brokkengird retreated backwards. The last thing to vanish

into the dark of the abandoned hold was his face. Drokki had a glimpse of gleaming eyes and gold, and then he was alone.

Drokki waited five minutes to make sure Brokkengird had gone before taking to his heels and running home as fast as he could.

Ulgathern-Grimnir gripped his new latchkey grandaxe tightly. The steel haft was still slippery with oils from the smithy. It smelled like home, and he felt a pang of regret. The doors of the Ulgahold were shut to him. The axe was taller than he was, toothed like a key. It would work as one too, once the lock had been crafted to fit it. For the time being there was no magma-vault for the meagre supply of ur-gold he had been apportioned, nowhere to hang his axe, nowhere to sleep. He had nothing.

And so I lead my people to beggary on the say-so of Drokki, he thought. Despite his disquiet, his heart told him he was doing the right thing. To say that to Drokki, however, was one effort too many, and he scowled at him instead.

The slot through the gates to Gaenagrik was a black, uninviting rectangle. Behind the short column of his people – those three hundred warriors, matrons, maidens and youngflames that had decided to come with him – was a tunnel with a collapsed roof open to the enemy, should they have the wit to look for it. They were vulnerable, front and back, and with nowhere to run to.

This was looking like a very bad idea.

'Where is he?' growled Ulgathern-Grimnir.

'Um, well. He said he would be here,' said Drokki.

'Did he now? You know he's a murderer?' said Ulgavost. 'Forty years ago Brokkengird was denied his eighteenth rune – more ur-gold than any Fyreslayer in the Ulgahold has had hammered into his flesh for centuries. He was accused of the gold-greed, and did not take it well. Brokkengird cursed our father, fought his way out of the hold leaving several dead duardin behind. Since then he's roamed the halls of Gaenagrik, killing whoever he comes across, and if they be duardin, taking their runes of power.' Ulgavost grinned sadly. 'If I'd have known what Drokki was about, I might have stayed. Brokkengird is a kinslayer, and insane.'

'Loremaster Kaharagun said the same thing about Hulgar the Farseeing,' said Drokki.

'Now then, Drokki, doesn't that tell you something when folks keep warning you about crazy people?' said Ulgathern-Grimnir testily. He shivered. His innate fire was a small warmth to hold on to in so grim a place. He sought out Amsaralka in the gloom behind him. She smiled at him nervously.

'You came. Ulgavost came,' said Drokki.

'Aye. I did. I'm beginning to regret it,' said Ulgathern-Grimnir. Ulgavost made a sour face.

'He'll be here. I made him swear. An oath will bind even a duardin as broke-minded as he.'

'I'm willing to hope, but it's far from a certainty, isn't it? I prefer certainty. Hope is fool's coin,' said Ulgathern-Grimnir.

The gate jerked, and opened wider. Grit squealed in the bearings of the wheel on the bottom, setting up an unholy racket. Ulgathern-Grimnir's hearthguard levelled their magmapikes.

'Ah, yes. I think that's him,' said Drokki.

A filthy duardin emerged.

'Brokkengird here,' he said cheerily.

'I am Ulgathern-Grimnir. You will show us the way?' asked Ulgathern-Grimnir as haughtily as he could manage. He watched the Grimwrath Berzerker warily – the mad Fyreslayer had enough ur-gold runes punched into his skin that he could probably slaughter his way through the lot of them. He glittered with power. Ulgavost shifted the weight of his twin axes on his shoulders, readying them.

Brokkengird scowled. 'Uppity young lord has Brokkengird's ur-gold?'

'Yes,' sighed Ulgathern-Grimnir. He weighed a heavy pouch in his hand. 'Twenty-seven runes, as you asked.'

Brokkengird took a step forward. Ulgathern-Grimnir snatched the pouch back, and stowed it in his pack. 'You get us to the Realmgate first.'

'Yes, little lordling,' said Brokkengird with a smirk and a bow.

Ulgathern-Grimnir's temper flared at his insolence. 'Where,' he asked Drokki, 'do you find these people?'

'Shhh!' said Brokkengird, holding up a finger to his lips. 'Quiet now. Enemy moving. They march on Ulgahold. Brokkengird has seen it! You are wise, crippled runemaster.'

'The prophecy!' said Drokki.

'Right,' said Ulgavost.

Ulgathern-Grimnir squinted at him in irritation. The door to Gaenagrik was open, and Brokkengird beckoned for them to follow.

'I only hope you're right, and this is no false gold hunt,' muttered Ulgavost.

'You know the way?' called Ulgathern-Grimnir softly after Brokkengird.

'Brokkengird know the way. Brokkengird want ur-gold. No gold for Brokkengird if not, eh? Not far now. Upper halls soon. Realmgate by the Thronecavern of the old fathers. This way! Quickly!'

Brokkengird hurried ahead and the column followed.

'Madder than a grot trapped in a bottle with fireants, that one,' said Ulgathern-Grimnir. He looked back down the column of duardin at the worried faces lit by dimmed runelamps. He couldn't see Amsaralka, and his heart beat faster. He had to stop himself from hurrying back to find her. Three hundred souls, all his to protect, that was the reality of being a runefather. They looked tired, but they could not afford to rest. They pushed on deep into the abandoned hold. It was much bigger than the Ulgahold, and would take many hours to cross.

Suddenly, Drokki frowned. 'Do you hear that?'

'What?' said Ulgavost.

'Shh!'

Ulgathern-Grimnir held up his hand. With a lurch, the column came to a halt. True silence descended.

'There!' said Drokki. 'Warhorns.'

They blew in the dark, back the way the duardin had come. A fearful chattering came after, the sound of wild laughter and wicked songs. It faded from hearing a moment, but Ulgathern-Grimnir knew it would only get louder.

'Curse it all!' he snarled. 'They've found us.'

At the sound of the horns, Brokkengird increased the pace. The column found strength from their fear and began to jog. It was a slow but dogged pace that the thick legs of the duardin could sustain for days, if need be. The tunnels rumbled to the thumping of their feet and the jangle of gold and weapons.

But the servants of excess were lithe-limbed and quick. They were gaining, their horns soon becoming louder, their songs chasing after the fugitives.

'Grimnir burn it! It's not going to be fast enough,' said Ulgathern-Grimnir. 'We need a place to fight them off. Brokkengird!' he shouted.

The Grimwrath Berzerker fell back to run beside the runefather.

'This very bad,' he said in his broken Grimnizh. 'Brokkengird tell to stripling runemaster enemy move soon. They move now. You should have come earlier.'

'We need to hold them back, to give Drokki time to open the Realmgate. Where can we make a stand?'

Brokkengird grinned. 'Brokkengird not here for battle, Brokkengird paid to guide.'

'I'll give you more ur-gold, Grimnir roast you!'

'Then this way, O lord of running duardin.'

Brokkengird took a sharp left, leading them onto a broad run of stairs that went up and up. The tunnel they occupied was high and finely made, although the vaulting of the ceiling was dangerously cracked, each piece held up only by the immense pressure exerted on it by the others.

Ulgathern-Grimnir's lodge was sprinting now, the few beardless children with them wailing in terror. The older ones tried to be brave, but the fire in their eyes flickered uncertainly.

There were nine hundred steps. Ulgathern-Grimnir counted them, his axe bouncing hard on his back. His lungs burned and the column straggled out. He kept his eyes on his feet, not wanting to look up and see the task that lay ahead.

The last step flew away under his feet and he burst into a vast hall built into the side of Gaenagrik Mountain. Ruddy light shone through tall slot windows, and the high mullions separating the apertures from one another were thick and angled, reinforced against earthquake and covered with protective runes.

The magic was dead, and there was a lot of damage to the hall – almost all of it, to Ulgathern-Grimnir's keen eye, down to the shiftings of the earth. There were signs of defacement to the statues and shrines in the alcoves along two walls, but otherwise it seemed that the forces of Chaos had moved on quickly after their victory a century ago, focusing their attentions on the living Fyreslayers of the Ulmount.

A huge dais dominated one end of the hall, with seats for the hold's highest lodge-lords. As the hold's heart, most of these had been smashed by the Slaaneshi, their pieces added to the scattering of rubble about the floor.

'Gate that way!' said Brokkengird, pointing to a round arch leading into another hall. 'This Fifthstair, only way in. All others blocked.' He pointed back down the way they had come. 'No other way to get here. Well, one other. Brokkengird go there now!' With that, the berzerker set off at a run none among Ulgathern-Grimnir's duardin could match.

'Make lines!' called Ulgathern-Grimnir. 'Hearthguard to the fore. Grokkenkir!' he called. 'Take the women and youngflames and go with Drokki to the gate! Can you get it open?'

Drokki swallowed hard and nodded. 'Yes, that is the easy part.'

'Good.' Ulgathern-Grimnir gripped his axe and looked down the stairs. 'We'll hold them here. Hurry!'

Drokki ran after Brokkengird through the huge round doorway into a second chamber. This was slightly smaller than the first. The run of windows continued along the mountainside there, and from this new position Drokki could see the peak of the Ulmount several miles away.

A road of cracked marble led down the length of the hall to another dais, this one crowned with a circular doorway that matched the first in form, but it was no ordinary portal.

'The Realmgate!' gasped Drokki.

The wall of the hall was visible twenty yards behind it. Unlike the door into the hall, which was fashioned from black granite blocks, the Realmgate was made of a dazzling white stone set with ur-gold runes that glowed with dormant magic.

'Aye, aye,' said Brokkengird. He had made the far side of the room, and stood beside an open stone door. 'Best open it quick, or everyone die, and that make Brokkengird angry, because Brokkengird get no ur-gold. See you soon, cripple priest!' he said, and dived through the doorway out of sight.

'What are your orders?' asked Grokkenkir. His Vulkite Berzerkers were restless behind him.

Drokki opened his mouth to answer.

'What shall we do, runemaster?' asked a maiden. This open show of fear set up a muttering among the duardin.

'This was your idea!' shouted an angry voice at the back. 'We're all going to die!'

The crowd surged forward around Drokki. All of a sudden they were shouting at him from every side.

'Silence!' bellowed a powerful female voice. 'Shivering with fright will do us no good!' Amsaralka pushed her way to the front of the knot. 'I'd suggest you, Grokkenkir, get half your Vulkite Berzerkers down the end of the hall to stop the enemy coming in, and the other half by the gate to stop whatever might be on the other side killing us if it turns out not to be friendly. And stop glancing back through the door at the others. I know you'd rather be in the fight with your lord, but this is honourable duty, protecting the young and maidens and those others who don't fight.'

'Of, of course,' stammered Grokkenkir, his cheeks colouring.

'Go on then, get to it!' barked Amsaralka.

Grokkenkir hastily bowed and began dividing his fighters. Amsaralka grinned at Drokki. He stared back. 'What? I'm going to be a queen. Don't see why I should sit at the back being quiet. Now you get about opening that door! I mean, runemaster.'

Drokki sketched a bow to her before trotting up to the Realmgate dais. Brokkengird was nowhere to be seen. He's probably waiting to rob our corpses of ur-gold once this has all died down, thought Drokki glumly.

He approached the gate. The runes inscribed onto the stones responded to his presence, calling out to him in voices only he could hear. Looking around guiltily, he unwound a bead book he had stolen from the Ulgahold from around his waist.

He began to read aloud, the beads clacking through his fingers.

Much to his relief, the first rune on the gate's array ignited with a fiery orange light. Encouraged, he read faster.

'Here they come!' roared Ulgathern-Grimnir, setting his stance firmly at the top of the stair and readying his grandaxe. 'None shall pass!'

A wall of pale-fleshed things came rushing up out of the gloom. Some were recognisable as human, others were so monstrous little trace of humanity remained.

They wore scanty clothing, most of it tight and made from soft leathers of terrible origin. The few iridescent plates of armour they bore were impractical, hooked directly into their skin. The servants of Slaanesh would endure any agony in pursuit of fresh sensation, and the range of horrible mutilations they had inflicted on themselves was dazzling in its variety.

Strong-smelling musk rolled up the stairs before them, making Ulgathern-Grimnir light-headed.

'Give fire!' he roared.

Rune-empowered magmapikes sang, conjuring gobbets of molten stone into their flared mouths, and spitting them forwards with great force. A wave of invigorating heat engulfed the front rank of Fyreslayers. They clashed their weapons on their slingshields and roared at the oncoming horde. The lava bombs smashed into the packed mass of enemy warriors, igniting several and splashing many others with searing molten stone. The Slaaneshi screamed in ecstasy at the pain. Besides the heat of the bombs, the mass of the rock did plenty of damage, knocking them back down the steep stairs where they tangled with their fellows, creating bottlenecks that the duardin were quick to exploit. Axes flashed out, felling dozens of daemons as they scrambled over their wounded fellows. The smell of burning flesh and molten rock drove away the sickening musk of the Chaos horde.

There was time for one more round from the magmapikes, and then the Slaaneshi were into the main duardin line.

Initially the Fyreslayers had the superior position. They swept their massive axes back and forth, hewing down the Slaaneshi methodically. The hearthguard retreated behind the front line, angled their weapons upwards, and continued to lob burning stone down upon the Chaos reavers. The stair's width clogged with butchered tribesmen and cooling rock. Perfumed blood ran down the steps, making them treacherous underfoot.

Ulgathern-Grimnir threw off a lilac-furred thing that grappled with him. It landed on all fours, displayed itself lewdly at him and scampered away. Ulgathern-Grimnir grunted in satisfaction as a glob of lava caught it square in the side as it ran, killing it instantly and setting the corpse ablaze.

'We might win this yet lads!' he shouted. 'Grimnir! Ulgahold! *Barakaz-dur*!'

The Chaos worshippers retreated down the steps. 'Yeah, go on, run off back to your silky pavilions! All mouth, the lot of you!' His crowing faltered. From the corners of his eyes he became aware of the blood of his kin. Fyreslayers kicked the corpses of their foes down the stairs. Their eyes glowed with ragefire. Cinders puffed from the mouths of the angriest.

Ulgavost came to his side from the left flank. 'Brother, we

should retreat while we can, get back to the gate.' He paused a moment. 'Were I runefather, that is what I would do.'

'Aye, well, you're not runefather, are you,' said Ulgathern-Grimnir.

'Fine,' said Ulgavost coldly. 'We don't have enough left to weather another assault like that.'

'I'm sorry, brother,' said Ulgathern-Grimnir. 'We're better off here, that is all. They've a steep climb, and nowhere to organise. It's the best position.'

'That's your decision, I suppose,' said Ulgavost, and some of the tension left him.

Drumbeats came from the depths of the stairs, the heavy tread of armoured feet behind them.

'Looks like they're not done with us yet,' said Ulgavost. 'I'll get back to the left.'

'Good luck, brother,' said Ulgathern-Grimnir.

'You too, runefather,' said Ulgavost.

The reavers had gone. The Slaaneshi elite came in their stead. Huge armoured figures trod the stair, their helmets blank and armour a riot of gaudy, metallic colours. As they came within a hundred steps, they locked tall shields together, and began to chant.

'Qualar Vo! Qualar Vo! Qualar Vo!'

'Let them have it!' shouted Ulgathern-Grimnir.

Magma pelted down onto the warriors, booming from shields and dripping onto the steps. The warriors came on unaffected, resetting their shields after every strike. They were the champions of Slaanesh, the lost and the damned, and they would not die easily.

They broke into a run at the last few steps and crashed into the duardin with such might the Fyreslayers were forced back. The advantage the duardin possessed was quickly gone, then reversed, for the Chaos warriors were so tall they struck down at the shorter warriors once they were on level ground.

Ulgathern-Grimnir swung his axe, cutting a purple-armoured warrior in two. To an untrained eye the grandaxe might have seemed unwieldy, too massive to be of much use, but the runes in Ulgathern-Grimnir's body gave him great strength, and he moved the weapon as easily as if it were a willow switch. He stove in breastplates with the heavy knob on the end of the haft, cut heads from shoulders with the broad key-head, and caught sword and axe blades in its slots and broke them into pieces with hard twists. None could stand against the young runefather, and the fire in his eyes was terrible to behold.

In spite of Ulgathern-Grimnir's best efforts, the Fyreslayers were pushed backwards, past the throne dais, towards the doorway where the vulnerable members of their lodge waited for Drokki to open the gate. Grokkenkir's warriors barred the entrance, but there were too few of them to hold the Chaos warriors back for long should Ulgathern-Grimnir fall.

'Come on, Drokki! Get that gate open,' said Ulgathern-Grimnir through gritted teeth.

The Chaos warriors chanted louder.

'Qualar Vo! Qualar Vo! Qualar Vo!'

'I am here, my children!' hissed a feminine voice. Quiet, as intimate as a lover's whisper, it nevertheless cut through the tumult of battle.

A daemon of Chaos stepped into the hall from the stairway. As tall as a gargant, its head was that of a cow, supporting a broad spread of blood-red horns. It had powder-blue skin, four arms, and carried three swords and a long black leather whip. Its hoofed feet were encased in shining boots tipped with steel. The chainmail harness it wore was immodest. Useless as protection, it accentuated the features of the daemon's mixed gender.

Ulgathern found himself entranced by its sinuous movements. A heavy smell of unwashed bodies and cloying perfume filled the hall. A dark passion rose in Ulgathern-Grimnir in response, distasteful and intoxicating. He fought it down, but even as he brought it under control he knew that everything that brought him pleasure in future would be tainted by this experience.

'*I am Qualar Vo, the Unredeemed.*' It pointed a long, painted fingernail at Ulgathern-Grimnir. '*Little duardin, so stubborn, so strong-willed, so boring. Let your passions flow, and join with me. Such things I will show you.*'

The Chaos warriors backed away as the daemon strode forward, hips swaying provocatively. The smell of it intensified, causing some of the Fyreslayers to moan, others to retch. A headache pounded in Ulgathern-Grimnir's head. The creature stood over him, its loincloth flapping inches from his face, and the stink of it made him dizzy.

'*So fierce! You should enjoy the finer things in life more. Pleasure is a generous master.*'

'Pleasure in depravity, in carving the flesh from your own body because your sensations have become so dulled? No, thank you,' said Ulgathern-Grimnir, and he was horrified at how weak his voice sounded.

'*I know you yearn to embrace me, to feel my tender caresses.*' A long, prehensile tongue slipped from the daemon's mouth. '*You are young to be a runefather.*' The daemon surveyed Ulgathern-Grimnir's small band of warriors. '*Another doomed offshoot of your race, sent off to grub about in the dirt for fragments of your god. It's simply tragic.*'

'You will not bend me to your will,' said Ulgathern-Grimnir.

'*No? Your brother submitted himself quite willingly.*'

'You lie!'

'*Then who opened the Realmgate into the Ulgahold, if it*

were not Mangulnar? Even now your kinsfolk die thanks to his treachery.'

Something snapped in Ulgathern-Grimnir. The fires of his heart were damped down by the thing's musk no more, but flared up, burning the fog from his mind. He swung his axe at the daemon, but it laughed condescendingly and moved lightly out of reach.

'How predictable. You little ones have always been so very dull, whichever world you burrow through.'

Qualar Vo raised an arm, and the Chaos warriors came surging back. From the stairs poured a horde of twisted tribesmen, flooding around the circle of duardin, a portion of them running for the door and Grokkenkir's berzerkers holding it.

'I loathe dullness,' said Qualar Vo. *'My aim is to remove its stain from the world. Dance the bloody dance. Let slip your passions, my children!'*

The Chaos warriors attacked, and Ulgathern-Grimnir found himself in the fight of his life. The daemon musk slowed his warriors, but invigorated the enemy. Ulgathern-Grimnir held his breath as he swung his latchkey grandaxe, swatting away the warriors. He was fixed on the daemon, but always it moved away from him, directing its endless swarm of decadent worshippers to attack Ulgathern-Grimnir in its stead. He hewed and hewed until his runes burned so hot they singed his flesh. Even with this magic, however, he tired, and his axe became heavier. He did not relent, ploughing on toward the daemon, but it was hopeless. His warriors fell, but the Chaos ranks did not diminish no matter how many he hacked down, and the daemon would not come within reach.

Nightmare creatures crowded him, their weapons and writhing appendages reaching out to attack.

Ulgathern-Grimnir's runes fizzled, the magic starting to fade.

'Ah! Grimnir cannot help you now!' said the daemon, and it presented its weapons and advanced on him. *'It is time we danced.'*

'Only now that I am reduced to my mortal strength do you come at me? You are a coward!'

'What need of honour have I? None. Another tedious mortal conceit. I would enjoy killing you as much whether you were a hero or an old woman.'

Qualar Vo leapt at Ulgathern-Grimnir. It brought two of its three swords down hard. The runefather lifted his axe over his head. It was cripplingly heavy without Grimnir's magic to sustain him. The swords slammed into the metal haft, driving him to his knees.

'Pathetic,' said the daemon. It raised its sword to strike again. *'Now you die.'*

The trumpeting roar of a magmadroth boomed from the stairwell, followed by a wash of fire.

'Then again, maybe not,' said Ulgathern-Grimnir.

Brokkengird bounded out of the stairwell, framed by a blazing ball of ur-salamander bile. Ulgathern-Grimnir marvelled at how high he leapt, his legs lent incredible strength by his ur-gold. The runes burned all over him with unfettered fire. His eyes and mouth shone as brightly as a forge's heart. The air wavered around him.

Brokkengird came down swinging. His axe was a blur, taking one of the daemon's arms off at the elbow. Stinking black blood jetted from the stump, but though it roared in outrage, the daemon responded immediately with its own weapons. Brokkengird moved so quickly his body was streaked with glowing trails of fire magic. He and the daemon traded blows furiously.

The sneer on the daemon's face shrank and vanished as it was forced back by Brokkengird's relentless attack. It lashed its whip round and round, seeking to keep Brokkengird away. The Grimwrath Berzerker grabbed it, and yanked hard. His muscles were so saturated in magic he had the might to challenge a Keeper of Secrets. Qualar Vo stumbled, falling to one knee. With a triumphant ululation, Brokkengird spun on the spot, sweeping his mighty axe around and down. The daemon's head tumbled to the stone, the black fluid that served it for blood spraying forth.

From the stairwell emerged a magmadroth, huge and furious. The black and red striping of its hide was instantly recognisable to Ulgathern-Grimnir; Grakki-grakkov, Tulgamar-Grimnir's mount.

'Tulgamar!' he called. 'Tulgamar!'

Ulgavost looked up at the name and saw for the first time the arrival of their brother. He shot Ulgathern-Grimnir a grin and charged into the tribesmen between their position and Tulgamar-Grimnir. Fyreslayers came in Tulgamar's wake, slaughtering all before them. The magmadroth stamped around itself, crushing the Slaaneshi under its giant clawed feet. It half-turned, its tail sweeping a dozen men from the ground and sending them crashing to their deaths against the wall. It drew back its head, its chest swelled, and it spat out thick bile that ignited on contact with the air, spattering a swathe of the enemy with fire.

'Grimnir! Grimnir!' shouted Ulgathern-Grimnir. His exhausted duardin had fought free of their knot. Most of the Chaos warriors were dead. What had been a fight for survival had turned in their favour and become an extermination. They cut down the remaining daemon-lovers without mercy.

Soon enough, Ulgathern-Grimnir found himself standing before Tulgamar.

'What are you doing here?' he said, grinning with relief. 'I thought you weren't going to come!'

'You know I considered it.' Tulgamar slapped the steaming hide of his mount. 'The choice was presented to me again, and this time in your favour, when Mangulnar opened the forbidden gate. Daemons and worse poured into the middle deeps, and at the same time they attacked the Hardgate, sending great beasts against it. Drokki was right. The hold has fallen, Ulgathern-Grimnir. We barely got out alive. We followed your trail, fearful of the daemonkin and of Brokkengird.'

The Grimwrath Berzerker gave them a cheery wave at the mention of his name.

'But then he brought us here, and, well. You know the rest.'

'What happened to Mangulnar?'

Tulgamar shrugged. 'I can only pray to Grimnir he found the reward he deserved.'

'Ranganak? Ulgamaen? Briknir? The others…?'

'All of them dead, or soon to be,' said Tulgamar-Grimnir sorrowfully. 'We have Marag-Or, and I have maybe three hundred warriors with me, double that of the folk from all the lodges.'

The ground shook, a sign of an impending eruption. The whole of Gaenagrik shuddered.

'The runemasters have called upon the Ulmount. They're bringing it down,' said Tulgamar-Grimnir.

'We have to go,' said Ulgathern-Grimnir. 'This way.' The three of them ran into the gate hall, hundreds of duardin streaming after them.

The Realmgate's aperture glowed bright. On the other side was the peaceful scene of a ruined city being reclaimed by forest; a hot, humid day bright with sunshine filtered through dissipating mist.

'Drokki! You did it!' said Ulgathern-Grimnir.

'Yes, yes I did,' said Drokki, sounding somewhat surprised.

'Where does it lead?' said Ulgavost.

'The city of Vharrashee.'

'Mannish?' said Ulgavost.

Drokki nodded. 'It was. No longer. This was Gaenagrik's main trading partner in the Mordash lowlands. That is why this gate went there. The Volturung hold is some way from there.'

Through the great windows of the hall they could see the Ulmount erupting. Lava fountained skyward, the amount of it and height it attained lending it the illusion of slowness. Orange tongues of fire ran down the mountainside. The ground shook.

'The mountain sings its songs of fury,' said Ulgavost softly.

Gaenagrik shook again. Rubble crashed down at the far end of the hall.

'It won't save them. It will kill us too, if we do not go through the gate,' said Ulgathern-Grimnir urgently.

Ulgavost nodded. Without another word, he stepped through the gate. On the other side he looked around, inspecting the ruins. Tulgamar-Grimnir barked orders that sent a large regiment of his own, fresher warriors after his brother to protect him.

Ulgathern-Grimnir roused his own weary people. 'Get them up. We need to leave. Now.'

'What kind of land is it, through there?' asked Tulgamar-Grimnir of Drokki.

'I can tell you… Well, I can tell you what kind of land it *was*, but what kind it is now? That we will have to see.'

'Are you sure Volturung still stands?'

'I have no idea.'

'Huh,' said Tulgamar-Grimnir. 'Oh well.' He stamped down on the thick scales of his mount. 'Huphup, Grakki-grakkov! Into the woods! You're going home to the lands of fire!'

The great ur-salamander rumbled happily, and plodded through the Realmgate.

Drokki and Ulgathern-Grimnir remained on the Ghur side of the gate, shepherding their relatives and followers through. Marag-Or came last.

Ulgathern-Grimnir grabbed his arm before he could pass through the shimmering skin of magic dividing one realm from the next. 'Tell me. If I had done as my father asked, and not listened to Drokki, would the hold have fallen?'

'Prophecies are tricky things, Ulgathern-Grimnir,' said Marag-Or. 'Often they contain the seed of their own fulfilment. Who can tell?' He pulled his arm free, and passed through the Realmgate.

Drokki went next, leaving Ulgathern-Grimnir alone in the shaking halls of Gaenagrik.

He took one last look at the burning Ulmount before stepping through to another world.

He never set eyes upon his home again.

II

Eight days after coming into the Realm of Aqshy, the Ulgaen lodges came weary and footsore down mountain paths to the Broken Plains. Through beastman-infested swamps and into the arid Firespike Mountains they had travelled. The mood of the lodges was mixed. In Aqshy they found much to delight them, and being in their ancestral realm lifted their spirits. In the swamps the air was as warm and thick as that of a forge, and pleasingly sharp in the mountains. But their thoughts strayed often to their lost kin. They had little food, and were alone in a hostile land.

So it was that when the plains opened up before them their hearts lifted. They were as broken as their name suggested, a country-sized lava flow that had been cracked by the movements of the earth into giant broken plates of stone, all tilted at thirty degrees, their raised sides pointing away from the mountains. They were all of a size – an endless sharp-edged landscape of black teeth salted with white sand. The plains

487

were featureless, but for a duardin causeway running down the middle of the plain parallel to the mountain range. The road was obvious from on high, but as they reached the plains it disappeared between the jagged stone teeth, leaving the Fyre-slayers to negotiate a labyrinth that taxed even their finely honed sense of direction.

The sun beat down mercilessly. In the crevices between the rocks there was not a breath of wind. It was hot enough to bake bread, and it made them sweat, fire-born though they were.

Though the journey to the road from the mountains was but a short part of their trek, by the time they reached it they were more exhausted than ever before, and coated with dust.

Ulgathern-Grimnir clambered onto the causeway. In one direction the road stretched away to the vanishing point, disappearing into the shimmering heat haze of the plains. In the other direction, where the mountains thrust themselves out into the desert, lay the Voltdrang of the Volturung lodges. It was many miles away yet, but so vast in scale that they could easily see it from their new vantage.

A whole mountainside had been refashioned into the roaring face of Grimnir-at-war. His curled beard cascaded down the rocks to merge with those of the plains. His craggy brows made a stepped series of battlements. His eyes were giant windows, also fortified, between a hooked nose topped with a rampart. The lower jaw of his roaring mouth disappeared under the stone. A huge throat went into the cliff. At the bottom of it was a massive pair of stone gates whose fyresteel reinforcements glinted in the sun.

Tulgamar-Grimnir's magmadroth clambered onto the road after Ulgathern. Ulgavost followed him. The three siblings stared at their goal.

'That's an impressive sight,' said Ulgavost.

'Aye,' said Ulgathern-Grimnir.

'What do we do? March up and knock?' said Tulgamar-Grimnir. Grakki-grakkov rumbled and yawned.

'I don't have a better idea,' said Ulgathern-Grimnir. 'Get everyone up on the road. It'll be quicker going, and better if they can see us coming.'

It took far longer to get their people out of the baking crevasses than Ulgathern-Grimnir would have liked. By the time all eleven hundred of them were on the road, the sun was going down and a strong wind was coming out of the desert.

'Get a move on!' shouted Ulgathern-Grimnir. 'We can't be stuck out here at night!' He turned to his brothers. 'Get the best we have up front. Let's look presentable. I want us to arrive as lords, not beggars.'

Arranged with as much dignity as they could muster, they continued on the last leg of their journey.

As they neared the hold, cairns appeared atop the rocks, singly or in twos and threes at first, then with increasing frequency until every tilted stone tooth was capped.

'Armour, and arms,' said Ulgavost.

'Um, yes,' said Drokki. 'They build them from the many enemies who have come against their fortress and failed.'

'I know that!' said Ulgavost. 'Everyone knows that.'

'His point is, the stories are true,' said Tulgamar-Grimnir.

'They're not just true,' said Ulgathern-Grimnir, taking in the endless heaps of bones and armour, and the massive face growing steadily before the column. Already it was big enough to swallow the sky, and they weren't even halfway there. 'They don't tell the half of it.'

They walked on into evening. The mountain reared higher and higher, Grimnir's face appearing titanically huge.

The Fyreslayers were already feeling daunted when a tremendous peal of trumpets blasted out from the Voltdrang. They blared across the silent desert. With no other noise to challenge them, they seemed to go on forever.

'The gates! They're opening!' said Tulgamar-Grimnir.

A muted cheer went up from the column.

The rattling of the gate mechanism came to them cleanly, again for the lack of any other noise to compete. Shouting and the sound of marching feet echoed around the wide throat of Grimnir, followed by more trumpets.

'Send Brokkengird to the back,' said Ulgathern-Grimnir. 'I don't want him coming out with anything regrettable.'

Brokkengird farted loudly. Beaming at himself, he turned about and marched away to the column's rear.

They were close now. Outside the hold the plain had been flattened and a town constructed. The buildings were all duardin-built, but sized for a mixture of peoples, as far as Ulgathern-Grimnir could tell. The place was ruinous, the buildings tumbledown, its defensive wall so full of breaches that the few parts still at full height resembled rough pillars.

'The Voltdrang seems inviolable at distance,' Ulgavost said beneath his breath, so that only Ulgathern-Grimnir would hear. 'These ruins tell a different story.'

'Their hold stands still,' Ulgathern-Grimnir replied. 'That is all that matters.'

It was there, in the central plaza of the ruins, that the Volturung Fyreslayers greeted them.

A great lord approached them, born aloft on a litter of gold and steel made in the form of a stylised magmadroth. Eight warriors carried it, their biceps studded with runes of strength. The lord wore more ur-gold than Ulgathern-Grimnir had ever seen on one duardin. His hair was easily four feet high, framed by an elaborate helm and crest of gold and jewels. He rode the litter standing, his hands clasped on the top of a double-headed rune-axe. Behind him marched four hundred hearthguard, all heavy with gold and ur-gold.

Horns blared one more time and the litter came to a halt on the other side of the square to the Ulgaen lodges.

Ulgathern-Grimnir nodded to Drokki. He stepped forward and bowed so low his crest brushed the roadway.

'O high and mighty lords of Volturung! We, the people of the Ulgaen lodges, have travelled many long days to meet with you. We humbly beseech you for aid. Our home is–'

'You're a sorry lot, and no mistake,' interrupted the Volturung lord.

Drokki stopped talking. His confidence evaporated.

'Runefather!' he began again, more weakly. 'We ask only–'

'Do you hear that? Runefather!' The Volturung delegation laughed loudly. 'Voltus-Grimnir wouldn't rouse himself to greet a bunch of vagabonds like you. I am his fifteenth son, Golgunnir. I suppose I must look like a runefather to you, paupers that you are.'

Golgunnir was old enough and richly decorated enough to be a runefather. Gold pendants hung around his neck in layers. His skin was studded with ur-gold runes. One or two more and he'd be a Grimwrath Berzerker, but Ulgathern-Grimnir was having none of his poor bearing, gold or not.

'Right then, *runeson*. I am a runefather, and I invoke the right of hospitality, and the rights of seniority.'

'You do, do you?'

'Yes. So shut up and do me the courtesy of listening. We come here to ask for sanctuary. Our hold was destroyed. Our people are homeless. Volturung is the great-great-great grandsire of our lodge. We return to our homeland and ask for aid.'

Golgunnir rudely looked away until Ulgathern-Grimnir had finished.

'What happened to your hold?'

'His brother opened a tainted Realmgate and let the hordes of Chaos come flooding in!' shouted Brokkengird.

'I thought he'd gone to the back,' muttered Ulgavost.

Ulgathern-Grimnir closed his eyes. His temper roared hot. 'We are your kin!'

'Ulgaen, you say? Never heard of you. Do you know how many lodges Volturung is father to?' said Golgunnir. 'Do you? Scores. There are nearly a dozen that claim the name Volturung in their title alone. We can't take every failing branch back. We're full, sonny.'

'You will address him as runefather!' said Ulgavost angrily. 'He and Tulgamar-Grimnir both.'

'I'm twice the age of your runefather. I've five times more warriors to command, and I'm reckoned the fourth senior of Voltus-Grimnir's sons. Now, my father is runefather, highest lord of all the Volturung kin-lodges, which I suppose includes you. Do you see what I'm saying? Your lot, you're a stripling lodge looking for a handout. That is not the Fyreslayer way. If you've got ur-gold to pay us to fight, then fine. If you have something to offer us for our mutual profit, we can talk. But you're not moving in no matter what, not if you brought me Grimnir's golden big toe and dropped it at my feet.'

'Do you think you might show me a little respect, young one?' Marag-Or came forward. 'I'm older than you by far.'

Golgunnir's attitude changed a little. He bowed. 'One as old as you, runemaster, is worthy of respect wherever he goes. I am sure space can be found, should you wish it.'

The gold beads woven into Marag-Or's beard clacked as he

shook his head. 'I'm sticking with family. They may not have much in the way of gold, but at least they have manners.'

Golgunnir's followers laughed again. The runeson gave them an angry look. A junior-looking runesmiter came to his side, and began to whisper in his ear, a concerned look on his face, he gestured at the Ulgaen. Golgunnir listened a moment, his face souring.

'He's getting an ear-burning,' said Ulgavost out of the side of his mouth. 'The bastard's been playing with us.'

Golgunnir nodded exasperatedly then flapped the priest away.

'My noble priest, Runesmiter Keskilgirn, reminds me of my father's offer.'

'There's an offer?' said Ulgathern-Grimnir.

'Yes, runefather,' he said disparagingly. 'There is room for you to settle, in a mountain three days to sunward. The Steelspike we call it, good ore land there. Nothing fancy: iron and lead and your other essentials, and you'll have to dig deep to get to the earthblood, but there's plenty for a duardin with a strong back and a will to bend it. It is outside of our current borders, but it's better than nothing. You are welcome to it in exchange for your fealty, and a pledge to maintain order in the valleys and hills around it. The contract's in the book.' He waved his hand at a richly bound tome, made with pages of pressed tin. This was brought forward to the Ulgaen. Drokki flicked through it and nodded.

A sense of relief radiated over the column. Ulgathern-Grimnir smiled broadly.

'Tell you father that w–'

Golgunnir held up a heavily ringed hand. A sly smile stole across his lips. 'Before you get too effusive in your thanks, there is one other thing you need to know.'

'Here we go,' said Ulgavost.

'Steelspike is infested with skaven. You want it, you drive them out.'

Golgunnir shouted out orders, and the horns of the Volturung rang. The Volturung Fyreslayers turned about, the gates of the Voltdrang commenced their slow opening, and Golgunnir's bearers began the delicate process of turning the litter around.

'Wait! We can't go now!' protested Ulgathern-Grimnir. 'Stop! You sully the customs of hospitality.'

'Oh, yes. Forgot. You can camp here,' said Golgunnir as the litter trundled round. 'You'll be quite safe. Chaos has grown tired of defeat before our gates. No doubt my father will send out food and ale.' He said this as if he thought it a poor idea.

'What if we fall in battle?' shouted Ulgathern-Grimnir. The litter was facing back toward the gates.

'Then your womenfolk, youngflames and such will be accepted into the lodge under the terms of bondage. They will have to earn their right to call themselves Volturung.'

'That is unacceptable!' shouted Ulgathern-Grimnir. The column was passing back through the gates of the Voltdrang.

Golgunnir laughed. 'It's all you've got.'

The litter passed through last. The gates clanged shut behind it, leaving the Ulgaen out in the rapidly cooling desert.

'The thin-bearded weasling,' said Ulgavost. 'We throw our lives away fighting their battles, and our wives and children go into servitude for who knows how long.'

'We'll sort them out, won't we, Grakki-grakkov?' crooned Tulgamar-Grimnir to his magmadroth.

'Little brother, Grakki-grakkov apart, I have no idea why father picked you as a runefather,' said Ulgavost, leaving the sentiment 'instead of me' unvoiced but heavily implied. 'If it's such a small matter why don't they clear it out themselves?

It's a convenient way to get rid of us and keep their honour. Times are hard, but still.'

'We'll see about that,' grumbled Ulgathern-Grimnir.

The gate horns sounded again. Smaller, subsidiary gates around the main opened and a stream of handcarts came out, marshalled by shouting victuallers.

'Well, at least they weren't lying about the ale,' said Tulgamar-Grimnir cheerfully. 'The day is looking up.'

Ulgavost shook his head and spat on the ground. 'A pot of ale and a hero's death. That's poor hospitality, and a poorer way to increase the weight of one's purse.'

The mountains around the Voltdrang were home to numerous holds. The Ulgaen's passage along the highways linking them brought a variety of reactions. Some among the Volturung lodges were sympathetic to their plight, while others were openly hostile, telling them their domain was full and that the Ulgaen should seek some other place to settle.

Ulgathern-Grimnir honoured those expressions of fellowship with small gifts of gold, and stoically bore the opprobrium of the rest.

As they proceeded, the mountains reduced in magnificence. The smattering of volcanoes became none at all. The Fyreslayers' affinity to the earth's heat told the Ulgaen that the earthblood retreated far underground there, almost out of notice. The last holds they passed were little more than outposts, modest in size and means. Nubby hills covered in sandy terraced fields replaced the soaring ridges and peaks. Farmers watched them from under their wide-brimmed hats, or ignored them as they drove their plough-goats to score the earth.

Two giant watchtowers closing the mouth of a shallow valley marked the end of the Volturung kin-lodges' territory.

Ulgaen-Grimnir and his brothers stopped to confer with the karl of the watch there, and were directed onwards.

'Be careful,' said the karl, a gruff but kindly duardin. 'Out there, the ratkin are thick. You might not see them, but they will see you.'

The road continued out into wild country. The valleys fractured into a wilderness of gullies. In response, the road climbed up to run along the ridges where the ground was easier. Behind them were the Firespikes, and ahead the hills became rounder and smaller, dropping down to reveal the Broken Plains once more. The desert conditions had softened, and the rocks jutted out now not from sand but from a heavy scrub of thorny trees.

One last mountain remained, looking over the plain: a small, sleeping volcano, as thin as a spear point. The outline of it was broken up by rickety-looking gantries and platforms, delicate against the far horizon. The smoke of industry rose from its flanks.

'Brokkengird smell rat-things,' said the Grimwrath Berzerker testily.

'There's nothing here, you maniac,' said Ulgavost. 'You can't possibly smell them at this distance.'

'Hey now, brother, best be careful, eh,' said Tulgamar-Grimnir.

Brokkengird sniffed at the air and scrambled off.

'Now look what you've done. Come back!' said Ulgathern-Grimnir. Brokkengird paid him no heed and vanished around a boulder.

'Bah, he'll be back. If not, good riddance. Looks like they've been busy over there,' said Ulgavost. 'How many do you reckon there are?'

'Thousands,' said Tulgamar-Grimnir.

'Tens of thousands,' said Ulgathern-Grimnir.

Grakki-grakkov growled.

'There'd be no shame in giving up, going somewhere else. It'd be better to swallow our pride than stir that lot into action,' said Ulgavost.

'Tulgamar?' asked Ulgathern.

'I'll do whatever you think best,' said Tulgamar-Grimnir. 'But Ulgavost does have a point.'

'N-no,' said Drokki. 'We have to stay here. What else can we do? Wander the world homeless? We can take it.'

'There are worse things than being a wandering lodge,' said Ulgavost. 'Assaulting the gates of that place being one of them.'

'Who said anything about a full frontal assault?' said Ulgathern-Grimnir. 'Are we not duardin?' He winked at Drokki. 'We go under it.'

'Lordling full of good ideas!' said Brokkengird, returning to the road. He threw a headless skaven corpse down at Ulgathern-Grimnir's feet. 'There'll be less of these to fight head on if we go underground. Clever little lordling.'

'Shhh!' said Ulgathern-Grimnir.

At his command, the Mining Fellowship ceased work, muffled picks stilled at mid-stroke.

'Douse the lamps!' said Ulgathern-Grimnir.

The two runelamps in the tunnel went out. Sparks of fire glinted in the eyes of the duardin. They stayed stock-still for several minutes.

A quietly tapped code gave the all clear.

'Alright,' Ulgathern-Grimnir whispered. 'Continue.'

The Ulgaen Mining Fellowship set to work again, timing their blows to the pulsing of machinery that resonated through the rock.

For three hours they toiled, the Ulgaen warriors keeping watch. Some of them thought they should use the runesmiters' magic to melt their way through the rock, though none dared say it. But Ulgathern-Grimnir needed the zharrgrim to save their strength for the task ahead, and he did not want to give the skaven advance warning of their approach. Magma tunnelling was anything but quiet.

'All change!' said Amsaralka. The Mining Fellowship stepped back from the rockface, rotating their arms and stretching their muscles out. A fresh band came forward and took up their tools.

'Let me help,' said Ulgathern-Grimnir.

Amsaralka smiled at him. 'Mining is not a leader's work. What would your warriors say?'

'They'd say there is a runefather who gets his hands dirty with his people,' said Ulgathern-Grimnir. They touched noses briefly.

'No, runefather,' she said. 'I'll not have you hacking away at the rock. One more day and we'll be through into the cavern. One wrong blow could bring the wall down before we're ready.'

Ulgathern-Grimnir took a step back. 'As you wish, my lady.'

'Soon we'll be done,' she said.

'Then the real work begins,' said Ulgathern.

Brokkengird strode along the rough road towards the Steelspike. His onyx greataxe was already slick with skaven blood. He sang a very loud, very rude song as he approached. Some three hundred yards in front of the main gate, he stopped and planted his feet firmly apart.

'Oi, oi, oi! Furry little thieves! Brokkengird is here! Brokkengird wants your mountain! Come out and give it to him, and maybe you keep your worthless heads!'

A small, sharp crack answered his challenge. There came the musical passage of a bullet through the air. It exploded into fragments ten feet in front of the berzerker.

'And Brokkengird knows how far silly ratguns fire!' He

laughed uproariously at nothing in particular. 'Come out if you want Brokkengird. He is not going anywhere.'

A dozen gun reports rippled across the mountain. The bullets came a fraction of a second later. Most reached no further than the first, kicking up a storm of stony splinters from the road. One buzzed towards Brokkengird, but he leaned out of its way contemptuously.

'Brokkengird better shot with rancid old grot head!' he shouted.

The gunfire stopped. The ramshackle gate creaked wide. A moment later, a regiment of tall black-furred skaven marched out.

'Oh good, you send your best out first. It is very boring when you do it the other way.'

The stormvermin broke into a clattering scamper. As they neared Brokkengird they levelled their halberds.

Brokkengird grinned widely. The ur-gold hammered into his muscles glowed. He waited until he could see the beady black eyes of the skaven warriors. Only then did he roar, 'Grimnir!' and throw himself forward.

Brokkengird exploded into the regiment. Ratmen flew everywhere. He tore through the middle towards the leader, hunched at the back. Their captain levelled a pistol at Brokkengird, but he cut the ratkin in half before its finger could pull the trigger. Bellowing incoherently, Brokkengird slew every last one of them. In short seconds, there was nothing but corpses littering the road, the sole survivor fleeing as quickly as it could back towards the gates. Someone shot the ratman down, then the guns turned again upon the Grimwrath Berzerker.

Bullets smacked into the corpses. Brokkengird did a little jig, dancing around their impacts. Waving his axe, he walked backwards until he was once more out of range.

Gongs and bells rang. More ratmen came out of the gates, hundreds of them this time, forming up in blocks with a discipline belied by their ragged appearance. They arrayed themselves in a curved battle line along the base of the mountain. They waited for their signal, filthy banners flapping in the breeze.

Then, with a clamour of gongs, the skaven swarmed forwards. Brokkengird howled with delight.

Brassy horns trumpeted out a belligerent march. Behind Brokkengird, Tulgamar-Grimnir's magmadroth roared. Two hundred Ulgaen warriors climbed out from their hiding places in the valley that the road ran through, and marched out to join Brokkengird.

The battle for the Steelspike had begun.

Drokki took Marag-Or's arm, although whether it was to steady the old longbeard or himself he was not sure. This was it, the final action. He sent a mental prayer to Grimnir.

'Now!' yelled Ulgathern-Grimnir.

Fifteen pickaxes, stripped of muffling rags, swung together at the wall. A hole opened up. A draft of stale air came through.

'Again!' ordered Ulgathern-Grimnir.

The Mining Fellowship hewed once more. This time the thin shell between their tunnel and the burrowings of the skaven gave way. Stone spilled into a broad, tubular corridor. The duardin flooded after it.

The tunnel was on an incline, curved in a way that suggested it to be a spiral. Chittering came from both directions. That from above sounded angry, that from below insane.

Ulgathern-Grimnir dragged his grandaxe through the hole. The tunnel was fifteen feet wide, broad enough to wield his weapon effectively. Days before, Drokki had hammered fresh runes into his muscles. Once again the grandaxe was light and easy for him to brandish.

A foul wind blew from the bottom of the spiral. The stench was indescribable. Drokki gagged on it.

'We'll hold the way here,' said Ulgathern-Grimnir. 'You do what you must, Drokki.'

'The stench is stronger that way, it must be the right direction,' he said breathing through his mouth.

'That will be where the skaven mothers are,' said Marag-Or, seemingly unaffected by the stink. He frowned at the young runemaster. 'Come now, Drokki, it's only a bit of rat smell. Show some backbone, my boy.'

Drokki nodded so hard his beard flapped, holding his breath just the same. The runemasters' escort of auric hearthguard and Vulkite Berzerkers fell in around them, led by Grokkenkir. They left Ulgathern to form up his warriors. The sound of tramping duardin feet echoed down the tunnel as the runefather led his war party further up the spiral.

A minute later the clash of arms rang out behind and above them.

'For good or for ill, we come to our greatest test,' said Marag-Or.

The corridor continued down and down, the battle noise growing fainter. The horrendous cacophony of squealings from the bottom became louder.

Drokki counted the revolutions of the spiral – five, ten, twenty. When he got to thirty-nine, it began to level out and ran straight. The stench had become so great it filled Drokki's body from the toes of his boots to the tips of his crest. Marag-Or stumped on, unperturbed, but the Vulkite Berzerkers and hearthguard swore and coughed. The smell was as thick as smoke.

Copper pipes emerged from holes to run along the wall. Water dribbled from the joins. Steam hissed out through imperfect patching. There was a sharp, dry odour beneath the overwhelming rat stench. It was similar to the sensation ur-gold brought, but far less clean. Drokki's spine tingled; he smelled warpstone, and it came from the water pattering onto the floor.

'It'll take forever to purify this mountain,' said Drokki.

'One thing at a time, lad,' said Marag-Or. 'We've got to take it first.'

The tunnel opened up. A vast lava chamber, empty of earth-blood, loomed large. A ramp led up the side to catwalks criss-crossing the void. Strange machines and thick pipes were dotted around the place. Brass troughs full of blood gruel, overhung with filthy spouts closed by spinwheel valves, were placed at regular intervals around the chamber.

These were the feeding stations of the skaven mothers. There were dozens of them, crowded around the troughs, packed together for warmth. Long, hairless abominations, they lay on their sides, useless limbs clutching at the air in pain and madness. Their bellies heaved with unborn young and their multiple dugs were thick with unclean milk. The naked, blind bodies of infant skaven squirmed over each other all around them, fighting for nutriment. Death hung heavily over the mothers. The crushed corpses of luckless ratlings lay about the floor, many half devoured. The skaven mothers' anaemic skin was streaked with dried blood and their own filth. From their gaping, razor-toothed maws came that endless, deafening squealing.

'Grimnir's holy fires,' breathed Drokki. The stink was so thick he thought he would choke on it.

'About there should do it,' said Marag-Or, pointing to the

centre of the room. 'Auric hearthguard, remain by the entrance. Grokkenkir, clear us a way.'

'Yes, runemaster,' said the karl. He and a half dozen of his warriors moved forwards and set to work, slaying the skaven mothers and stamping their pink young underfoot. They were merciless in what they did. The skaven were the ancestral enemies of all duardin, Fyreslayer or otherwise.

The mothers screamed louder, and thrashed about, trying to bring their snapping mouths into reach of their assailants. They did little but crush their own children. Grokkenkir hacked the head from one sickly monstrosity, then another, until a path of bloated, pale corpses carpeted the way to the middle of the room.

'Come on, we'll follow. Perhaps you should lend a hand?' said Marag-Or. Drokki hefted his axe in his good hand and nodded. He wanted very much for the squealing to stop.

Shouts came from behind them, and the runemasters turned back to see the hearthguard guarding the tunnel point to the rickety catwalks leading down from other tunnel mouths high overhead. There was movement up there, burly skaven beastmasters squeaking with rage at the duardin's trespass.

Marag-Or ordered the rest of the warriors that accompanied the runemasters to block the bottom of the catwalk. Then he readied his own axe.

'They'll hold them off, young one. This won't take long.'

Drokki buried his axe in the head of a skaven mother. He wiped blood from his face with the back of his arm and blinked.

Marag-Or nodded. 'That's the spirit.'

A skaven warlord screeched shrilly as Ulgathern-Grimnir drove his grandaxe's haft into its chest, crushing its ribs. It went down thrashing, bloody froth at its lips.

'Shoddy craftsmanship, that armour,' he said.

The clanrats of the warlord wavered, but held. Then another half dozen fell to Ulgathern-Grimnir's hearthguard berzerkers, and their nerve went. The Ulgaen surged forward as the skaven fled. The braziers attached to the hearthguard's axes whirled around on their chains, touching off fires on the ratkin's clothes and fur. The creatures fled, spreading flames among their fleeing fellows.

'Hold!' roared the runefather. Brass horns blared, conveying his orders. The duardin halted. The tunnel floor was carpeted with warm ratkin bodies.

'We've a moment, move these back down the line. Stop them using their dead as cover. Halvir's fyrd, come up front, let Brangar's lot take a rest.'

The duardin moved smoothly past one another. Footing became better as the corpses were passed down the line from hand to hand. The few Fyreslayers who had been wounded were helped back to the break-in tunnel, where the Mining Fellowship waited to tend their hurts.

Drums and gongs rang down the corridor. Typical skaven tactics, thought Ulgathern. They were seeking to exhaust his folk with repeated waves, uncaring of the lives of their own warriors.

But then, there were always so very many of them.

This time they came with firethrowers, four weapons teams skulking behind the front ranks of a skaven regiment.

'Ware!' shouted Ulgathern-Grimnir. 'Warpfire!'

He plucked a throwing axe from his belt and hurled it. His rune-empowered might sent it smashing right through the body of a skaven, but the first death took its impetus, and it bounced harmlessly from the shield of the warrior behind. Auric hearthguard with magmapikes hurried to his side from the back ranks and set up a bombardment. The skaven squealed as they were set ablaze and crushed by molten stone. One fire-thrower gunner was battered down by a hail of lava bombs, while his ammunition bearer became tangled by the tubes and harness connecting them, and he was crushed under-foot by the mass of skaven pushing from behind. Another exploded with a dull crump, immolating a score of ratmen. Ulgathern-Grimnir grinned, but when the fire blew out, the skaven were still coming.

By now the tunnel was thick with acrid smoke. Skaven burned everywhere. Still his hearthguard did not relent, pummelling the lead elements of the second wave with their magical weapons.

Then the firethrowers came into range.

Gouts of green-tinged fire burst outward. Skaven engineers played the jets back and forth, forcing the Fyreslayers to fall back, shields up. Several were caught, their screams turning to bubbling moans as their flesh sloughed away from their bod-ies in shrivelling sheets.

Ulgathern-Grimnir was at the heart of it. Warpfire, hotter than any natural heat, burst over his skin as the twin streams were directed at him. The pain was immense, but he refused to move. Grimnir's fire answered the flames of the skaven. His eyes blazed. His ur-gold runes burned with protective magic. Setting his shoulders directly into the jets, he marched forward. The pressure of the burning liquid was great and he struggled against it. His runes fizzed with energy. One gave out with a bang, overcome by the ferocity of the skaven weapons. The molten metal streamed down his arm, but Ulgathern-Grimnir refused to die.

He made it to the skaven line with a wild grin on his face. Skaven blinked and cowered, unsure what to do. The engineers shut the fire off before it was reflected back onto themselves.

Ulgathern-Grimnir's crest of hair had lost a good foot in height, and smoked vigorously. His skin was blistered and red, his wargear blackened. He lifted his arms to show that he was not seriously hurt, and laughed in their faces.

'I am Ulgathern-Grimnir, a runefather of the Ulgaen lodges. I was born of fire, forged in fire, and empowered by fire. Your little candle can't hurt me.'

He swung his grandaxe the full width of the corridor, its razor-sharp head felling a swathe of the ratmen.

With a roar the Fyreslayers charged up to their lord's side. This time, they did not stop, but advanced a step for every skaven they killed.

The ground rumbled. A hot wind blew from the depths. The Fyreslayers cheered.

'About time too,' said Ulgathern-Grimnir as the skaven were driven back. 'Get on lads, drive them up and out, we don't want to be in here when the mountain blows!'

'Aid me, Drokki!' called Marag-Or. His eyes glowed with yellow firelight. Ash sifted down from his mouth with every word. He slammed his staff into the ground. 'I call on the mountain! Bring forth your earthblood! Fill the hollow chamber of your heart! Purify yourself!'

The beastmasters of the birthing chamber fought ferociously against the Fyreslayers. They were bigger than normal skaven, incensed by the slaughter of the mothers, and took a heavy toll on the duardin. Drokki watched as a Vulkite Berzerker threw his bladed shield at a fresh party of skaven entering the hall by a secret tunnel, decapitating one and piercing another through the heart. The warrior gripped his axe and charged into the gap opened up by his shield, but was quickly swamped.

'Drokki!' called Marag-Or again. 'To me!'

Drokki hurried over to the ancient runemaster. The fires of his own runic iron flared bright in sympathy with Marag-Or's magic as he snatched it from its belt loop. He waited for Marag-Or's next beat, then joined in, pounding on the rock in time with his old master.

'I call on the mountain! Bring forth your earthblood! Fill the hollow chamber of your heart! Purify yourself!' they shouted together.

The ground shifted. A crack opened in the rock. Superheated steam roared out, cooking mewling skaven young by the score.

'Yes! Yes!' shouted Marag-Or. 'You can feel it, can you not, Drokki? The power of the earthblood. Feel it rise!'

'I call on the mountain! Bring forth your earthblood! Fill the hollow chamber of your heart! Purify yourself!' they shouted again. Their staffs slammed into the rock. Cracks ran out from their feet. The chamber quaked. The cracks widened into crevasses, the ruddy light of sluggish magma shining upwards from deep underground.

The skaven's sensitive noses twitched at the smell of burning rock. When another earthquake sent some of their feeding gear tumbling into the fires of the earth, they gave up their struggle, turned tail and ran.

'Everyone out!' shouted Marag-Or. He grabbed Drokki's arm. 'No more now, lad, we don't want this place to go the way of the Ulgahold. Enough to burn the vermin out, no more.'

Grokkenkir's warriors ran for the tunnel they had arrived by, dragging their wounded with them. The mountain no longer needed the runemasters' encouragement and set up a terrific shaking all on its own. Molten rock oozed from the crevices in the floor, pooling in depressions. The cavern became as hot as a furnace. Skaven mothers, living and dead alike, burst into flame.

Drokki led Marag-Or over the broken cavern floor as best he could, helping him over the wider cracks, kicking skaven dead and boulders out of the way. Grokkenkir beckoned to them from the tunnel mouth, his eyes straying over Drokki's shoulder at the rising tide of lava.

'Come on, runemasters! Just a little way further!' he cried.

Drokki stepped up the lip of the tunnel, and reached out a hand for the older runemaster. Lava filled most of the cavern floor and was creeping up the walls.

Marag-Or took his hand.

A shot rang out. Marag-Or's eyes widened in surprise.

'Skaven sharpshooters!' bellowed Grokkenkir and pointed to where a number of jezzail teams were lining up on the catwalks.

Marag-Or looked down at his chest. A wisp of smoke rose from beneath his war harness. Blood welled after. 'I'm done. You best get on, eh, lad?' said Marag-Or. He let go of Drokki's hand and fell back into the molten rock. His eyes closed as he sank into it, his skin blackened, and the fire took him.

'Runemaster!' said Drokki.

'We have to head to the surface!' said Grokkenkir, physically hauling Drokki back before he could jump into the lava after his mentor. A shot ricocheted off the wall and another shattered on the stone near their feet. 'Now!'

Brokkengird sang as he cut down skaven by the score. Try as they might, they could not harm him. What few scratches he took only enraged him. He drove into them, a one-duardin army.

Tulgamar-Grimnir rode his magmadroth deep into the horde, the great ur-salamander spitting fire into the ratkin masses and igniting them by the dozen. Fyreslayers fought in disciplined ranks around the magmadroth's feet, their axes cutting skaven down wherever they fell.

And yet still they were outnumbered, and the battle would have been lost, if two things had not occurred. Firstly, the ground's booming and rumbling turned into a fully fledged earthquake so violent that skaven went sprawling. Smoke belched from the mountain's summit.

Secondly, confusion took hold of the skaven still pouring from their lair. They began to falter, then to look behind themselves.

Ulgathern-Grimnir's fyrd burst from the gates, smoke belching after them, slaying skaven as they came. The runefather had lost many warriors, but those remaining fought ferociously and their arrival sent panic rippling through the skaven ranks.

'Forward! To my brother!' yelled Tulgamar-Grimnir. Grakki-grakkov reared high, pounding clanrats flat with its feet when it came down. Roaring, it broke into a lumbering canter, smashing ratmen aside as it ran for the gate. The Fyreslayers began to sing triumphantly. With trumpets blowing, they followed.

The skaven at the edge of the battle began to melt away. A few cowardly souls at first, then in great numbers.

The mountain boomed. Its smokes thickened. The Steelspike slept no more.

Brokkengird laughed. Today was a good day to kill.

The mass pyres of the skaven dead were still burning a week later when the rest of Ulgathern's people came to join the hold from their camp at the Voltdrang.

The Fyreslayers refashioning the gates downed tools and ran out to meet the column as it appeared from the valley approach to the Steelspike. Families were reunited before the new hold. Ulgathern-Grimnir and his brothers were glad to see a sizeable force had been sent to escort them by the Volturung, and that they were well fed, clean and happy.

They were less pleased to see Runeson Golgunnir.

The runeson came on foot this time, and was garbed for war. Still far too ostentatiously for Ulgathern-Grimnir's tastes, but at least he was dressed with fighting in mind.

'Looks like I underestimated you,' said Golgunnir. He looked around at the heaps of skaven bodies and gear. 'You did a good job. You reawoke the mountain. Crafty.'

'You thought we wouldn't win.'

Golgunnir shrugged. 'True. But my father thought you were in with a chance, or he would never have sent you. He's an honourable sort, my father.'

'You disapprove?'

Golgunnir nodded as he surveyed the mountain, the piles of scrapped machinery, the scaffolding around the gates where statues of Grimnir were already being roughed out in the rock. 'I do. I'll never be a runefather because of that. I've no faith in other folk. Still, at least I know my limits. Are there any tunnels left open?'

'A few,' said Ulgathern-Grimnir. 'We've flooded the deepest with earthblood, set warding runes all about those higher in the mountain. I don't want to plug them all, else how would we take the war to them?'

'That's what I hoped you'd say,' said Golgunnir. 'If I might have your permission, runefather, I will take my men hunting. The ratkin have regarded this land as theirs for too long.'

'I grant it gladly.'

Golgunnir gave a brief nod, hitched up his belt, and held out his hand. 'Welcome to the domain of the Volturung. Welcome home.'

Ulgathern-Grimnir clasped Golgunnir's wrist. 'If it's all the same, we'll be keeping the Ulgaen name. We are the last of our lodge-kin. Henceforth, we shall be Ulgaen-dumar lodge and Ulgaen-kumar lodge of Steelspike Hold.'

'Whatever you like. You keep your side of the bargain, we'll keep ours.' Golgunnir sniffed. 'There's something else too.'

'Oh?'

'An ambassador. He should be here, about... now.'

Golgunnir looked skywards and took three steps back.

With a rush of wings, a huge warrior in gleaming gold armour slammed into the ground before Ulgathern, as shocking as a lightning strike. Wings of brilliant white light dazzled the runefather, then were extinguished, the mechanisms that had projected them folding upon the warrior's back.

A stern-faced war-mask looked down on him. Ulgathern-Grimnir was sure this was a human male. He had never seen one so big who was not in the service of the four powers, but the energy that crackled around him was not of Chaos, he was sure of that.

'Hail, runefather! I am Seldor, Knight-Azyros of the Hammers of Sigmar. I come to you with tidings of hope,' said the angelic warrior. 'The gates to Azyr are reopened. The Storm-hosts march. Sigmar returns to free the realms from the tyranny of the Dark Gods.

'The war against Chaos has begun, and we seek allies.'

YOUR NEXT READ

LEGENDS OF THE AGE OF SIGMAR
by David Annandale, David Guymer, Guy Haley, Josh Reynolds,
Robbie MacNiven, Rob Sanders and Gav Thorpe

Delve into the forces that battle for control of the Mortal Realm with this
epic omnibus of three Legends of the Age of Sigmar books, comprising one
novel and nine shorter tales, focusing on the skaven of the Clans Pestilens, the
Fyreslayer lodges and the mysterious Sylvaneth.

For these stories and more go to **blacklibrary.com, games-workshop.com**, Games Workshop
and Warhammer stores, all good book stores or visit one of the thousands of independent
retailers worldwide, which can be found at **games-workshop.com/storefinder**

An excerpt from

BLACKTALON: FIRST MARK

by Andy Clark

CHAPTER ONE

Far to the north of the city of Hammerhal Aqsha, amidst the thick, sulphur-fed groves of the Heironyme Jungle, a village stood in ruins. If the place had ever had a name it was gone now, buried beneath the drifts of blackened fronds and sulphurous dust that were slowly reclaiming its buildings.

The bloated jungle moon loomed over a clearing that contained a few dozen crumbling structures. They stood within a rotting palisade wall, just enough buildings to raise the ghosts of streets between them and lend the town an impression of civilisation, of imposed order. Yet the fields outside the walls were overgrown by anyoi trees and strangler's twist, while the gaping hole in the village wall, and the hacked bones strewn amidst the ruins, put the lie to any notion that this tiny corner of Aqshy had been tamed.

Crouched amidst the jungle's fringe, Neave Blacktalon studied the settlement intently. The nameless village and all its hopeful, pious settlers were long dead. Yet the prickle on her skin beneath her resilient suit of gilded sigmarite told her that something else had slithered in to inhabit the carcass of their butchered dream. Something that lit the night with eerie witchlight.

Neave's senses were fully extended, alive to the slightest scent or sound, the merest vibration in the air. She reached out and felt the jungle around her, flitwings and diaphonids drifting through the canopy, treglyngs nosing between tree roots. She felt the strange movements within the slain village before her, long-limbed things stalking like wading birds, drums thumping a chaotic rhythm, unnatural beings cavorting. She sensed other movements amidst the jungle itself, but these concerned her less. Sigmar's gift tugged at her, the siren sense of her latest mark close at hand, the quarry whose presence she would always feel, no matter how near or far, until she or they were dead.

Neave was one with the world around her, and she tasted the Chaotic taint that soured it. It gathered thick on her tongue and made her scowl with disgust and anger.

From her right, she felt gusts of air stir the jungle foliage. She heard the sounds of subtle movement draw closer, something large doing its utmost not to be heard. She scented the tang of ozone through the jungle's sulphur. Curling her tongue, she gave a clicking signal: two low, quick sounds, a pause, then a third. The signal was returned, a moment before Tarion Arlor slid through the fronds of two anyois to join her.

'Don't tell me that Sigmar's finest Knight-Zephyros needs that damned signal to verify it is me, Blacktalon. I know you heard my approach,' said the Knight-Venator. Neave heard the smile behind the faceplate of his helm, and snorted with quiet amusement. Tarion was bigger than Neave, his bulky armour and its huge crystalline wings far less suited to slinking through the dense jungle.

'Where is Krien?' she asked. 'Didn't wish to tangle his wings amidst the foliage?'

'He is on high, circling well out of sight,' replied Tarion. 'Star eagles are not noted for their love of confined terrain.'

'Krien isn't well known for his love of anything, save you,' said Neave. 'Sometimes I cannot tell if he's your familiar, or you his.'

Tarion shook his head ruefully. 'Damn bird is lucky he's such a gifted fighter.'

'We may need him to be so very soon,' said Neave. 'Xelkyn is here – I sense his taint. The conclusion to our hunt draws near, but something feels wrong. What did you see?'

'Little,' confessed Tarion. 'It's a clear night and the moon is vast. Even distracted by ritual and blinded by firelight, I could not risk them looking up and seeing my silhouette against the sky. There's perhaps five or six dozen of his coven in the village. Stiltkin. Disc riders. Ogroids.'

'I do not see any sentries,' said Neave.

'I did not spot any from afar,' replied Tarion, shaking his head. 'Xelkyn is arrogant. He no doubt believes himself hidden in this remote location.'

'The sorcerer knows we hunt him,' said Neave, not taking her eyes from the village, from the warped kaleidoscope of vivid light that welled up from its heart, the weird shadows that danced across its walls. 'We almost had him in the Carathacium. You slew his Mutalith. He's a toweringly arrogant creature, but his mind is a barbed maze. He has *let* us run him to ground, Tarion. There's a trap here.'

'Be that as it may, he's conducting a ritual in there,' said the Knight-Venator. 'Look at the lights. Listen to the drums, the chanting. Feel the power gathering on the air.'

'You think that slipped my notice?' asked Neave wryly.

'You know what I mean, Blacktalon. He may be summoning

daemons, or opening a rent into the Crystal Labyrinth. If he slips away into the embrace of his master's realm, he'll be beyond even Sigmar's reach.'

Neave cocked her head, listening intently to the timbre of the drums, the tone of the chanting, shrieking voices. Some sounded human, albeit rendered bestial in their frenzy. Others were cawing and avian. From amongst them she filtered another voice, commanding yet brittle somehow, as though an insect were trying to form human words with mouthparts not meant for the sound. She knew the hateful voice of Xelkyn Xerkanos, favoured covenmaster of Tzeentch and arch-traitor to Sigmar's great city of Azyrheim, all too well.

'He does not sound panicked,' she said softly. 'Tarion, he sounds angry. Spiteful. Determined. Whatever Xelkyn is conjuring in that village, it is not an escape route. It's a weapon.'

'What then?' asked Tarion. 'He's your mark, Blacktalon. I merely hunt at your side.'

Neave paused and removed her helm, letting the foulness in the air wash over her skin, steeling herself against its touch. It thickened imperceptibly as she waited, like gossamer cobwebs caught on her flesh. She ran her gauntleted hand over her face, an unconscious gesture to scour away the invisible strands of Chaos magic that gathered there.

'There isn't time to seek aid,' she said, replacing her helm. 'Whatever Xelkyn is doing, his power builds by the minute. If we leave now, he will have completed his ritual and quite possibly vanished into the realmscape again long before we can return.'

'There's a lot of them,' said Tarion in a warning tone. 'You know we likely won't survive a headlong assault.'

'Neither will Xelkyn,' said Neave, steel in her voice. 'What's wrong, Tarion? Afraid of death?'

'Again? So soon after Gallowfall?' he replied. 'Could we not formulate some sort of plan that doesn't involve a suicidal headlong attack on a Tzeentchian arch-sorcerer and his entire coven? Reforging has its price…'

'And its boons. Did I not develop the talent of windshifting at will after my most recent reincarnation? What is that, if not a blessing from Sigmar himself? Besides, do you see another option?' she asked, easing her whirlwind axes from their sheaths and spinning them in her hands, refamiliarising herself with their weight. She had fought with the weapons until they were as much a part of her as the hands that held them, but it was a ritual she often undertook.

'No,' said Tarion after a few moment's frustrated thought. 'If he knows we are coming then any attempt at luring his force away or splitting them up will only alert him to our arrival.'

'Well then.' Neave rose into a crouch. 'Take to the air, do what Sigmar gave you the gifts to do, and if it is such a terrible inconvenience then… I don't know, try *not* to get killed?'

'Why in the realms do I hunt with you?' Tarion hefted his bow as coruscating arrows of lightning crackled into being in his quiver.

'Duty?' suggested Neave. 'Friendship? The deep-seated need to prove that you can keep up?'

'Just give me a few moments to get into position, Blacktalon,' said Tarion, and again she heard the smile behind the impassive mask of his helm.

'Be swift,' she said. Tarion spread the crystal-and-sigmarite wings that rose from the shoulders of his armour. Celestial energies glimmered through them, playing across the foliage like the promise of dawn, before he sprang skywards and punched up through the canopy with barely a rustle.

For all their repartee, Neave trusted Tarion more than any

other Stormcast Eternal in all of Sigmar's grand armies. He would cover her assault with a skill few in the Mortal Realms could match.

She glanced up, through the swaying jungle fringe, seeking the distant constellations that marked where the Realm of Heavens hung in the distant reaches of the void. Up there, somewhere, she knew that Sigmar looked down upon the realms and the battles his reforged warriors fought in his name.

'Sigmar, watch over me now and lend me your strength, that I might do your will and strike down your foes,' she murmured, before reaching out again with her huntress' senses. She felt the winds aetheric as they whirled across the lands, gave herself up to their ensorcelled power, let them flow through her limbs and course through her lightning-wreathed soul. Her eyes crackled with barely restrained power, and her heart beat faster as the thrill of the hunt welled up within.

'You may have laid a trap for Sigmar's huntress, Xelkyn, but you had better be sure you don't get caught in it yourself...'

Neave tore across the abandoned fields at such a pace that had any enemy seen her approach, she knew their eyes would have registered little more than a streak of displaced air and lightning. She cleared the village wall with an agile leap that carried her fifteen feet into the air, thumping down in the bone-strewn street beyond without missing a stride. Overhead, Neave caught a fleeting glimpse of Tarion, wings spread wide, storm-charged arrow nocked and ready to loose. The Knight-Venator was no longer trying to hide, and neither was she.

The street led towards the centre of the village, taking a left up ahead as it passed between the tumbledown buildings. In the distance, she saw Tzeentchian cultists clad in bright blue robes and grotesque avian masks wrought from gold. Their exposed flesh displayed forbidden markings and they bore the daggers and staves of minor wizards, while unholy fires sparked around them.

The enemy caught sight of Tarion. Shouting in surprise, they pointed skywards towards the swooping comet of the Knight-Venator's star eagle.

'Much too slow,' hissed Neave as she bore down on the cultists like a meteor.

Tarion unleashed a volley of lightning-wreathed arrows with impossible speed. They shot overhead as Neave charged. The arcing shafts lit the night white with their fury, piercing robed bodies and throwing cultists backwards as though they'd been shot with a bolt thrower. One man slammed into a building wall and was pinioned there, dangling and twitching as lightning cooked his flesh and set fire to his robes. Another took an arrow to the face and was catapulted from his feet to crash through the sagging doorway of a nearby hut. Such was the force of his impact that half the structure's roof came down upon him, burying the Chaos worshipper in an impromptu cairn.

Then Neave hit the cultists' lines. She leapt and spun, pirouetting through the foe with her blades angled outward. Blood exploded in fans as her axes bit through cloth, flesh and bone. Tzeentch worshippers were flung away from her, crunching into the sides of the derelict buildings or rolling along the street to lie in crumpled heaps.

The survivors were still reeling, frantic, seeking their assailant even as she hit the building at the street's end with her feet. Neave bent her knees, taking the shock of the impact and propelling herself back into the enemy like one of Tarion's arrows. She struck the head from one cultist and lopped an arm from another as she flew, before landing in a roll and coming up in a fighting crouch.

One cultist remained standing, drenched in the blood of his fellows even as their bodies crumpled, spurting, to the ground. He raised his stave with shaking hands and pointed it in Neave's direction. A crackling arrow slammed into his throat with such force that it passed clean through. She heard the man's heart stop as celestial lightnings coursed through his body and killed him even before his blood began to jet from the wound.

Wordlessly, she raised an axe to Tarion in thanks, then sped on towards the heart of the village. The drums had increased their tempo and the chanting had transformed into warlike cries.

'They now know we are coming,' muttered Neave to herself. 'It becomes more interesting from here.'

ABOUT THE AUTHORS

C L Werner's Black Library credits include the Age of Sigmar novels *Overlords of the Iron Dragon* and *The Tainted Heart*, the novella 'Scion of the Storm' in *Hammers of Sigmar*, the Warhammer novels novel *Deathblade, Mathias Thulmann: Witch Hunter, Runefang* and *Brunner the Bounty Hunter*, the Thanquol and Boneripper series and Time of Legends: The Black Plague series. For Warhammer 40,000 he has written the Space Marine Battles novel *The Siege of Castellax*. Currently living in the American south-west, he continues to write stories of mayhem and madness set in the Warhammer worlds.

Josh Reynolds is the author of the Horus Heresy Primarchs novel *Fulgrim: The Palatine Phoenix*, and the audio dramas *Blackshields: The False War and Blackshields: The Red Fief*. His Warhammer 40,000 work includes *Lukas the Trickster, Fabius Bile: Primogenitor, Fabius Bile: Clonelord* and *Deathstorm*, and the novellas *Hunter's Snare* and *Dante's Canyon*, along with the audio drama *Master of the Hunt*. He has written many stories set in the Age of Sigmar, including the novels *Eight Lamentations: Spear of Shadows, Hallowed Knights: Plague Garden, Nagash: The Undying King* and *Soul Wars*. His tales of the Warhammer old world include *The Return of Nagash* and *The Lord of the End Times*, and two Gotrek & Felix novels. He lives and works in Sheffield.

Nick Horth is the author of *City of Secrets*, his first Age of Sigmar novel. Nick works as a background writer for Games Workshop, crafting the worlds of Warhammer Age of Sigmar and Warhammer 40,000. He lives in Nottingham, UK.

David Annandale is the author of the Horus Heresy novels *Ruinstorm* and *The Damnation of Pythos*, and the Primarchs novels *Roboute Guilliman: Lord of Ultramar* and *Vulkan: Lord of Drakes*. For Warhammer 40,000 he has written *Warlord: Fury of the God-Machine*, the Yarrick series, several stories involving the Grey Knights, including *Warden of the Blade* and *Castellan*, as well as titles for The Beast Arises and the Space Marine Battles series. For Warhammer Age of Sigmar he has written *Neferata: Mortarch of Blood*. David lectures at a Canadian university, on subjects ranging from English literature to horror films and video games.

Guy Haley is the author of the Horus Heresy novels *Wolfsbane* and *Pharos*, the Primarchs novels *Corax: Lord of Shadows, Perturabo: The Hammer of Olympia*, and the Warhammer 40,000 novels *Dark Imperium, Dark Imperium: Plague War, The Devastation of Baal, Dante, Baneblade, Shadowsword, Valedor* and *Death of Integrity*. He has also written *Throneworld* and *The Beheading* for The Beast Arises series. His enthusiasm for all things greenskin has also led him to pen the eponymous Warhammer novel *Skarsnik*, as well as the End Times novel *The Rise of the Horned Rat*. He has also written stories set in the Age of Sigmar, included in *War Storm, Ghal Maraz* and *Call of Archaon*. He lives in Yorkshire with his wife and son.

David Guymer wrote the Primarchs novel *Ferrus Manus: Gorgon of Medusa*, and for Warhammer 40,000 *The Eye of Medusa, Voice of Mars* and the two The Beast Arises novels *Echoes of the Long War* and *The Last Son of Dorn*. For Warhammer Age of Sigmar he wrote the audio dramas *The Beasts of Cartha, Fist of Mork, Fist of Gork, Great Red* and *Only the Faithful*. He is also the author of the Gotrek & Felix novels *Slayer, Kinslayer* and *City of the Damned* and the audio drama *Realmslayer*. He is a freelance writer and occasional scientist based in the East Riding, and was a finalist in the 2014 David Gemmell Awards for his novel *Headtaker*.

Gav Thorpe is the author of the Horus Heresy novels *Deliverance Lost, Angels of Caliban* and *Corax*, as well as the novella *The Lion*, which formed part of the *New York Times* bestselling collection *The Primarchs*, and several audio dramas including the bestselling *Raven's Flight*. He has written many novels for Warhammer 40,000, including *Ashes of Prospero, Imperator: Wrath of the Omnissiah, Rise of the Ynnari: Ghost Warrior, Jain Zar: The Storm of Silence* and *Asurmen: Hand of Asuryan*. He also wrote the Path of the Eldar and Legacy of Caliban trilogies, and two volumes in The Beast Arises series. For Warhammer, Gav has penned the End Times novel *The Curse of Khaine*, the Warhammer Chronicles omnibus *The Sundering*, and much more besides. In 2017, Gav won the David Gemmell Legend Award for his Age of Sigmar novel *Warbeast*. He lives and works in Nottingham.

FURTHER READING

WARHAMMER AGE OF SIGMAR

Legends of the Age of Sigmar
Various

Eight Lamentations: Spear of Shadows
Josh Reynolds

Hallowed Knights: Plague Garden
Josh Reynolds

Overlords of the Iron Dragon
C L Werner

Nagash: The Undying King
Josh Reynolds

Neferata: Mortarch of Blood
David Annandale

Soul Wars
Josh Reynolds

Callis & Toll: The Silver Shard
Nick Horth

The Tainted Heart
C L Werner

Shadespire: The Mirrored City
Josh Reynolds

Blacktalon: First Mark
Andy Clark

THE REALMGATE WARS

WARHAMMER CHRONICLES